AutoFLICK

A Study of Whales and Cigarettes That Became a Novel

AutoFLICK

A Study of Whales and Cigarettes That Became a Novel

John R. Bancroft

Ecphora Press

Small-batch craft fiction from
Prince George's County, Md

This is a work of fiction. Names, characters, places, and incidents are the products of the author's imagination or are used fictitiously. Any resemblance to actual events, locales, or persons, living or dead, is entirely coincidental.

First Edition, Ecphora Press

ISBN: 978-0-9974350-0-9

Ecphora Press

PO Box 336

Hyattsville, MD 20781

www.ecphorapress.com

Member, Independent Book Publishers Association

Acknowledgements

Herman Melville inspired this voyage, and his contributions are everywhere in it.

Izzy owes deep appreciation to all the far-out characters of 1968 and 2002, who put wind in his sails and gave him things to write about, fictitiously.

Special thanks to S. Donovan, F. Solomon and the Glimpse Review Board, who manned the oars as needed.

And to my wife, who helps keep me afloat.

J.R.B.

ABSTRACT

This study sprang from a whimsy: the hypothesis that truth may be leaking through the lapses in awareness. Our research zigzagged doggedly. It was put to rest and resurrected. The data are random observations of generally unpremeditated actions: people throwing cigarettes from their cars.

The results are inconclusive. Most of the subjects did not explain their motivation, some denied that the event had occurred, and in many cases there was no opportunity to interview the subject.

We do not know how this behavior is influenced by environmental factors—the weather, the news of the day, etc.—or the kind of car being driven or the flicker's socioeconomic category. We collected as much of this information as possible, but so far have not discovered any statistical correlation with butt-flicking.

Field notes were recorded by my father, Rockwell Yardley, and by me. Some academicians have criticized my efforts to reconstruct his reports and the fact that in some cases we may have intervened in the behavior of the subjects, made inferences about their motives, and introduced selection bias in the sample.

They probably have a point.

Isaac Yardley
December 2002
Prince George's County, MD

1. Friday, June 7, 1968

1965 Triumph Spitfire

You can call me an only child and you will be half right. My mother had a child before she met my father. My half-sister, Katie, was several years older than me.

On the day of our first observation, I was riding with my father in his car from our gentle suburb, Acushnet, on the Pennsylvania slope of the Delaware Valley, heading to my summer job. It was already hot and humid, and soon the road would begin to soften underfoot and let loose the faint smell of asphalt hardened long ago by traffic and the passing winters. My father drove a 1955 DeSoto, a mastodon plodding toward extinction. Sunlight found pores in the windshield, ricocheted off the metal dashboard, and gathered old-car seasoning from the sagging cloth ceiling. We broiled tenderly on the car's vast upholstery.

I know now that there was something irregular about me then—a teenager who liked to get up before six in the morning—but this had not yet dawned on me. I was 16 years old, a high school junior, working for the summer as a golf-course maintenance laborer at the country club. I had caddied there on weekends since I was 13.

At the time we were riding to our work that June morning, I had no idea that a social science experiment was about to happen to me. Nor do I think my father set out that morning with a plan to start a long-term study of human behavior. However, he was a small-town journalist with a predisposition to gather facts, even inconsequential ones, because he believed that all facts have the potential to lead to truth. He was ready to follow any promising lead: a spiral-bound reporter's notepad waited in the gin box. He was never without a pen or pencil.

We were nearing Doylestown, the minor sun around which our suburb orbited. Ahead of us was a 1965 Triumph Spitfire. The Triumph driver flicked a cigarette from his window with slightly skyward trajectory.

"Hunh." My father grunted, a non-verbal conversation between consciousness and the self, the sound of someone pulling open an old wooden window stuck in its frame by layers of paint.

It is good to be on the lookout for the turning points. The entire project might have never gotten off the ground had I let that grunt crumble peacefully into the long, endearing hymn of unremarkable animal noise. Had I said nothing, we might have just continued on our way to work.

But we were too close together, even on the vast front seat of a 1955 DeSoto, for a grunt to just lay there in the space between us.

"What?" I asked.

"It's a small car, but it's got an ashtray," my father said. His forehead pointed toward the Triumph.

And still, we might have gotten away without this changing our lives had the passenger in the convertible not tossed his cigarette butt as well, toward the roadside. His was an on-hand curb flick; his lower arm hinged away from the car until his hand pointed straight toward the curb. With the butt teed up between his right thumb and middle fingernail, he shot the stub directly into the gutter.

Both my father's hands came off the steering wheel and his palms rotated upward, asking the unseen for an explanation.

"What the hell." Mysteries beckon whether we can solve them or not. "Get my notepad," he said, "and write down that license plate number."

At this point, I recognized the car in front of us. It was driven by a kid in my school, and I thought I knew the passenger as well. They were accomplished; they smoked cigarettes and were in the smart-kid classes.

I, on the other hand, was in the Boy Scouts.

I opened the glove box and pulled out the reporter's notebook.

"I know those guys. They're from my class," I said, wondering if this would matter.

The traffic had started rolling again, and my father was driving just a little more purposefully, following closer than he usually did. He didn't say anything for a minute; he was concentrating on the prey ahead.

"Why not just put the butt in the ashtray?" he asked no one in particular.

I improvised some Melville, "*Without a constant watchman, the hoisted sailor may cast adrift.*"

"Write down the kind of car, and who's in it and the time and date," my father said. Then he thought of something else. "And the ashtray in that car is up on the top of the dashboard. It's impossible to ignore."

Still, I did not dribble ink. Was I waiting for this to pass, knowing in my heart—where knowledge is certain—that it would not? My father had taken a baited hook that most people would have swum blithely past. I could have wriggled away, but it wasn't in me to leave him thrashing and dangling with a barb through his lip.

My father had been through a lot in the past few days. His older brother, James, a fair-haired spirit who lived in California, had suffered severe injuries in a calamitous surfing accident just a week before. My father had flown out there with his father—the two of them didn't get along very well—and brought my uncle back to a rehabilitation center near Philadelphia.

"What day is it?" I thought this might be relevant. I jotted down something about the weather, and the road we were on. When it comes right down to it, it's hard to know which details matter.

We followed the Triumph through town and past the street that went to the country club. It pulled into a gas station and parked near the office. We motored alongside, twice as much car as the two-seater roadster.

The driver pulled himself from the Triumph and paused, rummaging in his jeans pockets. His passenger stayed aboard. The driver found his money and went into the service station to perform a ritual at the cigarette machine, dropping coins into the large glass-and-chrome apparatus with about 20 brands sorted in columns, their state tax seals pointed toward the buyer. It was entirely mechanical. Up close, you could hear the coins find their way past the counters, and for 35 cents you could feel the heavy plastic knobs working actual levers and gates as the machine let free one pack that fell deliberately—after a moment's hesitation—to the aluminum delivery bin, sliding home like a base runner going through the motions even though there was no play at the plate.

My father did not smoke. My mother, a bartender at the country club, smoked occasionally to build her immunity.

Mine were the pure, virgin lungs of a Boy Scout, tainted only by campfire smoke.

The driver came back outside with his cigarette purchase. My father got out of our car, and I found myself getting out as well, staying on my side of the DeSoto, stage right in this absurd little drama, stretching my arms for no good reason.

My father said something, but he was facing away from me. I edged toward the front of our car for a better view.

"Yuh," the kid said, poised a third of the way into his driver's seat.

"You threw your cigarette onto the street about a half-mile back." This came like a question, but not definitively so. The kid waited for more information. "I wonder if you can tell me why," my father said.

The kid looked at me. Dim recognition flickered in his face. This did not help him figure out what my father was all about. "I dunno. I guess so."

"Yup," my father said, with detachment, as though he was reading a phone number out of a book. "In fact, both you and your friend pitched your cigarettes into the street at almost the same time."

"Did we start a fire or something?" The classmate looked my way again, as though I could explain this meddlesome adult. I sold my father out; the best I could muster was a sympathetic shrug.

"Nope, no fire," my father said. "Only litter. Your aim was good enough, you hit the street. I'm not judging," he reassured, "Only asking why. There's an ashtray in your car. I can see that."

My father, who was called Speedy by some, waited patiently in the warming summer morning at a gas station for a teenager he had never seen before to come up with a meaningful explanation for an act of trivial, probably unconscious, environmental disobedience.

"I don't know. Why does anybody throw a cigarette out of the car?"

"Yes, that's it exactly," Speedy was excited. "That's what I'm, what we, are trying to find out." He didn't look at me when he threw the plural nominative out there, but once you've been made a "we," you can't go back.

The Triumph passenger and the driver turned to look at me again. "You guys have too much time on your hands," the kid said.

"It's just that we all know it's not right." My father was not going to let this go. "It's not cool. Even the great prophet Television tells us not to litter." I heard an editorial coming on. "Maybe if we can understand why one meaningless thing happens, we can figure out why the others do."

My father and grandfather had retrieved Uncle James from Southern California just days after Bobby Kennedy was murdered for no good reason in a hotel kitchen. They were all Quakers, but Speedy had veered off track when he signed up for combat in the war. Even so, he was plenty rattled when Kennedy was killed. Even army basic training doesn't kill those Quaker roots completely.

"I don't know, Mr. Yardley. I'm sorry. I probably wasn't thinking." I was faintly surprised the Triumph driver knew my last name.

This was answer enough. Speedy nodded as though there was something there on the tip of his tongue that he chose not to let go. "Okay," he said after a pause. "Thanks for your time."

My dad looked at me across the roof of the car and shrugged as we opened our respective doors.

Back on the roasting front seat, he asked if I got the exchange, nodding toward the notepad and turning the key to ignite the ancient DeSoto.

"You know, LBJ says the North Vietnamese need to pull back in their war effort because we have stopped bombing their cities," he said.

My father smiled out the front window of the car at a thought going through his head. "The North Vietnamese negotiator said he would agree to stop bombing the U.S."

"That seems fair," I offered.

"People everywhere have difficulty seeing how their actions affect others," he said.

2. June 7, 1968

1963 Chevy Malibu

My father put the DeSoto into reverse, reached his right arm over the back of the roomy front seat and turned to look through the rear window. I turned my face so I could see into the passenger-side rearview mirror. Two guys looking behind themselves to where they were going. A red Chevy sedan slid into the filling area, piloted by a woman with blonde hair aloft. The coast behind us was clear, but we were stopped. I wondered what my father was waiting for.

The Chevy driver was smoking a cigarette. She could have taken a place at the full-service bay, but there was a growing do-it-yourself movement going on that summer and she had chosen the self-service bay. She got out of the car, the cigarette in her fingers, and headed for the office to pay for her gas. A step or two short of the door, she dropped her cigarette and squished it out with a twisting motion of her toe.

Ballerinas are all around us.

My father pointed to the notepad and asked, "Is that the same as throwing a cigarette out of the car window?" One scientist to another.

It dawned on me that this could turn into a thing that my dad and I did, that we would drive around and take notes whenever we saw someone throw a cigarette out of a car. And that we were on the brink of formalizing it, of giving it rules. I was also wondering when he was going to take me to work.

"Why do we care?" I asked.

"I would like to know why we do this," he said, as much to himself as to me. "Why we throw cigarettes out the window when all cars have ashtrays."

My father had been in a low-gear agitation since he had come back from the trip to gather up his brother in California, unsettled by what he found in Uncle James's apartment—or rather, what he had not found. The place had been stripped bare of any evidence of neighbors or friends, he reported. "I am sure somebody was there and redacted

Jimmy's life," he said to my mother and me. "There were family pictures, but no sign of any of his friends out there, and I know he had a lot of them. There was no phone directory, and there were places on the walls that looked like the time shadows of pictures removed. Someone was there before me."

Maybe that laid the groundwork for this inquiry about cigarette littering: He was in a truth-seeking mood.

The woman put sunglasses on as she came out of the gas station office. Her bracelets sparkled as she uncapped her gas tank.

"She didn't throw it out of the car while she was driving, but the cigarette ended up on asphalt all the same," my father mused, putting our car in park and turning off the ignition. "What are the boundaries here?"

"Dad?" But it was too late. He swung open his door and sprang back onto the gas-station macadam. Hands in his back pockets like a farmer sizing up livestock, my father ambled over to where the woman had stubbed out her cigarette on the way into the gas station office.

He leaned over and carefully picked up the spent cartridge, and examined it in his palm.

The woman studied her fingernails as the gas pump did its work. She looked up as my father circled around the back of her car, realizing that he was approaching her with his arm extended, palm skyward, as though he were panhandling among people with very poor eyesight.

She had no choice but to turn and face him. This time I stayed in the car, figuring there was nothing I could do to help the situation. It looked as though she was trying to disown any connection with the evidence my father was holding out in front of her. He stood his distance in an unthreatening way, but it looked like he was not taking "No" for an answer, even pointing once toward the spot where he had picked up the butt.

Her expression shifted from friendly disinterest to re-calibration of the scene and, finally, to annoyance. She looked away, trying to conclude her filling station experience as though he wasn't there, turning her back on him to settle into her car. She appeared to say something indirectly, with a slight turn of her head, as she cranked the ignition key and pulled her gearshift into drive. She barely paused at the street before barreling into traffic with a little more resolve, I thought, than she might otherwise have had.

My father looked after her disappearing car for some few seconds and then to the cigarette corpse in his palm. He dropped the butt into the trash can that was on the island of gas pumps and walked back to our car.

"She said it wasn't her cigarette," he reported, with some amusement. "Reason for throwing butt out of car: amnesia."

I wrote it down in the book as he dictated, adding "with drop-and-toe crush," to the account.

"The French government was on the edge of total collapse last week," my father said, starting the DeSoto engine again. He was a current events junkie. "Students and workers on strike, the economy at a standstill and the army unsure of what it should be doing.

"So what do you think the topic was for de Gaulle's weekly executive meeting?" he turned and looked at me with the bemusement that was at the core of the awe my father had for our species.

I did not know.

"French fashion models," he was pleased to say.

"Can you blame them?" I asked.

We had doubled the sample size of our study and began to establish the parameters defining the subject universe. We had no theory or government funding or plan for collecting data or even a good reason for what we were setting out to do, sailing the wide asphalt-and-concrete seas in search of whales spewing smoke and Lucky Strikes and Kools and Winstons, Marlboros, Chesterfields, Camels, Salems, Tareytons, Larks, Pall Malls, Newports and Viceroys.

Happy-go-lucky, Melville wrote, *neither craven nor valiant; taking perils as they came with an indifferent air; and while engaged in the most imminent crisis of the chase, we toil away, calm and collected.*

Eventually, he did get me to work on time that morning.

3. Sunday, June 9, 1968

1959 Buick LeSabre

My father was ferrying me to the country club to caddy.

Ahead of us, the driver of a buffed, two-tone bull of a car was smoking. In just a few days, we had begun trying to predict whether any given smoking automobilist would litter. There wasn't much useful data on the backs of their heads, but our working hypothesis was that people who flicked ashes out the window were more likely to throw the whole butt out in the street than those who used their onboard ashtrays.

The '59 Buick was a greaser car, but this one had a "Draft Beer Not Boys" bumper sticker. The driver drove faster than my father, who was an obedient trafficker. But that day, Speedy pressed uncharacteristically to keep up, stalking for a flick. Sometimes you have to wade deeper into the stream if you want to catch anything.

The driver smoked in bursts, taking two or three quick tokes on the cigarette, and looking more and more like he would throw. Soon enough, with the stub loaded between the middle fingernail and the pad of his right thumb, he reached across his body and flicked the butt well out into the opposing traffic lane.

I reached for the notepad, thinking the antiwar bumper sticker might be significant. I was raised by a pacifist, with an asterisk.

My father was the third of three Quaker sons.

His oldest brother, Desmond, volunteered for non-combatant service in World War II. He was killed driving an ambulance in North Africa.

The middle son, James, applied for civilian service as a conscientious objector and worked in a mental institution in Philadelphia. After WWII ended, he continued working in psychiatric wards and then signed up with the International Red Cross as a human rights inspector in Korea, and when that war ended he continued working in mental health on the West Coast until he got his head stove in by a surfboard.

As a young man, my father was so angered about what happened to Desmond that he volunteered for combat duty in the Army. This decision caused friction with his parents that never fully went away. He went into the infantry with no religious shield over his head. But by the time he got to Europe, the fighting was nearly over. He said it was the best decision he ever made because he met my mother over there.

In the army, my father also met a soldier who told him about Dick Mobius, a mythical apostle of Herman Melville who started an anonymous society with no leadership, no secret handshake, no dues, no organization and no mission statement. The sect is held together only by its oral tradition: memorizing passages from the tale of the white whale and spouting them when it seems appropriate.

The only path to this enlightenment is through repeated readings of *Moby Dick*, which my father was still doing long after that war ended and new ones began.

Some say that Dick Mobius was saved by his passion when the book, by its very thickness, blunted a round from a German soldier. Some say the book saved him by deflecting a dagger wielded by a hopping-mad Sicilian prostitute. Others say Dick Mobius used the text as a landmine detector, tossing it a pace or two ahead of where he was going.

The Buick veered off our bearing, but Speedy stayed on his mark, maybe because it was Sunday and he didn't need to be anywhere at any particular time. It could also have been the deliberate way the driver had thrown his cigarette from the car. This was the first time, but not the last, that we changed our course just to follow a flicker.

We tracked the Buick for about two miles along a road I didn't know very well. He pulled into a driveway splitting a gentle, sloping lawn dotted with grandfatherly trees that framed a colonial-era limestone building that was too big to be an ordinary house.

We watched the kid climb out of his Buick. I recognized him as another smoker from my high school, one who had just graduated. He wore blue jeans and a plain white tee shirt with a pocket that held a pack of cigarettes. He hitched up his pants and strolled to the front door.

To my surprise, we were getting out of our car, drawn along by the current, and following the kid past the sign in the lawn indicating that this was a Friends meetinghouse. Beyond a small vestibule there was a large room with whitewashed walls and wood benches varnished by a couple of centuries of Quaker rear ends.

There were a few dozen people inside. Buick took a seat on the back bench close to the door. We sat off to the side, also in the last row, where we could keep an eye on him.

Nothing happened. Then it didn't happen for a while longer. People rustled and then became still. By and by someone would stand and say something, or offer a sedentary comment, and sometimes it would get to be almost like a conversation.

The Buick smoker looked like he was serving detention. Not that I had ever.

My father was sinking in. He would nod slowly at something someone said and then he would close his eyes, rolling a thought over in his mind. At one point his hands rose to the back of the bench in front of us and I thought he was going to pull himself to his feet, but he just hung there.

I wondered if this had been his family's meetinghouse. I had never been to meeting with my father's family. There was no one there whom I recognized.

Virtually all of my association with my father's family was at his parents' home. He would take his wife and his wife's daughter and his son there a few times a year, as though it was medicine to be administered sparingly.

A woman across the meeting room stood up. She glanced our way as she began to speak—it could have been accidental—and then turned her attention to a neutral spot in the middle of the room. "We are all troubled by the death of Robert Kennedy," she said. "There are so many of us who have not found the light. We struggle for a way to reach people like Sirhan Sirhan, who have become too angry to reason.

"We have not always been able to keep as friends even those who were raised with this awareness in their own families, people who were nourished by the meeting of friends."

Her eyes stayed away from us, but I thought she was talking about my father. In the corner of my eye, I measured him, looking for confirmation. He was listening to her completely.

"Even so, I feel encouraged this morning," she said. "The love that moves the world can find its shape again and we can be made whole if we remember how to draw from one another." As she sat down, she looked quickly around the room, her cool gray eyes falling momentarily on my father and me.

Then it was quiet and still again.

It was attic dry and unhurriedly hot, with an un-ambitious stir in the air. The trees moved like semaphores, a pulse of summer morning sweeping around the meetinghouse. I felt very much at peace on the worn bench, awash in the patina of a community of deliberation built up over generations.

There was a string of sometimes connected, sometimes disjointed observations from people in the meeting. I was listening in on a conversation taking place on a carousel spinning around me, sometimes catching my own reflection in a mirror across the way.

Finally, an elderly man stood and called the meeting to a close. The people arose and began to mingle in private conversations of the moment. But my father was hustling toward the door. The Buick driver had bolted for the exit as soon as the meeting ended, and my father was walking purposefully to catch up.

The grass was still growing June-fresh and green, not yet beaten down by the foot traffic or the heat and lack of rain that lay ahead in the ripening summer. The kid walked straight across the lawn to the parking lot, ignoring the flagstone walk. My father followed his tracks, but I, ever the Boy Scout, stayed on the marked trail.

By the time I rounded the corner onto the parking lot, my father had engaged his target. The Buick driver seemed clearly not in a conversational mood, wanting just to get in his car and be on his way. He untucked the cigarette pack from its nest in his shirt pocket and tapped the top exactly against the base of his left thumb so that a staggered arrangement of cigarettes presented themselves. He lifted the pack toward his face and pulled the tallest one out with his lips. Smokers do have some skills. Pall Malls, I noticed, unfiltered.

He lit the cigarette with a stainless steel Zippo, studying my father's face. There was less deference than my classmates had shown a few days earlier at the service station, but this kid was older and already out of school. His car was exceptionally clean, the way a car can be if it's worth more to its owner than its market value.

He squinted a little as smoke drifted into his eyes, but when he exhaled he blew it away from my father. As I came up to them he was saying, "How the fuck should I know why I threw the goddamn cigarette out the window?" in a very matter-of-fact way.

"If you don't know, who would?" my father asked him. "You've got an ashtray in there."

"Maybe there's no getting rid of it like throwin' it out the window."

"It's a matter of degree, right? There's being done with smoking, and then there's being done with the cigarette."

"Yeah. Something like that. And maybe throwing it out the window lets pricks like you know that I don't give a shit about your uptight shit."

"I'm a prick because I stopped to talk to you after we came out of a Quaker meeting?" my father said, a neighborly challenge in his tone. "That makes less sense to me than throwing cigarettes into the street when you've got an ashtray right next to you."

"Hey man, get off my cloud—" The kid started to turn his shoulder.

"Cause two's a crowd, right?" my father said, filling in the blank on a Rolling Stones song.

The Buick driver paused, smiling reflexively. He took another drag on his cigarette. "So we've got that straight, is there anything else?"

"Now that you mention it, I'd like to know what brought you to this meeting. You don't seem the type."

"You mean 'cause I don't have flowers in my hair and bell bottoms and shit?"

"It's not the costume. You don't act the part."

"I ain't seen you here before neither, and I been coming for a while. Not even the regulars bother me anymore."

It was true that the "regulars" were keeping their distance, but some of them were watching, from a distance, as they assembled a picnic under the trees.

"So we're just a couple of misfits, aren't we?"

The kid drew again on his cigarette and carefully cleaned the ash from the end with the fingernail of his ring finger. "If you gotta know, I'm here cause of the fucking draft."

"You think you can get a conscientious objector deferment if you go to Quaker meetings?"

"I don't know," he looked down, now a little less certain. "I know I ain't gonna get one if I don't come. Cause I'm sure as shit not going to college."

"You know the draft board will interview you, and you'll have to convince them that this is your faith and that you can't serve your country by fighting? You don't just check a box on a form and get out of it."

"Like I said, they ain't gonna give it to me if I don't go to Quaker church."

"A word of advice then, friend," Speedy said. "The draft board is not the highest form of intelligence on the planet, but they believe they can sort out the fakers. When your day comes, you're going to have to stand up and convince them that, in your soul, you believe what you say you believe."

"That's what the other Quaker farts said when I first started coming."

"We have to make our lives reflect the truth. And there are moments when you have to speak the truth about who you are or you won't be believed," my father said in a confidential way, into Buick's ear. "I'm not saying you can't come to believe what the Friends stand for, or that you don't already. But you will have to live whatever the truth is that's inside you."

The kid looked down at his feet. He shrugged his shoulders and shifted his weight as though he was ready to leave, but couldn't pull himself away.

"If you go to Vietnam or you don't, either way you won't be able to duck the truth about yourself. If you manage to wriggle all the way through your life without speaking the truth, no matter how many Quaker meetings you go to, you will be wasting your time."

The kid leaned forward to drop his cigarette on the ground between his feet, a stream of smoke pouring out of him into my father's face. "I don't need another goddamn sermon," he said, his face hardening.

"We're just two friends talking," my father said.

His face tilted downward again, pulling closer to my father, as he ground out the butt with his toe. Then he turned resolutely toward his car.

We stepped back and gave him space. When he was behind the steering wheel, he backed up in such a way that the driver side of the car was closest to us, and as he shifted from reverse to first gear he looked at my dad with something that could have been a smile. He rolled slowly out of the parking lot and then gunned it on down the road.

My father and I didn't say anything for a minute, absorbing the warm Sunday morning, which is not like all the other mornings, no matter what the non-believers say. As we climbed into our car, I asked whether that last cigarette should count or not, since it was automobile-free littering.

My father didn't answer. Speedy backed us out the same way the smoker had gone. I didn't realize there was anyone nearby until we stopped. Through my father's window, I could only see her up to her neck, but I knew it was the woman with the gray eyes. Then she leaned forward so we could see each other's faces across the front seat. She held a bowl of potato salad in front of her.

"It was good to see you here," she said to my father.

"We didn't plan it," he said. To fill an uncomfortable lull, he added: "Irene, this is my son, Isaac."

"Hello," she smiled.

"You can call me Izzy," I said. "Everybody does."

"Isaac?" she repeated.

"My father wanted somebody to laugh at his joke about becoming a Jew only to find himself alone at temple on Christmas and Easter," I said.

"*I cherish the greatest respect towards everyone's religious observations*," Speedy chimed in, "*never mind how comical.*"

It's not always clear whether the rest of the world knows when Moby is being thrown their way. She smiled awkwardly and then became serious. "I am so sorry about Jimmy. How is he doing?" she asked.

"Not so good, I'm afraid," my father said. "I'm not sure my parents have him in the best place. But they aren't interested in my opinions."

"What do you mean?" she asked.

"My father made it clear that he is James's guardian and he will decide where he lives."

"We all have Jimmy's interest at heart," the woman said. "And I believe you and your father will come together on this." Then she looked inward to her potato salad. "Wouldn't it be nice to have some lunch with us?"

I was wondering if my father had forgotten he was taking me to the country club. "Thanks," he said, "but we are late already. Like I said, we hadn't intended to be here."

She seemed to have expected this response, but her eyes flickered all the same when she smiled. I couldn't say that they were flirting, but my father had a look about him like he was eating cookies that were supposed to be for company.

There was another lull. "It was good to see you," my father said.

"Will we have to wait another twenty years?"

I felt my father squirming. "I usually go to the Lutheran church," I said, jumping in. This was misleading because I only "usually" went there in the sense that it was the only church I had ever been to, but my attendance was anything but "usual." My father never went at all.

"I have heard Dr. Easton several times," she said, "he has a wonderful spirit."

"I mostly go because their Boy Scout troop has a cabin by a creek."

That made my father smile, and the woman named Irene did as well.

"We don't have the Boy Scouts, but we have a co-ed softball team," she said, leaning in a little closer. "Please know that you're welcome here any time," she said, backing away, giving us our getaway distance.

We pulled back onto the road and headed to the path we were on before.

4. SATURDAY, JUNE 15, 1968

1968 CADILLAC DEVILLE CONVERTIBLE

My father spent most of his army time in Europe cataloging unused munitions after the fighting ended.

The Army gave him a camera to point and shoot at the leftovers. One day he saw in his viewfinder a strikingly beautiful woman with an infant. He had some high school French to fall back on, so he thought it would take it for a spin.

She was, however, as American as he was. Her husband, a G.I., was killed in France. When the fighting stopped, she plucked herself up against the advice of everyone around her and took her daughter to find the places where their man had been.

They became friends. My father escorted her in his Army uniform and they read *Moby Dick* together. Eventually, he gave her all the money he had so she could get back home to Delaware. She was going to become my mother, though neither of them knew it at the time.

When his hitch was up, he returned home and used his veterans' benefits to enroll in college in Philadelphia. He was intended for civil engineering, but he detoured after he took a photojournalism class as an elective. He spent more of his free time taking pictures and talking to people than working out his slide rule.

One day, though they had not been in touch for three years, she showed up again in his viewfinder. He was taking pictures of kids visiting Santa Claus at a downtown Philadelphia department store, and they knew each other as soon as he stepped out from behind the camera to ask where to send the prints.

"You'll do anything to get a girl's phone number, won't you?" she said.

"*Young girls breathe such musk that their sailor sweethearts smell them miles off shore,*" he said.

They got married. He worked during the day and took classes at night. He ditched engineering and majored in history because, as he liked to say, it's where dead people live.

She was a waitress on the weekends and when he wasn't in class. He found a job with a local newspaper that was miles past where the four-lane road shrank to two, and eventually there was me. He still took pictures with the camera, but he discovered that he liked photography with words.

He and my mother were reading the paper when I drove away in my father's car that Saturday morning to caddy at the country club. The cigarette research notebook was on the front seat.

On the radio, Mitch Rider threatened to not be back at all as I pulled behind a 1968 Cadillac convertible, a long, low cruise ship on dainty wheels. The fins of the 1950s had been reshaped as upright buttresses on either side of a massive trunk that reflected the might and plenty of an empire that had conquered the world. It was a colossal, big-ass car.

The driver was smoking. The convertible top was down, but his thick black movie-star hair was unflustered. He was swarthy and polished at the same time; his left elbow was propped on the driver-side door.

I didn't have to follow him because he was leading me straight to where I was going.

At one point, the stub sailed into the street, tumbling end-over-end, as he motored along. There was a light becoming red in front of him and the turning lane was empty.

I pulled alongside. His profile was tanned and sculpted, sporting black sunglasses. He looked about my father's age. He glanced in my direction, absently taking inventory.

I surprised myself and said good morning.

He nodded slowly, acknowledging that ship-to-ship gamming was irregular, but not inappropriate on a quiet Saturday morning.

"I saw you throw your cigarette from the car back there," I said.

The corner of his mouth curled faintly as he faced forward, toward tomorrow.

"My doctor told me to quit smoking cigars." He made sure I heard him say this through my open passenger window.

"So you throw cigarettes from the car because you can't smoke cigars?"

"I'd rather be throwing cigars."

Then the light turned, and he launched his gleaming gold pleasure barge down the road. I slid into his wake and watched him ply the road, hempen whale-line whistling from the tubs in my father's lumbering DeSoto.

The 1968 DeVille has a massive, square-jawed hood with an unforgiving, damn-the-aerodynamics prow that's bolstered by a massive black grille. I had a good chance to study the front of his car because it was parked in the country club lot when I got there.

I logged in with the caddy master, and found a spot in the shade on a slope overlooking the sixth green to wait my turn.

"You're up." The caddymaster was standing over me, lightly tapping the soles of my feet with the toe of his sneakers. The sun was behind him, spraying light around the circumference of his silhouette. "You're going out with Mr. Winthrop and a guest."

Winthrop was a banker and some kind of big shot in the club. He was a dependably stingy tipper, a 14 handicap, easy to club and willing to spend a little more time than he should have searching in the woods for lost shots.

There was a monstrous bag next to his on the rack in the bag room, with a membership tag from a fancy club down the pike toward Philadelphia. I hoisted the thing onto my shoulder—it was lighter than it looked and well balanced—and picked up Winthrop's bag by the handle. I hauled them to the spot near the first tee ball washer where you could get a good view of the fairway and waited for the golfers to walk up the hill from the practice green.

The guest was the reformed cigar-smoking Cadillac driver. He chuckled flagrantly when he saw me standing with his bag.

"Did you catch anybody else littering this morning?"

"No sir," I said, "but I'm still watching."

The other two members in the group were sharing a riding cart. I heard enough of the introductions to guess that Winthrop and another member were teamed against the guest. His name was Vic Martine.

Martine's partner, a real estate agent whose name appeared on yard signs around town, teed off first, a short, controlled swing that launched the ball on a low line drive into the middle of the fairway. It rolled to a stop after about 220 yards, at the crest of a small hill just where the first fairway doglegged to the left. He could not reach the green from there, but getting par, which was an easy five, would not be difficult.

"How far is it over those trees?" Martine asked me. There was a stand of hardwood trees at the hinge where the fairway turned, the only defense of the dogleg. Big hitters would sometimes try to drive high over the corner. If they cleared the trees, they usually had a middle-iron approach to the first green.

"It's 230 yards to the tallest oak. You can pull it left around the corner and the green is reachable in two."

From where I was standing, I could see he was taking dead aim at the tall oak. He took a deep backswing and sprang into a persimmon explosion that launched a white streak, flaming across the lazy Pennsylvania sky dead for the big oak, bending gently left as it flew over its target. From the tee box, we couldn't see where it landed, somewhere well beyond the dogleg.

I had been caddying at that club since I was 13 and the only players I had ever seen take the dogleg on the first hole like it was a chicken wing were local golf pros at the club's annual open tournament.

The other players cleared their throats, and the standers-by behind the first tee muttered. Winthrop and his partner, who was on the membership committee, hit safely up the middle, ending up somewhat sheepishly close to the real estate agent's lie. Martine handed me his driver without looking my way as we walked down the slope from the first tee.

Martine was a sociable golfer, chatting with the others as they gathered around their first shots. From the top of the hill at the dogleg, we could see his ball far ahead in the middle of the fairway at a place that hackers struggled to reach in two. The others in the group did manage to get past him with their second shots.

He had a good lie about 180 yards from the pin, and I presented his bag with a little more curiosity than usual about his club selection. I knew what most members would hit from there, but I had no clue how to club him. He fingered his six iron and then pulled out the seven.

He ripped his second shot high and straight at the heart of the green, landing on the back third before it jerked back toward the middle of the green. This left him a 10-foot putt for eagle. Winthrop got safely on in three; the other two chipped their fourth shots from close range onto the green. Martine's partner, the real estate agent, got within eight feet of the hole, but Winthrop's teammate made a hash of it. Winthrop left his first putt short.

In other words, all three members took their fourth shots before the guest lined up his third. I didn't know what the game was, or what strokes were being given, but watching from the edge of green with the flag in my hands, I figured Martine had to have won this hole. He measured his putt carefully and hit an alarmingly firm stroke straight at the hole. It skipped over the cup and rolled almost as far on the other side as his first putt had been. He left the comeback for birdie a few inches short, while Winthrop coaxed in his par.

This did not seem to bother Martine at all.

And that is how the match unfolded. Off the tee and in the fairway, he he was sublime, finessing the wind and leveraging the terrain. Around the green, he was a lumberjack with a chain saw.

Sometimes he would use a club that clearly lacked enough firepower, leaving himself well short of the target. Sometimes he seemed to deliberately aim at hazards, as though this were just a practice round, out to work on his sand play or near-green approaches. Still, they were a merry foursome, and the guest's running joke, reiterated in varying forms, was that he was simply "doing his part to keep the club solvent."

I did not understand what this meant, but I believed then that I wasn't meant to understand everything. As we came down the 18th fairway, Martine stopped me and pulled a cigar from his golf bag, his first smoke of the round. "Is this okay with you?" he asked.

"The way you've been throwing strokes away out here, I doubt anybody would notice." This was not my usual Boy Scout manner, but I was disappointed because it wasn't often I caddied for a golfer capable of shooting par or better, only to watch him throw it away.

"For what it's worth," Martine said, "you can learn something about a man who wins that you won't see when he loses." He dropped his cigar on the ground and drilled a four wood that rose higher as it soared down the dead center of the fairway and then softly nested in the heart of the 18th green, eagle country again.

"But it isn't always clear," he said quietly as I headed off to tend to my other caddy duties.

When the round was over, Winthrop gave me his usual $2 tip. The guest gave me $25.

When I got home that afternoon, there was a package for me from the Boy Scouts. It was the booklet on how to earn a merit badge in journalism.

5. SUNDAY, JUNE 16, 1968

1959 MERCURY MONTEREY

I was still in the Boy Scouts that summer between my junior and senior years of high school. I had achieved the Life Scout rank and, on paper I was still hiking toward Eagle Scout. I had accumulated more merit badges than the 10 needed to qualify for Eagle. A few more were unfinished.

My scout uniform didn't fit. The pant legs were let out as far as they would go, and the waistband was tight. I stopped buttoning the top of the shirt. At my age, I should have joined the Explorer Scouts.

I was tooling along in my mother's Dart on assignment to fetch my sister and bring her home for our Father's Day cookout. When I left the house, my father was Dagwooding the living-room sofa, his nose buried in the back cushion and legs folded behind him.

Weaving toward the Schuylkill Expressway, I came up behind a 1959 Mercury Monterey in robin's egg blue. The fins were sloped distinctively at a 45-degree angle from the horizon, each one forming a wedge that pointed in toward the middle of the trunk.

In those days, the automobile was a canvas. The 1962 Monterey had its full share of chrome and fins that carried all the way to the front edge of the front door—in fact, the door handles were in the middle of the fin.

There was a woman in the co-pilot's seat, smoking a cigarette. Between puffs she extended her long brown arm lazily out of the car as though she were lounging by the pool, and casually tapping ash into the on-rushing breeze.

I followed the Mercury for about a mile before she finished her smoke with an index-finger flick from an underhand position. At the next stoplight, I pulled up alongside on the Mercury on her leeward side.

They were listening to the Poncho Sanchez version of "Watermelon Man." She had dark, striking eyes and a wide mouth. Her shoulders twisted slowly with the rhythm of the song and I could see the driver was nodding in time, his fingers dancing along the top of the steering wheel. There were three kids in the back seat, two of whom were waving their arms in the air over their heads.

A party on wheels.

"Watermelon Man" ended and the woman looked over at me in the quiet between songs.

"You dropped your cigarette back there on the road," I said, smiling, wanting to be helpful.

She was puzzled.

"Your cigarette." I pantomimed a smoker. "You dropped it back there on the road." I made a motion of a person flicking away a cigarette butt.

Her expression shifted a gear. She knew what I was saying. She just couldn't figure out why.

"Are jou some kinduva Boy Scout or something?"

By then her man was looking across the front seat at me, and turning down the radio. He was serious. The kids in the back stilled themselves.

"As a matter of fact, I am a Boy Scout," I said, "but that's not why I mentioned the cigarette."

You can never overplay the Boy Scout card. Time after time, complete strangers give you more room and edges are sanded smoother, if only by a millimeter or two. It may not be too late for you to join. Or say you did.

The light changed colors.

"I just wondered why you flicked the cigarette out in the road." I gave her the merit-badge smile.

"Well jou know tobacco don't smell so good. It smell bad in the car and for the kids."

The green light beckoned, but there was no one behind us, so we didn't move.

"So you threw it out to make the car cleaner?"

"Jes, it keep the car cleaner." This seemed to satisfy her husband, who pulled away into the open road.

I waited for the light to cycle through.

I wondered as I drove into the city whether I could use our cigarette-littering research for the journalism merit badge.

**AREA YOUTH STOPS MOTORISTS
TO DISCUSS CIGARETTE BUTTS**

Law-enforcement agencies are trying to gather information about an unarmed teenager who has been confronting area drivers about cigarette littering.

My half-sister was waiting on the front stoop of the West Philadelphia row house where she rented an apartment with two intimidating women who seemed to share a private amusement whenever I was near. I was not completely sure what a lesbian was (it's not covered in the Boy Scout manual), but I had an inkling they might have been some.

Katie was from the other side of hippie, the beatniks, a more inscrutable species that could fool you by looking almost normal. If sandals are normal in any kind of weather.

She climbed into the car and grabbed my head in both her hands and planted her older-sister kiss on my temple. We did not have a lot of common interests, but we were never far apart.

We went to visit Uncle James before heading home for the picnic. Perennially suntanned, exotic and effervescent, he was a version of my father unyoked by husbandry. I was stunned the first time I saw James after my father brought him back from California. He was barely conscious, sitting in a bed and unable to move or respond to us in any way.

I came to know Uncle James from the annual visits he made to visit his family back East. We would hang out in the back yard and devise our own constellations in the night sky from the available stars. Sometimes he would go out by himself and come back well into morning, sleeping late, laughing raucously at breakfast. I thought I was uncommonly lucky to have such an uncle, willing to play on the carpet with my trucks and listen wide-eyed to my scouting adventures.

Now, he had been deposited in a home for people who couldn't live on their own. My father said it was ironic that they couldn't put him in the hospital where my sister worked, a famous mental hospital founded by Quakers. James had made his career in mental health but because his skull was stove in by a surfboard, he had head trauma and not a mental disease or an addiction that would have qualified him for the Friends' home.

In fact, James's career had inspired my half-sister to go into nursing and work at the Quaker hospital where he could not be admitted.

But when Katie and I got there that Father's Day afternoon, Uncle James was not in the room where I had seen him before. We tracked down a nurse who said he was sitting with other residents in the social room. Katie and I looked at each other. As far as we knew, he had been in bed since he got there.

"How did he get there?" Katie asked.

The nurse shrugged her shoulders. "His new doctor said he needs to be around folks, so we propped him up in a wheelchair and moved him out wit the others."

"His new doctor?" Katie was more on top of this than I was.

"Dat nice doctor been in here a couple times this week."

We eventually found Uncle James sitting in a semicircle of men with empty faces in a room where sunlight washed over a linoleum floor.

"You have a new doctor?" Katie asked. But it was pointless; James was still lost.

My sister had met the doctor who was, apparently, now his former doctor, and had come away unimpressed. "I can't say a change won't help," she said, "but I wonder how it happened."

She looked at Uncle James for an answer. His jaw moved. Nothing came out.

After a half hour or so, we stood and leaned over him awkwardly, hugging a man in a wheelchair. Into my ear he mumbled something that sounded like "chatter nicely," but I figured I was inventing meaning for him.

"*You've got unknown worlds that empty into thee,*" I said. His eyes flickered with the strain of struggling vainly to command his voice. Then he quit and looked inward.

We checked at the nurse's station before we left, but there was no one there who could tell us about his new doctor.

On the way home, the car radio informed us that a golfer named Lee Trevino was on his way to winning the U.S. Open by beating some hacker named Nicklaus.

1961 Dodge Phoenix

My mother was a homecoming queen who married her high school boyfriend as he was shipping out for the war in Europe. Her talent in the Miss Delaware competition was yodeling. She played the piano, but she liked to say that anyone could do that.

Mother said that being a beauty pageant contestant has its rewards, though some people think it's superficial. She did not go to college or business school. After she and my father married, she worked at a swanky restaurant and taught herself bartending. None of this went over well with the Yardleys, who, she said, never got over their youngest son's decision to take up arms in the war.

When I got to junior high school, Mother started working behind the bar at the country club. She stayed in Miss Delaware form and sometimes, on winter nights, went out in the back yard and yodeled into the woods.

She was a great favorite of every guy who belonged to that country club. And most of the dogs in our neighborhood.

When Katie and I got home from visiting Uncle James, it was my mother who asked how he was.

"I didn't know he has a new doctor," Katie said.

My mother and father looked at each other and then back at us.

"A new doctor?" Speedy repeated. This was news to everyone.

"We didn't meet him, but the nurse said a new doctor is seeing him," Katie said. "Whoever he is, he told the staff to get James out of bed and in a wheelchair with the others."

"That's where we found him," I offered. In fact, he did look better upright, with other people around.

"How did he look?"

"Better, actually," Katie said. "Anything's better than leaving him in bed all day."

The three of us accepted Katie's views on medical matters.

"Where did this new doctor come from?" my father asked. Speedy had been concerned from the beginning about whether his brother was getting the right care. Of course, no one knew the answer.

"That's all we could get out of them, Daddy," my sister said. He never formally adopted her, but she still called him Daddy.

"Hmmm," he muttered, setting mental enzymes to work on this mystery. Anxious about James's health care, my father was still lobbying his parents to be named his brother's guardian, and he was getting nowhere. Grandfather Yardley—a stern, quiet man who rarely smiled—insisted in a very insistent way that he was his son's guardian.

"*Thinking is a coolness and a calmness*," Speedy said in Dick Mobius mode, "*but our poor hearts throb and our poor brains beat too much for that.*"

The fireflies were coming up from the lawn, and we had work to get to the next day. I agreed to take Katie home after the cookout, and she offered to drive the first leg. We were zipping south on the Schuylkill Expressway, all four windows rolled down in our mother's car so the summer evening rushed noisily all around us, when a 1961 Dodge Phoenix, an intergalactic traveler with bizarre wings and a space-age array of windows, flew past us, the driver's face partially illuminated by interior lights, a cigarette dangling in his lips.

"Follow that car," I said.

"Is this for your weirdo study?" she asked.

"We gotta see what he does with the cigarette."

She obligingly picked up the pace and slip-streamed into the left lane, tracking the Phoenix. It was the two-door model, with the wing starting just behind the door as a pair of parallel chrome lines. Its top edge leaned inward, over the trunk, creating a surface that faced up and away from the car. The wing itself was scooped out, but when it made the finishing arc it was still facing away from the car at an angle. The whole thing looked like a long, road-hugging flying fish.

It was also an open-road rocket, and Katie had to push the Dart to keep pace. The Doors' "Strange Days" was on the radio, a good soundtrack for logging sociological data. After a mile or so, the driver flicked his cigarette into the highway wind, and it hit the pavement in a miniature fireworks display, spraying red sparks splintering across the road.

"Now what?" Katie asked.

"Sometimes we follow them and ask them why they threw their cigarettes out the window."

"Okay." She took the challenge and pushed ahead into the middle lane, alongside the Phoenix.

We pulled even with the car, but we couldn't see the driver clearly. Katie turned down the Doors.

"Hey! Asshole!" she yelled. "You threw your butt in the road back there!"

"Fuck off, man," the driver replied, giving us the finger.

Katie gave him the finger back. I lifted my right hand out of the window and gave him my finger too.

It was my first time.

"That felt kinda good," Katie said, as she lifted her foot off the gas and we slowed to our normal pace.

7. WEDNESDAY, JUNE 19, 1968

1959 FORD FAIRLANE

I was hitchhiking home from work Wednesday evening because my father said he had some business to take care of and would be too late to give me a ride. It wasn't unusual for him to work in the evening, covering the school board meetings and candidates' debates that kept our seafaring life afloat.

I walked through town and when I got to the main street that led toward Acushnet, I began to walk backward on the shoulder of the road with my thumb raised in the direction of home.

Hitchhiking was not sanctioned by the Boy Scouts, who encourage just hiking wherever it is you have to go. That's why we have those clunky brown shoes. But in 1968, hitchhiking was a viable enterprise. There were still plenty of survivors from the hard times and the era of pitching in. Cars were capsules of private property, but people were more willing to share them with strangers.

I walked backward for a couple of blocks. It was usually harder to get a ride in the borough limits, even though cars were stopping and slowing all the time, than it was out by the Thanks for Visiting sign.

Fishing for rides requires careful aim, projecting innocence without vulnerability while appraising the approaching driver. Some want no eye contact; others will stop if you've caught them noticing you. Most pay little attention and you know early you have no chance. Sometimes you want nothing to do with them, and reel in your thumb and turn your back.

I thought I had landed a guy in an old Plymouth, but he pulled away just as I turned to walk toward his car. I spun around—no one owes you anything out there on the high road—and swung my thumb up in the air at an oncoming copper-colored 1959 Ford Fairlane Ranch Wagon. The driver, a girl, looked quickly in my direction and I felt the car's momentum downshifting for me.

It stopped just a few yards away. The girl was heaving clutter from the front seat to the back, hurriedly clearing away the debris to make a

place for me to sit. This was hitchhiker etiquette turned inside out. She
had a cigarette in her mouth. I waited patiently at the passenger door,
wondering at this unexpected turn of events. Girls driving alone never
stopped for hitchhikers. I looked at her through the rolled-down window and she leaned, twisting toward me so she could see up out the
passenger-side window. She wore a close-fitting blouse that was
opened far enough at the neck to reveal cleavage.

"Can you give me a ride to Fairview Road?" I asked, willing myself
to look away. I recognized her then as Juliana Madison, a girl from my
class at school. She was wearing glasses, which made her seem older
and possibly more dangerous.

She took the cigarette from her lips with her left hand and, without
looking, turned her shoulders and dropped it out the driver-side window into the street. I chuckled, which wrinkled her forehead as she
opened the door for me, leaning further.

"What's so funny?" she asked as we pulled away from the curb. "I
have to wear these damn glasses when I'm driving."

"It's not the glasses. You won't believe this, but I'm counting people
who throw cigarettes from their cars," I said, settling in. I was trying to
convince myself that this was nothing to get excited about: a girl of
sought-after proportions being neighborly to a boy from her school
who was known to be harmless. I didn't have a name for this encounter, but it was a big upgrade from eating lunch a few dozen yards apart
in a crowded cafeteria.

"Is that a Boy Scout thing?" she asked with gentle mischief. Our
paths had crossed from time to time, but ours was a big school.

"You never know. We are running low on old ladies waiting to cross
the street."

"What's so great about the other side of the street anyway?" She
had dark hair, cut short and she wore rings on her fingers. She was not
one of those girls who stand out in a crowd, but I usually was aware
when she was nearby in the whirling cloud of hormones at school.

"They can't help themselves. They've got chickens strapped on
their backs." I was looking at her thighs. She hung out with the hippie
contingent, such as it was, in our suburban fringe.

"So why did you throw the cigarette out the window?" Feeling
more comfortable, chatting her up in her family's '59 Ford.

"I get grounded if I get caught smoking. Leaving a butt in the ashtray would be pretty dumb." She was looking straight ahead, two
hands firmly on the steering wheel, following every rule of driver-

education class except the one about throwing cigarettes from the car, and giving me lots of opportunity to study her profile while she knew I was doing so.

There was a lightness in her voice, an intimation that we were sharing more than a ride into the sun on an early summer evening. I could feel myself responding to her in a physical way completely independent of the soundtrack going on in my head.

"Don't you ever do anything you're not supposed to do?" she asked.

In fact, I didn't. "I've been thinking maybe I should try." One hand on the wheel, she dug a pack of cigarettes out of her bag on the seat between us and offered it to me.

"Uh, no, I didn't mean smoking."

"No, you don't want to start out with the hard stuff." Smiling with a straight face.

"I thought about littering, but, ya know, I really don't want to. Maybe profanity."

She laughed. "Yes, that's a good start."

"Goddammit, yes, that's what I will do. I will start some damn swearing."

"How does that make you feel, now that you're dangerous?"

"My mind is spinning. I mean my mind is shitting swimming, the bastard."

"Fucking swimming. It would be better if you said your mind is fucking swimming."

"I need lessons. My parents don't swear. I think my sister does, but she's never around."

"What goddamn good is she?"

"Yes, the gosh-darn son of a bitch."

"Or something like that."

The Ohio Express was coming on the radio, ready to launch into its tribute to yummy. I was aware, even as a Boy Scout, that this was bubblegum. Yet Juliana was drumming her fingers and began to sing along. I did not understand the lyrics or what it means to have love in the tummy, and I began to fear that the moment we were having was fluttering away, like something written on a tiny slip of paper sucked out the window and blown down the highway behind us.

Juliana glanced at me, grinning and singing, completely at ease in herself. I wished I had paid more attention to this sugary concoction the first 600 times I heard it on the radio. I think I summoned up a grimace that looked only slightly constipated. Her eyes lingered on my face, road kill in the merciless rat race of courtship, and then she turned back to the road.

A form lumped up in my throat. I was suddenly aware of the scent of golf-course fertilizer and dried sweat. And pretty sure it wasn't coming from her.

No more cavalier banter. I was almost thankful that we were coming up to the turn-off to my house. At this point in a hitched ride, I would get out and walk the rest of the way unless I happened to get picked up by another inmate from our particular suburban cellblock. Where we lived, there were only two auto-accessible outlets to the rest of the world, and the other one was a less-traveled country road that connected only to more of its kind. I didn't know where Juliana lived, but I knew it wasn't back up in my neck of the woods.

"This is my street up here," I said.

"Your goddamn street."

Here is the wonderful, beautiful thing about being just one person and not everyone in the universe. You can lead yourself down a dismal, self-loathing path to utter desperation and the person you're sitting next to is still back there where you left her, sweeter than sugar, her tummy overflowed with yummy, and never having let you go.

"Yes. This is my goddamn street." Juliana was already turning into our subdivision and suddenly I was thinking about the tops of her breasts and her smoky breath and the fact that there was no one at home. I directed her to our house, right into our driveway, where there were no cars and only the looming unpeopled, unchaperoned house.

I had taken a stout girl who lived a few doors away to a school dance, but the outing seemed more like practice for when each of us would end up, separately, on real dates. Until then, I had never put my arms around the heavy fruit of promise in the air hanging like fuzzy dice from the rearview mirror. Juliana had wisdom and knew what to do. She had me.

Maybe she heard the thought forming in my head; maybe she was thinking something remotely parallel herself. Her mouth said, "I gotta get home," but she shoved the transmission lever up into park, not reverse, and turned to look at me.

"Thanks for the ride."

Eyes were talking for about 15 seconds. "Cool," she said. "Keep practice your cussing. I'm expecting to hear you swearing like a fucking sailor the next time."

"You are really a big help with that."

"A big fucking help."

"Yup, a big fucking help."

Another 10 seconds strained the eye contact. Something has to give, I thought, feeling around in the dark inside my brain.

Out loud, apparently, I asked her if she wanted to go out sometime. Apparently the voice of hormones was talking through me, because she nodded and smiled and said that would be cool. Juliana fetched a pen from her bag and took my hand in hers, turning the palm up, and I remember feeling the magic of her holding my hand in hers as she wrote her phone number on my palm.

I felt like a dope standing there in our driveway, waving goodbye to her with the hand on which she had written her phone number. But I was nevertheless a happy fucking dope, and I probably had a boner. She flashed the peace sign and drove off to her corner in suburbia.

8. THURSDAY, JUNE 20, 1968

1964 VOLKSWAGEN BUS

I was getting a ride home with my mother. On the radio, the newsman said Thailand had adopted a new constitution that day because astrologers said it was auspicious. The Thai national air force dropped flowers and popcorn from the sky. Buddhists played gongs and drums.

"Why don't we ever do anything like that?" my mother asked.

It was hot in the car and it would be hot at home. My mother was the only one of us who had air conditioning in her day, mixing cocktails in the country-club lounge, looking through oversized windows upon the pilgrimage of golfers thrashing away at the sod in the mad-dog sun.

She didn't need air conditioning to be cool; nature did not fluster her.

We were driving west toward home into the sun, still high and hazy, enjoying its longest romp of the year across the Northern Hemisphere. Afore our bow, a 1964 Volkswagen bus, in worn-out beige, was festooned with bumper stickers for the Soft Machine, a drug store in South Dakota, and Bobby. There were two rear hatches, one for the cargo/passenger compartment and one below to access the engine. It was an uncommonly tall passenger vehicle for its time, with side windows that seemed clamped on as afterthoughts.

The driver was smoking. I was hoping for a decisive action before the van might turn off our path. The VW was blowing smoke out the window, a statistically significant positive indicator.

We came to the last traffic light between us and home. In the van, the driver's right hand went to his mouth. The light turned green. He took another drag and flicked the butt past his left shoulder and into the street. The Volkswagen lurched straight ahead, and we steered left, to my disappointment.

It had grown quiet in the car while I was tracking the VW. As we rolled along the leafy entrance of our subdivision, I cleared my throat and announced that I was looking forward to going to go to a rock concert with a friend. This was a first for me.

My mother held that for a moment and then asked who the friend was. A new friend, I said, a girl.

"Do I know her?" she asked. I couldn't imagine how she could.

We were within sight of home. My mother was slowing the car so we wouldn't get there too soon. "Her name is Juliana."

"Is she cute?"

"Well, she cannot yodel, as far as I know."

A chuckle. "Does she know she's your girlfriend?" The car stopped in our driveway, but the ride wasn't over.

"We aren't there yet." My tongue felt thick. "I mean, we're friends and she's a girl."

My mother smiled her cool Miss Delaware smile.

Harpooned, I had called Juliana the night she gave me a ride home, before the ink was washed from my palm. She asked me on the phone if I wanted to go see the Doors later that summer and I thought she asked if I knew someone named Doris, which became my unfortunate nickname in our cozy, two-person universe.

"I guess I don't know her very well at all," I said, as we sat in the front seat of my mother's car, listening to the engine cool down. "She calls me Doris."

"That's different," Mother said. "Getting to know someone you already like is one of the nicest things there is."

She was remembering. "I felt that way about Rockwell from the start." There were years in her voice. "I grew up with Katie's dad and it was, well, predictable and easy when we got married, even though it was an awful time in the middle of the war. It was a marriage that I rushed into—we both did—and don't get me wrong, I loved Katie's dad and it would have worked out just fine for us."

She turned to face me. "But Speedy and I really found each other, thousands of miles from home, going in totally different ways. Or so it seemed at the time."

Neither of us wanted to get out of the car.

"It turned out we were going the same way," she said, reaching the back of her hand to brush my cheek. "I love you guys so much."

She withdrew the key from the ignition, and we climbed out our separate doors and took our time walking into the house. We made supper together, knocking around in the kitchen like co-conspirators, and when my father came home, she grabbed him in a not-so-casual way.

He was full of his day, lit up from a protest he had gone to at the Delaware Canal, the oldest of a once-common breed of enterprises that still had water and, in some places, working locks. He had gone to report on a rally against a proposal to fill in a stretch of the canal so developers could build roads and houses along the river.

My father was excited because a justice of the U.S. Supreme Court, a Minnesotan named William O. Douglas, was there to support the protesters.

"Justice Douglas said that trees and paths and waterways should have the same legal protection that people and corporations have," my father told us over our hamburgers and salad as the sun began to set. "He said the environment and all its parts should have standing to bring lawsuits in court. It was the damnedest thing I ever heard."

I was trying to picture trees in a courtroom.

"When I was a kid, we used to go fishing over there and no one gave much thought to the barges on the canal. And then one year, they weren't there. It was funny to have this big-shot Supreme Court justice and his newsmen and photographers and FBI spies making so much noise about preservation.

"Nobody can bring the barges back," he said.

Then something came to his mind. "I started to interview this guy who didn't seem like one of the protesters—his shoes just weren't right—and he started to tell me why he was there and then stopped. He asked me if I was undercover, which is the most bizarre thing anyone has ever asked me.

"I told him I worked for the paper, and he thought about it for a moment and said he didn't have anything to tell me."

9. Saturday, June 22, 1968

1960 Fiat 1100

It was gray and fixing to rain. I got up early with the expectation that I would caddy that day. Even for a Boy Scout, the weather was discouraging. There would be a few incorrigibles dragging two-wheeled golf bag handcarts behind them. If the rain got heavy, as forecast, the country club would refuse to put out the motorized golf carts, the godless nemeses of caddies. A few stylish daredevils would hire boys to walk the course with them while they tromped along under massive umbrellas.

But there would be few such lunatics out on such a day.

I heard thunder to the west, haunting and out of place before breakfast.

My dad came into the kitchen.

"Are you going to caddy in this?" he said, looking out the back window at the thrashing of the treetops.

"Maybe I'll go in later if the rain lets up."

"You could go with me to Washington?"

"What's there?"

"It's the closing of the Poor People's Campaign. They've had lousy weather most of the time it's been there."

My father had filed one story about the PPC a few weeks before, as trains of people headed from all angles toward an encampment on the Mall in Washington, D.C. A contingent of Puerto Ricans from New York City had crossed a tiny corner of our county, prompting Speedy to go ask what they hoped to accomplish.

Another gust pitched itself at our house.

"Okay, Dad. I'll go with you."

"Maybe you can get something from this for your journalism merit badge," he suggested. In fact, over the years I had done almost everything that was required for it in the normal course of my life: visit a newsroom, talk to an editor, and go with a reporter on assignment. What I had never done was write a news story myself.

We made peanut butter-and-jelly sandwiches and said goodbye to Mother.

My dad slung his arm over the back of the seat of the DeSoto to look through the rear window as we slowly backed out of the driveway. "We've got a stop to make first. I promised to give Irene Bennett a ride."

"Who?"

"We went to high school together. You met her at the Friends meeting."

I did not know what to make of this.

The streets were nearly empty. We cruised into Doylestown with the wipers earnestly slapping away at the storm. Speedy parked in front of a wood-frame house in an old neighborhood near the high school.

"I'll be right back."

He walked through light rain to her front porch and knocked on the screen door. He looked at home with what he was doing, but then, he usually did. He spoke to someone inside the door and then looked toward me.

The door opened and a woman stepped out. She locked her front door and turned around, smiling uncertainly. He gestured in my direction and his non-pointing arm embraced her, steering gently. They seemed almost like brother and sister, and I immediately decided that I belonged in the back seat. I got out of the car just as they were approaching.

"Irene, you remember Izzy," my father said.

"The nice Old Testament boy who tries to appreciate your sense of humor," she said, smiling and reaching to shake hands.

"Irene and I knew each other when we were your age," he said to me. "Our families go way back."

"Your father has tried to leave all that behind," she said, good-naturedly. "Maybe you and I can thwart him."

She winked.

I made my move for the rear door, muttering something about wanting to stretch out and take a nap. Miss Bennett and I gently collided trying to get around one another. Until that moment, the daytrip to Washington with my father's mysterious woman friend had seemed almost daring, an unpredictable experiment with unknown possibilities.

But when we bumped into each other I knew this wasn't about romance, no matter what might have been in the long-ago. Two auras can exchange a lot of data under the right conditions.

Once on the highway, I drifted in and out of a shallow, dozy kind of time passage. They were talking about Uncle James, whose first doctor had come back in the picture. Or maybe he never left. Over dinner that week, my father kept us updated on his efforts to track down the mystery doctor, all of which had so far led nowhere. No one at the rehab home seemed to know anything about him.

I drifted off for good somewhere in Delaware, I think.

Coming up for a gulp of awareness, I sifted through a folder of news photographs on the back seat. I recognized a stretch of the Delaware Canal, the waterway nearly 150 years old that sauntered from Easton to Bristol. These were photos of people marching and signs that read "Save the Canal!" and people making speeches.

In one of the photographs, I recognized Vic Martine, the country club guest whom I had caddied for. *Hunh*, I said to myself, and folded it up and put it in my wallet before sliding again into the drizzly highway ride. I missed the bridge over the Susquehanna and when I realized I was in Maryland, the adults were talking about the Poor People's Campaign. From what I could tell, it wasn't going so well.

When we got to the city of Washington, we parked on a street near the Mall. My dad got out of the car and leaned his shoulders across the roof, stretching out his arms.

"I've been sitting far too long," he said. "There's yellow lines down the middle of my mind."

A 1960 two-tone Fiat 1100 rolled to a stop next to us. The man inside had on a white shirt with two vertical stripes running from the collar to his waist, a slick black mustache and a white hat. He was smoking a cigarette and leaning across the middle of his car so he could see our faces.

"Are you leaving this parking place now?" he asked.

The 1100 was the upscale Fiat, not the cheapo shoebox on wheels, and yet clowns could have come pouring out of it at any minute. It was boxy, but smoothed on all its edges, with a brown panel running from the leading edge of the front door back to a modest fin. It had a dowdy shape saved by a streak of chrome along the flank that gave the car a forward lean, like it was going somewhere even when it was standing still.

"No, we just got here," my dad said, leaning into the Fiat's passenger-side front window. "Parking is hard to come by."

"Yes, I know," the man said. He had an accent, but I couldn't tell where it might be from.

Sure enough, the driver leaned back in his seat and tossed his cigarette out into the street.

"Pardon me, friend, but ya know you just threw your cigarette in the street," my dad said.

"It's okay. I am done with it," the man said. He was studying the street ahead for a potential parking space, and a taxi had pulled up behind him, honking for him to get moving.

"But you had options. You could have done anything with it. Why did you throw it in the street?"

"It's okay, mister. I am done with it," and he saluted the cabdriver behind him with his left hand out the window and started to move off before he stopped suddenly. "I'm sorry, mister; you want a cigarette?" he said, leaning toward my dad again.

"No, thanks. I don't smoke."

"You don't smoke, but you have all these questions." And the Fiat jumped ahead, resuming its quest for a resting place.

The sky was opaque and sodden, but it wasn't raining. We trudged to Independence Avenue and then a few blocks west until we reached the encampment.

The Poor People's Campaign had squatted down in West Potomac Park, declared itself Resurrection City, and sprawled across one end of the reflecting pool and toward the Lincoln Memorial. It was a village of plywood and canvas that should have washed away in a good stiff rain if not for the fact that it was mired in low ground with drainage to nowhere. When it rained, the swamp had no recourse but to wait at the bottom of the ramshackle settlement to be disbursed by people tromping through and methodically carrying away the mud between their toes.

The structures were of varying quality. Some looked as though they were made by knowing and caring hands, but many seemed to have been assembled by people who had never made anything more complicated than a sandwich.

Other structures were abandoned, a display of contemporary archeology in progress. The people who were still there had over the weeks bolstered their constructions to withstand Washington's unusually rainy summer. Their shanties were raised a few inches above the mud. The protestors who had decamped the city, and a lot of them had gone by then, left behind flimsier structures that were sagging into the muck as so many broken-down mammoths sinking tragi-comically into tar pits. The fittest, in fact, do persist. The rest surrender to the mud.

It was a pedestrian settlement, with no accommodation for cars. Chickens would not have seemed out of place. People milling about. There was a march to be got on in a little while, from the unvanquished Resurrection City to the Capitol.

It was Saturday and there weren't likely to be many lawmakers waiting around to hear what riled-up poor people had to gripe about that couldn't wait until regular business hours.

We stopped at a sturdy shelter where a mother and four kids were tidying up. Miss Bennett knew them, and there were enthusiastic greetings all around and the kids beamed at her, and at my father and me, as though it was the best treat to be entertaining visitors at their shack on this gritty June day.

They were from coal-mining country in West Virginia. The oldest girl was about my age. She was skinny and blonde and not the least bit uncomfortable about being on display in the muddy poverty museum while tourists like me wandered by.

You cannot tell what adults will do. Miss Bennett introduced me as someone working on a journalism merit badge; the topic must have come up in the car when I was napping. Before I knew it, the girl, who was named Charlotte, turned to me and said: "Do you want to interview me for your newspaper story? I've been interviewed before." Her younger brother and two sisters were watching me. The adults were wrapped in their own conversation.

"Well, so, where are you from?"

"West Virginia." I knew this already, but she didn't try to make me feel dumb for asking. "We came here on the Appalachian Train, which is not a real train. It was really just some busses that picked folks up in Tennessee and Kentucky and Virginia and country like that. We all came here to learn more about poverty and what we can do to help people get enough to eat and find good work and a decent place to live."

She had a directness and honesty that convinced me this was not an answer that she had been taught to give. Or maybe it was, but she believed it anyway.

I didn't know what to say or do. So I waited for her to continue the interview without me. At the time, I didn't know that acting dumb is actually a solid, time-honored reporting technique.

"I think the most important thing is to know that we are blessed with more than we need to accomplish these things," she said. "We have enough food. We have enough doctors and nurses. We have plenty of work to do, good work that will make us stronger. We can build or fix enough housing."

Suddenly I started talking. "Don't people complain about having to pay taxes and give handouts to the poor?" I grimaced when I said "poor" because I was afraid she would think I was putting her down. "I'm sorry; I didn't mean to say that you're poor."

She laughed. "Well, we're not. Not having a television set isn't what makes you poor. One thing we have in common with the poor is that we're not wasting anything. Actually, coming here has made me realize how much we really have."

I was still about 72 percent Boy Scout, but her positive outlook seemed a little creepy.

"On account of how everybody else here is poor too? I mean, not wasting anything?"

Her smile captured and gave me the sun. "You don't believe me, do you? You think I'm pretending to myself."

It was unnerving that she seemed pleased that I wasn't bowled over by it all. "Heck, I don't know." Which was the truth. "I guess I like living in a regular house more than a cardboard shack in the mud."

She reached out and touched my arm. Maybe that made it easier for the truth to flow through her to me. "Don't get me wrong," she said, "I greatly prefer living in our house back home. But if it weren't for this cardboard shack in the mud, we would have not have met. Am I right?"

"Well, there's something to that," I said. I was steaming up right pretty there in the early afternoon sun in the landfill west of the Capitol building.

I was vaguely aware that my father and Miss Bennett had drifted off along the muddy "street" that led down the middle of the encampment. But I was glued in my shoes, pinned down by the weight of the muggy sky overhead and tethered to this girl from West Virginia.

Molecules in the soupy air slowed and thudded against each other like constant tiny hailstones. My head felt exposed in the hazy sun and Miss West Virginia was looking around, anywhere but at me.

"Doesn't this heat bother you?" I ventured, finally giving in.

"It's been no picnic, I can tell you. Sometimes it cools off a bit at night, but really, we've had so much rain that it's nice when it stops. Even if it's yucky."

Heads bobbing perilously on limp bodies were swirling around us, a gentle heaving tide of sticky people in various stages of ornery, tired, stressed, fed up. It had been a long People's encampment full of setbacks from the leadership, a hostile and uninterested media, Speedy had said, and a government presence that was focused on containing the project geographically and politically. Neither Congress nor the White House wanted much to do with the campaign, and the District of Columbia was keen on preventing it from spilling beyond the public spaces of which it had been granted temporary tenancy.

"There's a nice place by the river where we cool off. You can also hang out in the lobby of Federal Reserve, but it's not open on Saturdays."

"The river sounds good."

To get to the river, ironically, we started by wading into the Reflecting Pool. The water was stagnant and embellished with more than the usual amount of human debris; it had been at the center of a massive rally a few days before, a day of marching and speeches and picnics that included a great deal more demonstrators than were actually left among the dwindling citizenry of Resurrection City. I felt as though I was slogging through a gigantic bathtub that had been most recently used by 55,000 people.

As we climbed out of the Reflecting Pool, we set our compass for tall timber to the northwest. Charlotte held her youngest sister's hand, while the brother stayed in front of us. The second youngest girl took my hand, but she was guiding me as much as holding on for security. The four of them seemed completely at home with what was going on around them, and we were soon enough outside the boundary of the Poor People's encampment and heading through a line of trees bordering the Mall.

Getting out of the encampment helped some. Reaching the trees made a bigger difference. By and by, I began to feel more like a part of the group, glued to them by the denominator of trekking in the same direction.

Charlotte and I traded resumes, about the parents we were with that day and the ones left behind. Her father was a union representative at a coal mine; I told her my mother was a beauty queen who tended bar. She was writing letters to soldiers serving in Vietnam, letters of encouragement and support even though she thought the war was wrong. I was keeping the grass flat and smooth so people with discretionary income could fritter away the hours chasing a white ball around the countryside.

We crossed 23rd Avenue and continued along a path that took us across a series of smaller streets and then almost to the bank of the Potomac River.

The river was brown from the rain and shipping jetsam that could have come all the way from West Virginia toward the sea. It was quiet and full of self-importance and the other shore looked far away— broader and fuller of volume than the Delaware I knew. We followed a path under a bridge overhead that spanned the river to Virginia and then slipped along a muddy little trail into a woods.

A few yards upstream of the bridge, we spilled onto a grassy clearing beside the riverbank. It was shaded by trees, and the moving water stirred the air enough to approximate a cooling effect.

The kids were immediately out of their sneakers and into the water, up to the bottoms of their shorts. Charlotte took off her jeans; she wore yellow underwear with green flowers. She looked over her shoulder at me, at my dumbfounded expression, and said, "Come on in."

I took off my sneakers and socks and arranged them with a Boy Scout's sensibility, but I hesitated long enough over the waist button of my khakis that my momentum stalled. I leaned over and rolled my pant legs up above my calves and then yanked them as far as they would go toward my knees. She was bent over, rinsing her arms in the river and paying no obvious attention to me. In case you haven't noticed, there is something about teenage girls in their underwear bent over.

The water was good. There was a gravel bar underfoot and the barely perceptible current gently washed between our legs. The kids dunked their heads in the water and started to splash one another. Suddenly the sky turned a shade or two clearer, and a lightness drifted from across the river like the first taste of something unbearably good that you knew would only come in small doses. Charlotte faced the direction from which the levitation came and arched her back, stretching her face into the fresher air, and raised her arms out straight from her shoulders, spreading sail to catch every square inch.

She was a skinny, sunburnt hillbilly with home-cut hair and tomboy muscles in well-worn, feed-store clothes, but there was a place in the pantheon of goddesses for her as well. I took off my shirt and tossed it onto the bank. I bent over and washed my arms and neck, and another freshet rolled across the river and upon us. She turned to face me as I waded to her and she reached toward me.

Clasping our hands, we slowly circled each other. The sky continued to lift, seeming to pull lightness up from the edges of the horizon. There were cars bustling across the bridge above us, but the sparrows in the trees were oblivious, pursuing their own agenda. I was looking into her face, but she was looking up into the sky.

"Charlotte, this is a wonder," I said.

"It is, isn't it?"

I doubt that either one of us had a very strong sense of who the other truly was, but that may be what made the magic of it. She was someone I had met less than an hour before; I think I had forgotten her last name already. I felt an urgency toward her on a level not described in the Boy Scout manual, but I knew enough to know that I wasn't in love with her; I was loving being with her there at that time, the muddy Potomac swirling between our legs, the kids chirping around us.

She looked into my eyes and smiled at me in a genuine, unfurnished way, but it was hard to hold the engagement for too long, I think, for both of us, and after a few moments we each looked away. I was thinking to myself—*is this real?*—and I looked back to her just as she was coming through the same portal. This time our earnestness was tinged with embarrassment.

Which broke the moment. My right hand let go of her left hand. We stood hip to hip looking upriver to where someone else's past was gliding toward us and we were about to bequeath it to the downstreamers. A moment differentiated itself from the others.

I turned and waded back to shore and lay down on the grassy bank. My eyes closed and the sounds of the kids splashing in the water drifted faster toward me. I felt more aware of myself as a transplanted species from Pennsylvania grafted temporarily to this family. A shadow crossed over me and I looked up at Charlotte, standing next to me, hands on her hips as though she were examining a plant form she hadn't seen before.

She knelt beside me and sat back on her haunches. Her hand began to trace the outline of my arm, then my shoulder, my neck and my mouth. She lay down next to me, our fingers entwined, and I slipped away.

For the second time that day, I woke up suddenly and from a deep spot, the kind of awakening that leaves you wondering how long you were asleep. There were two policemen standing on either side of us, and the children were lifting themselves ashore. I nudged Charlotte at about the same time one of the policemen, a heavyset, red-faced man who was fingering the handle of his club, was turning to me.

"Do you have some identification?" he asked. He was annoyed, though it was hard to tell whether that was just his professional style or whether he was pissed off about the weather.

I reached behind me for my wallet, but I was suddenly, roughly, pinned to the ground by his partner, who held me there with a club across my shoulders, pressed just hard enough at the base of my neck to shorten my breath.

"Let's take it nice and easy, kid," said the partner.

"Wallet's in my back pocket," I said. But I didn't reach for it.

"What else is there?"

I thought for a second, earnestly trying to figure out what else could possibly be in my back pocket. "Just my wallet, I'm pretty sure."

He eased up the pressure with his baton. "Why don't you put your hands behind your head and just roll over on your stomach."

Charlotte started to object, but the heavyset one cut her off. "Shut up," he said, without raising his voice.

I put my hands behind my head and the cop with the baton rolled me over on my belly and fished the wallet out of the back pocket of my khakis. Some moments passed.

"Long way from home, ain't you kids? What are you doing here?"

"I came with my father to the Poor People's March," I said. "We just came here to cool off."

"What about you," the big one said to Charlotte. "You got ID?"

"I don't have a driver's license," she said. "My sisters and I are staying with our mother at the camp. We are from Benton, West Virginia. We have been here since the PPC started, and we are fixing to go home tomorrow."

"So we got some protesters who couldn't stand that shithole anymore and went to the river to cool off, is that it?"

I wasn't sure if that was a question any of us was supposed to answer.

"Can I sit up now?" But I didn't move until the one near me with the baton grunted.

"It's against the law to swim in the Potomac River within the limits of the District of Columbia, and anyways it ain't all that smart."

"I didn't know it was against the law," I said. "We were careful and we were just wading. I have Boy Scout merit badges in first aid and water rescue."

"You must be pretty damn good if you can rescue people while you're sleepin' or makin' out with their big sister."

I decided it wasn't worth arguing either point. It was at that moment that I realized there were only two kids with us on the riverbank. I looked at Charlotte, who might have been counting as well.

"Uh, well yeh. I dozed off for a while. Honest, we didn't know we can't go in the river." It was just then that I saw her brother pull himself out of the water about twenty yards upstream and start to run away from us into the trees. Unfortunately, the big policeman's eyes followed mine and he saw him too.

"Hey kid!" he bellowed and for a moment it froze Charlotte's brother, but he quick enough took off across the path in the direction of the Mall.

The two policemen looked at each and decided it wasn't worth the chase.

"How many of you are there, and what are you hiding?"

"He's my brother," Charlotte said. "He's probably going home to Resurrection City."

"This is not good," said the one who was standing over me.

"Let's get them in the car and call it in," the big one said. "Now junior, behave yourself," he said, tapping my hip a little harder than he had to with his baton. "Let's not have any funny stuff."

Charlotte and I got back on our feet and we miscreants put on our clothes and shoes as necessary. She pulled her sisters close to her side as the heavy policeman nudged them along the path. The other officer had a firm hold of my left elbow, a strange feeling of someone taking control of my body, but he let me walk on my own as we trooped toward their squad car.

The two girls were placed in the middle of the back seat with Charlotte and me on either side. The doors were locked from the outside, and the policemen got in the front seat. The heavy one picked up the radio transmitter and called into the precinct station. He informed them that they had in custody four white minors who were detained for swimming in the river within District limits. He said they had intended to give us a warning and let us go, but a fifth minor, a male of about 10, had run away and failed to heed police instructions to stay the fuck put. Four of the five minors, including three of those in custody, were related. All five were participating in the Poor People's Crusade.

There passed a moment when the radio was silent. Then a voice instructed the policemen to bring us to the station, where they would figure out what the hell to do with us.

"See, the problem is we can't go into Resurrection City unless we see a crime or public-safety problem," the heavyset officer said.

He picked up a packet of cigarettes and lit one up. The windows were rolled down. He had my unwavering attention as we rolled off down the street.

10. Saturday, June 22, 1968

1965 Plymouth Fury

I was a little disappointed that they didn't turn the siren on.

The police car, a 1965 Plymouth Fury, took us along Constitution Avenue for a number of blocks. Although most of the crowds that had come for the big PPC march a few days before had melted away, there were still gawkers and everyday tourists shuffling from museum to museum. The four of us were crowded into the back seat, and Charlotte remarked that she and her sisters had not been in a motor vehicle in the six weeks since they had arrived at Resurrection City.

They were rediscovering life at the speed of internal combustion in stop-and-go traffic.

We turned off Constitution onto a less monumental street. At a stop sign, the policeman flipped his cigarette butt out the window.

"Officer." Obviously, I had been waiting. "Why did you throw your cigarette out the window?"

He slowly turned and looked at me with both eyes. "What goddamn business is it of yours?" The two peacekeepers until then had ignored us.

"This is gonna sound weird, but I'm doing a study." In fact, it had begun to seem less weird. "It's about, you know, why people throw cigarettes from their cars."

Silence in the police cruiser.

"Most people don't tell us," I added. "Or they say they don't know why. Sometimes they deny that they did it at all, even when it's as plain as can be. I think some people don't know what they did."

"My partner quit smoking and the smell bugs him," the red-faced policeman said, turning to face forward. I could feel the curiosity pouring out of Charlotte.

"Got it."

"Is there a merit badge for this?" the driver asked, and the two policemen laughed.

"There might be," I said.

The police parked western style, front bumper to the curb, in front of the precinct station, and they labored out of the car, wiping their brows in unison, and unlocked the back doors from the outside. They shepherded us into the station, where a desk sergeant was sorting through paperwork and a handful of police officers were standing around. It was barely any cooler inside. We were marched to the desk sergeant.

"These are the delinquents we told you about," said the heavy one.

"What am I supposed to do with them?" The desk sergeant was annoyed.

"Look, we were told to bring them in. Now they're your problem." The lean one flopped my wallet on the desk. Nodding at me, he said, "The kid's the only one who has ID. He's from Pennsylvania. The other three are sisters who say they're from West Virginia. The local address is Resurrection City."

"This is what I need, protesters," the desk sergeant said, and he pulled the driver's license out of my wallet to compare its picture to my face.

He tapped the license on the desk in front of him and turned to ask Charlotte, "What's your beef with the world?"

"Just displaced inside a jail," Charlotte said. She was not going to roll over. "People should think about what's important, not about the obsession of having things."

"Ain't there some communist country you can go to?" the desk sergeant said, for the benefit of his colleagues.

"If I was a boy, I guess I could look forward to getting drafted and going to Vietnam. But I'm just a girl, so I'll have to make do with being a prisoner of war right here," she said, leveling her eyes at him with a fearless calm.

The desk sergeant sighed. "Put the troublemakers on the bench while I call the CIA to find out what to do with them," he said, pointing with his pencil to an ordinary wood bench against the opposite wall. We were parked there, temporary ornaments in the vestibule of public safety.

We sat quietly absorbing the coming and going, gradually making our way to being less anxious, and almost relaxed and unwinding into familiarity. Gradually, the variations of foot traffic cycled through enough simulations to reach a little run of near emptiness in the vestibule. The two policemen who had brought us in from the banks of the Potomac had long gone. The desk sergeant was bent over paperwork.

It did not appear that he had called the CIA or the PTA or anyone else, and as the minutes ticked by, it seemed that no one in the D.C. Police Department had any lingering interest in us. He peered over the tops of his glasses at us once, but it wasn't clear he was actually seeing us.

I stood up. The desk sergeant kept working. Charlotte and her sisters stood up. Still nothing. I nudged one of the girls with my elbow and for a moment we four hung there on the cusp of uncertainty. Were we just going to leave?

We centimetered toward the door, pretending to look at the floor while I tried to keep the desk sergeant in my periphery. Suddenly, four policemen crashed in from the street with two men in handcuffs. All six were frothing and wild-eyed. One of the civilians had a bloody bruise alongside his temple.

We slid between the mayhem and the wall and squeezed for the exit. I glanced back at the desk sergeant, who now had more pressing public safety issues. We hurried outside for freedom.

As soon as we were out the door, we started walking faster and faster until we were running and jumping and shrieking and waving our arms in the air like the circus was coming to town and we were skipping school to watch the elephants get their toenails painted. As a lifelong Boy Scout, I had almost no experience with jailbreaks, but in those first precious moments, the way ahead was freshly paved and traffic free.

We had put two blocks between us and the police station when we heard the siren. It sounded like it was right behind, pursuing us. Charlotte and I and one of the girls froze; the youngest kept running. Soon alongside was the Plymouth Fury with our two policemen inside, but they were looking grimly straight ahead and pushing through the traffic to an emergency on the horizon.

We escapees held our ground. The police motored forward into the heaving traffic, weaving through cars splayed to the side, in the direction of West Potomac Park and Resurrection City. Charlotte rounded up her sisters and looked to me as though I would know what to do. The euphoria over seizing our freedom wilted when another police siren screamed in the distance.

"I'm scared," Charlotte said, under her breath.

We were orphans of circumstance, knowing our parents were out there, but not where.

"Let's go back to your camp," I said, thinking through Scout procedure.

"We got separated for a little while during the march this week," she said. "I'm nervous about Billy. He knows his way around Resurrection City, but if he wandered off somewhere else ...." Charlotte was finishing the thought in her head.

I think I had forgotten about the boy, but there didn't seem to be any point in going back to the river, since he was last seen running away from it. So we marched toward the PPC camp, about a mile away. We had become more subdued, tamed by the fear of being caught again, and the uncertainty about where the grown-ups were. And I'd eaten my last peanut butter sandwich in the car.

Two helicopters scurried overhead, beating their noisy wings.

We reached the foot of the Washington Monument and watched as a truck of National Guardsmen unloaded near the edge of Resurrection City. But they didn't go into the encampment itself. There were other police, including the blue-shirted city force, milling around the perimeter of the Poor People's Campaign.

We stood and watched from the higher ground near the monument, wavering in our commitment to going back in. I thought that I could find where my father had parked our car. At worst, I could just wait it out until he came back to look for me. The girls didn't have that option.

"Let's see if your mother is home," I said, and took Charlotte's hand. When we held hands in the river, there was rapture in our clasp, but as we walked down the incline toward the entrance to Resurrection City, all four of us linked together, we were holding on for courage.

It was nearing dusk; the sun hovered swollen and orange behind a veil of burnt smog beyond the river. People milled through Resurrection City, directionless and surrounded by the police outside. Although the Poor People's Campaign march the week before had gone smoothly, there was uncertainty about what would happen next. The city had suffered through two days of intense rioting after the murder of Martin Luther King just two months earlier. There was no shortage of smoldering fuses.

We gathered with a PPC posse near one of the public "buildings" in the encampment. They were listening to a man exhorting them to take their grievances out of Resurrection City and into the city of Washington.

"That's trouble," Charlotte said, and pulled us toward her family's home.

There was no one there, only stillness. We went from neighbor to neighbor. Few of them were around, and those who were had no news about Charlotte's mother or her brother. A gang marched noisily down the main street, cussing and calling for people to protest. Charlotte said she didn't recognize them.

"Now what?" I asked, more nervously than I wanted.

"Maybe we should stay here until someone can tell us where Momma is," Charlotte said.

That sounded good in theory, but I didn't like the feeling of standing still as the sun lowered and the universe came unglued all around us.

"I ought to see if I can find our car before it gets dark," I said.

"We will leave a note here and go with you." Charlotte went inside her family's shack and came out a minute later with a piece of paper that she pinned on the canvas flap that served as a door.

We walked to the south edge of the encampment, where there were police waiting. That morning, I remembered, my father had parked the DeSoto on a side street several blocks east of the Washington Monument and south of Independence Avenue.

It didn't take long to get to the place where I thought we had parked. But our car wasn't there.

Like a trap door in a magic show, my certainty disappeared beneath me. I floundered for the beacon that had guided me to that spot, only to find no familiar bearings.

We circled around a few adjoining streets, which looked more positively like places I had never been to. There was a hotdog vendor who was closing down for the day, and I won cheers from the rest of the urban pathfinders by proposing that we get something to eat. We ordered four hot dogs and a soda that we would split, and then I realized we had escaped the precinct house without my wallet.

"Oh, sir. We can't take this," I said, offering to hand back the wieners, although one of the girls had already taken a bite. "I'm very sorry. I forgot that I lost my wallet."

The vendor, a harried, middle-aged man, looked at me at first with disappointment, but then shrugged. Everyone should, at some time in their life on this planet, go hungry with no money. "I be here tomorrow," he said. "Just pay me when you can."

"But we're not from around here," I said, putting the soda and my hot dog back on his counter.

"Who is?" he shrugged, and pushed the hot dog back to me. "Can't use now anyway. It's better you should eat it instead I throw to trash."

And so we finished the hotdogs and helped him pack the rest of his things into the vending cart. There were two displays of the soda available at his stand that were empty cans stacked in pyramids on each side of the counter. I was surprised to see him pick up each pyramid as a whole: the empty cans were glued together, rather than stacked each time he put them out. This unexpected revelation led to another.

I had not thoroughly looked where Speedy had parked our car.

"We gotta go back one more time," I said, and we four trudged off again to the block where I had thought we had parked the car that morning. Some other vehicle was still in our spot, next to a sidewalk that was bordered by a low brick wall. There, atop the wall where no one would notice or disturb it, was a small pile of stones.

That I recognized as Speedy's statuary. Underneath the bottom stone was a slip of paper. In my father's handwriting, it said: "Car on 19th St NW betwn N and O." This is how text messaging was done in the old country, before the meddling Europeans showed up.

It took some walking, but we found the car just where my father wrote that it would be. There was a note attached to the windshield, saying he would be checking back at 6 PM, but the 6 PM had been scratched out and it now said 8 PM.

It was getting on to dusk, but I wanted to try to get the girls back with their mother. I expected that if we walked from the car back to the encampment, there was a good chance we would cross paths with my father. I had no wallet, but I did have a golf course pencil—*essere preparati*—and so I left a postscript on my father's note, letting him know what I was up to.

By then, the little sisters were zombie-trudging wherever Charlotte and I led them. As we headed south on 19th Street toward the Mall, an undertow began to pull us on.

We neared Constitution Ave., and a group of people approached from the east, chanting slogans against the government. We four instinctively drew closer to one another and slowed down, but the malcontents turned in front of us and took the same bearing we were on. There was no traffic; we were walking in the street.

There was a sudden uproar and the people ahead of us began to boil noisily and came to a stop. We four moved to the sidewalk for safety and climbed the stairs to the landing in front of someone's house, where we could better see the lay of the land. A dozen policemen were blocking the crowd from crossing into Resurrection City, ordering them over bullhorns to disperse and go home.

Outbursts from the people bounced around in the narrow urban canyon of buildings where we waited. Then the crowd quieted down long enough to hear something more from the police that outraged them.

The police became by degrees more insistent and less conciliatory, which caused the protestors to raise their decibel level and then, like a flock of geese that rise up as one on a signal, the people surged forward. At first the two groups just came chin to chin, growling at one another, but then the rear of the protest movement pushed the scrum forward into contact with the police. Clubs were unleashed. The police moved forward, flailing against the crowd, which quickly gave ground.

The civilians backpedaled, dodging the arcs of the clubs, and the police stepped forward to claim more territory. The protestors gave more ground slowly at first, and then suddenly the resistance broke and they turned and ran off past us, down the middle of the street.

We were the only ones left in the block with the police. Pretending that normalcy was restored, Charlotte and I and her sisters came down from the stoop where we had watched the encounter, like sightseers at Bull Run, and started down the sidewalk toward the encampment. The police immediately waved their clubs back toward where we had come from.

Not knowing what else to do, I raised my hand in the Boy Scout salute.

"What?" one of the policemen barked at me.

"Uh, we need to get into the camp, to find our parents."

"Resurrection City is off limits," he said. "We're shutting it down."

"Like I said, we must get in there to find our parents. We are supposed to be back before dark."

"You cannot go onto the Mall. There's already been some trouble and people are gettin' hurt. It's no place for kids," he said.

But he didn't draw a line in front of us.

"We'll be just as careful as can be," I said, and taking Charlotte in one hand and one of her sisters in the other, I started for the crosswalk that would take us over Independence Avenue into West Potomac Park. It was a moment of chutzpah, for which there is no merit badge that I know of, and I expected to be turned back.

But it didn't happen. We waited a short eternity for a traffic light to change to a crossing signal, and when it did, the police who were standing right beside us did not make any move to stop us.

"Be careful in there," one of them said.

Across the street, we followed a path through a wooded area. In the deep shadows, the air at last tasted cooler and cleaner. There were some city crickets, and as we emerged from the woods, we could see people milling around in Resurrection City.

We crossed the informal border between the Poor People's Campaign and the rest of America onto the baking mud that was slowly consuming the Resurrection. People were streaming east toward one of the main gathering points in the encampment, but we turned west and went straight for Charlotte's camp.

No one was home, but there was a new note pinned to the canvas door. Her mother and her brother were going to a community meeting at 7:30. Charlotte and the girls were to either stay at the shack or find them at the meeting.

This was a huge relief for all and there was sensation that things might be getting back to normal.

Charlotte guided us east toward the area where meetings took place, joining in a stream of humanity going in the same direction. A few hundred feet away, we could hear someone on a public address system. We slowed down as we neared the back of the herd. The crowd was packing in tight and began to surround us, forming a canopy. I could see very little, and I was the tallest one in our group.

A man was trying to calm the assembly, imploring the crusaders to hold on to what they had achieved so far through nonviolence. He was partially shouted down by some in the crowd, including two men standing a little ways off from us. Most of the people were listening attentively, but these two seemed to have already made up their minds. They were yelling angrily toward the stage.

I hoisted one of Charlotte's sisters up on my shoulders, where she could see out over the poppy field of heads. There were lights on poles around the outside of the area and on the stage, but it was hard to see in the middle of the crowd. Suddenly we were being pushed from behind, though there was nowhere to go ahead of us, and Charlotte had to pick up her other sister so she wouldn't get trampled.

People started to complain about being jostled from behind, and I noticed that the two guys who had been protesting the loudest were doing the pushing. Charlotte crashed into me but kept her feet, and I turned around looking for a way out. We were near enough to the back of the crowd and I was looking for a path to navigate back out, but then the sister on my shoulders yelled out for her mother and began wiggling around trying to steer me back into the center.

I turned in the direction she was leading me, and held onto Charlotte as tight as I could and we started to weave through the people with her sister as our gyroscope. It was slow going; we were squeezing through the densest core of the crowd, trying to wedge between people who had nowhere to go, negotiating each foot of passage. More than once I lost my grip on Charlotte and our journey was made more difficult by the spasms of the crowd. Up over my head, the sister began to yell out to her mother. I guessed we were getting closer.

Finally, the little girl dove off my shoulders and Charlotte's mother suddenly appeared in front of me, reaching up to take her daughter in her hands. The people around us spread out as much as they could, and Charlotte moved in front of me and embraced her mother. Her brother was standing behind his mother.

Suddenly I was out of place. They had been my family, or at least a family in my charge, but now they belonged again to each other. I figured I would work my way back to the car and meet up with my father.

Charlotte turned around quickly, her eyes soft. She reached her left hand around my neck and cupped the back of my head in her palm and slowly pulled us closer until our foreheads were touching and we were eye to eye, noses embedded in one another's cheek, her soft lips at the corner of my mouth. She held us there for a moment and then whispered "Thank you" in my ear.

We were being jostled in all directions and shoved forward. "It's been the best day of my life so far," I said.

She leaned back with our eyes locked. Then someone collided into us and her mother reached out, brushing her hand against my shoulder; it was as close as she could come to a hug in the increasingly restless mob.

The crowd packed in more tightly and I pulled one of the girls back up into my arms. It was all we could do to stay on our feet and close together; there was little hope of breaking free and finding a way out, or even where Out was. The crowd was rolling forward slowly, flowing around the small stage where the speakers had mostly given up. I had no idea what the point of this was, but I thought that eventually the molecules would diffuse and we would have a chance to work our way toward the edge of the mob and escape its gravitational field.

But for the moment I had to move with them or get shoved to the ground. Charlotte and her mother were nowhere around me.

We, the crowd, crashed ahead onto a city street, where there was more room, but I heard bullhorns across our bow: the police ordering the crowd to stop and return to Resurrection City. There would be no turning this mob around, but the surge slowed and then suddenly the front edge was hurtling backward upon me and Charlotte's sister while the rear of the column was still pushing ahead.

She and I were caught in the cross current.

There was smoke, a choking, acrid smoke that stung my eyes and someone bowled me over as I tried to clear my head. I was on the street, my shoulder crushed into the warm, hard asphalt. I thought I had knocked my head, but I was still holding the little sister close and my lungs felt as though I had dived into a sulfur bath. People were shouting, screaming all around us; I wanted to just lay there and wait for the fire and the madness to go away, but I knew I had to get to my feet and pull myself and the girl out of there. She was crying frantically, but the panic was slowing down in my head, sounding farther away. I got to my knees and held her face to my chest. Legs were rushing around us. I struggled to my feet, dizzily, picking up no signals from the Scout guidance system, lost and searching for a bearing toward safety.

Then my father appeared in front me.

He was holding a handkerchief across his mouth and nose, which he pressed onto my face. He took Charlotte's sister from my arms and said, "Come on, son," as though we were crossing to the other side of a sacred divide. My eyes and lungs were burning so that I could not see or breathe, but I felt my father's arm across my shoulder, steering us steadily through the chaos. My panic began to dissolve. Suddenly I was overwhelmed by relief to be with him again, but I also felt, for the first time all day, that I had been abandoned. It wasn't his fault that we had gotten split up—I had more to do with it than he had—but you can't always help how you feel.

He piloted us toward the south edge of the encampment to a stand of trees on slightly higher ground. Charlotte and her mother and her brother and sister were there, as was Miss Bennett. They had a bottle of water and some scraps of ripped-up cloth that we used to clean our faces and hands.

By and by, we learned that my father and Miss Bennett had found Charlotte and her mother just after the tear gas started to fly, and that

Miss Bennett had led them away from the confrontation. My father, the pacifist infantryman who had never seen combat, rushed back into the smoke, where some people were getting clubbed and others were throwing rocks at the police. He told me later that it was odd how purposefully he could move through the mayhem focused just on finding us, with a kind of immunity to the strife all around, and neither the police nor the protestors paid much attention to him.

"It was almost as if you could be there without being a part of it," he said. "*The profound calm only apparently precedes and prophesies the storm, and is more awful than the storm itself.* I think a street sweeper could have gone through there doing his job and no one would have interrupted him."

After a while, we who had been tear-gassed started to feel more normal. The police did not follow the mob into Resurrection City; it seemed that as long as the Poor People's Campaign stayed inside the ropes, the police would stay outside.

Yet the prospect of more trouble hung in the air, which, after a long, hot day, now had to try to cleanse itself of smoke bombs and tear gas.

We walked together back to the West Virginians' shack. My father and Miss Bennett tried to talk them into leaving Resurrection City right there that night as sporadic outbursts echoed around the encampment. But Charlotte's mother would not have it; she was intent on staying until the PPC formally decamped. They had return tickets on the Greyhound bus that they had purchased when they left West Virginia.

We hung out around their camp for a while listening to the sounds of a crusade coming to an end. Something cooler and fresher came in little tufts of air from the river as the adults talked about the future of the Poor People's Campaign, which was going to try to sprout again in other cities.

No one ever really asked us kids what we had been up to all day.

I was relishing my exhaustion and didn't want to leave. My father said it was getting to be time for us to head back to Pennsylvania; we had hours of driving to go before we would climb in bed. Charlotte disappeared inside and came back a minute later with a piece of folded-over paper that she pressed into my hand. I held her hand for a moment, but the awkwardness of saying goodbye, aggravated by the presence of adults, was hanging over us. We ended by muttering inadequate goodbyes.

We three Pennsylvanians started to walk to the east end of Resurrection City. I turned and waved. It was dark, but I imagined her there.

When we got back under the streetlights on 19th Street, I unfolded the paper. She had written her name and mailing address. I felt stupid that I hadn't given her my address.

Back in the car, on the highway, I free-fell into a dreamy sleep in the corner of the voluminous back seat of the DeSoto, cozy to the door.

"Look out, we're coming through," my father said as he pushed our car ahead into the passing lane, overtaking a line of slower-moving vehicles.

We whirled along the dark summer highway with all four windows rolled partly down, pulling noise and the smell of Maryland through our sails. On that day, June 23, 1968, the conflict in Vietnam became the longest-running war in U.S. history, moving past the Revolutionary War to claim the top ranking. Vietnam would last five more years.

Someday, I'm guessing, we might top that.

1957 DODGE REGENT

We were finishing dinner on the picnic table behind our house. Our lawn dissolved into the woods, which held in its bosom a minor Pennsylvania creek that grew from gully washes and insignificant streams and eventually made a small dent in the Delaware River not too far from the spot where, on average, the big river began to back up twice a day from the heaving oceans. My father was reminiscing about going to the canal when he was just small and watching barges loaded down with coal creep along at mule speed from the mines on their way to Bristol.

Unburdened, the barges floated lighter and higher on the way home. "I was happy for the mules heading upstream," he said. The business of carrying light and heat captured in rocks of carbon down the canal was over by the time he started going to school. The extraction of ancient carbon wasn't over—not by a long shot—but industry had found that it was more efficient to use combustion engines to bring the coal to market, instead of mules, men and gravity pulling barges over sleepy water.

"You could write about that for your journalism project," my father said. "Ask the old-timers what it was like. The editors love nostalgia." He paused to think. "It may even serve a purpose."

We could hear the phone ringing in the house. None of us wanted to leave the picnic table.

The phone was insistent. It rang for a while and went quiet. Then it started up again.

"I'll go." No argument from the folks, who were leaning together. Coolness gathered in the woods.

I carried dishes into the house, gently glowing from the long mid-summer sun. Again, the phone rang determinedly as I got there, years ahead of the time when regular people had answering machines. I tried to make it stop by carefully putting down the tableware.

It was Juliana. "Geez, I thought nobody was home."

"We were finishing supper out back."

"Do you wanna go to a concert over in Jersey?"

"I thought it was in Philadelphia." I was thinking of our long-term plan to see the Doors in Philadelphia.

"No, tonight. Now. A bunch of us are going to see the Fifth Dimension in Lambertville. Do you want to go?"

I knew what the Fifth Dimension was. I didn't know what a bunch could be. "When are you leaving?"

"In about two minutes. They just got here and we have an extra ticket so, like, how 'bout it?"

"Um." I didn't know what I wanted to say.

"You're coming, Doris," she said. "We'll be there in 10 minutes." The phone clicked off, and I stood looking at my end of it for a minute wondering who was holding the phone.

My parents were still at the picnic table. "Can I clean up the kitchen later? My friend asked me if I want to go to a concert."

They looked at each other. "I'll take care of the dishes, Izzy," my father said. "Do you need a car?"

I was already carrying a second load of dishes back to the house. "No, they're picking me up."

I swapped out of shorts into jeans and sneakers and a clean tee shirt. I was, ironically for a Boy Scout, unprepared to be a teenager. I heard my parents come in through the back door and suddenly felt anxious at the intersection of them and new people whom I didn't know, coming to take me to rural New Jersey.

I didn't have a lot of time to think about it because a 1957 Dodge Regent was rolling slowly in front of our house, making sure that it was at the right place. The Regent had a distinctive strip of chrome embroidering the top of the hood, a hood for the hood as it were, two wingy ornaments running north and south. Beneath this were thick slabs of chrome and an extra chevron on the leading edge of the car.

Another wedge of chrome across the top of the front window made the car appear to be wearing a fedora.

The Regent looked especially absurd repurposed for use by hippies.

I didn't recognize anyone. Juliana popped out of the back seat on the other side.

"Are you ready?" She was skipping toward me and I was taken aback by how glad I was to see her. Then she was before me, beaming, looking over my shoulder and I sensed that my parents were standing behind us. I turned. They were grinning, advancing toward us.

I introduced Juliana, and there could have been conversation except for the palpable sense of urgency coming from the Dodge. My dad said we ought to be going. "Up, up and away," he sang, and as I followed Juliana's swaying caboose to the Dodge, she turned and looked over her shoulder at him and smiled.

Names were tossed at me as we backed out of the driveway and I stuck my arm out of the window and waved over the top of the car to my home as we accelerated away.

A girl I did recognize was sitting on the other side of Juliana, and a third girl was between the two guys on the front bench. A late 1950s Chrysler product had room in the back seat for more than three teenagers, if necessary, but my whole being was in the places where my hip and thigh leaned into Juliana and the sweet air around her.

We gathered speed on the state road that would take us to Lambertville and caterwauled into the night. The driver lit a cigarette, but he used the ashtray in the middle of the dashboard, even though—maybe because—he had to reach over the girl sitting next to him. The radio was playing and my shipmates were talking about things I knew almost nothing about, but none of that mattered because as we rollicked through the Pennsylvania countryside, Juliana and I were slowly nestling closer together as though it were unplanned.

Thus was the pull of the species.

And then unthinkable tragedy happened. The kid riding shotgun lit a cigarette that I could tell was not store-bought and after taking a couple long gulps, he passed it over his shoulder to the girl behind him, who held it to her lips and inhaled deeply and passed it to Juliana, and I knew suddenly that it would be in my court and then she turned slightly toward me with her eyes glowing, sharing a treasure from one friend to another, holding the misshapen, fuming pumpernickel in front of me.

I was pretty sure I knew what it was, but I didn't know what I would do with it.

I looked from the joint to her wide-open eyes, which seemed dreamy and a little out of focus. I didn't want to pull back from us in any way, I wanted to dive in, even though smoking on a marijuana cigarette seemed impossible to me, with more merit badges than I would ever need to become an Eagle Scout.

I wasn't thinking about the Scout oath when I took the joint and held it awkwardly near my lips and faked inhalation around the edge of it. Some banned substance probably entered my anatomy, but I doubt that it made it to my respiratory system. I studied the joint in my fingers and handed it back to Juliana, who passed it ahead to the driver.

I looked out the window. Trees and farmers' mailboxes flew past just as they always had. There was a spicy aroma and I was thinking about things that I forgot as soon as they came to mind and then, demandingly, the joint came back to me, tinier now, a smoldering nub pinched between Juliana's fingertips. "You don't have to smoke it if you don't want to," she whispered.

I took the joint from her fingers and, giving it no thought, flicked it out the window. For the record, I did this in self-defense: I thought it was about to burn my fingertips.

My auto-flicking, however, did not go unnoticed.

"Hey, man, what the fuck!" Shotgun exclaimed. Suddenly all four of them were expressing general outrage. My first thought was that they were mad at me for tossing the butt out the window, starting a forest fire that would lead to social decay, to bunny rabbits and big-eyed fawns selling themselves for small change on the mean streets of Doylestown. Gradually, I understood that they were mad because I had committed the greater crime of wasting dope.

In one swoop, I had trampled the Boy Scout oath and the hippie code and alienated these people who were taking me to New Jersey and I felt like a small turd in a big toilet bowl, floating conspicuously with no place to hide.

Juliana put her hand on my thigh. "It was about spent anyway," she said loud enough for anyone to hear.

"I know, man, but jeezus," Shotgun said, glaring at me.

"Fuck that, man," the driver said. "Just fire up another one."

This struck Shotgun as an excellent solution and he seemed to forget almost immediately that he was pissed off. When the second joint came to Juliana, she didn't smoke any and just relayed it ahead to the front seat.

The rest of the way to Lambertville I played it as cool as an Eagle Scout in an opium den can and stayed quietly in my corner. Lightning bugs came up out of the lawns as we whizzed along two-lane roads just wide enough to have white lines painted on the edge. We rolled across the rickety bridge over the Delaware and then bounded north.

The Fifth Dimension—if you're ever looking for it—occurred for a few hours in a music circus, a permanent tent with seating 360 degrees around the stage in the middle. The house was nearly full. Some of the panels of the theater wall were rolled up so the night could breathe through and wash out the smoke.

I wasn't prepared for the volume of sound from the band or the precision of how its parts fit together. It was the first live rock concert of any consequence that I had been to, so I had no frame of reference. But as the songs rolled from one to another, I came to agree with the notion that this was a nicer place to be, in a beautiful balloon.

By surry-down time, Juliana and I had left our seats and moved back to where it was less smoky. The trains of trust promised better things for tomorrow; we were making out like our lives depended on it.

We pretty much kept at it all the way home. Until then, I hadn't known that I could be so hungry for something I had never had before.

I came up for air as our car jumped over the old bridge that arched over the Delaware Canal in New Hope, momentarily hanging us in the air, when I caught a glimpse of a tall man on the sidewalk with a string of coconuts carved into faces that hung from a yardarm of sorts.

By the time I got home, the only light left on in the house was in the hallway. But as I tried to creep to my room, my father softly bid me good night.

12. Tuesday, June 25, 1968

1960 Chevrolet Apache

I woke up remembering a dream about Juliana, sitting in the back seat of my father's big car, peeling layers of clothes away. I lay there a while, with dawn already full blast outside my bedroom window, savoring.

In the kitchen, my father looked up from his newspaper long enough to ask what the fifth dimension was all about.

"There were five of them who did the singing."

"It wasn't a breakthrough in physics?"

"Well, it was new to me." I was going to be taking physics in my senior year. I poured out my dose of cereal and sat down across from him at the little kitchen table.

I had a plan. "Can I drop you at work and take the car this afternoon? I'll come back and pick you up when you're done work."

This was an unusual request. Speedy thought for a minute and started to grin. "Wouldn't have anything to do with Juliana, would it?"

Actually, I was working on a different merit badge. "Uh, no. I was thinking about what you said about the canal. I want to go talk to the guys who run the barge." There was a single barge that toted tourists up and down a short stretch of the canal in New Hope. I had taken the trip once with the Boy Scouts.

"Sure, take the car. That's a start. They may know people who used to work on the canal."

I almost never drove either of our cars when there was a parent aboard. As he slid into the passenger seat, my father handed me an old 35mm camera.

"Sometimes I just point the thing at people without any film in it. There's a little privacy screen inside there," he said, tapping the camera. "People will say things when you're not looking directly at each other that they wouldn't otherwise say."

This was not covered in the photography merit badge, which I already had.

Not far into the ride into town, we came up behind a man smoking in a 1960 Chevy Apache pickup truck.

"I bet he's a tosser," my father said.

We were in the same bubble of traffic and, sure enough, he tossed his cigarette with a right-hand crossover move. Judging by the distance he got, it looked like a middle-finger flick, the biggest and strongest flicker of them all, especially when coupled with some wrist action. At the next traffic light, we were directly behind him and, unbelievably, my father reached over and started honking our horn. The eyes of the Apache driver ahead looked at me in his rearview mirror. Speedy waved at him through our windshield and then leaned out of the window and, not convinced he had gotten his message across, shouted for the man to pull over to the shoulder of the road.

The light turned and—this felt like the beginning of a train wreck—the pickup pulled over. I motored the DeSoto alongside and stopped, forcing the cars behind us to swerve around.

The pickup driver was thick and sunburned with a no-nonsense crew cut and a pummeled face. "What?" he growled.

"You dropped your cigarette out the window back there," my father said, talking across the space between their windows.

"What?" I think the pickup driver heard him right, but he just wanted to make sure.

"Your cigarette. You threw it out the window back there."

"So what?" He looked mad. My father was not a big person and he wasn't small. He had a swimmer's build and a bookish demeanor from spending so much time poised over typewriters.

"Can you tell me why? You've probably got an ashtray in your truck, so why'd you throw the cigarette out the window?"

It looked like the pickup driver was reaching down to where the ignition key would be. "Are you fucking nuts?"

"I'm doing a study about why people throw their cigarettes in the road. We checked our nets this morning and there you were."

"How would it be if I kicked your fucking study up your ass?"

My father thought this over for a few seconds. "I would record the motivation for the cigarette flicking as unwarranted hostility toward the universe." He motioned with both hands ahead down the road. "We won't keep you any longer. Thanks."

A car behind us had trouble getting around and began to honk angrily. Suddenly the pickup driver decided that we weren't worth any more of his time. He started his truck and shot ahead, spitting gravel back in our direction, and saluted us with the almighty finger.

I pulled over onto the shoulder so the cars behind us could get on with their day.

"Ya know, Dad, maybe it isn't such a good idea to confront people so early in the morning."

"We can't just ask the ones who look like they won't get mad. There is light in every one of us, no matter how ornery we are."

"Un hunh," I said, merging back into the pre-work traffic.

"Well, it's a theory," he said. "All the data aren't in yet."

I did not work overtime that day. At 3:30 in the afternoon, I drove my father's mobile research vehicle to New Hope, the tourist-artist colony alongside the hiftoric Delaware River. I found a place to park and enjoyed an unburdened walk, with neither golf bags nor grass mower, along the leafy towpath beside the canal that ran through town a few blocks west of the river itself.

The tour boat was between runs, its captain off having his supper, while a scraggly fellow about my age brushed down a pair of mules. I asked him if he knew anyone who had actually worked on the canal when it was still shipping coal.

"I don't, but Pop, he can rattle off about a dozen old farts what used to work the canal," the kid said. "He'll be back in about an hour and then I'll get to eat before we take the evening tour. You wanna buy a ticket?"

"I would, but I have to meet someone before too long."

"Yup, that's okay. We're here every day." I wasn't sure if he was speaking for himself or the mules.

"Have you ever met any of the old-timers?"

"Sometimes somebody will ask after the mules and how the lock is working and say he remembered when the coal barges come up and down here. Pop says he's old enough to have seen them, but he don't actually remember, no matter what speech he gives the customers."

The kid pulled a cigarette from the pack that was in his shirt pocket. "Anyways, he talks like he was mule and boat captain both. The stories he tells on the tour sure sounds like he was there, and that's what the people like, I guess."

"I'll have to stop back again someday when I have more time," I said. Then, while I was taking a few pictures of him and the mules, I asked if he had ever seen someone around town selling carved coconuts.

The mule driver laughed. "We call him Mighty Quinn. Just kinda showed up this summer. Pop thinks he scares the tourists, but I think he's cool."

"Does he live here in town?"

"I seen him going into Tripett's boarding house over on Mechanic Street." He pointed downstream, such as it was on the canal, and toward the river.

"Aha. Quinn, you said?"

"Somethin' like that. He's always singin' that song about the Eskimo, you know the one I mean?"

"You'll not see nothing like the mighty Quinn."

"That's the one, all right."

I climbed a staircase that led from the towpath up to the sidewalk on Mechanic Street. Walking down the slope toward the river, there was an antique shop and a thrift store and then a tottering old house with a sun-bleached, hand-lettered sign in the corner of one window that announced, unceremoniously, "Rooms."

The boarding house was smack up against the sidewalk, with a tiny front step and a long-neglected flower box under one of the street-facing windows that could have been an experiment in growing tobacco from half-buried cigarette butts. I knocked on the door. There was no answer.

The house within was still, almost like it was trying to be so. I knocked again. More quiet and then a feeble call from somewhere in the depths. Given enough time, an ancient, stooped-over man in slippers and housecoat opened the door.

He sized me up as a prospective roomer. "Yes?"

"Is there someone here who sells coconuts?"

Without a word, he turned around and called back into the house, "Quentin," with the frail commitment of an emphysema sufferer. Then he turned halfway back to me, already tired of attending to the door, and said I could come on in. "Quentin," he repeated feebly and, having given it his best shot, slippered off down a hallway.

I wasn't sure if I should stop or go, so I hung there in the in-between for what seemed like a long time, pretending to take an interest in the wallpaper. The landlord disappeared around a distant corner, calling one more time for Quentin. The wallpaper began to grow on me, and then there were younger, livelier footsteps approaching.

The hallway filled with a tall person and a bush of kinky hair. He was darkened by the sun, wearing worn-out Bermuda shorts down to his knees and sandals with no shirt. As he came closer, I realized he had tattoos on both shoulders and his upper arms. He was studying me closely, with a serious, skeptical expression.

"Do you sell coconuts?" I asked.

"Dey are not coconuts, man, dey are icons made from coconuts and other natural tings." I wondered if his accent was put on, if he wasn't just another white guy from the suburbs who was trying on a personality. He stared in a kind of challenging way at me with dark eyes.

"Even better," I said. "I can always use one of those."

"Hey, man, dat's one of my lines." Then a broad smile bloomed across his face and he slapped me on the shoulder, pulling me gently into the hallway. "I show you what I got." He turned and led me toward the light at the end of the hallway and then up a staircase covered with ratty carpeting to a landing where a door was open to the left. I followed him in.

It was a single room with a huge window as its centerpiece, six feet wide by four feet high, a matrix of small panes; it was hinged at the top and opened into the room and hooked to the ceiling. It looked out over a quiet stretch of a nearly waterless stream trickling through the heart of the town, surrounded by sycamores broken out with psoriasis and the miscellany that grows on the banks of pebbly streams in Pennsylvania. The window made the room seem nautical, as though it was a captain's berth at the stern of a 19th-century ship.

In front of the window was a large table filled with coconuts, tree roots, seashells, shucks of wild grasses, feathers, jars of marbles, shards of glass, baskets of buttons and beads, fishing line, a glue gun, coils of multicolored electrical wire, a jar of twigs, stacks of fabric swatches, a box of watches in various stages of disassembly, two pots of glue, several small jars of paint, spools of twine and ribbon, cigar boxes of various sizes and shapes, another glue gun, pens, pencils, markers, fish hooks, two coffee cans with assorted nuts and bolts, and other stuff. Embedded in the mayhem were a few half-built projects.

It was an artist's workspace, and the table itself was yet a work of art, I thought.

"Icons," he said, gesturing toward the table and then around the room, where icon coconut heads in various stages of completion were hanging from open beams in the ceiling.

"Icons of what?" I asked, trying to place this array in what little I knew of organized religion.

"Dat white man Phillip Ginder, he found the hard coal up there in Mauch Chunk back yonder in 1791, but nothing happened with the stone coal anthracitey, until the good Quaker Josiah White took rent of the place," he said. "He use mules to pull the wagons up the mountains to the mines and he let them mules ride down the mountain for free, eating their oats.

"The Commonwelt give Josiah a charter for the canals and the mines together so he could take that stone coal to the big markets. Alas, dem city people did not know what to do wit it; they had no stove to burned it. So Josiah White find a man to invent a stove that can burn it and then people realize this anthracitey keep house damn warm all up in the dark cold months.

"Before the canals, they ship the coal down the currents of the Lehigh River and Delaware River, and when the trip over, they sell the boat for wood. A lotta hard coal ship dat way until them two canals was ready and they barges and mules could go back and forth through the locks." He pointed out the window through the boughs of the trees to the canal.

"By and by, they make more canals, but in 20 years the railroad start to catch up with de mules and the barges. Still, the canal folk pretend that don't happen and keep floating anthracite from the mines 60 miles all the way to Bristol, through de Mexican War, and de Civil War and de Spanish-American War and de Fust World War before the last barge pay his toll in 19 hunnert and 31."

Quentin wasn't done yet. "Funny ting is, the railroad done in the canal because it run on dat same anthrocitey fuel coming out of the mines. But that old canal, he only just as fast as a mule team can pull the barge and Gawd call the water to the ocean, and when the floods come, it take a lot of work and money to put the canals right again.

"You don have to be some gawd or saint fo your work to be worth rememberin'. Every soul worth that," he said, waving his arm across the room. "These are icons of those people, dem boys who drove the mules along the towpath 13 hours a day while cap'n steered de barge, dem lock masters who lowered em down and raised em up, and them boat builders and storekeepers who kept the canals working long past their natural time. The miners dug that anthracitey out them damn mountains, and diggin coal is nasty work but not as nasty as butchering whales and cook him down on a boat tossing out on de ocean.

"Them canal men floated it down to folk's parlors and if you ask me they had de best of it, spite of all their troubles."

I asked him what troubles they had, but he said he had to get out on the street with his icons, as the foot traffic was picking up.

I took a couple of photos of Quentin and his workshop.

"You gots to peddle coconuts when their pockets still have some monies," he said, as I traipsed along behind him.

13. THURSDAY, JUNE 27, 1968

1963 RAMBLER AMBASSADOR

We were on our way to work, my father driving. A cream-colored 1963 Rambler broke the double-yellow no-passing lines and ripped past us on the left. A well-groomed gent behind the wheel in a crisp white shirt and bright blue tie was smoking fastidiously. He had short gray hair slicked into place, and the tan aura of a golfer, although I didn't recognize him from the country club.

He was using the ashtray. He didn't look like a flicker to me, but Speedy trolled for him anyway. The Ambassador had a refined, cavernous Rotary Club styling, yet it was also the fastest production sedan made that year. It appealed to successful middle-aged guys who wanted speed but not flash.

The trunk had remnants of fins, but instead of flaring up at the rear, they peaked near the back window, and then tapered down to the rear bumper. There was, predictably, a slab of chrome on the trunk.

The driver surprised me by pitching his cigarette aristocratically out the window. He had been smoking with his right hand, closest to the ashtray, but switched and threw straight down into the street, a left hand slam dunk.

We closed in behind him. "It's Ed McCafferty," my father said.

He was the publisher of the newspaper, my father's ultimate boss. We pulled alongside at the next light.

"Morning Ed," my father said, and his boss nodded our way. "I couldn't help but notice you dropped your cigarette out the window back there."

"Keen observation, Rockwell." There was a blank look in his face, as though he would rather not be talking to an employee, driver-to-driver, out on the open road. "Will we be reading about this in the paper?"

My dad laughed but pressed on. "You'll be the judge of that." The light changed and the Ambassador sped away before he could get to the question. We never caught up to him.

My father sometimes filed stories that were more than the editors wanted, that said more than people wanted to read. When he wrote stories that involved companies that advertised in the paper, he was careful not to advocate for them. He always asked people who had been arrested how they had been treated by the police.

Some of his stories never made it into print.

"Put McCafferty down as a Not Available for Response," my father said, nodding toward the writing pad as we turned into the driveway of the country club.

"What do think he would have answered?" I asked.

"*We can't let faith oust fact and fancy oust meaning.* We call 'em as we see 'em."

I told him I had a ride home after work.

The gears were spinning in his head. "Yes, I ought to look into something this evening. See you at home then," he said, and drove off.

We mowed the greens first thing in the morning on Monday, Wednesday and Friday, but most Thursdays I walked a mower around the course tidying up around the fairway trees and other tight places where the gang mowers couldn't reach. From this, I learned that if you keep your feet moving, you might think of something.

The places to be mowed were not contiguous ideas gerrymandered into a rational progression; they were a puzzle of unconnected notions. And there was the unpredictable intervention of the golfers. Whenever our paths crossed, I had to power down the mower and stand still, for in golf the ball waits for you, and the universe pauses for the golfer's coiling dance, assuming silent reverence.

I liked the being still part, and when I was caddying or working on the greens crew without power equipment, I sometimes closed my eyes to concentrate better on the breezes and the prayers of the golfers. Most of the layout of the golf course was outside earshot of any road traffic.

I came to the fourth tee, where the tee boxes were lined up, shooting-arcade style, one behind another and nestled in dense woods: the ladies, the regular tees and the blues. A small stream always full of water ran between the ladies' tee and the whites. The fairway opened up just in front of the ladies' tee and then, after about 30 yards, began to climb a steep hill. The green was completely hidden until you got to the top of the hill, about 300 yards from the white tees. There was plenty of room on the left, but the right side of the fairway was the property boundary, bordered by a run of trees and thick brush, behind which was a public swimming pool and the summer-long brining of youth in Coppertone and chlorine.

There was a group on the tee, a foursome that played together so much that they had formed a barbershop quartet—or it may have been the other way around—who called themselves the The Dufflinks. They were devoted cart-pullers, and I had never caddied for any of them. I shut off the engine and pushed the mower away to a respectful distance.

"I saw a fella drive the top of the hill here last week," said the tenor. "Some guest playing with Reynolds."

"An Italian guy with cigars?" said the bass.

"Yuh. He was tearing up the place."

I took it that they were talking about Martine, the guest I had caddied for. He had nearly topped the hill the day I caddied for him.

"Some big-shot developer looking for a friend on the zoning board," said the lead. "I don't think he even knows the territory."

"What's a guy like that want to join our club for?" the baritone asked.

"I heard he was behind that plan to put in a development over by the river," said the tenor. "I guess there is some serious money backing that project, and that fella looks like he knows where they keep it."

When I first started caddying, it was the ritual that interested me, the observation of honors on the tee and the devotion to determining who was away at all times.

As I graduated to caddying two bags, I became more focused on the geometry of the work: getting the bags and the right clubs to two golfers who may have hacked their way to opposite sides of the fairway. I enjoyed tracking errant shots as they rocketed into the woods by lining up markers and calculating landings. I think I might have made a decent dog had I been given the chance.

And when I started greens-keeping, I became more interested in the texture of the land itself, of the shades of green carefully shaped in the varying patterns of tee box, fairway, rough and putting green and the resident flock of brightly colored golfing fowl who pollinated the place with cash.

Strictly speaking, the members owned the course, but any nitwit can own something by mastering the laws of property. It takes more to be a steward.

Juliana had a summer job as well, working at a popular diner sheathed in aluminum. She had the lunch shift that day and had offered to pick me up at the club when my regular watch ended at 3:30.

The maintenance barn was an inheritance from the days when the country club had been somebody's farm on the edge of town. It was filled with equipment—mowers, tractors, three-wheeled jitneys for getting around—and a small mountain of 70-pound bags of fertilizer sold by the public works department of Milwaukee, Wisconsin, and manufactured by the good people of Milwaukee doing what comes natural to them.

I washed up more thoroughly than usual and sauntered down the lane toward the employee parking lot. Juliana was smoking a cigarette in her family's Fairlane parked under a tree.

She had her waitress uniform on and it was a little tight, which I later found out was by design, and the top two buttons were undone. It was hot, but having been outside all day I was used to it. She ground her cigarette out in the dashboard ashtray, looking at me with a smile in her eyes.

"You were going to throw that out the window, weren't you?" I said.

"And have the whole goddamn Boy Scouts of America breathing down my neck?" She fired up the Fairlane, and we rolled in a very well-behaved manner out the entrance road of the country club. I studied her thighs beneath the steering wheel.

It was soon clear that we were not going directly home. She drove us to a part of town I didn't know very well and turned us down a narrow alley lined with backyard fences, garage doors and trees. She stopped the car and then backed 90 degrees into a parking space tucked between two garages. A sign on one of them advised: "No Parking Aloud."

It was shady and quiet and it got a lot quieter when she turned the ignition off and the engine sputtered still. She carefully picked the cigarette butt from the ashtray and tossed it beside the car.

"Where are we?" I asked.

"This is my friend's place. He won't be home for a while and there's nobody here." Juliana reached under the front seat, released the lever that held the seat in position and pushed us back. As a short person, there was a lot of uncaptured legroom behind her when she drove.

She slid over to the middle of the front seat and lifted up my left arm and put it on the back of the seat and snuggled in.

I wondered how much of Milwaukee's fertile export I might have taken with me from the maintenance barn, but I was more absorbed in the smell of her. Beneath her own workday of shoveling food at people and taking cigarette breaks and whatever commercial scents she applied that morning, there was a whiff of the authentic Juliana.

We were grappling and tongue wrestling soon enough but my head was still in her smells, even more than the soft parts of her colliding with the various parts of me. This was a coalition of anatomy that was not the usual me. This me was less restricted by boundaries and spilling out over edges, entangled with another person living the same experience. We were not loud, but there was probably moaning, there may have been sighing, and there could have been grunts. We were lathering up on the front seat of the Fairlane when one of us, I'm not sure who, became aware of a white panel truck rolling noisily down the alley.

I leaned back away from her so pleasantly. She had left an impression on the far north of the inner side of my thigh. The two guys in the panel truck gawked at us as they rolled by, killing our momentum.

Juliana laid her head on my left shoulder and we held hands in my lap, breathing slowly. After a minute, she said she ought to be getting home, and I agreed that probably I should as well. In truth, I was just being agreeable.

She drove me to my house and in the driveway we lingered, but I was thinking of neighbors I had known my whole life. I promised to call her that evening and watched her backing out of the driveway, concentrating on her navigation, her waitress uniform a little more askew than it had been.

I plopped down on the bed in my room still inebriated with her, but as I closed my eyes I saw Charlotte up to her knees in the Potomac River, smiling in the sunshine, with her brother and sisters splashing around us. I felt us riding in the back of the police car through the steamy city, watching some other world pulse by, and launching like infants off the precinct-house bench to bolt onto the free sidewalks and run into the unruly protest and I realized that I had a story to tell and I was taken with resolve to write up my experiences at the Poor People's Campaign as a stab at my journalism merit badge.

An Eagle Scout is industrious and does not loiter about sodden with lust. I went into my sister's former bedroom, which had been converted into a family workplace after she moved out on her own. My mother's sewing machine was in there; my father had a desk with a type-writer that I used for homework.

It was an Underwood from before the days when typewriters were plugged into the wall. The keys weighed comfortably against the strokes, requiring a deliberate effort to launch a letter catapulting toward the ribbon of ink that was held in place, hammering uniform character spaces on the paper, the same room for upper case Ws and lower-case ls, like resistance fighters lined up for execution. No electricity-aided touch would do the job, and if you typed slowly enough—but not too slow to stall the machine!—you could feel the weight on the lever as the business end of the key raised up to do its work.

The carriage heaved along like a cartoon ear of corn, letter by letter until a chime signaled the end of the line. If you weren't paying any attention, or didn't have a clue what you were doing, you could jam up the keys when the carriage wouldn't advance any further.

The personal computer has made the soft return idiot-proof. On the Underwood, if you knew a little bit about what you were doing, you could adjust when the chime sounded. The carriage return was a fine little piece of chrome art, with a flange sized just right to make it an easy flip—like reaching down to shift gears on the bicycle—to start a new line, but you had to stroke it just right, not too impatiently or without conviction, to get the return you wanted, and there was mechanical feedback into your wrists as the gears rolled the paten over the top.

And as the page wore on, accomplishment waited at the bottom of the sheet of paper riding down its support and threading two rubber rollers. If you looked at the page—not the keys, students!—you could see where your thoughts were taking you.

I was working at the typewriter when my father came home, a little later than usual. He looked in the doorway, and I told him I was working on the journalism merit badge.

He paused for a minute as if he was going to say something, and then just smiled and turned back down the hallway. A little later, I heard my mother come in, and they were talking quietly in the kitchen as they made dinner together while I drummed gently on the Underwood.

I was most of the way through what I had to say about the PPC by the time my mother called me to dinner on the patio. Sitting in a folding chair with an aluminum frame and a weaving of plaid plastic, I sank a little lower as the fuel went in.

My father asked me what I was working on, and when I told him a story about the PPC a light skipped across his eyes and he looked down at his dinner plate.

"What did you do all that time on your own?" my mother asked. "Daddy said you were separated most of the day."

I told her a lot of the story about walking around the city and getting caught in the riot but I left out the part about the police station.

Then and there, in the loving embrace of my parents, I decided to live with my deception and, if I ever got to the Eagle Scout review, I wouldn't tell them about it either.

After doing the dishes, I went back outside and noticed the festive lights that surrounded our neighbors' swimming pool were turned on and guessed my parents were there. Our neighbors, one door over, were empty nesters who had made a standing invitation for our family to use the pool whenever we wanted. My parents particularly liked swimming without waiting an hour after eating.

The sky had darkened and the crickets were in tune and the fatigues of the day were unleashed heavenward. Fireflies were coming up as I walked barefoot over to the shadows outside the fence that protected the pool.

My parents were sitting on the cement edge with their feet in the water, resting between laps.

Speedy was talking about his brother. "He didn't look any better to me," he said to my mother. "I don't know who that mystery doctor is, or if he even exists. But we need to find Jimmy more help."

"And your Mother and Father don't know anything about this either?" Mother asked.

"So it seems."

It was distressing to think my uncle might not come back from this, that there is randomness loose in the universe that we can't do much about, that doctors and deities may or may not have any influence on the outcome.

And then my parents went back to swimming laps, my father underwater, my mother on the surface, as was their custom.

14. FRIDAY, JUNE 28, 1968

1963 CHEVY IMPALA

I took my news story about the PPC to work the next day, and Speedy said he would give the desk editor a heads up that I would drop by later in the afternoon.

After work, I slipped into the clubhouse to say hello to my mother. There were afternoon golfers unwinding and early birds showing up for dinner. I stood in the shadows at the end of the bar. Men were huddled in front of her. A guffaw of laughter rippled through their group portrait, realigning the faces and shoulders, and I could see for a moment Vic Martine in their midst, smiling self-assuredly. Then Mother said something witty that made everyone laugh again.

That guy gets around, I said to myself, and turned back into the kitchen without interrupting her.

I hiked up the hill toward the newspaper office in the center of town. It was darkening to the west. I recollected hearing something about rain.

The newspaper was in a quaint, three-story brick building across from the county courthouse, all dolled up with gingerbread. She was narrow across the shoulders, but went back deep, as far as she could into the town block, standing shoulder to shoulder with old townhouses converted to law offices.

I climbed the stairs to the newsroom on the second floor and looked toward my father's desk; he was on the phone. The room was noisy with the clacking of electric typewriters and reporters talking on the phone, but it was passed the deadline and there was a relaxed feeling in the newsroom, building for the next tide.

My father pointed toward the editor's desk in the corner at the front of the building. It grew darker outside and the overhead lights came on. The ceiling fans were spinning purposelessly. Gusts of wind blew across the room, scattering paper that wasn't anchored down.

My father's editor, Martin Brady, was a stoop-shouldered curmudgeon with a big head usually cocked to one side. Words tumbled out of the corner of his mouth as though they had nowhere else to go, and he had a habit of turning away before he finished his sentences.

His office was separated from the rest of the newsroom by a low wall topped with glass panels all the way around that only rose to about six feet. His doorway had no door. This created the illusion of being separate, but he could see everything that was going on outside, and the outside could see what he was doing. The assistant editor's desk was just outside his doorway, within shouting distance.

"Can I see Mr. Brady?" I said to his assistant. "My father talked to him about an article I wrote."

"Boss," the assistant editor called into Brady's aquarium. "It's Rocky's kid. Got something to show you."

I thought I heard something from the editor's glass box, but couldn't make it out.

The assistant editor interpreted for me. "Go on in."

There were two chairs in front of his desk, but one was piled with folders and papers. I wasn't sure whether I should stand or sit.

"Working at the golf course?" he said, eyeballing my sweaty shirt. "You have something for me to read."

"I'm trying for a merit badge for journalism. I hoped you could take a look at this," I said, offering my work by hand across the flotsam on his desk.

Brady took my folded-over sheets, swiveled to a slight angle and leaned back as far as the chair would allow. I stood before him trying in vain to read his expression. When he got to the end of the last page, he flipped back to the beginning and then tossed it onto the pile on his desk, somewhere between him and me. I couldn't tell from the geography of things whether I was supposed to pick it up or not. So I let it sit there.

"You had an interesting time, getting gassed and all." Brady finally said, without looking at me directly. "Who are you writing for here?"

"For the paper?" seemed like a good answer.

"This ain't a goddamn poetry journal," he said in a matter-of-fact way. "We're not selling them us. People read the paper to see themselves."

Oh goodness gracious, I heard Ishmael say.

"There are facts here that we could shape up into a story," Brady said. "But I doubt we would ever publish it. If you want to write a real newspaper story, you're gonna have to try something else, something people will want to read."

There was some dead air. "My father said I could maybe write something about the canal."

"Closer to home," Brady said, "but out of business for 30 years."

"There was a rally there a couple weeks ago."

"With Justice Douglas, yeah. The cock-eyed scheme to fill in the canal and build houses. Your dad covered that."

"And I met this guy who carves coconuts into heads and sells them on the street in New Hope. He calls them icons."

Brady looked at me for more.

"He says the icons honor the people who worked on the canal when it was still moving coal down from the mountains."

"What do you think?"

"I only saw him because I looked out the window of a moving car one night. And then I talked to a guy who works on the barge and he knew where Quentin, that's his name, lives. One thing led to another."

Brady tried to hide a smile, which made me think the adults had been up to some collusion again. "Serendipity is as powerful as gravity, Izzy. Don't ignore it."

"Should I write something about this guy, then?" I was already trying to remember what it was Quentin had told me.

"Yes," Brady was turning away and the words were spilling from the corner of his mouth. "A profile kind of story about this cat ... Where did he get this? ... whatchacallit icons? Why does he?" He was already on to the next thing on one of the piles in front of him. "You get the idea."

"I know where to find him." I said.

As we drove home into the dark sky, my father and I fell in behind a maroon Chevy from the post-fin era. It was wide and low with a heavy chrome bumper and rear lights set in a pair of small wings that launched out from the sides, a seaworthy vessel.

A woman was driving alone, smoking a cigarette that she carefully tapped outside the window whenever she came to a stop. My father said she was too ladylike to pitch the cigarette butt, but I bet the ashes as a prelude to throwing it overboard.

"She doesn't want any trash in her car," I said. As the light ahead turned, she held the cigarette between the index and middle fingers of her left and flicked it into the street. Another car slipped in between us, but my father continued to follow her, although it took us off our way home. She turned into the parking lot in front of a pharmacy and my father pulled into the parking space next to the Chevy.

"Ma'am," I said, leaning out of the window with my Eagle Scout smile. She was hurrying—it looked like rain could start spattering at any minute—but she paused on her way into the drug store and looked back.

"Could you tell me why you dropped your cigarette in the street back there?"

The woman was at a loss. "You're too young to smoke," she said, staring disapprovingly at my father.

"No, I'm not asking for a cigarette. I am wondering why you threw your cigarette out the window at the traffic light on Walnut Street."

She just shook her head and went into the drug store.

"A lot of people don't know why they do things," my father said. "Maybe what they need is a reminder," he said.

That night, after dinner, after talking to Juliana for a while on the phone, I sat out on one of the webbed lawn chairs feeling a thunderstorm gather in the sky. I had a plastic transistor radio, tuned to the very narrow groove in the dial that opened a portal in the radio spectrum all the way to Jean Shepherd on WOR in New York City.

Shepherd opened his show that night with strange music playing in the background as he read two poems by T.S. Eliot. There was thunder rumbling in the distance and I had the feeling you get when something is following you in the gloaming woods, a sense so tangible that the hairs stand up on the back of your neck. I wondered if he could feel the same storm system in his radio studio.

And then Shepherd read Elizabeth Bishop's "The Fish," whose "skin hung in strips like ancient wallpaper." There were already hooks in the fish's lip, signs of wisdom, so the poet let it go.

And then another piece by the same poet, about sailors steering around soulful icebergs as clouds warm overhead.

The background music, Shepherd explained, was from the film *2001: A Space Odyssey*. At the time I thought 2001 was impossibly far off in the future, well beyond the current horizon filled with ships and icebergs.

15. Sunday, June 30, 1968

1965 Ford Thunderbird

It was Sunday morning, a week after going to the Poor People's Campaign. I was out on the numbered road trying to hitch a ride to the country club. Some days the parents get up for you; other days they don't. There was not much traffic about, and I was walking backwards.

I reeled in an old-timer. He remarked that he didn't see many hitchhikers of a Sunday morning, and I said there weren't many cars either, so maybe the world was in balance after all. Ahead of us, coming in our direction, was a 1965 Thunderbird, from the generation after Ford had begun stretching the model out. The driver's left elbow was resting out the window. The T-Bird came at us fast and as we drew close the driver glanced in our direction and flicked a cigarette with his right hand, across his body, in our general direction, then flew on behind us.

"Sumbitch," my ride muttered, automatically, as if he wasn't thinking hard about it. I whirled around and saw the T-Bird, light blue with a white top, zoom away. There was no trace of a fin, just two wide banks of lights that narrowed over the license plate, with a scoop up the middle of the trunk.

The flick seemed intentional, a littering of opportunity. He may have seen us from a distance, as I had noticed him, and perhaps on a whim decided to shoot his cigarette butt at us.

The old guy who picked me up had a low opinion of golfers, and he didn't mind sharing this with me. I couldn't tell exactly whether he was putting me down for being part of the time-wasting, self-indulgent sect of golf, or whether he thought that I, as a caddy, must have shared his views. It turned out he wasn't too fond of hippies, blacks, women's libbers and homos.

In an abundance of caution, I did not bring up the Boy Scouts nor confess that I was a poverty protester who had escaped police custody and was in grave danger of enjoying modern poetry.

The caddies were in a rambunctious mood when I got to the club. Two boys had already been sent home for pulling down another kid's pants and pushing him down the hill toward the ninth green. No golfers were harmed, but the incident was observed from the first tee and the indignation flew like 18-year scotch down the chain of command, from the members to the pro to the caddy master.

"He had it coming, he's such a retard," an eyewitness kid told me.

"*Always go to sea as a simple sailor*," I observed.

"Yeah, but he is a fucking retard," the kid insisted.

By and by, I was called to carry two bags in a foursome, with the other two golfers riding a cart. One of the cart-riders was Winthrop, the banker. He was the cheapskate kind of player who didn't mind asking a caddy who wasn't actually working for him to replace his divot if the caddy was standing too close by.

It was an unremarkable round, the kind that made me wonder what golfers saw in this. In any given outing, almost any golfer will do something that exceeds his customary mediocrity, his par. Honey, I hit a hell of a six iron on the seventh, he might say. But to the unwashed masses at his dinner table, this fleeting excelsior was irrelevant. And it would likely be disremembered by the time he got back at work on Monday.

Maybe the silent firing of brain paths illuminated by his rare solid shot had a therapeutic effect on the rest of the organism. Or maybe he just couldn't think of anything better to do on Sunday mornings.

These were golfers who barely acknowledge the caddy's existence, and the round was running true to form when, as the five of us stood together in a loose semicircle on the twelfth tee waiting for the group ahead to move out of artillery range, Winthrop suddenly turned to me and asked what I thought about Martine.

"Who?" This was a stall; I knew whom he meant.

"The guest you caddied for a couple weeks ago. You had my bag as well."

"He had a great round. I haven't caddied for him since then."

"Do you think we should admit him to the club?"

This was a bizarre question for a member to ask a caddy. The other three were staring at us.

"I really don't know, Mr. Winthrop, it's none of my ...."

"I know he gave you a ridiculous tip, probably because he thinks I'm cheap. So it is your business if he's going to play here on a regular basis."

I looked down the fairway, wishing the group ahead would move on.

"Give the kid a break, Ron," one of my golfers said, taking a practice swing right in our midst, clearing away some of the debris. "It's the membership committee's job to look at these applications. If you make him the right offer, I'm sure you'll get to finance his deal, whether he thinks you're cheap or not. You're just pissed off because you butchered your approach on the last hole."

The other two golfers chuckled at this the way golfers do and Winthrop gave it up. For the rest of the round, I kept as much distance as I could from him. Later, while I was helping the member who had intervened on my behalf look for a lost shot, he muttered that Winthrop was having trouble at his job.

When it was over, I decided to go another round. Sunday afternoons posed a high risk of catching married couples—or even worse—one couple by themselves, trying to balance the psychological terrors of golf and wedlock all at once. I preferred working for a group of women over a mixed foursome. By themselves, women played a game with less yardage and fewer demands on the caddy. We only had to smile at one another while I enjoyed their cool and pleasant scent, even in the crucible of summer.

Fortunately, the mixed foursomes usually rode carts.

I didn't have to wait long. A younger caddy and I were called for a threesome, and as we rounded the corner to the pro shop I recognized Martine's bag in the group that would tee off next. I told the caddy master I would take it and he gave me the bigger of the two other bags—balance is more important than weight—and gave the lightest one to the kid.

I recognized both bags, owned by a pair of old guys who played together all the time. Caddying them was about as easy as it got; they wore out the middle of the fairway, hit the ball about the same distance and knew the yardage better than they knew their wives. The three of them came out of the pro shop, spikes clattering on the flagstone, Martine enjoying a joke with the old-timers.

It was an odd grouping because the two long-time club members played side by side, as they always did, while Martine laced his drives fathoms beyond theirs. He had an easy grace, waiting with interest as they hit their fairway shots, saving his congratulations for when somebody actually did something noteworthy.

He seemed to me to be someone you definitely would want in your country club, a likable guy who befriended others without trying too hard. He fit in well with the old guys and there was something about his approach to the game that seemed honest and straightforward like theirs.

The three of them went into the clubhouse after the ninth hole, while the kid and I trudged out to a tree that was about 200 yards down the 10th fairway, the spot where caddies waited. We looked away as the mixed foursome in front of our group hacked their way along.

When our group came out, Martine teed off first. He launched a rocket that was on us instantly and gained altitude as it whizzed high and mighty overhead, and streaked away down the center of the fairway. I sprinted out from under the tree to see if it would land, and there was a moment when I thought I had lost it. Then a thin white trail fell from the sky in front of the green.

I turned around and looked back at the tee, where Martine was casually walking off the elevated launch pad to wait while the others took their turns.

My other bag hit his tee shot about 220 yards up the middle of the fairway, but his friend uncharacteristically sprayed wide right into the practice range. It was not out of bounds over there, but he would have to navigate a line of trees to get back on course. The kid marched off to meet his golfer while I set up next to my member's tee shot.

When Martine arrived, he was smoking a cigar and sipping from a tall plastic cup filled with a cloudy, ice-filled drink with a lime wedge floating in it. Martine handed me his driver. We waited quietly, the sun was starting to slant a little softer in the sky, while the member in the practice range deliberated and then punched something low with a half swing that managed to bounce back into the fairway.

My old guy may have fooled himself with his club selection. He didn't hit it very well and came up short of the green. We waited again while the refugee from the practice range lined up his third shot and, suddenly looking a little tired, clunked his ball awkwardly off line. As it bounced toward a greenside trap, Martine muttered James Brown under his breath to the golf shot in flight, "Get up-pa, stay on the scene."

My member was a few feet behind Martine's tee shot, which was the longest I had ever seen on that hole. Hitting his third, the old fellow had been lapped, but he made up for it by running a perfect chip across the green that rolled hard into the flagstick and rattled into the cup.

"Oh, baby," Martine said, clapping him on the shoulder. The old-timer tried to play it cool, but he couldn't hold back his grin.

Then Zeus struck again, reaching down and touching the other old guy in the sand trap. From the cloud of sand spraying off his wedge, the ball jumped green-ward, landed softly and rolled like it had no-where else to go but straight into the cup, barely touching the pin. He thrust his club skyward in exultation and did a little jig on his way out of the trap.

More James Brown. "Can we hit it and quit it?" Martine sang.

Martine was only a few yards off the edge of the green and he pulled out a seven iron. He put his cocktail and his cigar on the grass near his ball and studied the path ahead before lifting his pant leg by the crease in his slacks and settling over his shot. The four of us watched frozen as the club clicked perfectly and the ball rose up on a gentle arc.

While it was still en route, Martine said, "This isn't as easy as it looks. You guys didn't leave much room in the cup." His ball sauntered up against the flag and tipped into the hole.

The two old guys actually yelled and pointed to the cup that held a miracle par, an unexpected birdie and an eagle. Martine handed me his club and picked up his cigar and drink.

"That was something different," I said.

Neither of us moved, enjoying the moment. "Did you hear about the track meet last week in Sacramento?" he asked.

I had not.

"Including the preliminary heats, there were 10 different runners who equaled or beat 10 seconds in the 100-yard dash," Martine said. "Three of them were timed at 9.9 seconds, and one actually had a 9.8 that was thrown out because there was a little too much wind when he ran it."

The others were heading for the 11th tee and we started after them, slowly.

"The world record has been stuck at 10 seconds since 1960, and then all of a sudden—in one day—three guys beat it, and a few others tie it." Martine sipped his drink and started walking. "The officials thought maybe the track was short, so they re-measured it. Turns out it was 4 inches too long.

"You have to be prepared to be amazed," he said.

"This place seems too easy for you," I said, wondering where this was coming from. "Why would you want to join this club?"

Martine stopped at looked at me. "Who said anything about becoming a member?"

Once you're out on thin ice, there's not much to do but see if it will hold. "I heard Mr. Winthrop say something about you joining. I really don't know anything about it."

"A lot of business takes place in these clubs with guys like Winthrop," Martine said, with an edge in his voice. He was thinking. "I've asked about joining, and that's one reason I'm trying to meet a lot of different members," he said, nodding toward the two codgers ahead of us.

"And I'm a spiritual tourist," Martine said as we arrived at the next tee. "This is where looking has brought me today."

16. MONDAY, JULY 1, 1968

1962 OLDSMOBILE EIGHTY-EIGHT

Things were quiet as my father gave me a ride home from work. I was thinking that we spend a lot of time, as a species, staring at the ass ends of cars. A white blur streaked past us in a passing zone on the two-lane road.

The driver was smoking. My dad accelerated to keep pace. From a distance, the fingerprint of the late-model Oldsmobile was in focus: the wide flat trunk with fins that leaned out about four inches at the end of the car.

There was an oval carved into the rear with pointed corners that extended straight back. The taillights were flat and compact; a minimalist chrome bumper. The Olds logo, a rocket emerging from an "88," was in the corner of the trunk. Sometimes a rocket is just a rocket.

Along the way, the cigarette came flying out of the front window. A man in his mid-20s was driving, a burly, well-tanned arm jutting out the side window.

We were never able to catch up to him to ask the question. When we reached the point of no return, the Olds went straight and we had a left turn to go home. We turned.

"We'd like to know a little about you for our files," Speedy hummed under his breath.

"What's that, Dad?"

"At some point we may find the same car or the same driver in our sample," Speedy said. "Maybe we should mark them, the way biologists tag species in the wild for study."

In the National Geographic, the savannah science guys always shot the wildlife with tranquilizers before they stapled tags in their ears. I wondered if this is what my father had in mind.

"It can't be permanent—we don't want to tamper with the evidence—and we may have to tag them without their knowing." I was used to the fact that my father often thought out loud.

"You mean put a mark on the car, right?" I said, trying to lead the witness.

"Maybe the crayons that used-car dealers use on windshields would work on a bumper ..."

I should have stepped in there with something to change our bearing, but I came up empty.

"Or something else," my father said, "like a bumper sticker."

I was afraid to ask.

"I flick butts." Speedy seemed pleased with this.

"I guess that would show them," I said.

When we got home, Mother had some news that I thought would divert my father from his crusade for the truth about butt-flickers. A doctor who was a member of the country club had stopped by the bar to ask about Uncle James.

"Is it common knowledge there?" my father asked.

"I've mentioned it to a few people, you know, our concern about his progress." Mother explained.

"And what did this doctor have to say?"

"Dr. Matthews actually has seen him. He's the one who suggested that they get him out of bed and socializing with other people. He said he was only offering to help. He said he would talk to Jimmy's primary doctor if we want."

Matthews was a cart-rider. I wasn't sure what this said about his professional acumen.

Speedy mulled this over. "He's doing this just because you work at the club?"

"Yes, isn't it great? I mean, he made it clear he just wants to help out. He said brain damage cases are very difficult to treat ... but it's his specialty."

"This is terrific," my father said. "And I thought I would be the one with the surprise tonight."

"You have something up your sleeve," Mother said, tugging their midsections a little closer. I was thinking bumper stickers.

"I propose to take us to the Music Circus in Lambertville to see Duke Ellington."

I couldn't remember anyone in our family ever mentioning the music circus before Juliana and I went there for the Fifth Dimension.

"We haven't been over there in years," my father said. "If we don't go now, we could someday find out that things ain't what they used to be."

And so we finished supper and spruced ourselves up and took our places in my mother's car, with my father driving. We bounced across the county road toward the river, and after a few miles my mother slid closer to him and my father stretched his right arm over the back of the seat, creating a nook for her to settle into. She whispered a secret in his ear and I could see in her face the reflection of his smile. I fell back through time to when I was a very young and just tagging along for the ride of their lives.

I liked the Fifth Dimension, but it was clear that Ellington was much longer off the tee. I am not smart enough to understand jazz, but I discovered that I could swim in it. They started with a number that even I, an unschooled, overgrown Boy Scout, recognized, but then dove into unfamiliar and haunting territory, trombones softly calling into the night, a saxophone responding from the silky woods backed up by more brass, against the steady drum brush and bass, a trumpet spraying notes across the music circus, always in control but on the verge of mayhem, a trio reeling them back into the woods; the tempo quickened behind a clarinet spreading its wings, fucking with the rhythm and shimmering as a heavy wave of brass and brash stomped forward, all bold and reaching a crescendo.

They had me, and I was gone for the next hour.

"They were on their game tonight, weren't they?" Mother said when it was over and we were suddenly back walking under the stars.

None of us wanted the evening to end, and so we stopped for ice cream at the frozen custard stand near the entrance to the music circus. Crickets flailed industriously in the fields surrounding the theater, and the people who were standing in line with us were talking quietly, weaving all of ourselves into the summer night. There was vacation in the air, even though most of us were ankle-deep in another work week.

We sat in the car and ate our ice cream with the windows rolled down while the parking lot gradually emptied, fat American tires rolling contentedly across the gravel crunching a tune about leaving without upsetting the balance of things for those who lingered.

Then it was our turn to set sail on the state highway. I curled into the corner and listened to the night rushing past us.

17. Thursday, July 4, 1968

1967 Plymouth Valiant

The garage door was open to the warm morning, like a cave dwelling that looked over a quiet meadow. My father was rummaging around in a pile of boxes.

"Can I get a ride in with you today?" I asked. The greens-keepers were off; the caddies were not.

My father always covered the Fourth of July parade and the patriotic speeches made by dignitaries on the steps of the county courthouse. He would write a story that might or might not get published, but they always used his photos.

"Don't we have a roll of masking tape somewhere?" he asked.

I pointed to it, not far from his nose. "What's it for?"

"Bumper stickers." When he found what he was looking for, he tore off a small beige strip, walked out onto our sunlit driveway and put it on the bumper of the De Soto.

He stood back in review. "Sure, I'll be going in soon," he said, and then peeled the tape away from the bumper, bending down to inspect it at close range.

"Perfect." Turning to me, "Is my permanent marker in there?"

When we went paddling, my father wrote poems with an indelible marker on the hull of the canoe. He had covered quite a bit of the inside of our Grumman, and some of the exterior. Haiku was his favored form.

I retrieved the marker from the box of paddling stuff and walked it out to him.

He wrote "Yardley" on the strip of tape and put it back on the bumper. Sometime long ago in an earlier life, I was an Egyptian boy holding chisels for a carver hammering hieroglyphics into palace walls.

Independence Day was busy at the country club. I could have risen early and hitched to town to caddy in the shotgun tournament that went off at 8:30. But I didn't.

I may have been sliding toward perdition.

The parade didn't start until 11. I idled around the house until my father was ready to go. Juliana called before we left. She was at work at the diner. People in the ancient times had to wait to make their phone calls until the rest of life—jobs and so forth—was out of the way, and the pay phone on the wall was not in use.

"This is excruciating," she said. "It's dead as hell in here. It's too hot for breakfast. I made two dollars all morning."

I thought of her leaning over a table to set down coffee and plates of steaming eggs and bacon, girly beads of perspiration on her chest.

I told her I was going to caddy in the afternoon, even though this seemed increasingly unlikely even as I was saying it. Then I heard myself asking her if she wanted to come to our house for supper. There was a pause on the line.

"You don't happen to have a swimming pool, do you?"

"Our neighbors do."

"Seriously?"

I told her it was so, adding that we had carte blanche to use it whenever we wanted.

"Why the hell haven't you mentioned this before?" she said rather pleasantly. And then she had to hang up and get back to work.

My dad and I were soon rolling toward town. The masking tape and poetry marker were on the front seat. Ready for action.

"You should know this if you're going to get a badge in journalism," he said. "It is all about getting nearer to the truth."

I had heard this a thousand times from him.

Speedy continued. "The Army has abandoned our base at Khe Sanh, the same one where we lost 200 men in a siege by the North Vietnamese this winter. We were darn near overrun, but they sent in reinforcements and held on to the camp, which the Army said was strategically important.

"A few weeks ago, the Army told the reporters in Saigon that we were going to pull out of Khe Sanh, but the information was under embargo. You know what that means?"

"Not exactly." Actually, I had no idea.

"It's a game the government plays. They give information to reporters that they are not allowed to publish until the embargo expires."

"Why do they do that?"

"The official reason is that they want to give background to reporters without giving it to the enemy. Some people think it's a way of trying to influence <u>what</u> reporters write, more than <u>when</u> they write it. Anyway, a reporter from Baltimore published a story before the embargo was over saying that the Army was getting ready to pull out of Khe Sahn."

"What happened to him?"

"They pulled his press credentials, shut him off from all official information," Speedy said. "In the long run, it's probably no big deal; he'll get his credentials back or his newspaper will send someone to replace him. A lot of people doubted the Army's explanation for why we fought so hard to keep the base in the first place, and it wasn't at all clear why the North Vietnamese committed so much to try to take it. Propaganda is a big part of war."

I wondered if the Army gave medals for propaganda, or for being wounded by it.

"The North Vietnamese delegation to the peace talks in Paris went to the horse races this week, just to make people wonder what the hell they were up to," he added.

"Or maybe they like horse races."

"Exactly."

At a red light, we pulled alongside a new Plymouth Valiant. A woman about my mother's age was smoking a cigarette. She blew the smoke out the window. Her Valiant was a two-door coupe in luminescent aquamarine, a boxy trunk with suggestive, miniature fins. The woman didn't look like a thrower, but you never know.

"Let's see where this goes," my father said. When the light changed, he hesitated long enough for the Valiant to pull ahead of us. The driver seemed to be done with her smoke; her right shoulder dipped slightly as though she might have been grinding out the burning end in the ashtray.

As we were slipping in behind her, the cigarette came flying out the window. She appeared to toss it with her right hand, across her body.

She pulled into a shopping center and wheeled toward the supermarket. We followed her, which was beginning to feel a little less creepy, and parked a few spaces away. She gathered up her things and pulled down the visor to check her face before she opened the door and slid outside. She walked around the back of her car and toward the market.

My father slowly pulled out of our parking spot and rolled behind the Plymouth and then stopped. He tore off a length of tape about 16 inches long and stretched it temporarily across the steering wheel, uncapped the marker with his teeth, and inscribed "I FLICK BUTTS" on the tape.

"Slide over and take the wheel," he told me. "But don't start driving until I say so."

He pushed the gearshift into park and got out of the car, closing the door softly behind him. As I pulled myself behind the steering wheel, he ducked below sea level in the parking lot, into the underwater of tires and side panels and grills below the windowed auto world where the top third of motoring humanity is visible. I watched him carefully place and smooth his homemade bumper sticker on the Plymouth.

He stood up and turned to me. "Go ahead. I'll come around and get in the other side." He was a little breathless. I wondered who this man was.

Once he was aboard, I knew enough to drive out of the parking lot as normally as I could.

"Far out," my father muttered as I steered us back into law-abiding traffic.

This cattle-branding episode melted the little go-to-work resolve that was left in me. I decided to tag along with my father at the parade instead of lug golf bags for four hours.

We found a spot near where the parade formed up, and worked our way along the edge, stopping to take photographs and talk to people, watching the high school marching bands marching and Boy Scout troops trooping, and Kiwanas kiwaving from popped-open convertibles, and policemen on motorcycles, and veterans of foreign wars, and fire trucks and ambulances, but no Dr. Seuss critters, or elephants decked out in velvet, or clowns juggling flaming torches, or girls in skimpy outfits on prancing horses, or any of the good stuff that would have made the parade better, *much less a sober harpooner parading the streets of our Christian town.*

It came to the speeches in front of the courthouse; I was surprised to see Martine on the platform in a dark business suit, one leg crossed atop the other, the very model of civic focus. My father was in front of the stage, invisibly taking photographs the way photojournalists invisibly do. Unless you happen to notice them.

After the parade, I sat in the newsroom and listened to my father type up his notes. There was no edition that day, and we were alone. Speedy was lost in what he was doing, putting his electric typewriter through its paces, daring the ball of letters and numbers and symbols to fall behind.

Juliana did not come over for dinner, but she picked me up later at dusk. We went to town and met up with a movable party of high school kids and college kids home for the summer on pilgrimage to the vast grassy lawn surrounding the old tile factory where the town fathers staged their annual fireworks display. We moseyed, by unspoken agreement, to a quiet spot beyond the frontier of the crowd near a clump of trees. There were other teenagers with the same idea back there, hormonal pyrotechnics.

Juliana was having her way with me, guiding me to places I hadn't thought to explore on my own. There were fireworks in the sky overhead that seemed to draw us together into the light. And it was more than light. It was lightness.

1959 DESOTO FIREDOME

I was riding home from work with my mother, and in front of us was a 1959 Firedome, nephew to my father's car, another winged experiment from the Ike fantasy world. Viewed from the rear, it hefted a barrage of thick chrome fittings and a large insignia that included a keyhole for the trunk. On either side, three protruding circular taillights were stacked on top of one another with a chrome V jutting over the top. It had two radio antennas, one on each side of the trunk, and a low, wide wrestler's stance.

This particular vessel had a bumper sticker that said: "Stassen '68—Why Not?" The former governor of Minnesota was on his fourth campaign in pursuit of the Republican nomination for president. He had at that point in the summer of 1968 rounded up just one delegate, and there were only a few weeks until the party convention in Miami. After the RFK assassination, the Secret Service assigned an agent to guard him.

It was said this protection was the biggest crowd Stassen had attracted so far in the campaign.

A perpetual anachronism, Stassen would keep running, in 1980, 1984, 1988 and 1992, and you can judge for yourself whether his country would have been better off in any of those years with a liberal Republican president committed to peace.

The middle-aged gent in the DeSoto was Stassen through-and-through, in a dark suit and white shirt, hair combed carefully across the top of his head. We were driving alongside, and I was surprised to see him light a cigarette with the car lighter.

"Mom, we're gonna have to stay behind this guy," I said.

"Did you know your father is putting stickers on cars now?" she asked. I wasn't sure whether she disapproved or was amused. However, she did slowly descend into the gravitational field of the Firedome.

Were Speedy and I gradually subverting the universe?

I did not think a Stassen man would be a cigarette litterer, but he was. Just before our turn, he dropped the cigarette straight down the outside of his door and kept rolling off to his Tomorrow Land.

We did not join the Stassen movement.

"Uncle James seemed better last night," Mother said, wheeling toward our neighborhood.

While I was making out with Juliana at the fireworks in town, my mother and father had taken Uncle James to a big fireworks display in the city. In fact, it was the first year I hadn't gone with them.

"He tried talking to us, about people named Sidney or Grant. It was all mixed up. Daddy says he has no idea what he was talking about," Mother said. "He was with the other patients in the social area, the way he was when you and Katie went to visit. The nurses said Dr. Matthews had been there and talked with James for a long time."

"So maybe this new doctor is helping," I said.

"Jimmy seemed to like the fireworks, but maybe it was too much. It's so hard to see him like this, his life all bottled up inside."

My father came home with the paper under his arm. He had a story in the A section, and they used his photos from the Fourth of July parade.

It was the second time I saw a picture of Vic Martine in a photograph taken by my father. He was in the corner of a shot of the mayor orating above a podium festooned with patriotic bunting.

"Do you know him?" I said, pointing at Martine.

My father studied the picture. "I was aiming to catch the mayor looking intelligent, which isn't as easy as it sounds, and not paying much attention to the rest of the faces," he said. "I have talked to him before, somewhere."

"He has been playing golf at the club," I offered. "And he's a cigarette thrower."

My father looked again at the photograph. "He is?"

"I put him in the log one day when I had the car. Followed him all the way to the country club and ended up caddying for him."

Speedy snapped his fingers. "He was at that canal rally. We were chatting about the proposed development. When I pulled out my notebook to ask him where he stood, he clammed up."

"What did you do?"

"I said we could go off record, but it didn't matter. He shut down."

1957 CHEVROLET BEL AIR

It was plenty weird being driven to the monthly Boy Scout meeting by my girlfriend. Juliana wanted a date that night; I felt that I ought to go to the Scout meeting. The compromise was that she would chauffeur me.

Our Boy Scout troop, sometime in its mossy past, built a log cabin on a thumb of wooded land in the curve of a creek. When I got started, the cabin was the most interesting thing about Scouting: a large, single room with a cement floor and a hearth. No church basement for us, no sir. And you could not drive right up to our cabin; cars had to park on the other side of the creek and the Scouts walked across a footbridge to our sanctuary.

When Juliana and I drove into the parking area, the other Scouts were disembarking from cars driven by moms and dads. I looked at her just before I got out of the car, wondering what she would do while I was in the meeting, when she suddenly reached her hand behind my neck and pulled my mouth to hers.

I felt a thousand eyes on us, but a Scout is prepared to do a good deed every day.

She looked at me, our eyes only inches apart. "I'll just hang out here with the moms," she murmured.

Slinking out of the car, I adjusted things in my crotch as discretely as discretely as I could while trudging across the bridge.

At that point in my Scouting career, the guys in our troop who were my age had quit or graduated to the Explorers, and a number of them had long since been beatified as Eagles. I was losing my place on the ladder; kids younger than me were already being crowned.

This did not bother me. I liked working on the merit badges. The final step did not seem important.

And when I recited the Scout oath with the rest of my troop, it still rang true. What is so bad about a vow to do your best, to help others, and to become physically strong, mentally awake and morally straight?

My mother and I sometimes went to the church that sponsored my Scout troop, mostly to justify my membership in the troop. We were not church people. When I was in the second grade, I was marched with the rest of my class once a week from our public school to Bible study at a nearby church, where a well-intentioned woman fed Christian awareness into our heads, until my parents, and specifically, my father, found out about it. After that, I stayed with a small subset of students back at school, in a formless classroom, until the others came back from god study.

At the Scout meeting, we pledged allegiance to the flag and the stipulation that we were members of one nation under god. I moved my lips over that phrase, but never actually said it.

The pledge wasn't formally adopted by the federal government until after World War II, and it didn't get the "under god" part until a little later, after the Daughters of the American Revolution and other social clubs clamored for its inclusion. In 1954, President Eisenhower endorsed the change. Ike had had the good sense to be raised as a government-fearing Jehovah's Witness, but during his presidency he became a Presbyterian, like Ishmael. I don't know where Stassen stood on the issue.

Ironically, activism by Jehovah's Witnesses helped get a court ruling that students cannot be compelled to participate or even stand for the pledge.

"There is another kind of dirt that won't come off by washing," our troop leader was reading from the Scout handbook. "It sticks. It is the kind that goes below the skin, that sinks into your mind." A boy—or a president, I thought to myself—has a hard struggle fighting that kind of dirt, keeping his thoughts clean, the handbook advised.

"By forcing your mind to occupy itself with things that are good and true, you will be able to overcome temptations and will be at peace with yourself," the Scoutmaster read, and I don't think it was accidental that he looked my way. But there was nothing about Juliana that seemed not good or untrue, and the Temptations were a popular Motown group, not a dangerous surge of hormones that needed to be suppressed.

I was listening to him, but there was a running counterpoint in my mind. I thought about my father writing I FLICK BUTTS on strangers' cars, and I knew that night that the Boy Scout handbook was only a map, even a serviceable one. In the end, you have to make your own compass, as Captain Ahab did.

I was never going to claim my Eagle Scout designation. Getting an Eagle badge may have meant more to the Boy Scouts than it did to me.

But I was still the oldest Scout on deck, and so I stood next to the Scoutmaster while he handed out merit badges and acknowledged the migration of Scouts upward through the system. If there was one thing the Boy Scouts excel at, it's doling out commendations. You couldn't swing a dead cat in that room without hitting two or three people, at any given time, who were getting or bestowing awards and saluting one another.

When we were done with the ceremonies and the Scouts were storming the cookie table, the Scoutmaster cornered me and asked again when we would have the personal conference, the last hurdle to getting the Eagle badge.

I liked this man and it was hard not to. He put in a lot of time long after his son had grown through scouting and moved on to the rest of his life. But he hung in there, stuffed into his adult Scout uniform and trying his best to help us be prepared.

"Well, I've got somebody waiting for me tonight," I said.

He rolled his eyes and grinned. "I saw her," he said, and saluted me. "Call me and let's finish this Eagle badge. You have been done with all the requirements for some time now."

Instead of saluting, I reached and shook his hand. "Tonight is my last meeting," I said.

This did not seem to surprise him. He took my grip and put his left hand on my right shoulder. "Good luck, Isaac," he said.

"I'm not gonna stop being a scout," I told him.

As I walked over the bridge to the parking area in the trees, I thought about the times I had crossed over that creek, but never with the particular anticipation of that moment. All four windows of the Fairlane were rolled down and Juliana was smoking a cigarette in the car with the AM/FM radio turned down low and melting into the sounds of the woods.

When hiking, a Scout learns to turn around every now and again to see what the landmarks along the trail will look like on the way back. As I opened the door to her car, I looked to the cabin, light bursting out of every window and door, memorizing the scene so I would recognize it on my way back.

"Are you ready to go, Scout?" my girlfriend asked.

I said I was, and she lit the engine and we rumbled back to the road. We gathered speed and Juliana kept pushing the gas, hurtling us faster along the deserted country road.

We pulled up at a four-way stop sign, and a '57 Chevy Bel Air arriving at almost the same time paused only briefly and then shot across our bow through the intersection. There were teenagers inside and they were smoking.

"Follow that car, please," I said.

The people in my life were getting used to this, and Juliana didn't even blink. We turned to follow the Chevy, a heavy, boxy carriage with modestly long skirts and an abrupt windshield that wrapped slightly around the sides of the front cabin. Its distinctive forehead leaned slightly into the wind, and a flat, jet-plane hood ornament steered it streaking down the road ahead.

The '57 Bel Air was a popular car for teenagers, reliable and roomy and of an age that middle-class dads no longer saw as suitable for the family car.

A passenger flicked his cigarette, a dramatic fling into a cornfield that may have sailed several rows deep.

We followed the Bel Air a little ways, but our hearts were elsewhere. We gave up and headed down a dark farm lane tucked between a cornfield and a line of trees, where we worked on the merit badge in French kissing, an unexpectedly easy one to earn.

20. WEDNESDAY, JULY 10, 1968

1963 FORD FALCON

After work that Wednesday, I walked into town. Heat was building during those days, too ornery to go away overnight, leaving a gritty edge for the start of the next day.

I was going to stop at the diner and get an iced tea and then hitchhike home. Juliana had the dinner shift. She would be too busy to idle with me, but I liked to see her at work. As I entered the diner, she was taking an order from someone in a booth. She suddenly put her hands on her hips and struck a pose, leaning to the side enough so that I could see that the customer was Vic Martine.

They laughed heartily. The air conditioning sent a chill up my back.

I hesitated in the doorway before taking a stool at the counter. The waistband of my work pants was sweated through.

I studied the menu, embalmed in a heavy plastic binder, like it was the bar exam. Another waitress slid in front of me, fussing with something behind the counter. Without looking up, she said Juliana would be back in a minute to take my order.

"I just want an iced tea, please," I said.

The counter area before me still needed some mopping, and the waitress attacked it with a dish towel, forcing my elbows into a hasty retreat. I leaned back, my hands dangling with no sense where to put themselves, waiting exposed while the waitress-who-was-not-Juliana polished up, threw down a paper placemat and laid out the cutlery in one motion.

Then my girl brushed past me. I don't know whether I could tell from her scent or from her softness or the quiet whoosh of her waitress shoes on the floor. Maybe we were getting to the point where we could feel each other nearby. In the background, on the jukebox system that played throughout the diner, Neil Diamond said we could make our own bright lights.

"You got the way to move me," Juliana said.

I wanted to reach for her but held myself back. Mr. Cool. "Just stopping for tea," I said, thinking that I needed a new speechwriter.

"You came to see me." She flitted around behind the counter, rounding up supplies for another foray to the booths. The other waitress served up my beverage.

Juliana loaded up a tray with beverages and paused to look me in the eyes and smile.

"I did," my rhetoric improving. "I did come to see you."

"I know," she said. *I felt deadly faint,* Ishmael said, *bowed and staggered beneath the piled centuries of human love since Paradise.* Then she was gone, into the flow of the diner.

I didn't want to stare after her, but pretending that iced tea is interesting is harder than it sounds. I compromised and spun my stool 62 degrees to the left so I could watch her without looking at her. I saw Martine look from me to Juliana, who was approaching his booth. He looked like he was putting two and two together.

As she delivered his order, I had an intuition that he was asking about me, though he never took his eyes off her. Juliana did not turn in my direction, but her shoulder was tilting my way.

She lingered there a minute and then moved off to the next table. I looked away, but not before crossing glances with Martine.

I swiveled back to the counter and meditated upon iced tea.

She was coming close and swept around to the working side of the counter. "You know that man?" She didn't look up at me.

"I've caddied for him a couple of times."

"He asked if me and you want to work at some party he's having."

This did not immediately make any sense to me. I pictured myself cutting his grass and Juliana carrying glasses of iced tea to his aunts and uncles. "Work at a party?"

Juliana seemed almost exasperated. "Wealthy people hire people to work at their parties. Parking cars. Serving appetizers, cleaning up the plates. And so fucking forth. He said he knows you."

"Ah, yes." The light coming on. "He's not a member, and he's probably too good a golfer to join our club." And, I thought, he sometimes shows up in my father's viewfinder.

"Who cares if he's any good at golf?" she said, turning to load her tray at the serving window into the kitchen.

But that's just it, I thought. "He's the best bag I've ever carried," I said to her back, with little hope that she was hearing me.

"What should I tell him?" She paused, holding the decision up between us for me to make. She wanted to do this. I was unsure, but curious.

I swiveled slowly to my left. He was reading a newspaper, probably indifferent to us. "Why not?" I said.

Then Juliana was gone on her next sortie and quickly the diner was filling up with real customers who were going to spend more than the price of an iced tea just to chat up a waitress. I drained my glass to the ice cubes and waited for her to come back.

"What did he say?"

"I haven't talked to him yet. Look, it's getting a little busy ... can I call you later?"

Dismissed, I perceived a meaning in her offer to call, not to get together. Those sweaty pants. Nodding, I scooted for the door and looked over his way. He remained immersed in the paper. I gave the Scout salute to no one in particular, pushed through the door to the landing area outside, through the second door and down the steps to ground level.

I walked past the last traffic light on the street that merged into the road that led home, and pivoted to face the oncoming traffic. It was a good, wide, graveled shoulder that I knew well—an easy place for the drivers to pull over. Sitting at the light, they had plenty of time to decide whether they wanted to give me a ride. Or not to.

The doubting hitchhiker, perhaps lacking confidence in his thumb-bait or skeptical of the generosity of strangers, hedges his bet by walking backward, thumbing all the while. The hitchhiker who has given up all hope turns and marches toward his destination, offering his left thumb in a backhand hitch. This is a self-defeating strategy: if they can't see your face, it is too easy to ignore you.

But the hitchhiker in a state of grace stands his ground, faces the traffic, smiles confidently into the windshields of the oncoming traffic, picks out his mark and gently jerks his thumb like a trout fisherman. He is confident and disinterested, accepting the fact that most drivers will not stop but religiously sure that one will.

Sometimes it's his father.

I didn't see him in the line of cars waiting at the traffic light. He found me first and steered onto the shoulder, leaving a clear route for the rest of the traffic to go past and within a few feet of where I was standing.

"Where are you going?" he asked.

"Home, I guess."

Speedy was in a good mood. He had been to see Dr. Matthews that day, and came home aloft on the notion that his brother was getting the best care available. "I think he's gonna get better; I think he already is getting better," he said, gripping the steering wheel enthusiastically.

We rolled back onto the thoroughfare, slipping in behind a black 1963 Ford Falcon. It was a modern, compact car in its day, sleek and flat. "Futura" was written across the back of the trunk, with an emblem above and a slash of red-bordered chrome beneath, speared in the middle by a circle. Wings on either side pointed out, rather than up, curling over the round red taillights. The bumper below curved sympathetically, framing the taillights like burning rocket exhausts.

It was no jet car. It looked a little like a layer cake.

The driver was smoking, and we motored past our turn to stay on his trail. He looked to be in his mid-20s, a plain khaki work shirt, a working-class hero. I could see a chunk of his face in his rearview mirror; he held the cigarette in his lips for what seemed like a long time and then took a long draw and threw the butt out the window with conviction.

As whalers hath before us, we lowered for him.

Eventually the Futura pulled into a roadside tavern, where the parking lot was about two-thirds full of cars left by men who deserved or needed a beer, or two, before facing the dinner table.

The driver was climbing out of his car as my father slowly rolled up beside him.

"Evening, friend," Speedy said. He paused.

"Do you remember throwing a cigarette out your window a little ways back down the road?" My father had an uncommonly polite and neighborly way of asking complete strangers if they might be assholes.

The Futura driver looked at us, trying to put it together.

"I dunno. I might have." More curiosity than antagonism in his voice at that point.

"Maybe you can help us figure out why people throw cigarettes into the road when there is always an ashtray."

The subject considered the question for a minute and then shrugged his shoulders. "I don't remember if I did or not. I did just have a smoke and if I threw it out the window, it was because I was done with it."

My father's hand reached to pick up the roll of masking tape on the bench between us. He ripped off a piece about a foot long and slapped it on the dashboard in front of him. He pulled the cap off the marker with his teeth and wrote in block letters I FLICK BUTTS on the tape.

"Thanks, that helps a lot," he said around the marker tip. "I don't want to bother you again, in case you throw another cigarette out your window."

"It's no trouble, man," the Futura driver said, and started to turn toward the tavern.

"Would you put this on your car, you know, to show you've already participated in the research?" Speedy offered the curling tape out the window.

The Futura driver took a less friendly look at the homemade bumper sticker and then at my father. "We're gonna have a problem if you put that fucking thing on my car," he said. He stated this in a matter-of-fact way, as though he were a grocery store clerk telling us the price of lettuce.

"That's why I always ask first," my father said, still holding the sign out the window. "You can pull it off any metal surface without any residue for ..." he looked at his watch. "At least 17 days."

Oddly, the Futura driver didn't take the two steps necessary to punch my father's nose. Instead, he reached to take the piece of tape from my father's hand and studied it for a minute before handing it back.

"I don't think so."

My father took back the sign. "Thanks for your time," he said. "Are you sure?" He made it sound like it was too good a deal to pass up. "You can put it anywhere on your car. It'll come off whenever you want and won't leave a mark."

Unexpectedly, the subject reached again for the tape, and my father put it in his hand.

"Thanks, friend," my father said. "You're really helping a lot."

The Futura driver looked quizzically at the homemade bumper sticker and a grin crept up at the corners of his mouth.

"What the fuck," he said, and turned back toward his car. We watched him slap it on the trunk flap and he looked our way, almost as though seeking approval, and then swiped his palms together three times, in the pioneer's gesture of job well done.

21. Sunday, July 14, 1968

1960 Volkswagen Beetle

Juliana was not working that day. This thought was on my mind as I stood hitchhiking to the country club early in the morning. I had a hankering to go with her into the woods, to get ourselves into the sunshine and the leafy shade on a trail to someplace.

But first I would go a-caddying. I would be useful and earn money and save it. Thrift, a Scout cornerstone, had a more robust sense for the Vikings before they turned the word over to the English. To them it meant grabbing hold of life and taking it for the full ride: the condition that happens when you have thrived.

A Volkswagen Beetle approached. There were few better chances for hitchhiking success than an approaching people's car. This feature is not mentioned in the owner's manual!

The bug crawled to a stop in front of me. The driver—a college-looking kid wall-papered with hippie accessories—timed his landing so that I had only to walk a step or two to the passenger door.

The 1960 bug has seats like dining room chairs bolted onto the cabin floor and the classic, unadorned VW dashboard stamped from sheet metal—a few white knobs, a dash of white trim across the middle, a solid white steering wheel (his interior was blue), the single speedometer behind the steering wheel and the AM radio. He had upgraded to an eight-track stereo attached beneath the dashboard.

It also reeked of smoke, although the windows were all wide open.

"Where you going, man?" I wasn't sure it mattered how I answered. He was singing some of the right words to a Dylan song.

"To the country club," I said. I pointed down the road in the direction he was already headed. So we rode nonverbally, him grooving to the music, me imagining what Juliana did for pajamas. I was getting the hang of this.

About halfway to town, he pulled a hand-rolled smoke out of his shirt pocket and lit it with the cigarette lighter that was alongside the little pull-out ashtray. He took a long drag and offered it to me. At that moment Dylan declared that he wasn't gonna work on Maggie's farm no more, that he had woke up in the morning praying for rain, and it occurred to me that I too had looked for rain that morning out my bedroom window.

I boy-scouted the joint when he handed it to me, holding it near my lips and taking a deep breath of mostly clean, god-fearing air from around the edges. I was happy to pass it back and forth with him, for I did not think it right to let him be alone with his cannabis at such an early hour and on such a beautiful morning.

After the last pass, the VW driver had smoked it down to about three-eighths of an inch, and after considering it for a moment, flicked it out the window.

"Hey. Do you want a bumper sticker for your car?" I asked. Of course, I didn't have a roll of tape or a marker with me.

"Sure, but what kinda bumper sticker is it? I'm not into politics, man."

"It just says I FLICK BUTTS. My dad makes them."

"Cool. I'll take one." I regretted not actually having anything with me.

"That's the problem. I don't have one with me."

"Sure, man, that's cool. Whenever."

He dropped me off near the country club. I thanked him for the lift and watched the people's wagon skitter off onto the road, its button-down rear end with two understated taillights and an agrarian chrome fence-bumper with the distinctive curved rear window and air vents to cool the engine in the back of the car.

Wingless, it was the anti-car. I had forgotten to ask why he flicked. Free the roaches, man.

Though I had only pretended to smoke, there were blue and yellow cartoon birds singing around my head and shoulders as I rambled to the pro shop.

I didn't have to wait long for a caddy job: half of a foursome of youngish members. I was working with another caddy and it turned into an unmemorable round except that we were held up at almost every stage of the game by the group in front of us, which included the banker Winthrop. They should have let us play through at the first par three, but they kept their heads down, ignoring us.

Winthrop and his group were making each other finish every putt according to protocol, and at one point they spent several minutes searching for an errant ball off the sixth fairway, a perfect opportunity to wave us through. By then, our golfers were grumbling about it a lot.

At the turn, our guys somehow got past Winthrop's group while the other caddy and I were sitting under the tree alongside the 10th fairway. I noticed Martine was teeing off on the first hole with the club pro and two big-shot members.

By the time the round was over, the morning had turned hot and sticky. We settled up with the golfers and hauled their clubs to the storage room behind the pro shop and cleaned the irons in a bucket of grassy water, wiping off the woods with towels that needed cleaning more than the golf clubs did.

When I went back outside, I watched Martine's group hit onto the ninth green. I hung around under the shade near the first tee and watched him lob a nine iron to within 10 feet of the pin.

He measured his putt and pushed it right of the hole. Then he looked up at me, 80 yards away, in a non-accidental way. He shrugged his shoulders in my direction and turned to mark his ball.

I went in the back door of the kitchen and said hello to my mother and when I came back outside, he was lingering nearby, studying his scorecard.

"How are you hittin' them today, Mr. Martine?"

"Not too bad. Paying my dues," he said with a smile. In the background, a Brueghel's landscape of curious cultivators farming the grounds with golf sticks.

Out of the blue, he said, "Do you know about Fosbury?"

The name was familiar.

"He's a high jumper who goes over the bar upside down, facing the sky." Martine threw his arms above his head and mimicked a man floating on his back through the air. "It's the damnedest thing, but he makes it work. He qualified for the Olympics at seven feet one inch. The next best jump was five feet, 10 inches."

Then I surprised us both. "Were you going over backward when you yanked that putt?" I asked, nodding toward the ninth green.

He looked me straight in the eye. "I thought I read something that wasn't there," he replied.

Neither of us said anything during a moment that seemed ripe for moving off on our separate courses.

"You and your waitress friend are going to help out at my party?"

"Yeah, well, what's that all about?"

He looked down at the scorecard in his hand. "Kids always need money. The guests are mostly business contacts. They feel important if there's somebody to park their cars."

"I guess we will," I said, and he nodded.

Then I left, hiking to a pay telephone booth at a gas station. I dialed up Juliana's house, navigated around her mother, and fell headlong into her voice. Sometimes I felt more connected to her talking on the phone than when we were wrestling in the front seat of her car. I said I thought it would be fun working at Martine's party.

But she wasn't interested in such far-off things. "I want to get away," she whispered. "Take me someplace."

"I'll see if I can borrow my dad's car," I said. "But first I gotta get home."

Sundays can be hard on hitchhikers. The family men, even if they might pick you up on their own, universally drive on by when they have their entourage with them. I quickly gave up the faithful approach and became a doubter, walking backward and then surrendered altogether, turned and jogged home the rest of the way.

After a shower, I sat with my father and two sandwiches at the picnic table in our back yard. I asked if I could borrow the car. But he was more interested in a news story about Che Guevera's diary, which the Cubans claimed to have.

"Is it a true copy?" my father asked rhetorically. "They say the original was a mess. Che's handwriting wasn't so good to begin with, and the manuscript was dirty and stained with sweat. But how did Castro get it?"

He looked at me as though I might have an opinion.

"There are at least two kinds of truth," Speedy said. "There is truth that is accurate, an objective reflection of reality. In the Cuban diary, Che includes dogs and chickens in the causality count of his enemies. That sounds true to me."

He took a bite from his sandwich and put it down on the plate. "And then there is truth in being faithful to your family or yourself. It strikes me, a thousand miles away and never having read the thing, that this Cuban diary might be true on that score too." He took another bite.

"But how do we know how many enemy chickens Che and his men actually killed?" I asked.

"That might be the less useful truth," Speedy said through his sandwich. "Maybe Che just set out to write a *hideous and intolerable allegory,* and used a diary because it was the only empty book he had handy," my father mused.

Juliana's family lived in a split-level in a subdivision parallel to ours. She met me at the front screen door in sandals, cut-off jeans, and a loose white top with a wide neck.

She reached for my hand and pulled me inside. It was quiet and pleasantly warm and it smelled different than our house, the way other people's homes do. There were windows open everywhere. She guided me to the kitchen, where a short, dark-haired woman was almost done cleaning the counter.

Juliana's mother seemed genuinely pleased to meet me; I had the impression that she knew more about me than I did about her.

We whiled away a few minutes and then I was being steered through the dining room and down the stairs and out onto the back patio, where a swarthy, pot-bellied man was watching the Phillies on a small black-and-white television set. He wore plaid, old-guy shorts and a sleeveless undershirt. He and his cigar were making proper use of a nearby ashtray.

We shook hands and he sized me up in one undisguised sweep.

"Is that a baseball game?" I asked. I had never seen anyone watching television out of doors.

He looked at me a second time and smiled. "I thought you were some kinda Boy Scout."

"Yes sir, I am. At least for now. Juliana wants me to change my ways and grow my hair."

Her father grunted, but re-focused on the tube. We lingered through one more unsuccessful Phillies at-bat, and then Juliana pulled me away authoritatively. It was liberating to get into the car together.

The great advantage of older cars with bench seats is that we could sit as contiguous beings, flesh-pressed to one another as we motored away to a creek to the east. In the spring, it roared for a few miles into the Delaware River, but in summer it became a sleepy, watery path from one pool to the next.

The creek was dammed at a state park, and just downriver it swept in a horseshoe around the base of a set of cliffs that rose 200 feet out of the woods. As Cub Scouts, we would camp in the state park but spend all of our time exploring the cliffs and the creek, where the only trails were the ones made by people going where they wanted to.

Through the state park and along the road that crossed the top of the dam we went, and up the steep old country road barely a lane-and-a-half wide on the other side. At the top of the hill there was a time-worn farm road to the right; cornfields on one side and woods on the other.

The DeSoto gently bounced over the ruts in the farm road and I eased her into a spot off to the side where it would not be in the way if a hay truck happened along. We left the car and found the path that led to the top of the cliffs and danced along its edge.

I held Juliana's hand in mine, and she said, quietly, "Oh," when we got to the topsail promontory, the perch that overlooked the sweeping curve of the creek far beneath our feet and the woods climbing uninterrupted to the opposite horizon.

We stood for a few minutes not saying anything in the bright sunshine and then tracked along the top edge of the cliffs until the path slid back into the trees and eventually began falling, steep and twisting, off the shoulder of the rocky facade. I should have cautioned Juliana to wear something sturdier than sandals. When I stopped at the top of a rock staircase to help her down, her face was tense and her grip anxious.

It took us several minutes to get down and I held her most of the way. She was strong enough, and not clumsy, but she was careful. I began to feel more stupid and irresponsible for leading her into this so unprepared. We had to stop several times and face the rock wall, climbing down ladder-style.

At the bottom of the cliff, the trail started to flatten out. We picked our way through the woods and the terrain relaxed and led to the edge of the creek. I could feel in her hand that she was unwinding and could see humor coming back in her face. The creek, where we found it, was in a pool; on the other side, the shady side, there was a long slab of granite that tilted from the woods into the water. We crossed at the riffle that separated our pool from its upstream parent and then walked along the rock slab. It was shady near the trees, but the sun warmed the gray and purple granite at the water's edge.

"Do you want to go in?" I asked.

"I don't have a bathing suit," she answered.

"We don't need them today. It's Bastille Day," I said, pulling the tee shirt over my head and unbuttoning my shorts. "*Allons, enfants de la patrie,*" I sang. "The day of glory has arrived."

And then I was standing naked beside her, more than a little surprised by my revolutionary spirit, feeling the July sunlight and the warm breath of the woods and the algae and the rocks holding the slow-creeping water in front of us. I didn't know whether she would follow, but I understood that having made the invitation I had to give her as much time as she needed to respond.

I am certain that I had a quite ridiculous look on my face while I waited for her to decide, hanging out there, as it were. She looked me over slyly, unable to suppress a smile. I committed to not looking away from her face.

"You are going to have to go in the water and look the other way," she said, fingering the top button on her blouse.

That was all the direction I needed. I turned and walked down the rock as it submerged into the still creek, gathering a veneer of moss as it went deeper, open fissures along the way, the occasional rogue out-cropping, and only the vaguest sense of a current sliding incrementally toward the next lock that marked the gravitational bottom of the pool, a languid, summery chunk of Pennsylvania hung up on its way through the woods. I found the edge of the rock shelf a little over waist deep and crouched down until my chin was in the water, then slowly pushed upstream for a few easy strokes in the shallow water, not wanting to put too much distance between us. Then I turned back.

She was already in the water, crouched down to her shoulders in the deepest part of the creek. I drifted toward her as though the current alone was pulling me. She had an expectant and confident look, watching me carefully as I stood, waist-deep, and walked across the slippery and sloping slab.

Standing in front of her, I offered my hands, palms up on either side of my hips, and she bit her lip as though she was jumping off a cliff and put her hands in mine and slowly stood up. We had groped plenty in the car over the past few weeks, but we had not stood before one another in the fading afternoon light with nothing between us but water-bugs bouncing off the surface of the creek. A ripple rolled out from us across the water, catching sunlight and refracting it into scores of dancing lights around her.

There was lust under the water, for sure, but from the waist up I was entranced by the way her neck gently curved onto her shoulders. I leaned forward and we kissed and slowly lowered ourselves into the creek and clutched one another under the water, the only lubricant we would ever need, finding ourselves, recognizing parts long forgotten in the other—hey, you've got one of those too—whose hand is that anyway?

And so it went on, magically, drifting in a current close to still, pushing us gently toward the inescapable downstream. The sun leaned lower, raking through the leaves and limbs of the forest, striped in shafts of light driving poetry across the surface of the earth.

Until we were not alone. I felt tension in her embrace and pulled back and saw the new look in her eyes and I turned to where she was looking.

Two Scout-aged boys stood slack-jawed beside the neat piles of our clothes, wondering how lucky they were.

"Fellas," I said. "You're gonna have to find your own swimming hole."

"This is where we always go," said the one who looked, marginally, less dumbstruck.

I could tell there was nothing to be gained by staying in the water and giving them uncontested control of dry land. I began to scale the rock slope, facing them directly, with the water quickly falling down to my thighs, knees, ankles. I watched their eyes and of course they couldn't look away and of course I was jutting forward like a 16-year-old should.

"Nothing personal, guys, but I'm really going to have to insist that you clear out." Still marching toward them, now out of the water.

One, then the other, bent and scooped up our clothes and turned to scamper away, and there was no point in talking anymore. The game was on as they dashed for the trail in the woods from whence they had come.

Prepared, I had kept my sneakers on when I went into the water. A naked guy in sneakers looks significantly goofier than one who is altogether clothing-free, but it was a practical choice (unseen hazards lurk in murky water) and prudent and probably faithful as well. As I chased after them, I ignored the clothes that fell from their ransacking and chose one of them as my target.

He had scooped up Juliana's clothes and was the first one into the woods. I had traction and righteous purpose on my side. I pushed past the one with my clothes, brushing him off the trail. My target was the quicker of the two, and I had to chase him longer. But I was settled into the race, content to measure his speed and track him down in time. Then, he stumbled and slammed howling into the ground, and I felt sorry for him. That must have hurt, I thought, and closed in before he could collect himself.

"Have you had enough now?" I asked. He didn't know what to say, as his friend came gasping along. Now in close quarters, we all three measured the situation. They seemed a little tough, but they were younger than me. More significantly, I was clearly lunatic enough to chase them naked through the woods, which can be a strategic advantage.

They abandoned their stolen goods and darted off, stopping a few yards away to yell profanities back at me. I waved to them cheerfully and gathered up the mix of her clothes and mine scattered around the trail.

When I got back to the pool, she was still in the water and looked to be shivering. I laid her clothes carefully on a sunny spot on the rock ledge.

"You can use my tee shirt to dry off," I said, putting it beside her pile and then turning to face the woods while I pulled my shorts on over my sneakers. I heard her come out of the water and I kept my back to her until she came around in front of me and handed me my tee shirt.

"Thanks," she said, but we did not look each other in the face.

"We can go back the way we came, but it's a kinda hard climb up the cliff," I said. "Or we can take the longer, easier, path to the road and then back over the dam to the car."

She shrugged wearily, ready to have this over with. I chose the longer, gentler path back to the car. So we set off on the trail where I had run down the delinquents.

It seemed a longer hike than it actually was. My brain was busy generating a lot of thoughts, but we didn't speak much. The trail through the woods was a one-lane affair; I paused often to make sure she was close behind, and most of the time she looked through me to the path ahead.

It was a welcome change to break out of the woods onto the road that led through the park and across the dam back to the east side of the creek. Now that we had more room, we walked side by side, and I was washed in relief when she tucked her arm around my elbow. We climbed up the hill on the other side of the bridge, and I didn't let go of her until we got back to the car. I opened the driver's side door and held it open for her and she turned and put her hand behind my waist and pulled us together, still not saying anything as she held us there for a minute.

I did one genius thing on the drive home. Dusk was upon us, and I was hungry. Instead of heading directly back home, I drove down into the village where our infamous creek joined the Delaware River, and followed the river road to a hamburger and dairy stand. We each had a sandwich and shared a milkshake and fries, and gradually it began to seem funny, and we laughed over the checkerboard vinyl tablecloth.

A little farther down the road, from the car I saw the tourist barge on the canal, reaching its upstream limit and pausing while the driver brought the mules around and walked them downriver until the slack came out of the line and the barge inched back to port.

She buried her head in my shoulder on the open road, windows down, rolling on the power of an American-made V-8 engine through the firefly Pennsylvania night. Life can be pretty good, I thought, if you're not afraid to show your penis every now and then.

22. Wednesday, July 17, 1968

1967 Volvo 122S

After work, I hoofed into town to see if I could catch a ride home with my father. But he wasn't in the office; they said he had gone to interview a man who had miraculously survived an automobile crash in which the car had flipped over, pinning him inside. Speedy would go home straight from the interview.

Brady waved me into his office and asked me how my article about the canal was coming along. I had been too busy skinny-dipping and laboring for the country club set to follow up with the coconut salesman of New Hope.

"Um .... I haven't done anything yet on that."

My father's editor stared at a pile of papers in front of him. "The story isn't going to write itself." He was annoyed; his bald head was turning crimson. "Are you gonna do this or not?"

Not for the merit badge. But there were echoes in those mules and the creaking barge and the suburban cannibal peddling coconut-head icons. If that was all that remained from decades of floating coal fresh-dug out of the mountains down to the shivering, dark city, then maybe it ought to be told.

"I think there is a story in the canal," I heard myself saying. "Something about lifting that fuel up and floating it on the water."

I'm not sure either of us knew what I was trying to say. But Brady wasn't going to be ungracious about it.

"Just don't take all damn summer getting it done. Listen for a while. Then write. This isn't the *Atlantic Monthly*. We got used cars and appliances to sell." He picked up some copy in front of him and a blue pencil and leaned into his carving. "Pulitzer's never been around here," he said, nodding toward the newsroom, "I can fix almost anything once it gets to me."

I walked past her diner on the way to my hitchhiking spot and we waved through the large plate-glass window.

I caught a ride soon after hoisting my thumb homeward, from a kid in the class ahead of me. We knew each other a little, but the radio was turned up and by mutual agreement we had little to say.

A cream-colored 1967 Volvo 122S zipped past us, soft and pillow-like, with rounded edges. The lines recalled the softer shapes of 1950s American cars, scaled down to a European fit. In Sweden, the car was called the Amazon when it was rolled out with a sinewy feminine form. In America, it was the first car sold with front safety belts. Just before the 1967 model year, Volvo cut back the chrome to only the bumper and front grille. In another cost-cutting move, the car had no passenger-side sun visor. Let their eyes fry!

What made the car at hand especially noteworthy was that on the bumper, right below the rear-mounted gas cap, was an I FLICK BUTTS bumper sticker. I leaned forward in my seat and asked the driver to come up a little closer.

"What the hell's that?" he said.

"It says 'I flick butts,'" I told him. "I've seen one before."

Amazingly, it seemed, the young woman driving the Volvo was smoking a cigarette and dusting ashes out the window.

There was a traffic light a couple hundred yards ahead, the only one we would come to until he dropped me off at my road. I could see that we might catch red. The plan came to me; I didn't go looking for it. "If she stops at this light, I'm gonna get out and ask her about that bumper sticker," I announced.

"What?" It was a lot for him to process. There was, all around us from the radio, Trogg love, and the feeling growing.

"Just make sure you come to a stop. If I'm not back, go ahead and leave without me."

I stared at the light as we zoomed closer and when the Volvo was about 50 yards from the intersection, the green turned to yellow. She may have been a carefree, cigarette-smoking young Amazon, but she was, after all, driving a Volvo and she yielded to caution. Blessed are the risk averse, for they shall pay lower insurance premiums in heaven.

The red brake lights flared at the ends of the Volvo's tail feathers and she stopped a little suddenly. We were still rolling when I bolted from the car and ran to the passenger-side door of the Volvo.

I leaned my forearms on the window hole in the door. The Troggs were in her car too. She was pretty, a few years into her 20s, having a nice late afternoon, enjoying her smoke, not particularly fazed to have me looking in her window like one of the principal characters in *The Wizard of Oz*, who show up year after year at the end of the movie to greet Dorothy as she awakens.

"Hello," I said.

She was looking at me, smiling faintly and unalarmed. "Hi," she answered.

"Can you tell me where you got your bumper sticker?"

She smiled wider and blew a plume of smoke out the side of her mouth, away from my direction, tapping the cigarette out the window. "Some guy gave it to me for throwing my cigarette into the street." Like it was a prize. There was a pullout ashtray in the middle of the dashboard, but it was closed shut.

"Did he ask you why you didn't use the ashtray?"

She did a double-take, looking at me again, trying to figure out how we knew each other. I smiled at her, a bookmark my father had laid down in the currents of smoking automobilists. Looking at him through a stranger's reflection, I loved him as much as I ever had.

"Yes, that's exactly what he asked me."

"I thought so. What did you tell him?"

"I told him the truth. There is an ashtray in this car, but there's no cigarette lighter. So I don't use the ashtray. I always throw my butts out the window." To make sure I understood, she then threw her cigarette out the window.

"And then he gave you the bumper sticker."

"Exactly." Without looking, I could tell the light was going green and I backed away from the window in the passenger-side door. She turned away from me then, refocused on the traffic and the rest of the driving-and-smoking life ahead of her. The Volvo pulled out of the intersection, spinning down the road all Nordic cool, unapologetic for being un-American.

My driver paddled forward with the current, slowing for me to jump back in. I think he was so curious about my daring approach toward an unknown woman on the road that it completely trumped my violation of the universal code of hitchhiking: Never abandon a ride unless the benefactor-driver is too weird to abide.

"What was that, man?"

"I had to ask her about the bumper sticker. You know, where she got it." I slid a little lower in the seat, searching for a slouch.

"So, where did she get it?"

"Some guy gave it to her." He was pushing ahead quickly to catch up with the Volvo, as though we now had some connection to it.

"What did she look like?"

I thought she was entitled to scientific anonymity since she had twice fallen into our sample of cigarette litterers. "She's married," I said, though in fact she did not wear a ring.

We hung on her rear bumper all the same, although I could not decipher what he hoped to gain from it. But I was soon back in hitchhiker mode, neither roiling the waters nor stirring the pot, sinking into the free seat I had. As we came to the place where he would let me off, I reminded him. Outside, as I turned back to thank him for the ride, I thought he looked both grateful that the Volvo was slipping away in the traffic stream and reluctant to see the fantasy evaporate.

I walked the rest of the way home feeling affection for Juliana, for an alternative to wistful, speculative, and impossible chases after unknown women driving in cars.

Both Yardley family cars were in the driveway, a comforting sign. I walked toward the front door, but as I drew close something felt out of place, and I held back before I went in.

I could hear my mother and father talking inside, louder than usual. Suddenly they were other people, tense strangers who had emerged from parts of them I didn't know.

"You're making more of this than there is," my father said. It seemed he was trying to calm her down.

"Then why did you do it?" she answered, colder than I think I had ever heard her sound. "And why did you make a point of telling me?"

"Because being truthful with you is what I do," he said.

"That's a cop-out," my mother responded, almost bitterly.

There was silence in the house; they were in the kitchen, the room of passion. I was frozen momentarily, afraid to hear what came next, certain that I had no choice.

Then, without notice, the silence had a different quality, written on the wind, and I pulled open the front door.

They were standing close to each other and her face was buried in his shoulder, his arms pulling her tight to him. "It's everywhere I go," I thought to myself.

"The Czechs planted hedges near the graves of their first president and his son, who everybody thinks was killed by the hard-line Communists," my father said, as though he were singing a poem. "The bushes spelled out the words, 'Truth Prevails,' because the hard-liners had tried to scrub history from their memories."

My mother pulled her face away from him, and I sensed that they knew I was inside the house. "Melville said that God spoke to the whale and told him to bring you to the warm and pleasant sun and all the delights of air and earth," she said, "and spit you up on the dry land." Her voice was warm.

"*My ears were like sea shells, but instead of murmuring the secrets of the ocean, I was doing the almighty's bidding, preaching Truth to the face of Falsehood*," my father said, practically laughing.

"Honesty is a moral cop-out," my mother said, pinching his ribs with both hands. "Nobody wants you to tell them everything."

"Truth prevails, honey. It's all gotta get out there." He winced from her pinching but opened his arms to the universe.

Then we all three became aware that the spaghetti sauce was plenty ripe, and whatever they had been arguing about was cast overboard.

23. FRIDAY, JULY 19, 1968

1967 JAGUAR E-TYPE

Juliana was talking to my father in the living room when I came out of the shower that evening, a towel wrapped around my waist, digging a fingernail into a sudsy earhole.

"Is this what I wear to park cars?" I asked.

Juliana looked at her watch. The universal language of telling someone there's no time for such nonsense.

Soon enough, I was in a white shirt and black pants, sitting beside her on our way to a rich guy's party. I was puzzling out whether this was a date or not when she asked me how my parents met.

"In France, after the war. My mother jokes that she at first mistook my father for a handsome British officer she had met a few days before, but by the time she realized her mistake he already had his foot in the door." Mailboxes flew past on a country road.

"My father always says at this point in the story that it is a far, far better thing to have been mistaken for a handsome British officer than to have never been one at all."

She laughed happily and then said she couldn't figure out why her parents were together.

There was an awkward quiet. "In the army, my father also got hooked on *Moby Dick*, and I'm afraid he passed the addiction on to me." Then I told her about Dick Mobius, and she took her eyes off the road when I said I had read the book seven times already.

"The one about the nutty captain and the fucking whale?"

"Yup." This is why we don't often reveal ourselves.

"Are you trying to memorize it?"

"Just parts. The story is that Dick Mobius had the whole thing down. The rest of us just collect pieces."

She shook her head.

The directions to Martine's house were typed on white stationery that had his home address printed at the top. Her Fairlane skittered across a part of the county that I didn't know very well, where Paleozoic rocks have coexisted with modernization, past gentlemen's farms and old family homes on roads with little commercial traffic and no stoplights. We were heading east toward the Delaware River, but not by the main road, and were soon beyond the frontier of our school's territory and into tonier, more genteel country.

And so we turned onto the River Road and began looking carefully for a secluded drive that led to Martine's house.

After gliding up a winding hundred yards through some trees, we came to his house, an elegant stone manor nestled on a slope. A guy in black trousers and a white shirt directed us onto a close-mown field. Juliana took off her glasses and got out of the car while it was still running and headed for the house as assuredly as though she had done this sort of thing before.

I slid behind the wheel and pulled the door shut. Across the field there were already a handful of cars parked side-by-side up against a rail fence. The parking attendant waved at me and pointed yonder to where Juliana's car was to go. The field was lumpy, not regularly used for parking. The Fairlane sighed and moaned to the far corner.

I walked determinedly back to the gathering of valets. There were four of us, including one who was in charge. I assumed that I was the only one who didn't know what he was doing.

It was still early, party-wise. When cars came in, I was told, I would give a numbered ticket to the driver and put a matching ticket under the windshield wiper. If the traffic slowed down, some of the valets would go into the house to help with the party.

Our leader made a point of telling us that all tips go into the jar, and everyone would get an equal share. No one bothered to introduce themselves.

There are scoutmasters everywhere. "The last thing we need is valets getting fucked up," the valet-boss said. "This party is for the guests. The money is good and there will be leftovers ... when it's over."

A dark blue Buick LeSabre rolled up the driveway and stopped in front of us. Four starlets in party regalia, each more glamorous than the one before, got out. They were oblivious of us, sharing a private joke.

One of the valets clipped a numbered ticket under the windshield and handed the other to the driver. She looked at it, shrugged her shoulders and let it float from her hand to the ground. She turned and skipped after the others, who were teetering along on heels down the slate walkway to the main entrance to the house.

The valet was unflustered. He retrieved the slip from the ground and took it with him into the car, pulled the door shut and steered off into the field.

At first, the cars arrived intermittently, only one or two at a time to be parked, and then things picked up and suddenly we had a backup of cars. I hustled back from parking one car and the head valet handed me a pair of tickets and pointed to a red sports car that had just stopped.

It was a 1967 Jaguar E-Type convertible, a long, eccentric shape with alien headlamps notched like cod's eyeballs set in a cone of glass that somehow fit into the low-slung profile. There was an elevation along the middle of the hood, but the car was not about edges; it smoothed into its facets, a haunch over the rear wheels, an open, oval mouth like an inflatable sex doll low on the front. The roof was down and the cabin was wide open to the summer air.

The Jag glowed in the evening light. Somehow I got to the door handle before the driver did, and opened it slowly as he turned to me with an amused look. He was a confident, contented man somewhere in that vast expanse of his third or fourth decade on the planet, with slightly roguish long hair and a tennis court tan. He was smoking a cigarette.

"Help the lady first," he murmured, as though we were, in our separate stations, working toward a common purpose, and I realized that I had failed to survey the tee shots properly. He took a last drag on his cigarette and dropped it on the ground between us and mashed it out with a loafered right foot, lingering there and giving me a chance to get where I was supposed to be.

I handed him a numbered slip and looped around the back of the car. His passenger was studying the visor mirror, applying a finish coat to her face, and I wondered if this delay was just for my benefit. I opened the door for her and she swung slender legs onto the asphalt. I must have seen the next part in a movie: I offered my left hand while I held the door open with my right and she rewarded me with a beguiling smile that made me think a fellow could get used to this line of work. She took my hand, gently, and rose from the car, sweeping past me in a fragrant cloud.

I wished Juliana was at hand as it came to me. *Who would think that such fine ladies and gentlemen should regale themselves with an essence found in the inglorious bowels of a sick whale!*

I closed the door slowly; it seemed weighted to find its own way solidly home. I followed her, mesmerized by the swaying flowered skirt that swished from her hips and looked up in time to see the driver's eyes, smiling, admiringly, into hers.

I clipped the second numbered paper under the windshield wiper and then settled into the driver's seat. In the middle of the leathered dashboard was a little drawer that served as an ashtray. It was closed.

I pulled the door shut and closed my eyes, sensing the evening ambergris. I had never before sat in a handmade car; this was the way automobiles and carriages were built before a lightning bolt struck Henry Ford and he created a market by giving people jobs that allowed them to buy the products they pushed through the assembly line.

I found the handbrake and slid the gearshift into first. Even at a snail's pace, there was a low, throaty purr all through the car as we pawed across the parking field and headed for the next open space. Once in its berth, I shut off the engine and listened to the Jaguar settle down to sleep. Behind me, the party sounds were picking up in the house, but in front of me the evening was filling the woods from the bottom up. I wondered if I should put the convertible top up, but after searching for a few minutes I accepted that I had no clue how to do that.

There would be more cars. I stayed outside with the valet scoutmaster when the two other guys went inside, and the incoming traffic never really stopped all night long. At one point, there were people starting to leave while others were still arriving.

Somewhere along the dial when I wasn't looking it became late, later than I was used to staying up, and I had been up since six that morning and pushing a lawnmower at seven. But it was pleasant sitting on a wooden fence stile with the valet boss. We were on slightly higher ground and looking down from a moony field at the house seeping light and laughter and humanity, listening as the live band played a jazzy kind of rock and roll, shepherds of sorts, keeping watch over our flock.

I was content with what I was doing, smoothing the comings and the goings, trotting off to the lines of cars when one had to be retrieved, bringing each one to life, wheeling it out of its space and cruising as dainty as a hippopotamus across the field to the departing guests.

During a quiet moment, I headed up to where Juliana's car was parked. I peed through the rails in the fence and then slipped into her car and began rummaging around in the glove box, where I eventually found a packet of tissue papers and a tube of lipstick. I wrote I FLICK BUTTS in coral red.

I walked over to the Jaguar and thought of leaving the ridiculous bumper sticker inside, but then I chickened out—or got smarter—and crumpled it into my pants pocket.

I did not have a watch, but it was well into the morning. The band had packed up and gone; the party was being fueled by spinning vinyl. The energy in the house was winding down. The two other valets were ready to leave and the boss doled out their shares of the tips. I was no expert, but I thought they were drunk. The scoutmaster valet asked if I wanted to go home, but I told him I was having fun and, besides, my friend was still working in the house.

It was cooling and there were sleepy, empty times between guests reuniting with their cars. Two girls in white shirts and black skirts stumbled out of the kitchen door and wobbled to their car at the far end of the parking field. I heard an owl in the woods. We moved the remaining assortment of guest cars still scattered around the field closer to the driveway.

Two men and a woman came around the corner of the house, linked at their shoulders. As they crossed under the light at the end of the walk, I could see that it was Martine with the Jaguar couple. They were leaning on one another, but walking steadily.

I waited for the Jaguar man to hand me his ticket even though I knew which car was his.

"This is my friend from the Doylestown club," Martine said, pointing to me with an open palm.

"A fine fellow," the Jag driver said. "He had the decency to admire Marcia's ass when we dropped off the car." The two men laughed, not coarsely, and Marcia looked me straight in the eye with a bemused smile.

"At your service," I said, and bowed slightly.

They laughed again, and Martine put his hand on my shoulder. I was leaning to go fetch the car, but he held me back.

"You're going to miss your tip if you go now," he said. "Roger is going to give us a stock to buy."

The Jag driver was looking me over, ciphering something in his mind. "You can't ever say where you heard this, or tell anybody else." Then he stopped. Martine was looking at him, but he was looking at me.

"Scout's honor," I said, holding up the three-fingered salute.

"Integrated Electronics incorporated yesterday in California. The guys behind it are from the Traitors. They'll go public in a couple years and when they do, you should buy at any price."

None of this meant anything at all to me.

Martine took a twenty-dollar bill out of his pocket and pressed it into my hand. "I'll take care of it," he said.

I was dumbstruck. It was too much, as though he was paying for something I didn't even know I had done. I put it in the tip jar on the way to get the Jaguar.

There was a starter button on the dashboard that had to be worked with the key. There was a not unpleasant dampness in the cabin from being open to the sky all night. I flicked on the lights and eased toward the driveway.

Juliana had joined Martine and the Jag driver and his date. Draped over her shoulders was a jacket that was too big for her.

"Sorry, I didn't know how to put the roof up," I said, pulling on the parking brake. I bounded around to the passenger side, but Marcia had already let herself in. Her man pulled the hood up over the car and they were soon rolling down the driveway toward the river road.

Martine said it was time for Juliana and me to go home. The valet scoutmaster and I split the accumulated tips, and I put my arm around Juliana's waist and walked her to the passenger door of the Fairlane. When I got behind the wheel, she curled next to me and fell asleep.

Juliana slept the whole way home to her house, and I think she was probably sleeping still as I helped her into the house. I got her to the nearest sofa and took off her shoes.

I was wide awake as I drove her car home to my house.

1962 CHRYSLER 300

The Boy Scouts prepared me to stand vigil through the night and park cars until dawn, among other things. As Robert Baden-Powell said, being prepared means being prepared for anything. Some say scouting is trivial, a thing invented to keep boys from masturbating. But the Boy Scout manual at one time was the fourth most widely published book in English. Scouts are everywhere, a trained insurgency standing next to you at the checkout line and pausing to let you cross the street, waiting for the call to duty, even the retired ones, like me.

Don't say you weren't warned, motherfucker.

But even Scouts sometimes lose their bearings, and I was lost that Saturday, waking up around seven, barely having gotten to sleep, stumbling for the power to think on my way to the kitchen. Habit pushed me to make my usual pre-caddy breakfast before I realized there was no way I was going to work. I detoured face first into the living room sofa and began plowing dreams. Intermittently, a parent would pass by, remarking on the condition I was in.

Around noon, I struggled off the sofa and went out to the vegetable garden to pull weeds, aiming for each one very deliberately, my fingers digging for the roots. My father and I barbecued hamburgers for dinner.

Speedy mentioned that he had seen our neighbor throw a cigarette from his car window and that he was intending to bumper-sticker him that night. This was the same neighbor who let us use his swimming pool whenever we wanted.

"Shouldn't we ask him first, Dad?"

"Ah, he'll know it's us."

Speedy and I sat at the back of the house and watched the sky turn indigo when he started talking about his visit with Uncle James that afternoon. "He was wearing that beat-up old robe he got in Korea while he was with the Red Cross. He looked happy, and almost like he knew where was, and more like himself than at any time since the accident."

My father paused to think. "On the way out, I checked in at the nurse's station and they said he was scheduled to move to a new room in the next couple days, apparently because Doc Matthews thinks it would help."

"Sounds like he's getting better," I said.

"I hope so," he said, and we watched the sky turn a little darker.

Then he stood up with his roll of masking tape and black marker and said it was time. We slipped into the woods from a trailhead at the back of our lot. We could have just walked across the lawn; there was only one property between our house and the cigarette-throwing, pool-sharing neighbor. We were being surreptitious for its own sake.

I followed my father single-file along the narrow path in the woods that connected the back yards of all the houses on our street, whether they knew it or not. He seemed to glide through the underbrush with barely a rustle, as though his spirit had left his noisy, bulky body behind.

It was dark in the woods, closer to the beginning of things, but soon enough we were turning toward the light on the back porch of the neighbor's split level. As we approached the house, Speedy turned around and held his forefinger to his lips. It was sometimes hard to tell which of us was the bigger kid.

Then he crouched low and scurried out of the shadows and along the side of the fence around their pool and across their lawn toward a great oak tree off to the side of their house. He paused—I couldn't make him out very clearly in his hiding spot—and then bolted a few yards farther to hide behind a massive snowball bush.

I followed his steps to the oak and waited there for his next move. Just beyond the snowball bush was our neighbor's red 1962 Chrysler 300 glowing under the light over the garage door. I bent low and stole up behind him, leaning on the small of his back.

Window air-conditioning units churned relentlessly, the only noise coming from the house. We would have no warning if someone came out.

He pointed me to a holly tree at the entrance to their driveway. "You can see the front door and the garage door from there," he whispered. I slinked passed the Chrysler to my lookout near the curb.

Evolution had winnowed away the fins on the 1962 Chrysler 300, but it still had the long, low-slung body and exaggerated rear end of its ancestors. There was a run of chrome that started under the rear window and bracketed what was left of the caudal fin and then returned toward the front of the car over the wheel. There was a tricolor badge where the dorsal fin had been. And a small fortune in chrome slathered all over.

Speedy crawled on all fours to the back of the car. He pulled a length of tape from the roll and pressed it to the fat chrome bumper and then inscribed it: I FLICK BUTTS.

He scampered to join me behind the holly tree. For a moment, we both tried to squeeze into its shadow, which was barely adequate to hide one person.

I thought we were going to reverse the whole procedure and melt back into the woods like good guerrillas, but my father simply stepped into the street and stared up at the stars.

It occurred to me that a better hiding place than the holly tree would have been in plain sight, at the end of our neighbor's driveway, listening for owls.

As we walked home, I was craning my neck and trying to put together the rest of Ursa Major from the Big Dipper, a puzzle I never really sorted out. People have been seeing a bear up there for over 10,000 years, I thought to myself, but I'm darned if I can see it. And in another 50,000 years, they say, the Big Dipper won't be there at all. You can doubt planet change all you want, but the universe is moving on no matter what you believe.

25. SUNDAY, JULY 21, 1968

1966 FORD GALAXIE 500

Juliana and I had a plan to go out Sunday afternoon, but I decided I would first try to pick up a round in the morning. I was a little later than usual and I missed the first wave, but soon enough the caddy master said there was a guest asking for me, and I knew he meant Martine.

Martine was going out with three members who were not, as far as I knew, anyone special in the club. I was carrying Martine and John Peleg, some kind of lawyer who usually rode a cart. The other two were dedicated cart-pullers.

He was chipper and funny and engaging. The members relished being out with this golfer from another planet who had become a sensation at the club, like a comet that orbits once a generation. After not too many holes they were laughing at his jokes and smiling and ribbing each other and they were really playing. Believe it or not, a lot of folks are out there going through the motions because that's what they do on Sunday mornings.

But it seemed there was something more going on, and then I overheard Peleg say something about "zoning matters" in a conversation with Martine. I wondered if they were talking about zoning along the canal.

"I'm very interested in that," I heard Martine say, but then my caddying duties took me out of earshot.

Later, we were working down the 18th freeway. Martine had driven his tee shot over the defenseless dogleg, shortening an already suspect par five into a feasible par four. The cart pullers were losing steam, struggling as the heat wore them down, and Peleg was still away after two swings that were, for him, decent. He really wanted to go for the green, which lay behind a water hazard. As I grounded his bag near his ball, he kept looking at Martine's tee shot, still a few dozen yards ahead. His hand crawled from the eight iron, his layup club, to the four, and I wanted to tell him not to get in over his head.

He went with the four, which should have been enough, but his swing was tense and hurried and he hit it so badly that it whimpered to rest short of the water, the outcome the same as if he had laid up, but with a dismal score for artistic merit.

We walked ahead to Martine's lie and waited there as he idly skimmed the top of the grass with the blade of his eight iron while the cart-pullers hacked their way along. The last to hit sent a low line drive whizzing near us, far off line, out of control. For a moment I saw Martine roll his eyes, a grimace bolted across his face but streaked away into the galaxy without leaving any tracks. He was too cool to show anyone up.

"Are you clubbing these guys or are they making this up on their own?" he said so only I could hear, looking down to address the ball at his feet.

Then I broke another rule. In the middle of his takeaway, I said, "Did you ask to play with them, or did they ask for you?"

It didn't affect his stroke even a little; a high, soft draw that settled comfortably into the middle of the green.

"This is a business outing, getting to know the members." He handed me the eight iron in exchange for his putter. "Lawyers aren't interesting, but they have their parts to play."

We had to stop for one of the cart-pullers, who smashed a middle iron past the green, and then the other one, who sent his ball into the pond. Peleg chipped safely over the water and as I traded clubs with him he asked me to help the cart-puller fetch his ball from the pond.

All three of the members were ball-retriever golfers—they carried telescoping aluminum harpoons with wire baskets on the end—acknowledging that they were going to need them often enough. Not all golfers are that honest.

I fished three balls out of the pond, and it didn't really matter whether any of them belonged to the cart-puller. The foursome managed to finish their putting without my service on the pin, and I gave the pond balls to the cart-puller who took them, I thought, a little too eagerly. Then the four of them were shaking hands and climbing the hill to the pro shop.

I took my two bags into the storage room and cleaned them and brought Martine's back outside. He was standing by himself, watching someone out on the course.

He gave me a $20, which was twice the going rate, for both the bags. I figured he must have offered to pay for the caddy. The three members were gone.

"That was a weird foursome," I said.

Martine bent down to poke around in a compartment in his golf bag. "I want to settle up with you and Juliana for the party." He was holding out two envelopes for me.

"We made a lot of tips, you know." I watched my hands taking the envelopes from him. One had my name on it, the other had Juliana's. The contents felt like cash.

"You're going to go to college or buy a car or get pregnant or something," he said. "You can't be paid too much for your work."

"That wasn't exactly work."

"Well, no cars or guests were lost. That's what you were paid for." He was smiling, in no particular hurry to go anywhere.

Then a strange thought came rushing through the filter. "If I bet this on you in a golf match," I said, holding my envelope up in front of him, "would you play to win?"

A smile took the corner of his lip. "An investor." His eye twinkled. "A man of my calling."

I had a savings account in a local bank that was working up the courage to install a drive-up teller window. I probably lost more change in the dryer than I earned in monthly interest. "You mean Integrated Electronics?" I remembered the name, had no idea what it was about.

Martine chuckled. "That's not in play yet, but there's a way we can build up your wages and have a few laughs," he said, nodding to the envelope. "And you won't have to bet on my putting to improve."

He pulled a sawed-off golf course pencil from his back pocket and wrote something on the envelope with my name on it. "Give me a call Friday around six if you're interested," he said.

It was a telephone number. "Interested in what?"

"Investing at the track," he said. He smiled and lifted the bag onto his shoulder and started toward the parking lot.

I went home thinking what a strange breed adults are. I showered and called Juliana and she said she would be over soon, but I was a little surprised when the 1956 Dodge Regent full of longhairs rolled into the driveway.

Again, I wedged myself behind the driver, thigh-to-thigh with Juliana. By that time, we had a mutual occupancy treaty when it came to the spaces between us.

I didn't smoke the joint when it came my way, but was tugged along, a hook in my lip, feet dragging in the sober world with a passport stamped to get where my Dodge-mates were at.

Man.

The eight-track stereo buzzed of electric stringed insects and a gypsy. He was on the road again, as the miles slipped along in a haunting, magical cadence, a harmonica winging across an empty landscape.

We cruised along to New Hope, our sunny, antique-bohemian Mecca by the river, where even Manhattoes sometimes stooped to visit. People were licking ice cream cones and strolling the crowded sidewalks, looking in shop windows. The water in the canal was antique too, thick and sleepy. Eventually we found a parking place and scrounged in our pockets for change to feed the parking meter, never coming close to a jackpot.

We marched on the sidewalk, my arm on Juliana's swaying hips.

Like the rest of the marauding tourists, we got ice cream. We went into curio shops and stared at hash pipes and tee shirts, alternately putting them down and extolling them as state-of-the-commerce.

I found myself in a hippie haberdashery with Juliana. A shopping demon I did not see coming had taken possession of her. She was looking at a tabletop of miniskirts, holding them up against her waist.

Eventually Juliana found one that worked for her and moved her attention on to me. Apparently, I had to have a pair of bell-bottom pants. I didn't have anything closer to a hippie uniform than dungarees and tee shirts. It would take years and years before faded Boy Scout uniforms were cool, and that would last only briefly.

"You've got money from the party," she said, sweeping away any argument I might have against buying a pair of pants I didn't have any desire to own.

They seek him here, Ray Davies sang, and they seek him there. We looked at a lot of pants: stripes and jeans and polka dots and paisley. Paisley! When I pictured myself in these fantastic things, I thought I was looking at an advertisement. Eventually, I tried some of them on in a dusty changing room and paraded about for Juliana's inspection with no shoes on. None of it seemed like me, a scout who was too old to be one, who practiced Thrift because that's what we sons of failed Quakers do.

Eventually I chose a pair of grotty blue- and white-striped bell bottom pants that clung weirdly around my hips and set sail at my calves and unfurled themselves onto the floor. For a moment they felt like something I wanted or even needed—a token to get me through some cultural turnstile. It almost seemed like a good idea as I carried them to the cashier, though the choices by then had all run together in my mind. I don't know whether I chose the pants I chose or they had chosen me.

They seek me here; I seek them there.

The cashier was snapping gum and never looked up at me. Somewhere in the universe, a style had been created, or evolved, and it had led to the manufacture of this pair of pants put on sale in this store and I had walked in with the right amount of money and the right size hips and an appropriate number of legs of the correct length.

I dug out a clammy wad of folding money—held together by a tie clip from my mother's father—and separated the necessary paper and handed it to the cashier, who was staring at my homespun system for storing money. I ought to get a new wallet, I thought. The pants went into a bag, were pushed at me across the battlefront of commerce and we were heading out of the store. Enriched by a new pair of fancy pants, I felt dedicatedly happy for a moment, high on the acquisition of merchandise.

We stepped out of the store blinking in the sunshine. The afternoon began to disintegrate around us, yielding to evening. Suddenly I was dissatisfied, regretful, and a little grumpy. The bag of pants was weighing me down, damping the light.

And then there was Quentin with his coconuts, recognizing me first. "What?" he asked, and baked into the inflection was the question: If you have money to spend in there, why haven't you bought from me an icon? We came nose to nose in an eddy of tourists staring at his inventory.

"Buddy," I said, more happily.

He grabbed the parcel from my hands and pulled its contents out for his inspection. *"When a country dandy joins the great whaling fishery, you should see the comical things he does upon reaching the seaport,"* Quentin bellowed. *"He orders bell bottoms to his waistcoats, straps to his canvas trouser."*

Quentin looked very pleased with himself. Of course, I thought, he's Dick Mobius to the core.

"Shipmate, you've saved me a mighty burden," I said.

There was a public trash bin nearby on the curb, where I deposited the bag and the new pants. When I turned his way, Quentin had been drawn away on the current of tourists, his full sail of coconuts running before the wind on a bearing away from mine. Lightened again, I turned to track down my merry contingent.

I looked into a passing automobile. Someone scrubbed the fire from a cigarette in the small collapsing ashtray mounted in the back of the front seat. One less cigarette butt for the road, I thought, and that's how it ought to be.

It took nearly a block of weaving through fun-seekers before Juliana noticed that I wasn't carrying the bag of pants anymore. She asked me what had happened, and I told her that I had decided to return them.

At that moment we were strangers. She likely calculated that I could not have actually returned them to the store, but she said nothing and merely turned away. It didn't matter what had become of them; I had rejected them.

I held back, watching her melt into the crowd. On the periphery, a woman's hand languidly reached out from the starboard side of a 1966 Ford Galaxie 500. There was a smoking cigarette in her fingers; she tapped the ashes deliberately into the street. And then she dropped the cigarette into the gutter.

The Galaxie was a modern box, all crisp and hard angles. A starry formation in the middle of the taillights harkened to a constellation of astronomical magic where navigators dreamed. I set down the reason for the cigarette littering as ennui.

The car had New York tags.

1965 BUICK RIVIERA

It had become sublimely hot in summer's foundry. I woke up at the edge of dawn, crooked on a lawn chair that folded down nearly, but not exactly, flat, out on the back patio, where it was cooler than in my room. On the other side of the house, the giant red sun pushed its way up from the horizon, sullen, poised to squash the sliver of coolness stored up through the dark hours. Before I was done with breakfast, the morning was already uncomfortable, breezeless and short-tempered.

I pushed a lawnmower all morning as it got hotter and a smattering golfers fought the good fight, trying to keep their grips dry by pulling their club handles between their legs, somehow a little like the way dogs clean themselves on the grass.

Lunch in the shady, cavernous maintenance barn suggested that there might, after all, be such a place as heaven, though it may be only slightly more pleasant than an average day of waking life. Roused from my lunch stupor, I was sent out to weed sand traps, most of which had no shade and were relentlessly efficient at converting sunlight to radiant heat for the purpose of parboiling seasonal greens-keepers.

Country clubbers golfed by sullenly, some tugging their gear on two-wheeled carts. There weren't many caddies around on weekdays, and none that day. The jaunty little motorized golf cars looked the saner choice; they made their own breeze and offered a way place to carry beverages.

I came to a fairway trap that was rarely in play on the 16th hole and settled into a patch of faint shade from a tree 20 yards away. I dreamed that Juliana and my father were dancing together. I was glad when I realized, still dreaming, that this was a dream.

My unintended nap boiled away. I sat up and drained my water jug and looked at the sand pit carved into the Pennsylvania countryside. Sitting with my arms around my knees, I could smell my sneakers.

A golf ball came hurtling from heaven and thumped into the turf a few feet away. I stood as tall as I could and looked toward the 14th tee, where a threesome was looking in my direction, searching for a shot gone awry.

I waved and pointed to the ball. In my career as a golf course worker, many shots had landed around me, but I was never struck by one. On the greens-keeping crew, we could never tell when incoming were on the way—we didn't get the same courtesy, the pointless "Fore!" that golfers sometimes yell to each other. The caddy fared a little better in that his attention was at least focused on the golfers, rather than the grass.

I trudged light-headed on to the next sand trap. I stood beside it, staring into the harsh white sand, searching for weeds. There were none. I had apparently dozed myself into a perfected universe.

I transited a straight line from where I stood to the maintenance barn and took the most direct route to my destination, even walking across the ninth green and through the creek that ran alongside it.

When I arrived at the maintenance barn, I realized that I had overshot the mark and missed quitting time. I wondered if someone had come out to tell me the shift was over, found me sleeping by the sand trap and left me to my reverie.

I punched my timecard and leaned over the water hose at the barn door, slurping almost cool water off the top of the stream, savoring the taste of rubber and summer. Bottled hose water isn't so good, but fresh off the tap—if you've let the foul part run through the coils—is a treat.

It was an early shift for my mother, so I figured I would go home with her. I walked the flagstone path to the kitchen door of the clubhouse; the outdoor world had by then been nearly abandoned, leaving our patch of the planet to those who had nowhere to hide.

With the heel of my right sneaker I reached to stop the screen door before it slammed behind me. I nodded to the guys working in the kitchen, which was, for once, cooler than the outside world. I pushed through the double-hinged doors into the bar of the clubhouse dining room.

Mother was leaning back against the ice machine behind the cluster of beer taps at the center of the bar. Two old members sat at the bar, nursing beers. The tables were set for dinner, but it was early and the only dish being served was the machine-cooled air that made the dining room feel like the penguin house at the zoo—cool, in a birdy, clammy way.

She looked at me and smiled her genuine smile, but then she was drawn forward to refill a golfer's beer. She could have been stirring drinks for councilors while discussing foreign trade, passing looks at every suave old man.

The country clubbers saw Miss Delaware, but she saved yodeling, her pageant talent, for the trees and me and Speedy.

She looked my way and pointed to her wrist. I found a stool at the far end of the area behind the bar, separated from where she was waiting out the end of her shift at center stage.

By the time you get to be an old Boy Scout, new distances start to seep into life, the slowly dawning awareness that the other is someone different than had been known until that time. My mother had an edge on me: she had already been through this once with my half-sister. And from an early age I was aware that there were unseen players in our family story, that there had been acts before I came on stage.

And I reckon there will be some after I exit.

When her shift ended, we walked together through the kitchen into the wall of late afternoon heat. I was glad to be back outside, where the honest sun resumed the baking dry of me.

Riding beside her in the front seat of her 1964 Dodge Dart, the vents drawing air through the cabin and the windows open all around, she asked me if I was going to see Juliana that night.

"I don't think so," I said, on the edge of saying more but not sure how to do it.

After some silence, I added, "She's mad at me."

Mother took her eyes off the road with the look mothers get. "You can always fix things if your heart is right." Her hand reached out on the seat between us.

"It was dumb," I said. So dumb that I didn't want to tell her that I had bought a pair of pants I didn't want and then threw them in the trash and that we had barely spoken since, even for the hour or two we were together the rest of that afternoon.

As impossible as it was to tell her this, I knew that my mother knew best about the romantic stakes. And so, staring straight ahead at the bumpers of the cars in front of us idling through a heat wave that buckled asphalt, I coughed up the whole embarrassing narrative of bell-bottom Sunday.

"That _was_ dumb," she said, shaking her head. "But I've heard dumber. We've been married almost 20 years and we're still finding potholes. I love Rocky dearly, but sometimes I just want to run away to Maienfeld."

Switzerland was not an option for me. "I don't know what I should do." It creeped me out a little that I was sort of enjoying being miserable.

"Your dad's father says the way through these things is to let your life speak. If you listen, your life will tell you what to do." I chewed that over for a minute, trying to figure what it meant.

"You just have to talk to her," she simplified.

The proof of a Scout is in the way he acts, in the things he does. A real Scout is a fellow who can and is and does.

Of course, there was a car ahead of us. There usually is. It was a 1965 Buick Riviera, the last run of the first generation of a car that aimed for the fabulous lifestyle of the Cote d'Azur. It was futuristic, wide and low and long. A refined fin bolted at an angle from the back of the front door, hit its apogee after a foot or so and then curved leisurely toward the stern.

The driver, a woman, pitched her cigarette, with an impatient overhand motion.

Instinctively, I looked at the seat between us and then at the back seat, but of course my mother wasn't carrying bumper sticker material.

"What do you think?" she asked, nodding across our bow toward the Riviera.

"The driver is impatient. She may have flicked because they're late, or because she's frustrated. Having a fancy luxury car hasn't been as fulfilling as she hoped."

A moment of quiet.

"You're really giving this a lot of thought, aren't you?" my mother remarked.

27. Friday, July 26, 1968

1965 Maserati Sebring 2

Juliana thought I was mad at her, and I thought she was mad at me. Making up took place on the old sofa in the basement recreation room at her house. When we came up for air, we called Vic Martine from the wall phone with an unusually long cord and said we would like to go to the racetrack with him.

And so on Friday I got my father's car and picked up Juliana and we bounced along now familiar roads and headed to the rich man's house with a tree-lined driveway. This time we parked in the driveway, as guests, instead of in the field.

It took a while for anyone to answer the doorbell. Then Martine appeared, an unbuttoned shirt over swim trunks and sandals. He had a beer in his hand and led us out to the swimming pool, set in a slate patio.

Martine disappeared back into the house. A wiry Asian man in a white Nehru jacket came outside and asked if we wanted something to drink. Juliana asked for a martini as though she had been doing this all her life. I wanted to rewind that moment to confirm that I had heard right, but the houseman was waiting for me to speak. All I could come up with was iced tea. He was gone like a vapor, leaving me to wonder at Juliana, settled into a lounge chair, crossing her legs, closing her eyes in the sweet scent of evening from the woods mixing with the aroma of pool chlorine.

"A martini?" I asked.

"I never had one until the night we worked here. The bartenders made us drinks when we weren't busy." This was new information, and I tried to picture my Juliana knocking down cocktails with bartenders.

I was never going to keep up.

"I think I also had a Manhattan and a Gibson," she added, "but I can't remember which was which."

She looked beautiful and unattainable, and then she reached out and took my hand. "I'm just trying to get them straight in my mind," she said, smiling innocently. I was sitting sideways on the lounge chair next to hers, admiring the way she took residence there like a model in a French painter's fantasy. The air above suddenly lifted a few foot-pounds, became less dense, opening a path in the air that only we could ascend. Was this heaven, I asked myself, meaning not the luxury that surrounded us but the intimacy that we were concocting beneath the opening sky.

The man in the white jacket came back with her martini and my iced tea. I watched her lips as they cautiously approached the rim of the glass, slowing down as she came closer and the slippery concoction tilted forward. A sip spilled over the edge into her mouth, the glass moved away and a gasp flashed across her face; her head wagged involuntarily from side to side. She laughed at herself, her eyes widened and then she leaned determinedly back into the drink.

"It's that good?" I couldn't believe that it was.

"Pretty as a daisy, but look out," she purred.

Juliana was gaining ground on her drink when Martine emerged from the house in gray slacks, a dark blue shirt unbuttoned at the top and brown outdoor slippers. It was then that I noticed the particulars of Juliana's outfit, a white summer dress and sandals, and became painfully aware that I was a caveman who had thrown away the only pair of fancy pants I ever owned.

The houseman was better dressed than I was. It was no longer clear what I was doing there, and it wasn't about to get any clearer.

Martine said we were going to meet an "expert" at Delaware Park, a racetrack about an hour away.

"There aren't any sure things at the track," he said. "Jockeys fall off. Horses forget to run. But we'll have some kicks and probably walk out of there with more than we go in with." He put his hands in his trouser pockets, waiting for me, apparently.

"I'm not worried about the money," I said. "I'm sure you know what you're doing with that."

He shrugged. "There are no sure bets, no matter what they tell you in Sunday school."

"I didn't go to Sunday school," I said.

"Neither did I," he answered, still waiting for something.

"*Give us, ye gods, an utter wreck, if wreck we must,*" I said, borrowing from another Melville, and reached my hand to Juliana. She downed what was left of the martini in one determined gulp.

"I couldn't have said it better myself," Martine said, lighting a cigarette. And so we retraced our steps through the plush living room and out the front door and along the front walk to the garage. Martine summoned the door to open electronically. As it slowly lifted, I expected to see the weighty ass of his Cadillac DeVille.

Instead there was a sleek, two-door that I could not name. It had a tight, wingless rear that looked like a suitcase, with a subtle crease wrapping across the top of the trunk. A modest bumper, a bulging package of three rear lights mounted on each side and the Maserati badge. Two chrome exhaust pipes pointed improbably at an angle into the night sky.

It seemed alive in the fading light, at a standstill, promising to fly off into the night at any moment.

Martine was smoking as he backed slowly from the garage. I opened the passenger door and determined that Juliana had to sit in the front. So I squeezed myself into the back.

When she flipped the back of the front seat into riding position, I was embalmed in deep, dark-red leather, trimmed in gray. It was more comfortable than it should have been, even if there had been some place to stow my legs.

The dashboard was polished gray, with "Maserati" between mid-dash air vents and a bank of toggles and sliding switches. There was a grab-bar for the passenger, homage to the vehicle's conception as a racing machine. No radio.

Martine wore driving gloves and in that car, one of fewer than a hundred ever made, it did not seem an affectation. He took a drag on the cigarette and threw it onto his driveway. Mentally, I attributed this flick to "car too refined to smoke in."

Power poured through the design, right through its buttocks and shoulders into the endoskeleton. I don't think we ever went over the speed limit, but from time to time he loosened the reins and gave the car some pace. Once, as we hurtled through a bend that mortals would take more cautiously, Juliana reached for the grab-bar and turned to Martine, her profile lit up with excitement, centripetal force bending us in our flying jewel box, leaving behind a trail of burnt testosterone.

The windows were open, sunset streaming through the cabin. At times I forgot myself and briefly thought that somehow I belonged in that car. Being in the back seat was like looking through a window from the outside, theoretically part of the car but experiencing it secondhand, moments after the real occupants had already been launched through the threshold of the present into the future.

The hour's drive went by too fast.

At the racetrack, Martine stopped at the valet parking booth. We valets and caddies can be a jaundiced lot, but there was no point in trying to play it cool with a Maserati. One valet went around to Martine's side; another opened the door for Juliana, but his eyes were on the machine. He held the door for me while I awkwardly unfolded legs that had gone wobbly.

The first valet took the car away.

"How come you don't drive that to the country club?" I asked.

"That's for driving, not business," he said, pulling out a cigarette and cradling it over his lighter.

We went through a pair of gates and up an escalator to a large, open space with a view over the track on one side, a bar and lounge area next to it, and a line of windows like teller stations at a bank. People were queued up at several windows.

We followed Martine across the space and down wide stairs with short risers that brought the track slowly, step by step, into more complete view. I was dazzled by the brilliant green oval of grass in the middle of the track, glowing in the lights, framed by the reddish brown of the track itself. I was used to seeing grass tenderly nurtured to look and feel like a carpet, rolled and mowed to a precise nap, fed and inoculated against the ravages of weeds, bugs, and germs. The infield of the track looked the match of any fairway we had, and it was bejeweled to a fare-thee-well by a ring of lights around the track.

Staring at the grass, I fell behind. Juliana had to come back and fetch me. "Time has come today," she said, taking a gentle hold of my elbow, sweetening her command. I looked at her and grinned, thinking she too was awed by the beauty of the lawn, of what people can do if they hire enough students and Puerto Ricans to educate their grasses. In her eyes, there was a reflected understanding; she probably didn't see what I saw, but she could see that I saw something important.

"We're over here," she said, pulling me magnetically between tables that were arrayed along a low railing that overlooked the track.

Martine was talking to a waitress as we arrived at the table. "And something for my friends," he said.

The waitress waited for us to sit down, tapping her pad with her pencil, looking deliberately away from us. I let Juliana slide into the seat across from Martine, next to the railing, and took the chair next to her.

"I'll have a Manhattan," Juliana said, looking away immediately to the track. The waitress never blinked. I should have been ready for that one, but my mind had blanked up again.

"Just an iced tea, please," I said.

Repetition is the resort of the unprepared. The waitress turned and resumed her journey through the sea of waiting, hungry and thirsty patrons.

The horses came out for the race, brimming with possibility, a pageant of silky riders and handlers, men cajoling reluctant athletes into the starting gate, as a quiet fell around us in the stands. The murmur turned to the moment at hand and, bam! in a click of time, the gates flung open and the pack burst forward in a frantic dash for speed.

Juliana leaned onto the railing, her hands clenched at the top, psyching the mass of muscle and flying hooves faster on around the near turn, and I wondered how much of it she could actually see. Without her glasses, which she left behind at every opportunity, she could see the up-close world just fine. But the far-off was a blurrier thing. Across the back stretch, two horses were pulling away, stringing the rest of the pack behind them and then they all hurtled around the far turn, a third horse broke from the pack, trying to gain on the leaders. The announcer's voice rose as the race came to us, and people stood, pressing forward, and the powerful smell of prayer mixed with cigar smoke and beer on a summer night, laced by the scent of money. Horse bettors take it personally.

The third horse caught one of the leaders, but the wrong one. The cagey fellow who had been hanging in the draft of the leader for most of the race found an extra gear and glided past his rival with 50 yards to go. It was too late for the challenger to catch him.

I don't know whom Juliana was rooting for; she fell back in her chair and looked at us as though she had been the one galloping with a lightweight Cuban on her back.

Martine stubbed out his cigarette. "I never make a bet without Nicky," he said, whistling a plume of smoke into the night air.

Nicky, it turned out, was a short, pudgy woman of indeterminate age who chain smoked. She arrived at our table shortly after that first race, wearing a man's yellow fedora, a plain white shirt and black slacks that were a size too small. Martine introduced us, but she barely looked our way. She was studying the tote board in the infield of the track just beyond the finish line, where the lineup for the next race was listed.

She was packing a sheaf of papers in a notebook that never left her grasp as she sat in the fourth chair at our table, across from me. We might as well have been garden furniture, but I didn't feel slighted because she was paying no attention to Martine either. The drinks arrived in plastic cups, and Nicky muttered "Schmidt's" out of the corner of her mouth without ever looking at the waitress.

Juliana turned and tried to get a conversation going with Nicky. "You come to the races a lot?"

"I fucking live here, sweetie. It's my job." She was comparing the board for the upcoming race against pages from her notebook, a mishmash of newspaper and magazine clippings, sheets of hand-scribbled notes on lined paper and an assortment of cocktail napkins, cigarette packs turned inside out and other make-do writing surfaces.

Martine sipped his cocktail. "Are we in this one?"

"Honeypot will win, but she won't pay enough to make it worth the risk," Nicky said. "I like Blue Mercury to show, but there are better races ahead."

Martine turned and studied the board. "I'll put $100 on Blue Mercury to show. Do you want to put some of your money on it?" He was addressing Juliana, who turned to me but too quickly, and actually had to back up her gaze to bring me sight. This time it was Manhattan, not the lack of glasses.

The Boy Scout manual doesn't cover this. I shrugged. "Sure, put some of our money on whatever you're betting on."

This pleased Juliana, who picked up her fancy cocktail with one hand and squeezed my thigh under the table with the other.

Martine pulled a money clip out of his pocket, peeled off two $100 bills and slid them over to Nicky. "Two tickets, $100 and $40, on Blue Mercury to show."

Nicky picked up the cash without really looking at it, took up her notebook and bustled away from the table. Leaving the three of us vacantly drumming our fingers. Juliana lit a cigarette and charged into her drink.

When the horses came to the starting gate, Blue Mercury seemed the smartest and strongest and noblest of all of his or her kind, partnered with a fearless jockey with incalculable nerve and sporting insight. It was, after all, the second horse race I had ever seen in my life.

Now Juliana and I had a rooting interest, and we hollered like rubes when the gates flew open. Martine barely stirred, sipping at his drink and absentmindedly twirling his cigarette lighter in his fingers.

Our champion did not escape the pack, seemingly content to let two brown rivals carry the lead around the first turn. It became difficult to find our man-horse team across the back stretch in the heaving fury of pounding legs and bobbing haunches. I enviously glanced at the two horses fighting for the lead, wishing we had chosen a more willing competitor. And then as they neared the far turn, a small black horse bolted from the crowd and began to close on the front runners as though they were walking. A cheer rose up from the grandstand as he caught the leaders and swept past them.

By the time he rounded the final turn, the little black had a substantial lead; the two horses that had led at the beginning had fallen back into the clump of indeterminate non-winners.

I might have missed it altogether had it not been for Juliana jumping out of her seat and waving her arms in the air as Blue Mercury came a-storming out of the pack with about 20 yards to go. He would not catch the black horse, but my heart swelled to see him give such effort with no chance to win.

Blue Mercury finished second. This is when I learned that you can win a bet without winning the race.

Nicky came back to the table with two separate piles of money that she carefully set down in front of Martine before sitting down to study the board behind the finish line. Our horse had only to come in among the first three and our $40 wager would pay $58.

We sat out the next race because Nicky said she didn't like the odds on the favorite, and she liked the jockey even less. The favorite competed early for the lead but faded to third and seemed content just to run along with the others.

"Lazy shit," muttered Nicky.

If we listened carefully, we might have heard the gears grinding in our handicapper's brain as she flipped through her notebook. Martine was watching her with a bemused smile; Juliana was studying the bottom of her plastic cup, sucking on what was left of the ice cubes.

Nicky came out of her trance and recommended betting two picks, Phantom Rudolf and Porch Child, as an exacta with a box, whatever that meant.

"When Nicky says it's a good bet, I go heavy," Martine said, pushing the money pile in front him and adding two $100 bills from his roll. "Let's make that an $800 quinela," he said, looking in my direction. "How much do you want?"

I faltered. Nicky seemed impatient. I looked at the two small piles of money that I understood were our winnings from the first bet. "Put half of it on what you just said," I said.

Martine raked through the money and shoveled separate piles toward Nicky.

Then some Scout mechanism kicked in, or maybe it was my inner journalist; I wanted to know more about this. I started out of my chair and then stopped and turned back to Martine. "Can I go with her?"

He signaled for the waitress. "Keep your distance. Nicky works alone."

I weaved through the people milling around the betting windows and spotted her in a line that had only one bettor ahead of her. I edged too near to her. She turned suddenly.

"Back away," she snarled under her breath. "You and your girl-friend are in way over your heads."

Suddenly, *a confluent small-pox had in all directions flowed over her face.* "You've shipped with him then?" she said.

"What do you mean?" I asked.

"*What's signed is signed,*" Nicky said.

I know a prophet when I hear one and stepped back away from her. That's when I discovered the racing form, or more exactly, stacks of them piled on small tables designed for standing to, rather than sitting around.

Nicky walked past me close enough that I couldn't miss her, and I fell in behind and followed her back to our table. When we were seated, she leaned across the table. "You can't make bets here. I can't make bets for you, nobody can. So for chrissake, don't do stupid shit that makes it look like I'm making bets for you. You're not the first kid to do this, and really the track doesn't give a damn how old the money is, but they gotta look like they're obeying the law."

I nodded. I got it.

Martine was grinning, amused by my situation, and Juliana was staring at the horses being brought to the starting gate. Phantom Rudolf was in red, number one. I couldn't even remember the other horse we were betting on, and then the gates flew open and they galloped up to speed, edging for the rail. We, the humans, spurred them on around the first turn. As they took the far corner, number one began to pull ahead, fighting with a group of three other horses, tearing desperately down the back stretch and inching away from the pack.

As they rounded the far turn, the grandstand stood. Phantom Rudolf was looking strong. The race was strung out and suddenly our pick was racing headfirst for us, the jockey slapped him once or twice on the hip and he bolted forward, steaming down the stretch, pulling ahead by one length and then by two, and with the finish in sight he still seemed to be gaining speed. Two horses struggled for second, a couple lengths ahead of the rest of the race.

The crowd around us seemed upset. Phantom Rudolph had been listed fourth when the race went off, and the favorite did not even finish in the top three. When the announcer read the winners, I was surprised to learn that Porch Child had finished second, just as Nicky had predicted.

"How did you do that?" I asked.

Nicky looked at me as she was getting up and she tapped her notebook. "I study the crap out of the horses. I talk to people. The favorite was overrated and I thought all along Phantom Rudolph was the best in the field." She pointed to the racing form in front of me. "Read that. I haven't seen anything worthwhile in the next race, so play this one in your head."

With that, she was off to the betting windows.

"Nicky likes to pick up the winnings right away," Martine said. He blew a cloud of cigarette smoke into the night air.

"But how did she know which horses to pick? How did she pick the second-place finisher?"

"It could have gone either way for us, as long as those two horses were first and second." His eyes turned away, focusing on the person who was sliding up behind me. It was the waitress. She put a paper napkin down in front of Juliana, took away the spent Manhattan and replaced it with a fresh one. She performed the same maneuver with Martine's drink and paused for a moment. My iced tea was hardly touched, as was Nicky's beer.

Martine handed her a folded bill, which she seemed pleased with, and she departed for her next table. Juliana was already leaning in. I stared at the racing form, but I was reading the same information over again and none of it was penetrating my thick brain. Then Nicky was back at our table, sliding two stacks of money in front of Martine.

In my head, I threw imaginary darts at the racing form and picked three horses. It was a good race, and only one of my picks finished in the top three. Juliana was shouting for her new favorite, every bit as excited as she was for the race we had bet on.

We played the next race, but placed just one bet, on the favorite at 3 to 2. It struck me as lacking in ambition, but Juliana and I made up for it by betting $300, about three weeks of take-home pay, on a single horse. We won, and the night became less real.

Juliana worked toward the bottom of her second racetrack drink, and suddenly leaned into my chest, her hand slithering electrically along the inside of my thigh.

I noticed that Martine was studying us, not too subtly. I put my arm around Juliana's shoulder, but I was distracted, thinking about what I should do rather than what I was doing. The quiet at our table turned awkward, as though we were four strangers waiting for a bus, suddenly aware of one another.

"So what do you do for a job?" I asked Martine.

"Haven't we had this conversation before?" he said, a little smile in the corner of his lips.

"I'm working on a new merit badge," I said. "How to Get a Maserati."

"That's right, the Boy Scout." He was nodding, and drained his drink, scouting himself for the waitress. "I'm an investor. I've got a few things going on, some of them are big projects that take years to develop and others are short-term trades." Behind me, the waitress must have beamed her attention our way because Martine made the helicopter finger gesture around our table, indicating another round of drinks.

"To get a Maserati, start by understanding that you are your biggest asset. Whatever it is you're good at, if it's mowing grass or carrying golf bags, you have to find a way to leverage that talent."

Nicky chimed in, "CallYourName is worth something."

I turned around and saw that a horse by that name was now at five to one.

"I don't think she can win, but she'll start strong and the rest of them might never come around," Nicky said. "But if she's passed, she'll fold."

Martine shrugged and slid a $100 bill toward her. "Let's bet to win." But he never looked my way to see if I wanted to ride along, and Nicky was quickly off for the betting window.

"The thing I like about the stock market is that you can bet against other investors if you think they're overpricing a company. Horses are all about faith," he said. "That's why I could never make a living at this"—he waved at the track—"the way Nicky does."

CallYourName started slow and never made much headway. As Nicky had predicted, she settled back into the herd, lacking whatever gumption it took to get to the front.

The waitress brought another round of drinks; Juliana eagerly traded in her used one. Martine didn't seem any more troubled by losing the last bet than he was excited about winning the ones before it.

Nicky was sure about Black Fabulous, going off at three to one, in the next race. Martine pushed the whole stack of money in front of him toward her, even before she had a chance to explain her thinking. They both looked at me, but I was unwilling to risk everything we had won to that point.

"I guess half of what we have there," I said, looking at the separate stack of money that represented the winnings I shared with Juliana.

He nodded, and sorted through the bills, doling out a separate stack for Nicky to whisk away to the betting window.

Juliana was leaning devotedly over her Manhattan, another cigarette burning by itself in the ashtray she shared across the table with Martine. He was watching her, but he glanced away when our eyes met.

"I have an investment in Nantucket. It's a run-down fishing island off the coast of Cape Cod, but there's a guy buying property there and trying to convert it into a vacation spot for rich people." He took a sip of his drink. "I like his thinking. He bought the ferry that services the island and then raised the fare. The plan was not to make money on the ferry, but to discourage poor people from going to Nantucket.

"If you make it more expensive to get there, the idle rich will want to go," he explained.

I tried to remember what Ishmael paid to get to Nantucket.

"It could work," Martine said. "But then there was a rich widow in France who bought up a shitload of property in a little town in the country, and sank a fortune into restoring everything to its original condition. She turned the town from a collection of rotting buildings into an historic artifact, a place celebrating its past and preserving ancient culture.

"But the people who lived in the village revolted," he said. "They wanted their hillbilly life; they didn't like living in a museum."

"What happened?" I asked.

"The widow gave up. She said she couldn't deal with people who had been corrupted by modern times."

The drinks were going down faster. Juliana's head thudded to the tabletop.

Martine made nothing of this. "She said she wants her tombstone to read, simply, 'Nuts.'

"I've actually been to that town," he said, "around the time you were born. I was researching an investment in a Swiss drug company. The place was a dump. But the Swiss deal was my first big score after getting out of the Navy and the beginning of how I got my Maserati," he said, grinding a half-smoked cigarette into the ashtray in front of him. "Just goes to show there's no substitute for personal experience."

At the racetrack, nobody flicks their butts into the road, perhaps because it's too fucking far away.

28. Friday, July 26, 1968

1966 Ford Mustang

The sure thing was a dud. It held the lead most of the way through the back stretch but was caught on the far turn and lacked the heart or the fuel or the inspiration to hold off two challengers around the far turn. Nicky was visibly upset—I had no idea how much she was betting—and even Martine was annoyed by the loss. Our pick galloped down the stretch, running with weights on its ankles, unable to make any kind of move, slowly drifting further behind. It finished fifth.

The money was an abstraction, but there is something tangible about winning and losing, even vicariously through a far-away horse and a rider I would never know.

Juliana never picked her head up from the table, merely turning to stare through the railing. A noise like snoring came out of her and she bolted upright.

"Do you think she's okay?" Martine asked me, as though she was a piece of abstract art.

My girlfriend pulled her drink close to her chin and met it halfway, slurping the melt at the bottom of the cup. Some fucked-up Scout am I, I thought, realizing that she was crashing.

My one-size solution to most problems is to hike somewhere. "Let's take a walk," I said, putting a hand under her arm and lifting gently. Her arm slid limp through my grip. A more committed effort got her to her feet, but drunken legs gave out and she crash-collapsed back to the chair.

Nicky and Martine stared at us. I bent over and placed Juliana's left arm around the back of my neck, holding her wrist firmly with my left hand, and wrapped my right arm around the small of her back and searched in vain for a firm grip on her dress. I had to settle for a tight hold under her rib cage and hoisted sail again, slowly raising her to her feet.

"How much longer are we going to stay here?" I asked.

Martine said there were just two races left.

"Do whatever you think best with that," I said, nodding at the wad of our money in front of him. Juliana found a tentative balance in her legs. "We're gonna walk around a bit. Can we meet you where we came in?"

"Get her to drink water," Martine said, but his words were thickening and slushy at the edges. "See you in the winner's shircle."

Juliana and I stumbled away from the table. Once I got us pointed forward, we managed a more efficient potato-sack walk. Bettors were staring, and I figured they all knew she was drunk. I was ashamed for both of us, vowing that I would never let this happen again. We weaved through the crowd toward the escalator in search of fresher air.

I found a grimy snack bar on the ground floor where we got a cup of water. Juliana had a few sips and mumbled that she needed to go to the bathroom. I steered her to a women's rest room, but I did not think I could let go of her and so I did the unthinkable and caddied her into the ladies room.

A few women were gathered around the washbasins and the mirrors. The clan sensed invasion and readied to defend its turf, but their mood changed when they sized up Juliana's condition. One woman held open the door to a stall, but as Juliana and I neared the entry point, the water got too deep for me. I maneuvered Juliana around so she was facing the right way and then instinct took over. Juliana freed herself, wobbling a little, and gently pushed me back outside the stall and began to reach under her skirt and I wondered if maybe there is god at least in the most intimate places. I turned away and pulled the door closed.

The women looked at me, as relieved as I was. Two of them were studying Juliana's feet under the door, and the other nudged me toward the exit. "We'll help your friend from here," she said.

As I crossed the threshold, I figured I had sunk about as low as I could. I loitered around the entrance to the ladies room like a regular scoundrel, feeling oddly liberated and avoiding eye contact with the people who passed my way. Finally, one of the women came out of the sanctuary and put her hand on my forearm. "She'll be out soon. I think she'll survive."

I had been projecting self-disgust onto the people around me, people who were a lot more forgiving and seemed to take our condition in stride. *The swinging lamp oscillating in the room inside my head held its position relative to the healing world around me*, and I couldn't take my eyes off it, even if no one else could see it.

Juliana came out of the restroom under her own steam. Her face was flushed pale, her eyes swimmy and tired, but there was a plucky smile on her lips. Her arms were folded in front of her as though she were cold. We fetched another pail of water and walked outside, where the cool darkness of night and fresh air began to do its work. I told her that I was sorry, and she looked at me with a question, and whispered that she was glad I was there to hold her. This is the awful weight, accepting love when you're not worthy.

There was a roar from the racetrack, and soon the patrons began streaming past us on their way to the parking area. We had to wait a while before Martine and Nicky came out. He was weaving unsteadily and fumbled for the valet parking ticket. In the harsh light above the valet stand, he didn't look as smoothly assembled as before. Nicky headed off wordlessly to the self-park area, leaving us in an awkward silence, our feet stuck in the sand while the tide of gamblers washed past and out to the sea.

When the car came back, Martine put his hand on my shoulder and pointed to the driver's side. "Get us home, old scout," he mumbled. "There's a blanket in the trunk." He dug into his pocket again and pulled out a thick wad of money and pushed it into my hand. "We got lucky in the rast two laces," he said, pausing for his brain to catch up with some thought that got lost on the way. His eyes were red and watery.

I looked at the money, wondering what to do with it. Martine dove into the back seat as though this wasn't the first time. As I lifted the trunk, I noticed that he had vanity license plates that said "Delstyn."

In the trunk, there was a soft, neatly folded blanket. I held the door for Juliana, who leaned forward to let me drape the blanket around her shoulders and then sank back into the plush leather, leaning endearingly toward me.

The Maserati and I became a partnership, riding gears into curves and reaching for the wind as we pushed ahead on the straight runs. I remember coming to a stop at a red light and feeling the night catch up to us from behind, turning to look at Juliana, who was smiling with half-opened eyes. I felt goofy for enjoying it so much, but it was hard not to get sucked in by the fantasy when the owner was passed out in the back seat and there was nobody but we church mice manning the cockpit.

The journey home seemed timeless, and then it wasn't.

A few miles from Martine's house, along the curving and dipping River Road, we cruised up behind a 1966 Mustang coupe just as the driver flicked a cigarette onto the road, where it exploded in a tiny fireworks display. We purred ahead like a confident Italian weightlifter, operas of horsepower in reserve, riding on his left taillight, waiting for the road ahead to give us a passing lane. When it did, we lifted off like a rocket, passing the Mustang, and Juliana leaned toward the open window.

"You dropped something back there," she yelled as we accelerated into the open road, and then the empty night. "Everybody's making love or else expecting rain," she sang to the wind.

When we got back to Martine's house, I stopped the Maserati outside the garage and turned off the ignition.

I left the wad of money on the passenger seat after Juliana and Martine got out. If I could throw new bell-bottom pants in a trash can, I could leave a few weeks' pay in a rich guy's car.

Driving home in my father's car was a letdown, though I tried to tell myself that it wasn't.

29. TUESDAY, JULY 30, 1968

1964 CHEVROLET CORVAIR

The diner where Juliana worked was a popular place. It was only a few blocks from the high school, and—since the fast-food chains had not found us yet—high school kids went there. But respectable grown-ups went there, too; some of them had gone there as teenagers themselves. Men who worked in town would go for lunch, families showed up for breakfast on the weekends, and couples dropped in for casual suppers. There were only two kinds of coffee, and it came in only one size, and there was no take-out menu.

But it wasn't the only diner in town. There was another one, similar but sited on the other main axis running through Doylestown, closer to auto-body shops than lawyers' offices. In truth, I had never been in the "other" diner, although there was a kid in the Scout troop who praised it.

My mother had worked the lunch shift at the country club that day and offered to take me home after work. When I had finished mowing enough grass and pulling enough weeds and raking enough sand, I met her in the kitchen. She said she wanted to pick up bread at a bakery that was slightly off our usual path home.

Mother said Speedy would be getting home late because he was going to see Dr. Matthews. "The people at the hospital said he's already paid to move Jimmy to a private room and he has hired new therapists. We thought he was just offering to help, volunteering his time, but now it seems like he's paying for this."

This was worrisome. "Your grandfather is as much in the dark as we are," she added.

"But I thought you talked to Dr. Matthews."

"Not since he asked if he could look in. I haven't even seen him since then."

The bakery was next door to the "other" diner. I sat in the car while Mother went inside. It was late in the afternoon, and I was dozing a little. I thought I saw my father coming out of the diner. He was right behind Miss Bennett. I had not seen her since the Poor People's Campaign.

They walked together to a car that wasn't my father's and navigated separately to the opposite doors; my father was saying something clever to her over the roof; I could tell by the look in his eyes that it was one of his droll observations. Her back was to me, but I imagined that she was enjoying the joke.

They got in her car; she backed slowly out of their parking space; the windows were rolled down and she was talking, though I couldn't hear any of it. She slowly turned her car and headed to exit the shopping strip.

My mother's car was just four stalls away, but my father apparently had not noticed it. I didn't know what to make of finding them together at a diner when he was supposed to be meeting with the doctor. Mother came out of the bakery, and I decided I would not be saying anything to her about it until I figured it out.

We pulled out of the strip mall lot and fell in behind a bright green 1964 Chevrolet Corvair, a car-of-the-year pick when it was introduced as the first American-made rear-engine car in 1960. Although it would later incur the wrath of Ralph Nader, the Corvair influenced car design by ending once and for all the obsession with wings, and introducing the flow-line design using convex surfaces. At the time, it was an oddity, flat, low and wide with air vents in the hood over the engine in the back. The back of the car wore a lid.

The trunk was in the front!

The 1964 was the last model year Chevy offered the Corvair with a gasoline-powered heater. It looked more American than the VW Beetle, against which it was competing, but there were few in the school parking lot. It was the flying saucer your weird uncle—the one who was a ham radio operator—drove and bragged about.

This one had a bumper sticker that read: Waiter! What Is This Nitwit Doing in My Soup?

The Corvair lurched a little bit at the start, the sign of a manual transmission. I was thinking about my father before I noticed that Mr. Corvair was also working on a cigarette. We were following him out of a red light recently turned green when he quickly threw the cigarette out into the street with his left hand, and then grabbed the steering wheel.

"He had to litter because he was shifting gears," I said.

Later that night, I went out to my father's car to put my Corvair entry into the logbook. Scribbling in the front seat of his car, a breeze blew through the open window. I turned around, sensing someone behind me outside the car but there was only the moonlight. My parents were around the back of the house, and I thought about the evening a few weeks back when I had come home to find them arguing and then quickly making up in a giddy way, in the kitchen. It was slowly dawning on me that life was not always perfect for them, and that our souls *are glued to our flesh and cannot freely move about with running great risk of perishing, like ignorant pilgrims crossing the snowy Alps in winter.*

That day, Ron Hansen, a shortstop for the Washington Senators, made an unassisted triple play, catching a line drive that two base runners didn't think he would get to. He stepped on second and, with momentum carrying him, chased down the runner who was trying to retreat back to first and tagged him out. It was the first such play, which are rarer than perfect games, in more than 40 years.

30. Friday, August 2, 1968

1959 Ford F100 Pickup

In midweek, Juliana told me over the phone that Martine had invited us to his house on Friday evening. This happened at her diner.

I wasn't keen on the idea. On the phone, I dragged my heels, but I didn't dig them in. It dawned on me that she might go by herself. In the end, that bothered me more.

She came to get me after dinner on Friday. I told my parents we were going to a party at a friend's house. There might have been something in my delivery, but Mother looked at me cock-eyed as we were leaving, as though she was holding something back. As I was.

I decided to make the best of it, that being with Juliana was all the reward I needed. It was a pleasant evening, a great time for a drive over country seas, the windows rolled down, the corn growing tall and rich, upholstering the landscape.

Ahead of us was a 1959 Ford F100 pickup, the model that pioneered the full-width pickup bed, paired with a roomy cabin and the absence of a running board. It wasn't new by any means in 1968; the gutter along the top of the back window already seemed quaint. It was the truck that began to make trucks more like cars.

I wouldn't be mentioning this if there wasn't a woman driving the F100 with a cigarette in her left hand. She wore a plaid shirt with the sleeves rolled up and held the cigarette between her index finger and middle finger just at the knuckle. There were two small heads next to her. The truck had some travel on it, but it was cared for; in all likelihood it lived on a working farm. I was quietly watching the prey in front of us, and Juliana knew without my asking to stay close without tailgating.

As scientists, even mere social scientists, we weren't supposed to influence the behavior of the subjects.

The pickup truck driver was flicking her ashes out the window, and seemed uninterested in actually smoking the thing. The truck had a heavy duty, no nonsense bumper. FORD was embossed in raised letters in the tailgate, which had a curl at the top. The cab had a visor over the windshield. The gas cap sat on a neck that jutted out behind the driver's side door. Nothing about it was particularly aerodynamic; its built-up front end and heavy grill seemed to ride low in the waves like a tugboat.

She had stopped smoking and twirled the cigarette around in her left hand so the lit end was cupped in her palm. She was shaving the embers with her fingernail and when it appeared that the fire was extinguished, she pinched the end of the cigarette and tried to toss it back into the bed of her truck. But she misjudged the wind and the spent soldier bounced off the side of the truck and tumbled onto the road. I thought I saw her look back in the left mirror and then quickly up into the rearview mirror, but the truck kept rolling along.

"What was that?" Juliana asked.

"I think she was trying to toss it into the truck bed. She didn't want the cigarette butt inside the truck because of the kids, but she didn't want to litter it either."

"She flicks butts, but needs to work on her aim," Juliana said. I had turned to look at her profile, wondering if I was in love.

Martine's estate was eerily quiet as we rolled up the driveway for the third time. The garage doors were closed. It wasn't dark enough for the outdoor lights yet. We stood together and knocked on the heavy wooden door, peasants calling on the lord of the manor.

The houseman answered the door with an empty expression. He immediately looked down, holding the door open and gestured through the living room toward the wall of windows that looked out over the pool. "Pool," he said.

Martine was on the patio at a glass-topped table with an umbrella sprouting through its navel. He was bent over, studying a beige-colored box from which a pair of wires fell off the table to the ground and ran across the patio and into the house through an open window.

He looked up at us joyfully, pointing at the contraption on the table. "This is Victor Electrowriter," he said, pleased with himself. In his hand he held a pen-like device that was attached by a wire to the box in front of him. Coming closer, I could see that it said "Victor Electrowriter" on the front, and had a large red idiot light on top.

No tail fins, however.

Nevertheless, I was hooked. "What is it?" I said.

"Trying to figure out whether this is worth investing in," Martine said, studying the device. "You use the stylus to write on this pad," he said, picking up the pen and drawing a peace sign on a pad on the top of the machine. "You push the 'send' button," and he pushed a button marked, appropriately, SEND. "The Electrowriter somehow takes a picture of this and transmits it over the telephone." The machine was grumbling away as Martine pointed to the wire running from the device into the house.

"At the other end, there's another machine that prints a copy of the picture." He turned and called into the house: "Lee, bring us the picture." In a minute, his assistant came back with a piece of paper that had Martine's hand-drawn peace sign on it.

"How does that work?" I asked.

Martine shook his head from side to side. "I have no idea, but I don't need to. The system has been tested in adult education projects. It has been used to teach Hebrew to people who live in rural areas, but the company really wants to sell it to businesses. They think engineers and architects can use it to send complex diagrams over the telephone."

At that point in time, the fax machine had not been introduced to the market. If you wanted more information about the Victor Electrowriter, you had to send a letter through the U.S. Postal Service to the company in Chicago. Your mail might get there a little quicker than usual if you included the new zone improvement code, but most people were not yet brainwashed into using them at that point.

"It's hard to tell whether they're actually leading the wagon train into the future," he said.

I was still piecing it together. Draw on machine, point to wire, man brings paper from house.

"It's your future," he said, looking from the machine to Juliana and me. "Is anybody gonna to use this? Or will something better come along?"

I had not a clue.

Juliana's opinion was: "We want to go swimming."

She did not wait for a response and started around the edge of the pool to the bathhouse on the other side. I was still puzzling over the machine.

Then Martine changed the subject, and I had the sense that he had waited until she was away. "Why did you leave the money in the car?" he asked.

I balked because all I knew were the small parts of whatever the truth was. I felt guilty about enjoying the racetrack and being excited by winning money and driving the Maserati, and a little unnerved about how much Juliana enjoyed it all. "It didn't feel like it was mine," I said.

"A buddy of mine from Korea said man is a money-making animal," Martine said. I was enough of a Dick Mobius to recognize the phrase, but I wasn't sure that Martine did. This was like seeing a car with your father's bumper sticker on it.

"It's wired into us," Martine continued. "Turning away from it will just make you broke."

"My father doesn't make a lot of money, but he's not broke," I said.

Martine kept his attention on the Electrowriter. Then he leaned back from it and pulled a cigarette from the pack that was sitting on the tabletop. He flipped open his stainless steel lighter, thumbed the wheel that turned against the flint and brought it to the end of his cigarette, taking a long draw and snapping the lighter lid shut.

"Honor that," he said, without looking up. "But you'll have to be your own man and he will turn out to be something different. You pick up people through life and you help them," he nodded across the pool to the cabana, "and then it's no joke. You're nobody till somebody loves you."

This seemed odd to me, since there was no visible sign that Martine was attached to anyone other than himself.

"You have a family?"

"Not in the usual sense," he said.

At that moment, Juliana emerged from the cabana. She did an exceptional job wearing a bikini. Other than our skinny-dip in the creek, I had more knowledge of her shape in my hands and arms than I had in my visual understanding.

Martine was watching her coming around the pool. When I surveyed him in my periphery, he looked down quickly at the machine.

As she laid a beach towel on the back of a patio chair, she looked at me and then him, measuring the state of things.

Then she was diving into the deep end of the pool and I knew that I could not abide this situation, me and Martine under the silly poolside umbrella, watching Juliana swim about.

Alas, I was not prepared! "I didn't bring anything for swimming," I said aloud to myself.

"You can find something in there." Martine nodded toward the cabana.

In the bathhouse, a mood clung to the upholstery, an uncomfortable smell. Juliana's clothes were folded neatly on a lounge chair, one of three that were oddly arranged around a small coffee table. It was dim; the last gasps of sunlight were pushing through wide venetian blinds.

In a chest of drawers I found several swimsuits that seemed clean. I pulled out a pair and stared at the mesh lining inside. I had read through the Boy Scout manual several times. There was no guidance on wearing some else's swim trunks, laundered or otherwise.

I had little interest in swimming, but I wanted very much to be with her in the water. The lesser evil seemed to be wearing another guy's swim trunks.

So I did. I found the baggiest pair that would fit—after pausing briefly to ponder one rig that was little more than a painted jock-strap—and pulled them on. Tried not to think about who had been in there before.

I folded my clothes and placed them carefully next to Juliana's.

When I came out of the cabana, Juliana was hanging on the edge of the pool, talking to Martine, who sat smoking at the table with a clever look in his face. I dove into the deep end. I ranked third among swimmers in my family, but I had merit badges to prove I knew my way around a pool.

Juliana swam to me. For 10 minutes or so we were, at least in my mind, back in the creek, almost unaware of Martine, the sun crouching to squeeze through tree limbs, the subtle stench of rich-guy pool chemicals and wealth and slate surrounding us. Not so unlike the natural rub of creek scum, only a different flavor.

Martine never came into the pool, but I felt his presence more and more. It began to feel like Juliana and I were swimming for an audience, dance partners in an aquatic audition of some kind, or primitive life forms jerking about on a microscope slide.

The water was going sour and I pulled myself out, not knowing whether she would follow. I hadn't the forethought to bring a towel with me from the cabana, as Juliana had, so I took my seat with Vic Martine and the Victor Electrowriter and simply air dried.

The houseman showed up. Martine asked if we wanted something to drink. Juliana piped up from the pool, her face beaming, asking for a whiskey sour.

Again, who was she?

I said I would have one too.

"Truth serum for all!" Martine said.

It occurred to me that he might already be drunk. I never saw it coming at the race track.

"*In landlessness alone resides the highest truth,*" I said, "*so it is better to perish in that howling infinite than be ingloriously dashed upon the lee, even if that were safety.*"

Martine looked like he didn't get it. They usually don't. Then the fellow came with a tray of drinks and Juliana arose glistening from the pool, a freshly washed peach goddess. She wrapped herself in the thick towel she had brought from the cabana.

It went downhill from there.

"You're a revolutionary Boy Scout, right?" Martine said. "You should know the Republicans have a plan for dealing with troublemakers like you at the convention in Miami Beach."

I played along. "What's that?"

"If senior citizens try to come over from Miami to stage protests, they're going to pull up the drawbridges over Indian Creek. That will keep the angry old people from disrupting the coronation."

"How deep is Indian Creek?" I asked.

He chuckled.

Juliana seemed hell-bent on inebriation. She fairly gulped down her drink and held the empty glass like a flare above her head, signaling for more. The towel came half undone from around her shoulders and she made no effort to restore it. The houseman returned with another round of cocktails.

"What's Deltsyn?" I asked. I was thinking about the license plate on his sports car.

"Oh, a lesser prophet," Martine said, staring into space.

I lost a couple of moments there. Martine asked Juliana if she had ever considered modeling, and suddenly I couldn't take it any longer. I took my second whiskey sour into the house to study the receiving end of the Electrowriter, as if a sign might come through it from the other side.

The stereo inside piped music onto the patio: Harry Belefonte singing "You jump in the saddle and hold onto the reins" and Juliana stood up and began dancing by herself in front of Martine, the towel now down on the patio.

I gulped from my second whiskey sour and woozied back outside. I couldn't remember my intention, watching her. When the song ended, she collapsed laughing into her chair and Martine applauded. She finished off the drink in front of her like it was water.

I drank my potion in one manly gulp and dove in the water. By the time my face broke back into the air, hot blood was flushing into my face. Two or three strokes put me at the far side of the pool. I turned around and hoisted myself up on my elbows on the edge of the deck. I could have been in the Himalayas, at the Natu Pass, where Indian and Chinese troops were facing off. Each side had loudspeakers poised across the border. The Indians played propaganda in Mandarin from five thirty to six thirty every morning. Then the Chinese preached their version of the truth—in a classical Hindi that none of the Indians understood—for the next few hours. And so it went, over the day, each side blasting the other with bad translations of the truth. At one thirty in the afternoon they both ended their broadcasts. At no point did they interrupt one another.

My girlfriend was looking briny, but at least her head hadn't collapsed on the patio table yet. Another round of drinks had appeared beside the Electrowriter. I felt unhinged, and probably lost track of time, but at least I was above water and had not so far done anything too stupid.

But there was still plenty of time.

I pulled myself out of the pool and reeled into the cabana. I sat for a while on a chaise lounge and watched them through the blinds, and began to consider whether I still existed. I fought for my center of gravity against the swimming inside my head.

I got a towel and dried off. It felt weird to be naked in his pool house, watching them through the jalousies, drying my crotch. Not unpleasant. Just weird.

I put my clothes back on, unsure what I would do next. I wanted to see how this disaster would unfold, but I also wanted to go home and start over. Back on the slate patio, I shuffled around to the table. He was smoking; she was sipping. A fresh drink was waiting there for me.

"We ought to be heading home, Juliana."

She did not respond.

"C'mon. It's time to go. I gotta get up tomorrow."

She looked at Martine over the top of her drink. "Let's stay a little longer, Doris," she said.

Martine was staying out of it, at least on the surface. I didn't know what strings he was pulling under the table.

I do not know how to argue with people or wage emotional warfare. I have no power of manipulation; I cannot even make water evaporate.

Smashed, upset, clutching for familiar bearings, I could not be mad or bully her because I believed that I was the only one who could make me angry. Everybody, especially Juliana, knew that if I ever got in a brawling mood that I would probably stop, if the opportunity arose, to help an old lady across the street.

"I think we should go now," I repeated, quieter than the first time, sensing already that I was giving myself two equally crappy options: stay until she was ready to leave, or leave her there. I could think up good reasons for either plan. There was a long silence when I thought she might actually be coming around, but the longer it lasted, the more it felt like setting concrete that left both of us with no choice.

I reached my hand out to shake hands with her, a gesture that confused both of us.

"Go ahead and light up the town," I said, letting those damn Rolling Stones do my talking for me. I turned my back on them. I was walking drunk, half realizing what I was doing as though I was in a movie about myself. I did not go back in the house but walked around the outside, singing, "You're gonna come back, baby, knocking right on my door."

I didn't believe a word of it.

Then it was just me with myself. It was a long walk home. But I have never had a problem with long walks, by myself or in a troop.

Gradually, with the unrelenting placement of one foot in front of the other, the alcohol burned off.

I did not turn around to pitch my thumb for a ride at any of the vehicles that sped intermittently toward me from behind. Each time their headlights illuminated the way forward and then left me with my night.

The miles turned slowly underfoot. Heading west, I was helping the earth's rotation, spinning us a little closer to the next sunrise. It was a pleasant night for a hike, even if the road was narrow and, for the most part, lacking a shoulder. But I was glad to be on the road again. I stopped a few times to look up at the stars and tell myself that we, Juliana and me, could work through this. I knew from the AM radio that teen romance ends.

At one point I thought I felt the Fairlane fly past me on the road, but I convinced myself that if it was her, she hadn't recognized me chunking along the road.

The heavens rotated as I hiked. A few miles from home, I sensed another person without a vehicle around him, someone running toward me over the blacktop, unwavering. He made no sign that he even saw me. I stopped and watched him disappear around a turn in the road, two strangers in the middle of the night, wondering if I had seen him at all.

At last I turned down my street in a walking trance, giving up all hope that she would track me down in her automobile.

This was discouraging. It was some unknown hour of the dark morning. I slid into my father's car and pulled out the notebook. I noticed that he had tagged a cigarette litterer that day, a 1965 Chrysler that he followed all the way to the supermarket on his way home from work. Usually he left some note about the driver, but that day he didn't.

I wrote in my entry about the conscientious pickup driver who tried to flick her butt into the bed of the truck after carefully extinguishing it. I was glad that people sometimes had good reasons for the things they did, even if they weren't such good things.

31. Sunday, August 4, 1968

1963 Pontiac Grand Prix Sport Coupe

I was supposed to be going with Juliana and her hippie friends to see The Doors in Philadelphia, but we had not spoken since the swimming pool at Martine's.

I got up brightly, before anyone else in the house, and hitchhiked into town. I was sent out with another caddy almost as soon as I got there, an early round with four better-than-adequate golfers. It was quiet and summery, gradually burning off the dew.

When the round was over, I popped through the kitchen and showed my face behind the bar. My mother's shift had just started, and she was talking to a golfer sitting at the bar. It didn't register, at first, that she was talking to Martine. The sonofabitch was everywhere.

I turned and retreated before either of them saw me. *I have sat before the dense coal fire and watched it all aglow, full of its tormented flaming life; and I have seen it wane at last, down, down, to dumbest dust.* I was pretty sure they hadn't notice me.

I didn't want to caddy another round and I didn't want to go home. When I got to the state road that went through the middle of town, I turned east toward the river, and put my thumb in the wheel of fortune.

Didn't know where I was going, so it didn't really matter that it was Sunday afternoon and no time for hitchhiking. And that, my friend, is freedom.

After a while, a middle-aged, nearly bald guy picked me up in a battered Ford station wagon. Neither of us said anything, and when he asked me where I was going, I said the first thing that came to mind, New Hope, because it seemed like the right distance away. He muttered something about going through that way, but I really wasn't listening.

We stopped at a red light on Main Street right before the road sprang across the bridge into New Jersey, and he asked if it was a good place to drop me. I said yes and got out of the car and suddenly wondered what I was doing there. The ice cream eaters and bell-bottom buyers were already out in numbers. I drifted through them toward Mechanic Street.

The landlord didn't seem surprised when I knocked and asked for Quentin, though I was taken aback when I was told he was on his way down, as though I had been expected. Then Quentin came clattering through the hallway into the dusty sunshine near the front door carrying two strings of carved coconut heads.

"I'm going to meet the canal people," he said. "Thou art welcome to the meeting."

I didn't know what he was talking about, but I fell into formation. Outside the door, he went around the side of the boarding house and returned with his icon cross, a one-by-four nailed at a 90-degree angle to a two-by-two that he carried in a holster around his waist that was, I thought, originally meant for carrying flagpoles in marching bands. I waited while he draped the icon strings to his yardarm, thinking about a kid I used to know who was an altar boy.

We traipsed along through the gathering crowd of tourists, who gawked a-plenty at his display of carved heads, but apparently he wasn't ready to start merchandising, because we brushed past them and then turned down a narrow alley that I hadn't noticed before. We pivoted on a corner into a leafy lane that ran parallel to the river, close enough to smell the moving water. I followed him to a hole-in-the-wall with a sign over the door that said "1931 Café."

Inside, there was a very small counter, three booths against the wall and a handful of round tables in the middle of the room.

The café was empty except for four old folks gathered around the table nearest the window at the front. A puddle of sunlight gathered there, exhausted from caroming through the glass from outside. Quentin leaned his array of coconut heads against the wall near the door and then steered straight for an empty chair at the table.

There was one more chair, which I took. The four old codgers looked at me over their coffee cups.

"Dis Boy Scout want to learn about old days on the canal," Quentin said. Pointing at me.

Slowly one of them, a slight and withered gent with white hair and a scraggly beard, cleared his throat and began remembering aloud. He told a story about having to captain his family's barge when he was young because his father took ill. When he got to Bristol to get weighed—the boatmen's profits were based on how much higher the barge floated after unloading—he was paid in a crowd of older men, some them rough-looking, and scared that he was being cheated. The agent was impatient, but he fought for his ground and insisted on going over the books a second time. He had to been to school some, and his father had shown him how to do the plusses and minus, but his brain was froze up. He stammered and wanted to cry but just kept saying over and over that he was getting shorted. Finally, the agent gave him a few dollars more and he ran all the way back to the barge and hid the money under a floorboard near the potty.

Then a weathered woman rocked forward. The Delaware Canal was the nicest, she said, and sometimes fancy people would pay for a ride to the next lock. She remembered once a party of young people of means from New York joined their empty barge going light upstream from New Hope. It was during Prohibition, but they had gin that they sipped as the mules moseyed toward Lumberville. Her father told her to stay away from the passengers, but she saw two of the men kissing each other as the barge passed beneath a bridge.

Another old fellow said some drunk fellers tried to piss on their boat as they glided under a bridge. But he conceded that bridges was mostly useful; the boatmen used them to get to the towpath for various purposes. But the stylish way to get from boat to land, he said with a grin, was to vault over the water using one of the long poles that served a variety of purposes on the barges, though it took a little practice. He admitted that he got wet more than once and landed in his share of mule shit.

Once they got going, like a barge behind a good team of mules, the old canal people glided through their memories. They told us about the conch shell horns that boatmen used for signaling in the dark, and about the inns and stores along the canal like the River House at Lock 9, which took overnight guests and sold whatever goods the "inner man" might need. Ferries that crossed the Delaware to link up with canals that went to New York. An old yarn about a great flood in June 1862 that washed out the canal, but the canals were running again by the end of the year, even with so many men away for the war. Some said there was a mythical stretch of canal up into the mountains with locks 30-feet high that had somehow vanished, proving perhaps that the universe had a few things up its sleeves.

They were excited because the commonwealth had been rebuilding locks along the canal that summer, and they were seeing their past come back to life, if only for tourism and public recreation. Almost from the beginning, the railroads had commercially triumphed over the canals, but the Delaware Canal kept delivering coal into the early years of the Depression, despite the floods and roughnecks and men trying to pee on them from bridges.

My head was brimming with the lost folk culture of floating coal to the city, where men would burn it, spewing the Industrial Revolution into the sky as I staggered from the dusty café into the street and found the state road running west back home. It took three rides to get home, and the last one was a 1963 Pontiac Grand Prix Sport Coupe, one of the early edge-line designs, crisp, precise surfaces and smaller headlights and wheels that emphasized the inner space. My driver was a mulish looking guy in his early 30s, shoved incongruously into a white button-down shirt with short sleeves and a hard-knotted tie gripping at his throat. He was smoking when I got in the car, listening to the baseball game on the radio and not even mildly interested in me.

He threw his cigarette into the road in disgust when a Phillies batter struck out with men on second and third, squandering a potential rally. In my mind I attributed the flicking to over-eagerness at the plate, with the go-ahead run on second.

When I got home that evening I was impatient to get through dinner as quickly as I could and get up to the Underwood in the unused bedroom and bilge pump as much canal lore as I could. I was consumed by the idea of people toiling valiantly and giving their lives to feeding civilization's insatiable hunger for light and heat.

I didn't figure this was going to get a merit badge, but of course by then it didn't matter. So the next day I slid my work across the front seat of Speedy's car when he dropped me off at the country club.

32. FRIDAY, AUGUST 9, 1968

1952 CHEVY DELUXE

Summer trudged along. Juliana and I talked a little on the phone, but we did not get together. She sounded far away on the wire, unattached, and it made me wonder if it had always been like that with her and I simply hadn't noticed. Neither of us brought up the weird way our last date ended.

Talking to her on the phone in the dark kitchen—we only had one telephone—I could pretend things were still right between us, or that they could be made right again. I didn't want to know what happened after I left Martine's house, and I was content to let myself think that it was her car that whooshed by me on the road, and she had not recognized me.

But it was hard to reconcile that thought with the remembrance of swimming bare-naked in the creek and wrapping her in a blanket for the ride home from the racetrack.

My father told me that Brady, his editor, had offered to talk to me about my article on canal life, so I hiked downtown after work to the newspaper office and climbed the wide, squeaking staircase to the newsroom with ashtray ambiance. Speedy was studying his notebook, concentrating on his typing.

I slid past the deputy editor's desk slow enough that he would be sure to see me, and poked my head in the semi-private space around Brady's desk. He was talking to a reporter and took note of me. I waited my turn leaning against the doorframe outside his office.

My mind drifted, catching on the occasional steeple, shredding away chunks of cloud.

Brady summoned me from his desk. "This is more like it, junior." He held my latest effort in his hands. "We're gonna have to clean it up some, but it's a nice feature. Just a couple things, though." He was more focused on me than he had been the last time.

"We need the names of these people, and their ages and where they live now. Where did you talk to them?"

"My friend, the guy with the coconut heads, took me to meet them. We were sitting around in a restaurant, like the story says." I hadn't thought to ask for the names of the old canal hands, much less how old they were. They looked old as mules to me.

"You're going to have to get their names or we can't use it," Brady said, passing my story back across the desk to me. "And get some goddamn pictures of them and the canal. Fresh photos of these people, or old family photos, if they have any. If you can't do it, get your dad to help. Tell him you think these people might be warmongers."

I didn't get the impression he was serious about the last bit.

Brady smiled, quickly. Then he stood up, pulling his waistband up under his old-guy belly. "What do you think about Nixon?"

Honestly, I didn't have an opinion on him. People said he had locked up the Republican nomination for president. My father and my sister were both for McCarthy; my mother rarely talked about politics. I thought Nixon's hair was funny.

"I'm not old enough to matter," I said.

"It's hard to believe that sonofabitch is a Quaker. He must be one of them fighting Quakers," Brady said, "a Quaker with a vengeance." I pictured Richard Nixon with a staff and angry white beard, in a robe, with lightning flashing around him, leading his people through the desert.

Brady came around the desk and clapped his hand on my shoulder. "You know what they're saying around the convention now?" He paused. "'Spiro Who?' And they say Republicans have no sense of humor."

I didn't get it, and I guess it showed.

"Nixon picked a nobody as his vice president," Brady explained. "Spiro Agnew, the governor of Maryland. The smart alecks are making fun of the fact that nobody's ever heard of him, that the biggest thing he's ever done is win an award from *Men's Hairstylist and Barber's Journal.*"

Agnew also had led the fight to repeal Maryland's 306-year-old law barring interracial marriage. Later, he shut down Bowie State University when a student protest got too rambunctious.

Usually when I was in my father's office I felt like a kid, hanging around with the grown-ups, but with my edited-up newspaper story in hand and marching orders to go out and finish it, I thought I had risen a notch. I headed to my father's desk, but he was busy and said he needed some more time before he would be ready to go home.

I asked him quietly if he could pick me up at the diner. He winked and gave me two thumbs up.

Juliana smiled, a little awkwardly, I thought, as I headed for a spinning seat at the counter. The booths were separate planets, where the context was the people you were with, the jukebox, and the view out the window. But at the counter your nose was cheek-deep in the diner's business, the waitresses were on display, and the busts of the kitchen staff up to their eyebrows acted out their short-order opera through the pass-through puppet window.

Juliana poured my iced tea, and business was slow enough for her to linger, but we had difficulty making eye contact. I wanted to say I was sorry I had left her at Martine's, but I couldn't find the right words for it, and in truth I was sorry that I wasn't more sorry.

"What have you been up to?" she asked.

Missing you and feeling crappy, I could have said. Instead I mumbled something about meeting with the editor at the newspaper about a merit badge. That brought her eyes to mine, and there was disappointment in them. I should have corrected myself—it wasn't about the merit badge—but I didn't. Maybe it was better if I just let the reasons pile up, I thought.

"How about you?" I asked.

"There's a bunch of us going to see Gary Puckett on Sunday," she said. This seemed at first like an opening to slip back in, for another ride in the '56 Regent, sitting thigh to thigh with her again and, perchance, to grope and wrestle when the show was over. Something's wrong between us, I thought, and we're afraid to let our eyes meet. I realized that she hadn't really asked me to go with her.

And then the awkwardness really fell on us.

She looked at me, her hands busy behind the counter.

"I love you, Juliana," I said quietly, not looking at her. Then, desperate to fill the quiet, I added: "I don't really know what that means."

She started to say something, but I might have been afraid to hear it. "Besides," I interrupted, "we have a family thing on Sunday." This was a lie and probably poorly served. I wasn't sure whether she knew that Saturday was my birthday.

She turned to fill a tray at the kitchen pass-through and did not look back. I knew this wasn't the time or the place, and I swiveled on the stool and walked out through the revolving door.

My father was just pulling into the parking area as the revolving door pushed me outside. I felt like walking home, I wanted my life to just go on ahead without me and I would catch up with it later, but I plopped into the passenger's seat. He asked me how Juliana was and I muttered something uninformative and sighed more theatrically than I intended, and turned to look out the window. We maneuvered into the traffic.

Speedy was in a good mood. "I think I'm getting somewhere on this business about Jimmy," he said. "Matthews tried to tell me that it was a group of club members who were paying for Jimmy's new room and the extra therapy sessions. But when I asked him why, he said they were just interested in the welfare of your mother's brother-in-law. He is not a very good liar."

It was a little annoying that he was in such a good mood. "So when I asked him why they wanted to be anonymous, he said they didn't want their identity known because they were afraid that other needy cases would come calling. When I offered to keep the secret, he said a newspaperman might have a hard time doing that."

We were behind a two-tone 1952 Chevy Deluxe, by then a fuddy-duddy in the social order of the road, round and from the glory years of the Baroque period, finned, and imagining itself to be aircraft. The view from behind was a solid chrome bumper that seemed too close to the road and an oversized bubble trunk that rose with self-importance and big enough to hold a small pony, with smooth wings on each side that bowed in deference to the mighty trunk. The rear wings finished off wheel covers that were completely separate from the raised panel that started at the back door and grew into a massive sidewall, capped with the front headlight. The hood over the engine was its own time-worn Appalachian hilltop, presiding over an overdone constellation of chrome. The windshield was in two pieces, with a chrome bar joining them together.

An older, dark-skinned man with a felt hat was driving, calmly smoking an unfiltered cigarette in his left hand. He was an ash tapper, hence, a possible buttflicker. We stalked him from a polite distance, but close enough that no other traffic could get in the way. Soon, we were off the bearing for home.

My father wasn't done with his story. "But today I found somebody at the club who said the money is coming from just one person, some widow whose husband was in a bad car crash, went in to a coma and then died after a few weeks," my father said as he studied the Chevy.

I didn't know what to say. "I don't know who that could be," I offered.

"It wasn't too hard to find it in our archives," he said. "Some woman named Crick."

That rang a bell for me. "I'm not sure I know her."

"I don't think it's gonna be hard to get in touch with her," he said.

The Chevy approached a covered wooden bridge and edged to the shoulder of the road to wait for an oncoming car to come through. Just as he was entering the bridge, his right hand came up, waving as though he was trying to shoo a bug, and then his left hand got involved and he must have dropped the cigarette because he bolted up in his seat and the next thing we knew he was pitching the cigarette butt out the window like it was a grenade. He pulled onto the one-lane bridge and we slid up the entry to wait until he cleared to the other side.

The bridge spanned a narrow creek. As the Chevy Deluxe crawled forward into the sunlight, we eased into the wooden tunnel, sun splintering through the cracks between the boards of the bridge, glimpsing the summer-dry creek below, and then we too rolled out into the sun.

We followed him up a narrow road that climbed a steep hill and through a gap in the ridge. He turned onto an even smaller road that seemed almost abandoned, and I wondered whether my father would follow him down the rabbit hole. I had covered most of the country roads I could get to by bike or foot, but I didn't recognize this one. That's about all it took for me to stop feeling sorry for myself about Juliana.

My father stayed a nine iron behind the Chevy. At first there didn't seem to be any reason for this road to be, no farm fields or driveways or buildings at all, but of course there is always a purpose and, some believe, a reason. On my side, there were unruly trees posted with no trespassing signs and contained by a half-hearted barbwire fence. My father's side of the road was fenced as well, but there was more open space, and as we turned a corner in the road the Chevy was waiting for us, pointed back in our direction.

There was just enough room for us to squeeze by and he was studying us as my father rolled to a stop, driver to driver, so close that neither of them could have opened his door.

"Evening," my father said, nodding. The Chevy driver was unmoved.

"I noticed you tossed a cigarette out of your car back there at the bridge."

The Chevy driver's eyes narrowed. "Are you following me or something? This is private property back up here, and you don't look like you know the territory."

"Well, yes, we did follow you here, for science. We're studying people. We don't care much about property."

This wasn't scoring any points with the Chevy driver, who showed no intention of pulling forward. An uncomfortable, anxious moment.

"Do you remember throwing the cigarette in the road back there by the bridge?"

"Maybe, but I don't see it's any business of yours."

"It looked like maybe you were swatting at a bee."

"I don't like to smoke in them bridges. I can handle the flies all right."

"But why throw it out in the road?"

"Listen, mister, that's just the way it went down. I told you, I don't like to smoke in them bridges. That's all old timber been soaking up oil and fumes for a long, long time." He was warming up a little.

"I appreciate your time," my father said. "You've been very helpful. I've got something for you for helping us out." He reached around to the back seat and picked up his roll of masking tape and thick black marker. "It's for your car," he said, tearing off a piece of tape and writing I FLICK BUTTS on it and handing it across the short distance between us.

The Chevy driver studied the strip of masking tape for a minute and handed it back. "I don't think so," he said, glaring at us. "Now if you're done wasting my time, I gotta be somewheres."

The problem with this arrangement is that we were both pointed in the wrong direction, with only inches to spare between our gunwales. We inched ahead—Speedy was studying his outside mirror closely—and then around the curve in the road we saw a driveway. Beyond that, the road twisted on farther into the woods. We turned ourselves around in the drive and started back out.

The Chevy was backing up toward us and, again, we edged past each other carefully; now I was face-to-face with him and I nodded, wishing we had left him alone. After we squeezed past each other, I looked in my outside mirror and saw him pull into the driveway. I noticed my father was watching him as well.

In the research journal I wrote "Historic preservation" as the reason for his cigarette toss. Then I added: "May have been bee-induced."

33. SATURDAY, AUGUST 10, 1968

1965 TOYOTA CROWN COUPE UTILITY

My father always gave me a book for my birthday. This started when I was one, my first *Moby*, which he read to me at night for years.

I did not go caddying on my 17th birthday. Speedy and I drove to his brother's convalescent home, my first visit since Uncle James had been moved. According to my father, he was doing better, mumbling parts of words and feeding himself, clumsily.

We loaded a thermos with ice and lemonade and took three waxed-paper cups and stopped to pick up cupcakes, my uncle's favorite treat, at the bakery where my mother and I had gone when I saw my father and Miss Bennett. About six times as we stood in line I thought about asking my father about that day, what he had been doing there with her, but I could never figure out how to phrase it so it didn't sound like an indictment. Mostly, I didn't want to know.

On the road, we came up behind a smoker putting along in a 1965 Toyota utility coupe, one of those oddball concoctions that started off in the front like a normal coupe and changed course behind the front doors to become a pickup truck. It was one of the first Toyotas exported to the U.S., from the second generation of Toyota Crowns that were, ironically, intended to evoke the majesty of the Chrysler Imperial with a grand, wannabe front grill that looked particularly odd on the front end of what was basically a runt-size pickup truck. It landed on our shores just when we were bickering with France and Germany over tariffs they had placed on the import of American chickens. In retaliation, we imposed the so-called chicken tax on imports of brandy, potato starch and light trucks.

Which may explain why real Americans don't drink Courvoisier.

The specimen before us was loaded with two surfboards. The driver, a shirtless fellow with long blond hair and golden tan, held a cigarette in his right hand. He was tapping the top of the seatback along with the music and then, when it became irresistible, drumming with both hands on the steering wheel.

The cigarette flew out into the wind from an overhand right-hand flick. We caught him at a red light a little ways down the road. I was closest to him.

"Hey man, why did you throw your cigarette in the road?" I shouted over the Jefferson Airplane roaring from the coupe end of his Toyota.

"Her rattlin' cough never shuts off," he sang, tuned into the music. Then, in good timing, the signal turned and he putted away from us.

"It's hard to carry a cigarette when you're surfing," my father said.

Uncle James was sitting in a wheelchair beside the window in the shared sitting room in the new suite where he lived, staring at the floor. He seemed to recognize me, which felt like the best thing that had happened between us in a while; although I wasn't sure he had many of the details pinned down. Speedy asked him if he wanted to go outside, more as a social formality to which James made no response. My father took the grips at the back of the wheelchair and piloted him toward the door.

I carried the cupcakes and lemonade and two birthday gifts, one of which was supposed to be for me from Uncle James. My father described to his brother what we were doing and where we were going in considerable detail, trying to put words to whatever experience James was having in his busted-up head.

Outside there was a walled-in garden area. Carp lounged in the shadows of a shallow pool like wealthy degenerates. We parked Uncle James and pulled up chairs for ourselves and watched the fish, while my father continued describing the action, filling in the gaps with memories from their youth, casting for anything that would bite in his brother's mysterious mind.

"It's Izzy's birthday today, Jimmy," my father said. "We've got cupcakes."

I opened up the bakery box of cupcakes and presented them to Uncle James. The icing was sweating a little from the heat, and I thought my uncle's eyes opened a little wider.

"It was the custom," my father said, *"when a great battle was gained there, to barbecue all the slain in the garden of the victor."* Speedy carefully took one of the cupcakes from the box and broke off a corner and raised it to his brother's lips.

"Barcabube be slain," James mumbled, or something like that. In his day, Uncle had been a pretty fair Dick Mobius.

We ate our cupcakes while the carp sauntered about in the dark water. I washed mine down with a cup of lemonade and opened the book from my father, *The Day of Saint Anthony's Fire*. It seemed an odd choice, a detailed history of an outbreak of mass hysteria in a small town in Southern France.

"This happened right about the time you were being born, which I thought was interesting," my father said.

"What's it about?"

"For a few days people suffered from hallucinations and psychosis. The local doctors thought it was ergotism—poisoning from moldy flour—but the disease is so rare, and it hadn't happened for such a long time, that no one knew what to do about it."

"Eventually it goes away?"

"Well, the symptoms do, but some people in that town were scarred for good." He looked at his brother, who likely wasn't getting any of this. Speedy wiped a cupcake crumb from James's chin. "Apparently, their experiences were similar to the effects of LSD, which was discovered only a few years before all this happened by a researcher not so far away who was working with ergot."

I guessed that the book may have been a review copy sent by the publisher to my father's newspaper, rather than something he had gone out and bought specifically for me. Even fallen Quakers are penny pinchers.

The other gift, the one supposedly from Uncle James, was a pair of bell-bottom trousers.

My father was smirking. "Somebody thought you might need a pair," he said.

We sat for a while in the sun, listening to the chatter of wrens. Some other visitors came out with their inmates, but most of them found it too hot and went back inside. After a while we pushed James back inside to join a circle of men in the big social room who were waiting for the next thing to happen. He looked at me when I shook his hand to say goodbye.

Driving to my sister's house, Speedy was excited about the visit. He was convinced that James was getting better. "We owe a lot to this Mrs. Crick," he said. "I gotta talk to her."

"But I thought she wanted to be anonymous," I said.

"Well, I can pretend I don't know who she is."

We went by my sister's house, picked her up and headed home. The four of us put dinner together and ate at the picnic table on the back patio.

Just as we were finishing, Juliana showed up with a cake from the diner where she worked. I thought my parents did a remarkable job pretending there was nothing remarkable about this, but knowing glances were flying around like nobody's business.

When we finally had a moment alone together, I told Juliana how surprised I was.

"This has been in the works for a while," she said. "Your mother asked me to come for dinner, but I had to work. They are really nice."

"When I was little, every time my father talked about headlines I thought he was saying head lice." I realized this was apropos of nothing. "I thought you were mad at me."

"Maybe, but you owe me a swim in this fabulous pool of yours."

And before I knew it, my parents were announcing that they were taking my sister home and I was asking if we could go for a swim in the neighbor's pool and my father said that I should check with the neighbor. As they were getting into the car, Juliana was coming out of hers, with a towel and her swimsuit under her arm and I was following her into the house like a puppy. I showed her to my sister's old room as a place to change and while I was changing could not stop thinking about her in there, however briefly, with no clothes on.

We walked holding hands across the intervening backyard—none of us had fences—to the house with the pool, where the old couple was quietly watching the moon bouncing off their cement pond. They were glad to have people using it and quietly faded into the shadows as we slipped into the water.

Juliana and I stayed in the deep end, elbows up on the lip of the pool, talking about nothing in particular and stopping to slip underwater and see how long we could kiss before one of us would come bursting up for air.

As birthdays go, this was not a bad one.

34. Sunday, August 11, 1968

1966 Plymouth Barracuda

I caught a foursome that went off early that morning to beat the August sun. This strategy sounds good on paper but usually means morning humidity.

I was worn down when the round was over, and my thumb wasn't working and I ended up walking all the way to Acushnet, roughly the same distance as caddying another round without the golf bags and the time it took to watch them hit golf balls and then go find them.

When I got home, my father asked if I wanted to see a movie that evening. Really, I just wanted to take a shower and eat something and find a shady place to collapse. We were far enough into August that we could hear the hooves of summer galloping relentlessly toward school. I was thinking of how to answer when he said the movie was in New York.

"We're going to New York to see a movie?" It was a two-hour drive, plus some.

"It's the North American preview of a new Beatles film!" he said in a hammy announcer's voice. "I got review tickets from the newspaper."

Mother was going, and Juliana was working that evening. If I didn't go to New York, I would be hanging around the empty house by myself.

So it would be the three of us. I took a shower and as I was drying off I smelled the charcoal briquettes through the window. But when I went into my bedroom and lay down, the day got the better of me.

There was a tapping at the door, and the light in my room was different, bluer and cooler.

I pulled on a pair of khakis and then remembered that I had new bell bottoms that seemed like the right thing to wear to the North American premiere of a new Beatles film in New York. I wondered if there would be any actual Beatles there.

My father had barbecued chicken and there was cornbread and coleslaw and bean salad to eat as an early supper before we piled into the car. My parents had become their other selves, people who go to

New York for a show. We tooled through Doylestown and picked up the two-lane U.S. highway that crossed the heart of New Jersey on a mostly straight line toward New York City. The farther we went, the more momentum the party gained; behind us, the sun was easing westward toward where the buffalo roam. The road became four lanes, swirled around a few rotaries and joined up with bigger highways. New Jersey thickened like pasta sauce as we hurtled for Manhattan.

I glimpsed the city skyline just before we dove into a tunnel, and then came out the other side, suddenly there, in the vast urban canyon lands. Leaning my head out the window, I took the city in the face.

By then it was dark. We rolled along block by block, doggy-paddling with a school of yellow cabs. My father seemed to know where he was going; my mother and I were enjoying just being there. Finally he steered us into a small parking lot and told the attendant we would be back around midnight.

We walked a few blocks smeared with human debris and came to a building with a gaudy marquis hanging improbably out over the sidewalk and a two-story sign overhead proclaiming it to be the Fillmore East. Outside, a motley cast milled about. The sign read: "Magical Mystery Tour, a Benefit for the Liberation News Service."

My father talked to some people in the entrance to the theater and came back to us. "There's a party we can go to before the show," he said, pointing across the street. He took my mother's hand and headed out into the street as though he owned it. They were going to jaywalk through a cataract of mad traffic and I had no good choice but to keep up.

The only bar I had ever been to was the one where my mother worked, in the safe and antiseptic country club. But I followed my parents into a crowded, smoky city saloon where people were packed in shoulder to shoulder. I found a spot along the wall, not far from the door and watched as Speedy guided my mother toward the bar and ordered drinks for them.

They were soon enough sipping beers and chatting with people around them whom they could not have known. That's what they were good at.

The conviviality became more loudly convivial. I noticed my foot was tapping to the music beating through the din of laughter. Standing nearby, a guy a little older and taller than me, who seemed out of place.

He nodded in time with the music and then before I knew it, we were on the same page, sharing this experience.

More people pushed into the bar and then the tide began to turn and people started leaving. My new friend said something about it being time to go to the Fillmore, and I remembered that was the name on the theater. Somehow my parents were gliding out the door with a group of boisterous people. I thought it best to keep them in sight.

Unbelievably to me, the whole party crashed across the street in the middle of the block, riling cab drivers into a horn-beeping frenzy. Enough people who don't give a damn can change traffic. There was a logjam of people outside the theater, spilling into the street, and then the doors opened and we streamed inside. Nobody ever asked for tickets.

There was a movie screen set up on the stage. The house lights were up and it was noisy with people talking. And smoking. And drinking. I sat with my new friend a few rows behind my parents near the aisle. A joint came down the row. I waved it around in front of my face and passed it along. I figured that if the police came and arrested everybody in there for possession that I would at least have something with more swagger than unlawful wading on my criminal record.

Then the lights went down and after a pause the screen crackled to life. My first impression was that this was an elaborate home movie for which someone had, hurriedly, taken the trouble to design costumes and sets. While a narrator spoke over the film, Ringo and a very large woman called his aunt were walking up a treeless city street. She stops to rest. "For goodness sake," Ringo says, "will you stop that sitting down?"

I thought this was funny, but no one else seemed to.

There was an anxious quiet in the theater. I did not know it at the time, but the film had aired on British television over the previous Christmas holiday. It was a dud, everyone agreed.

The Beatles were riding a bus with two tour leaders, a wide-eyed and overly excited man in a white outfit and a woman trying very hard to be mysterious. Some of the people on the bus were more creepy than funny. It's a fine line.

Then Paul sang "Fool on the Hill" while standing on the top of a hill. Again, I was the only one laughing when he came skipping down the slope.

My new friend became agitated during a long scene in which a military man spewed gibberish in a movie set made to look like a cheesy office. A matador worked with a stuffed bull, and an inhuman sound came from my neighbor. There was an instrumental version of "She Loves You" playing over a tug of war among kids out in a field, but the camera angles kept shifting, shredding the little bit of continuity the scene had going for itself.

A few people close to us turned away from the movie and started talking among themselves.

There was some kind of race involving the Magical Mystery Tour bus, which was on the verge of tipping over, and people running on foot. I heard my friend gasp "What the fuck" in exasperation. Back on the bus for a moment and then the scene jumped to a laboratory where the Beatles fussed about in wizard costumes. Instead of musical geniuses, they looked like guys who were in this film because they had lost a bet, and I could feel another slice of the audience turn away from the film like a slab of glacier calving into the sea.

Back on the bus, mercifully.

Then, Paul on the beach pushing a midget around on a bicycle to an instrumental version of "All My Loving." This soothed my friend, momentarily. Then, he was undone by the walrus scene. "What the hell!" he yelled, and slapped two corners of his skull. "Is this a fucking movie or real life?" People turned around to look at him. I tried to assure him that it was a movie, but I don't think he heard me. The song ended with a group of people dressed as eggs walking single-file under a large white sheet, following the bus.

My friend was shaking his head from side to side. His leg was twitching. The movie was again back on the bus. Ringo was freaking out, and his aunt advised him to not get "historical." I thought we were getting back on track, but then we watched John, as a waiter, shoveling food at a patron in a motorway restaurant.

The whole cast piled into a small white tent pitched in a field, like a circus trick with too many clowns climbing into a car. In the tent they watched a movie: George performing "Blue Jay Way." This annoyed my neighbor considerably, but not me. I had noticed a stagehand running in the background of the scene with a fog-making device. When the movie in the tent ends, the magical mystery tourists get back on the bus, which runs over the tent.

I thought for a moment that my neighbor had simply given up, but when I looked at him I saw that he was deeply entranced. The tourists had gone into a nightclub where a band—the Bonzo Doo Dah Dog

Band—performed "Death Cab for Cutie." By and by, a stripper joined the act. This calmed my friend.

The finale featured the Fab Four in white tuxedos on a lavish Hollywood musical set, soft-shoeing down a massive staircase, lip-synching to "Your Mother Should Know." All around them dancers swirled in crinoline skirts. It was really quite beautiful, I thought, and comforting. Then the music segued to "Magical Mystery Tour" and suddenly the cast (and others, including children) began to run towards the camera in a crescendo.

The narrator came back. "This was the Magical Mystery Tour," he said. "I told you. Goodbye."

The credits began rolling, and there was a smattering of applause. When the house lights came back up, my friend was crouched in the aisle, his arms wrapped around his head, rocking fetal-like. This, I surmised, was not good.

When I leaned over to ask if he was all right, there was no response, as though he had checked out and left his body there on the floor of the Fillmore East.

"What's wrong with your friend, man?" a very hippie guy said to me.

"I don't know. I don't think he liked the movie."

"What's he tripping on?"

There were many levels on which I couldn't answer this question. I just shrugged.

People were milling around chatting. He was still on the floor when my parents found me. "What do we have here?" my father asked.

"I don't know his name. He was acting weird during the movie, like it was scaring him or something, and then he just collapsed on the floor."

To my surprise, my father crouched down next to him. "Are you tripping?" he asked.

The kid peeked over his shoulder at my father.

"Was it purple blotter paper?"

The kid nodded.

"When did you drop?"

I couldn't hear what the kid said, but my father looked at his watch. "This is going to be okay," he said. "How 'bout if we hang out together here for a while?" The kid didn't fight it when my father took his hand, and then Speedy reached his other hand to me and Mother took my other hand and we three knelt down on the floor, closing the circle with the kid. The four of us settled into an impromptu orbit while people milled around us. Inch by inch, my nameless friend began to sit up and look around.

"Sometimes in the first hour or so it can get scary," my father said. "You just have to be brave about it and go ahead. Your head is moving way faster than the rest of you, faster than you usually go, but you are still here in your body and everything will get back in step pretty soon. My advice is to accept the fact that things are temporarily not normal. But that's because of the acid, not you. People get freaked out all the time, even without taking acid—at least you've got an excuse."

"What was that movie about?" the kid asked.

"When it started, nobody knew exactly where they were going, and one idea just led to another. I think they were trying to find something in the clutter. *There is a sweet mystery about this sea, whose gently awful stirrings seem to speak of some hidden soul beneath.* You couldn't figure it all out if you were straight, so you might as well relax."

The kid was staring, suddenly love-struck, at my mother, who had that effect on people. He blurted out, "You're so pretty," without any hint of self-consciousness.

This was not news to me or my father, but we liked to hear other people say it. I don't think my mother minded it at all.

"You know, I met a young woman here tonight who is planning to protest at the Miss America pageant next month in Atlantic City," my mother said. "She's with the Liberation News Service, and they're going to make a newsreel about the objectification of women. When I told her that I was a contestant at the Miss Delaware pageant years ago, I don't think she knew exactly what to do with that."

"You were Miss America?"

"No, I didn't even come close," Mother laughed. "A lot of those girls were really intense, and I was just there for the adventure. It did make me feel pretty."

"Wow, a real Miss America."

My mother and father laughed. "Something like that," she said. "But it's time for us to get up from the floor, motherfucker."

And she and my father pulled the kid to his feet. He was looking somewhat more at ease, but unwilling to give up the circle of hand-holding. "I have an evening gown competition in a few hours, and we are miles from home," she said.

We stood around with our new friend, chatting him up, trying to signal where the landing strip was. Eventually we got from him that he was actually there at the show with some other people who were on the same trip, whom we found mercilessly ripping through a bag of potato chips. Our nameless friend forgot all about us the moment he rejoined his tour group.

We were walking in the cool city evening back to the parking lot, talking about how strange and unpolished the film was, and not much of a match for the music. I asked Speedy how he knew what to say to the kid, and he told me his brother knew all about that sort of thing from his job.

At that point, a fire-engine red 1966 Plymouth Barracuda rolled down the street with a smoker behind the wheel. He seemed to flick the butt almost directly at us, although it was an off-speed pitch that landed away in the middle of the street. "Hey," my father yelled, and then the light turned red in front of the Barracuda. My mother and I watched in amusement as Speedy loped off to do more research.

He went right up to the driver's window, put his hands on the top of the door, and started a conversation we couldn't hear. The Barracuda driver did not seem particularly annoyed. For all I know, there may be special rules in effect at a certain hour of the night, especially in highly concentrated urban spaces.

The 1966 Barracuda was a spaceship car, a sweeping fastback window pitched over angled lines and squared-off heirloom fins. Light on the chrome, it featured a bold, forward lean toward a boxy front end that plowed shark-like through the road ahead. It actually looked a little like a barracuda.

The light turned green and the Plymouth swam away, leaving my father still standing in the street. He danced past traffic coming from behind him and rejoined us, breathless, happy.

When I was young, I never needed a puppy.

"He said he throws his cigarettes in the street because the bums want to smoke too," Speedy said, smiling broadly. "You don't hear that one in Doylestown."

We didn't have bums in our town, or at least none that I knew of.

On the way home, I fell asleep in the back seat, listening to my father sing "So I let out my wings and then I blew my horn. Bye-bye New Jersey, I become airborne."

35. SATURDAY, AUGUST 17, 1968

1964 AUSTIN-HEALY 3000 MARK III

I hitchhiked into town early in the morning and got dropped off about a mile away from the country club, a pleasant walk on a morning that was cooler and drier. The sun was swinging around more southerly on the compass.

I had been reading the weird book my father gave me for my birthday and realized that August 17 was the day the good people of Pont-St.-Esprit began their descent into psychedelic hell.

Good weather brought the golfers out in numbers, and there was a mixed-foursome tournament with a shotgun start, meaning each group started at a different tee. The caddy master pointed me to two bags that belonged to a pair of older guys who played together all the time, usually as a team, and finished each other's sentences. There was another kid carrying the two women's bags.

Eventually, I noticed that the name tag on one of the women's bags said M. Crick. She was an athletic woman somewhere past the mid-century mark, as best as I could tell, with a cheerful determination. Of course, I couldn't say anything to her about my uncle because nobody was supposed to know.

She was likeable enough, although she didn't look like someone who had enough extra money to pay for the care of invalids she didn't know. Her golf bag was well used, and her clubs weren't anything special, as far as I knew, and she seemed, well, normal. Of course, some people advertise their bank accounts in their golf outfit, but a lot of golfers stick with what makes them comfortable.

So much the better for Uncle James, I thought.

After the tournament was over, I waited for another round and after a while went out with a threesome, a walker with two guys in a cart. It was a snappy round trying to keep up with the motorized cart, and the course was fairly open.

When it was over, I was pleasantly worn out. There were still groups going off for nine holes, but not many caddies. I was cleaning clubs in the member bag storage when the caddy master poked his head in and asked if I wanted to shag balls.

This was usually a last resort. The money was pitiful, and you were basically a live target. I looked over the caddy master's shoulder. Martine was waiting in the pro shop.

"He's not even a member," I said.

"He just joined. I told him I didn't think there was anybody around, but I guess he saw you in here." The caddy master looked like he wanted to go home himself. "You don't have to. You been out twice already."

"Another half hour won't kill me."

I went into the pro shop where Martine was looking at golf clubs. "You need someone to shag balls?"

He said he wanted to work on his short irons. "I can pick them up myself," he offered.

"I'll shag balls for about a half hour and then I gotta get a ride home with my mother."

He paused and then looked at me. "Your mother?"

"She works at the bar. You've met her, Suzanne Yardley."

"Oh," he smiled. "I didn't know her last name."

So we headed side by side without saying anything, down the hill and around the back of the 18th green, past the swimming pool of squealing country-club children to the driving range. I propped his golf bag up on an iron stand. He dumped his bag of practice balls on the ground and began to loosen up. I jogged out on the range with the empty bag.

The whole trick with shagging balls is to stay at an angle so that you don't lose the shots in the sun.

Martine started with his short irons, snapping shots on high trajectories that would pause at a corner in the sky and come rushing to a thump on the turf beside me. As long as I could see the launch, I had a decent chance of reading any bend in the shot.

He worked his way back through the irons, and the landing area began to spread out. I lost what I think was a four iron and was surprised to hear it plunk down a few yards behind me. Martine must have seen that I had lost it because he held up his arms questioningly. I just turned and hustled after it. After that, I hung a bit farther back from the mortar fire.

After about a half hour he waved me in. There were a few balls scattered here and there to pick up on my way in. When I got there, I reached for his golf bag, but he shook me off and took it on his shoulder himself, leaving me with just the ball bag. It felt a little funny, being from the forecastle, to carry a lighter load than the country club member. And then he invited me to have a drink with him on the patio, where a waitress came and asked us what we wanted.

I needed something to say.

"I saw you in a photograph my dad took over at the canal a few weeks ago." I wasn't sure why I brought this up, except that I had been thinking about taking photographs for my canal story.

The waitress came back with my lemonade and his gin and tonic.

Martine was flipping through the deck of memories in his head and found one that matched. "I was there when Justice Douglas was there. I know there were reporters around, but I didn't realize anybody was taking my picture."

He looked at his drink. "What's your interest in the canal?" he asked.

"I'm writing a newspaper article about the old-timers who used to work on the barges."

Then I asked him what I really wanted to know. "Why did you let Juliana get drunk at your house?"

"This is going to be in your story about the canal?" He was trying to make a joke.

"No." I wasn't.

"Of all people," Martine said, "I am not the one to stop anybody from drinking. But I would rather see a kid stoned when there are people around to take care of her and make sure she gets home okay."

He paused a few seconds and then asked what may have been on his mind all along. "Why did you leave her?"

I fidgeted with the paper napkin under my lemonade. "I should have stayed to make sure she got home okay, but I was pissed. You let her drive home that night." I think I glared at him. "I saw her bombing along the road while I was walking home."

Martine thought this over. "That wasn't her. I had Lee drive her home."

"But her car ..."

"It was her car, but she wasn't driving. He is a long-distance runner, a marathoner. I met Lee at the prison camp at Koje-do in Korea during the war. He deserted the North Korean army by running over a hundred miles across the front to the south. Since he's been here with me, he's run every road in this county, mostly at night."

"So he drove her home and then ran all the way back to your house?"

"That's what he does."

"Is he going to run here today and drive you home?" I looked at the cocktail in front of him.

Martine half smiled. "I had it bad and then a friend of mine helped me back to dry land. But I guess the undertow got me."

There didn't seem to be a lot more to say and so we sat there quietly finishing our drinks. I was glad when it was over.

Riding home with my mother, we pulled up behind a creamy 1964 Austin-Healy 3000, the biggest and most lavish of the line, though small compared with most of the other fishes on the seas in those days. It was originally intended to be a peppy, poor man's Jaguar.

Two teenage girls wearing bathing suits were smoking in the front seats; the top was tucked under the convertible cover. They were poster children for the good life.

The Austin-Healy had an un-American trunk, a half clamshell curving down to the bumper. The brake lights and running lights were mounted on top of each other, where the fin would have been had it been born in the U.S. instead of an Italian design studio. The trunk was well-fitted, with matching chrome hinges at the top and a svelte lock at the bottom. The car was signed in raised chrome script at the lower right corner of the trunk, like a painting. It was the last model in the Austin-Healy line; the Healy part of the hyphenation left the partnership in 1968.

The girls held their cigarettes on well-tanned arms out at a distance from the car. There was little doubt what would happen when they became bored with smoking. At the next stop, one after the other, they dropped the cigarettes from their hands, laughed at some joke, and zipped away when the signal changed.

"What are we going to do about that?" my mother asked.

We caught them at the next light, the last one before the road left town. I was feeling something, and got out of our car and trotted up to the passenger side. They were girls from my school, wealthy, popular girls. They were wearing bikinis, looked fantastic, and knew it. All I had going for me was that I was clearly deranged or, at best, interplanetary.

"Hey," I said. They stared at me. I could feel the light changing. "Why did you drop your cigarettes in the road?"

The girls looked at each other and laughed, two princesses tucked in soft brown leather. "Where else could we put them?" the driver said, looking down at one another's bikini tops. "We didn't want to get ashes all over." And they were gone. I waited for my mom to roll ahead and pick me up.

"They are wearing bikinis. I guess that means you can do whatever you want."

My mother smiled. "You know, the bikini was invented by a French engineer right after the war. It was named for an atoll in the Pacific."

I was picturing a Frenchman with a slide rule trying to figure out how to cover and support key female features with as little fabric as possible.

"We started testing nuclear bombs on Bikini right when the swimsuit was invented. We set off 23 bombs; the last one was just 10 years ago." My mother pulled a cigarette out of her purse and lit it. "The U.S. government this week said it is now okay for the people who lived there to go back." She inhaled and blew smoke out the window on her side and then looked at me.

"Promise me you will never go anywhere that's been used for testing nuclear bombs, no matter what the government says," she said.

"I won't, Mom."

"I can tell you one thing," she said, tapping ashes into the ashtray.

"What's that?"

"LBJ did not ask Lady Bird if it was all right to let people back on Bikini, and you can bet he won't send his kids or grandkids there."

36. Wednesday, August 21, 1968

1959 Lincoln Premiere

I told my father that I had caddied in a foursome with Mrs. Crick, but had not talked to her much. He was full of questions that I couldn't answer.

Speedy agreed that it would be better if Mother talked to Mrs. Crick, without letting her know that we knew she was the secret benefactress, and to tell her in general terms how grateful the family is that someone was helping Jimmy and that he seemed to be getting better.

I wasn't sure he could stick to that plan, but I hoped so.

Summer was changing. The heat was drying out, the sunlight softening.

I was hitching home from work. A 1959 Lincoln Premiere, one of the biggest cars ever built in America, was heading my way. It was the hard top, a dull bronze body and white roof, quad headlights, a pair stacked on top of each other with a huge, low-slung massif of chrome anchoring the front of the car to the road. The Premiere rolled halfway off the paved road onto the gravel shoulder where I was standing, a luxury yacht from a lost harborage of car design. You could not look away from its wings, which took off from the back wheels, jutting from the frame of the car like epaulettes on a Rushmorian military costume.

I opened the door to a spacious interior in brown and white leather, a steering wheel that looked a yard wide in diameter, a dashboard without borders. The driver, a man in his early 30s, was smoking a cigarette. He was also crying.

Not sobbing; tears were tracking down his cheeks and his eyes were red. He was not trying to regain his composure.

"Are you okay?" I asked.

He wasn't making any move to resume driving, and I wondered whether he had actually pulled over to give me a ride or was simply stopping in despair.

He pointed to the radio with the cigarette smoldering between his fingers. "Did you hear what dey did?"

My first thought was that someone else had been assassinated. "Who?"

"The fucking Russians. Dey invaded Czechoslovakia." I was dimly aware that things were happening in Czechoslovakia, that there had been protests and upheaval in the government. But I couldn't pick it out on a map, and 1968 was lousy with revolutions.

"Those poor Czech bastards thought dey had a deal with the Soviets, just like we did, but Russians don't like the smell of freedom, even socialist freedom," he said, his voice thick.

"I'll be honest with you," I said, fascinated by the cigarette that was burning down closer to his bare knuckles. It had no filter, so he could smoke it as far as he dared. "I don't know anything about Czechoslovakia."

He turned his blurry look at me, ready to gush.

"I am Hungarian. I come to this country in 1956 on U.S. Navy ship sent by Dwight D. Eisenhower." He pushed the ivory colored knob of the gearshift attached to the steering column counterclockwise a couple of notches to put the car in park. He threw the cigarette butt over his left shoulder into the road.

"I am a socialist, but I am not so socialist to refuse help from your Republican president to live in America. In Hungary, the Russians invaded us. But before that, we had democracy for about 10 minutes after the war ended. Then the Stalinists took our government from us slice by slice, like cutting off a salami." He made slashing motions with his right hand across his left arm. "Soon dey had control of state police, ran the country and sent our money to Moscow because some of us had been allies with the Nazis. But that's a fucking nother story."

He reached in his shirt pocket and pulled out a new cigarette and pushed the car lighter into position to do its business.

"This lasted seven years." He waited for the lighter to pop out and raised the glowing coil to the end of his next cigarette. A whiff of smoke blew toward his eyes, but he soldiered through it. "We became a very poor country and nobody was happy, not even the bosses. Stalin died and suddenly again birds were singing and flowers colored.

"We had a reformer, though not a very good one, not as good as the Czechs had this summer, and on 23rd October 1956, students at university made a union that was prohibited. I marched with them in Budapest and we took down the statue of Stalin. Only his boots were left, and we put Hungarian flags in them.

"Then we go to radio building, which had state police in it. Dey don't like crowd of 200,000 crazy Hungarians, so dey start shooting at us. But we don't go away. The army comes, but they would rather be with the people, so dey tear the red stars from their hats and won't help the police. We are singing 'We won't be slaves,' which is forbidden by the puppets.

"The whore government asks the Russians for help, and the tanks came, but dey don't really do much. Just like when tanks first go to Czechoslovakia this week. Our reformer makes a new government, even with some non-communists on it, but we are still a socialist state—we just want to be our own nation and manage our own affairs—like the Czechs now."

A long exhale of smoke into the vast expanse of the Lincoln. "For a few days, it is the hunky dunky. Russians say this can be worked out peacefully. Same now for the Czechs; dey think dey made a deal with the Russians a couple weeks ago. Dey promise to be good socialists, and this is sincere." He stopped for a moment and thought about something.

"I don't know what made the Russians fuck the Czechs. For us, people say it was a mob that attacked party building and killed some polices. Dey showed newsreels of this in Russia and sudden it's no good anymore to let Hungarians think dey are free socialist people. The tanks shut down Budapest, shoot everybody. New government takes over. Birds stop singing."

Neither of us said anything.

"What about your family?" I asked.

He sighed. "I was 22 and trained as metalworker. My father told me to leave, find a new life in a free country because Hungary would only be prison. He said I should send for him when I am settled. I left home with a suitcase and walked to the Austrian border. In refugee camp, I was put in a group going to America because I said I had uncle here. I didn't, but nobody checked. So I was put on Dwight D. Eisenhower's navy ship and sent to New York City."

"Did you get your father?"

He spoke as if he had lived that pain so many times that there was only numbness there. "No, he died a few years after I leave. Momma is still there, but she don't want to go anywhere now. It's a shame because Hungarians are good socialists, just not very good Russian slaves."

He sucked again on the cigarette and turned back to the steering wheel, a little more at peace.

"*What are the sinews and souls of Russian serfs and Republican slaves but fast-fish, whereof possession is the whole of the law,*" I mused. The driver looked at me and shrugged.

"Can I ask you one more question?"

"Sure." He had pulled the transmission lever back into drive and was sliding into a space in the traffic, the cigarette clenched in his lips.

"Why do you throw your cigarettes in the street?"

He looked at me and smiled. "Hey, motherfucker, I'm a little anarchist, too."

This is how anarchism made it into the study, already overrun by atheism.

1955 DeSoto Fireflite

When I was more with Juliana, Fridays were an open horizon of northern lights exploding in possibilities. It had turned around so quickly, and I had to try to remember why I was not with her as much, even when were together, and that was not so fucking easy to do.

Hitching home from work, I could not catch a ride home. I thought I had a couple of bites there in the early evening light at my usual spot, but every time I looked, my hook was bare.

It was so bad that my dad stopped for me.

"Wow," he said. "How long have you been at it?"

"Seems like hours, but it was probably 20 minutes."

"Even I had second thoughts."

I knew what he was talking about. It had been a long, hot sweaty day at the country club and I was feeling every bit as bedraggled as I looked. Beside Speedy in our dusty DeSoto, I shifted to autopilot, relaxing in the stream of the air blowing through the open windows.

A car suddenly rushed up alongside us on the driver's side, tooting his horn. The driver was waving. My father hit the brakes, allowing the two-tone (pale green and forest green) 1955 DeSoto Fireflite—the same year as my father's—to rumble ahead of us, without a lot of room to spare before oncoming traffic whizzed toward us from the other direction.

The driver was waving his left hand out the window. "I know this guy," my father said, and then I noticed that he had an I FLICK BUTTS bumper sticker. The Fireflite had a magnificent chrome bumper with two vertical pieces nearly a foot high that stood like sentries on each side of the license plate holder. A large V was over the keyhole, and an arching "Desoto" at the point where the trunk curved toward the rear window. Its fins were nothing special, but it had an oversized constellation of lights over slabs of chrome that wrapped around the fin. The car reminded me of the shoes Harry Truman might have worn with a tuxedo. The best part was the grille, a toothy shark grin in a forward slant with excessive chrome around the hood latch. Trails of chrome flew back along the front fins from the headlights.

The Desoto driver suddenly lit a cigarette, and my father laughed, waving to him from inside our windshield.

"I met this guy a couple weeks ago and he was really happy, excited even, to get the butt-flicker's bumper sticker. 'Sock it to me, man,' he said."

I turned and got the research logbook from the back seat and flipped back a few entries. There in my father's handwriting was the time and date and type of vehicle and the simple note: "Subject appears to really enjoy everything, including throwing things."

"So do we give him another entry, or just note it with this one?"

"Well, he hasn't thrown it out yet." But Speedy had just finished this observation when the cigarette went somersaulting out into the middle of the road. For good measure, he threw a bottle of some kind out the passenger window.

"I'll give him extra credit on his first entry," I said, noting the date of the second sighting and a citation that he was still enjoying throwing things. When I looked up, he was gone. I held the logbook on my leg for a minute, thinking about all the happy smokers out there, driving along with the whole world for an ashtray.

"I saw your entry in there about the Hungarian," my father said.

I re-pictured him, crying through clouds of smoke. "I felt stupid for not knowing anything about it. The Hungarians or the Czechs or any of it."

"The Czechs had a mostly independent kingdom within the Holy Roman Empire," my father said. "They had a university, and a Czech priest named Jan Hus started a reformation around 1,400, a century before Martin Luther. 'Seek the truth, hear the truth, learn the truth, love the truth,' Hus said.

"The Bohemian nobility adopted this reformed vision, but Rome didn't like it. The church lured Hus in, tried him for heresy and burned him at the stake. Then it declared crusades to stamp out the Hussite movement. The crusades flopped, and eventually Martin Luther covered a lot of the same ground as Hus.

"After World War II, the Allies let Stalin have Czechoslovakia as a puppet state. Now, the Russians are trying to crush them again. A Czech journalist wrote that it is the Russians, not the Czechs, who are at the crossroads of history, with tanks and hungry soldiers who don't understand why they were sent there. A slave cannot be a friend, he said, and a tyrant cannot have friends."

We were almost home.

"During the riots outside the Democratic convention, while the Chicago police were beating up the First Amendment, someone held up a placard that said 'Welcome to Prague.' McCarthy told the demonstrators he was happy to address the government in exile."

After supper that night, I called Juliana's house, but her mother said she was still working at the diner. She asked me how I was in a way that was more than just something people say to one another. I told her I was doing all right, and there was a pause before she said Juliana would be home around 10. It sounded like a suggestion.

I decided to walk over to her house, which was a couple of miles away. I spent a lot of time walking that summer, behind lawnmowers, lugging golf bags around those 18 flags. *As I was thus walking, uttering no sound, except to hail the men aloft, sometimes insight would emerge from the tossing or rolling of one foot in front of another.*

Her house was mostly dark when I got there and the Fairlane was dozing in the driveway. I didn't know where her bedroom was or much about the layout of the house. It was a split level built over a basement that opened out onto the back yard, which was lower than the front. Lights burned in separate corners of the house.

I scouted around the back and I was not surprised to find the black-and-white glow of the portable television casting creepy shadows on her father's face. He was staring into the screen, out there in the August night, with a beer can in hand.

Her dad was only a little startled when I stepped out of the night into his cathode-ray campfire. Maybe this happened to him all the time. "We are getting killed by the fucking Braves," he said, as though we all took communion in the misery of the Phillies, with just one National League trophy to show for all those years of trying.

I came around and looked over his shoulder. Little men in gray were scratching themselves and spitting while they waited for something to happen in the timeless ballet of inspirational geometry that is modern American baseball.

"Is Juliana home?" I asked.

"I dunno. Did you see the Ford?" Then something bad happened again in the television and he groaned. But he was unable to tear himself away from the suffering.

"Yup, it's in the drive."

"Then she's prob'ly in her room." He couldn't tear himself away from the unfolding Phillies disaster.

I circled around to the front of the house. A picture window was lit up, but I guessed that it was her mother sitting in the living room. The other light was in a back corner, and on my way there I came across a ladder stored along the side of the house. All of a sudden, it seemed like a good idea to hoist the ladder and peep into the lighted corner window.

Gentle reader, please note that this is usually not a good idea.

However, insurrection was a thing in those days. I raised one track of the ladder to the appropriate length and managed to lean it with little fanfare against the house, right below the beckoning window.

At that point in my life, I was a lot more familiar with work on the surface of the earth. So climbing the wobbly ladder was enlightening. Each rung brought me closer to the Beach Boys, spinning around on Juliana's record player. Though the middle rungs were wobbly, the climb became more stable at the top and even seemed the right place to be. She was lying face-down on her bed, her foot keeping beat.

Happy times together we could be spending, I hummed along.

I waited until the song was over, and then tapped on the window frame just loud enough to be heard.

Again, it was hard to surprise these people. She looked up, but couldn't tell what was going on out in the dark on the other side of the screen. Like it was an everyday thing, she got up and came over to raise the screen.

"Look at you," she said, leaning forward to be kissed. There are some tactics that work nearly every time. Our lips lingered there, remembering.

"I'm sorry I left you at Martine's. I should have stayed."

"I got home all right," she said. I could see in her face that it had upset her. "But I couldn't figure out why you left."

"I don't know myself." I wondered at that point what I was doing on a ladder at her window.

"Then you told me you love me," she said, her eyes brimming, "and you left before I could even turn around."

"I'm sorry about that, too."

"Sorry that you love me, or sorry that you left so quickly?"

"I am okay with how I feel about you, but I maybe should have waited till I knew what I was talking about."

She thought that over. "Until you knew what the fuck you were talking about?"

"Yes, that." We smiled at each other.

"Just because we're in love doesn't mean we have to always agree, you know," Juliana said.

That plural pronoun was one of the most wonderful things anyone had ever said to me.

"Do you know what our highlight has been, so far, for me?" she asked.

I was sifting through possibilities, glad that there was a "so far" in there.

"Skinny-dipping in the creek."

"Before or after the criminals tried to steal our clothes?"

"I mean all of it. As we were walking back to the car I kept thinking to myself, 'Where's he going to take me next, the black hole of Calcutta?'"

"Sheesh, I wouldn't know where to begin."

Having climbed as high as I could on that ladder, I lingered there with her, the two of us like a pair of idiots, making out through her open bedroom window. And yet when I climbed back down the ladder, I wondered if we had gotten as high as we would get.

38. SUNDAY, AUGUST 25, 1968

1948 FORD

I thought that if I waited until another Sunday rolled around, I would be able to find Quentin and the canal people back at the café mulling over old times. I borrowed my father's camera and figured I would leave it in the pro shop while I got in a round of caddying.

The fishing was lousy that morning. Although I had my thumb in the current of traffic early, I had miserable luck. Finally I gave up and started walking backward, the summer sun climbing up my back. When I got to the country club, there were a number of guys ahead of me in the caddy queue, and the only way you got to jump ahead of your spot was if a member asked for you specifically. It was warming up quickly, and it was discouraging to watch so many foursomes go off with electric carts.

I finally got a round, but was a plodding, tedious business with a foursome that was making a mess of an only passable morning. Then, when we were on the sixth hole, the sirens on the county jail began shrieking like ravens, disrupting church services and peaceful family breakfasts and children looking in their gardens for worms and married people staring past one another in the living room.

The jail, one of the oldest penitentiaries still operating in the state, was adjacent to the country club property. Once in a great while, someone managed to escape, and the usual first choice was across the open spaces of the golf course.

Police swarmed in from the dead-end residential street at the top of the hill, though none of us on the golf course could see any escaped prisoners. The protocol was that we were to stay where we were until the jail gave an all-clear signal. I sat on the firm bottom of my biggest bag in the middle of the fairway sniffing for the fallout of chaos erupted from a dusty granite cell.

I was half hoping my golfers would abandon the round and head to the clubhouse, but after a long half hour the jail siren sounded the all clear. The interruption did nothing to improve the quality of play in our foursome. In fact, they were making a bigger hash of it than before the social order temporarily came unglued; and after one of my golfers made a particularly ghastly approach shot, I think I actually muttered, not completely under my breath, "For the love of Pete, take a lesson."

I was never sure whether my client heard this, or whether he was so disgusted with his play that he pretended that I didn't exist for the rest of the round.

By the 18th hole, we were all glad it was over, caddies and golfers alike. I took my money—the golfer-who-needed-lessons gave me a 50-cent tip. I wanted to give it back, but didn't, and instead retrieved my father's camera and headed for the highway.

But this day wasn't going to get any better. It took some time before I caught a ride in a battered 1948 Ford. It was the last of the post-war Fords, a remnant of classic automobile architecture made at a time when the industry was already shifting to more modern soft-shell designs. In a year, Ford would blast right through the frontier to rocket designs with the 1949 model. The driver wore farmer overalls. There were piles of stuff in the back seat, and the seats were frayed. He had pop-riveted sheet metal onto the floorboard beneath the front passenger seat, and I could almost feel the road rushing like rapids under my feet. It had triangular jib windows in the front doors that could be pointed against the current to blow more air into the cabin, and there were outdoor vents from the hood into the leg space. It was summer, and getting on in the afternoon, but the overall sensation was not unpleasant.

We rode in silence for a while and then he offered me a cigarette, which I declined, and he finally asked where I was going. I told him the river, and he said he wasn't going that far, but then he ended up driving me into New Hope anyway. As I got out of the car, he seemed to be finishing with his cigarette. I asked him if I could throw it away for him.

He looked at me with a queer expression, old farmer blue eyes burning bright from a deeply sun-burnt face, his hands gnarled by a lifetime behind a tractor wheel. He took another draw on the cigarette and handed it to me, who was still standing in the open door. "Help yourself," he said.

I got out of the car and looked back. "I was going down this dusty road, like Woody Guthrie, feeling I didn't want to be mistreated," I said. "And then you stopped and picked me up."

"Those whistles blow for all of us, son. You just take her easy."

"Do you ever throw them in the road?" I asked, looking at the fuming cigarette in my fingers.

"That ain't right," he said, pushing the floor-mounted gearshift into first, waiting for me to close the door.

"Can I take your picture?" I asked, dropping cigarette to the ground at my feet and fumbling with the camera. He took off his straw hat and licked his palm and pressed it against his forehead and smoothed back his thinning hair. I was struck by the paleness of his forehead and the top of his skull, the result of years spent under the straw hat on the seat of a tractor. He had a two-tone head, which I photographed, mostly for practice.

The ancient Ford rumbled away and I stepped firmly on the cigarette before I picked it up. I tried flicking it from short range into a trash can on the sidewalk, and missed. I retrieved it from the street and dropped it in the trash, a car flick by relay. The motive, I thought, was just trying to help a fellow do the right thing.

I headed for where I thought the Yoder Café was, but it took me longer than I expected to find it, and I had to retrace my path a few times. This was embarrassing for a recent Boy Scout alumnus, especially as I had the merit badge in orienteering. Eventually I found the café.

Which was closed.

I peeked in the windows on the street, and it was empty inside. I found my way around the alley behind the café to its back door. I knocked for a while, to no avail, and then tried the door. It was unlocked.

I went inside, into the kitchen, where two men were cleaning up. They did not seem particularly surprised to see me.

"The café is closed?" I asked.

They both nodded.

This put me way off the path I thought I was on. We three stared at one another.

"Jou looking for somebody, man?" one of them finally asked.

I asked whether the old canal people had been there.

This was nonsense to the guys cleaning up the kitchen.

"You know, some old people who come every Sunday?"

They looked at each other and shrugged their shoulders. "We don't know who come here or who don't," said one of them.

I nodded and started to turn, then stopped myself. "What about the guy who sells coconut shells?"

This they understood. "No, man, we ain't seen Quentin today," said one.

Strangely, this felt like progress on my foolish enterprise.

Less lost, I navigated to Quentin's rooming house, having little faith that he would be there since the streets were flush with potential icon buyers. And his landlord looked at me as though I had washed up on shore in a hurricane.

"*Landlord*," I whispered, "*is the harpooner here?*"

"Oh, no," said he, amusedly, "he's away."

So I went exploring the streets of New Hope, and after wandering a while I spied above the masses Quentin's crosstree some ways down the street where I tread. He saw me coming.

"*Like an ignorant pilgrim crossing the snowy Alps in winter*," he said, lowering his rack of coconut skulls below its optimal merchandising level in the great open-air marketplace of America.

I clapped his shoulders with both hands.

"What brings thee here?" he asked.

"I was hoping to talk to the canal people again, but they weren't at the café."

"No, they aren't there anymore," he said, twirling his crosstree of coconut skulls for the tourists.

"Can I find them? I need to get their names."

"Well, I don't know. Sometimes they are there; sometimes they aren't."

"And if they aren't there?"

Quentin shrugged, his coconut skulls dancing aloft. "Then they are someplaces else."

I took his picture and watched him pitch icons to a foursome of giggling teenage girls. I drifted away, and headed to the towpath and caught a barge full of tourists heading upstream. The mule-driver nodded to me; I guessed he didn't have so many interactions with canal historians such as me. I asked if I could take his picture and he said sure, so I photographed him and the barge of tourists and his father, the captain spinning yarns, and the mules. In their harnesses, they looked like four-legged caddies.

On my way to the state road that wound back to Acushnet, I passed a sidewalk newspaper box for a local paper, not the one my father worked for. Above the fold was an article about the plan to build a new subdivision along a stretch of the canal south of town. I figured Speedy would be interested in this, since he was still following the story. I bought a copy of the paper, folded it in thirds and stuck it under my arm, which gave me a rather scholarly look.

It took even longer to get home by thumb than it had to get there. I was beginning to lose patience with the goodwill of my fellow man.

1968 CORRECT CRAFT SKI NAUTIQUE

It was our family tradition that on Labor Day weekend we paddled down the river and ate sandwiches from a picnic basket and jumped in the water whenever it pleased us. Before I became a Cub Scout, the four of us rode in one big canoe. By the time I made Tenderfoot, we had become a fleet of two canoes, and when I went into the Boy Scouts, my mother and sister began to drive along the river road and wave as my father and I floated by.

When I took the merit badge in canoeing I got to know more about it than my father did. One day I got in the stern and waited for him to get in the bow, where he could clown around and drag his paddle in the water and chatter to the other people out on the river, knowing that an Eagle-Scout in the making was steering us safely downstream and providing most of the power, doling out strokes with a drummer's precision.

Our voyage that year came on Saturday, high noon in the Labor Day weekend. My sister came home the night before and we all took the day off. I woke up later than usual and puttered around in the garage, getting the canoe gear together while the others made lunch.

It was the last of August, full of sun, dry and breezy, the kind of day that blew you toward a balmy evening and a healthy appetite. We tied the canoe on the roof of the car after breakfast and drove like in the old days to a put-in on the Delaware River near where the canals of the Lehigh and Delaware once met. The gradient was low and the paddling was leisurely. Both sides of the river were settled with mostly older houses, some of them old enough to remember men digging the ditch for the canal or even the heady smell of revolution against a distant king. A lot of them had become weekend places for wealthy people.

The river had enough depth to make it easy to avoid grounding, even late in the summer. Within just a few hundred feet, Speedy and I came to a wing dam we knew well and as I steered us to the funnel of water pouring over the center, the least risky path, my father raised his paddle over his head with both hands and let out a yell.

Just below the wing dam, we floated under a footbridge upon which my mother and sister were waiting for us, tossing lobelia blossoms our way. They turned to the other side of the bridge as we slid below, and my mother called out to tell us how good we looked. "That must be why they're going so slow," my sister said.

For most of the trip we hardly needed to paddle at all, if we didn't care how long it would take. I could not just drift, but my father could. I liked making propulsion; he enjoyed floating. After a couple of miles, we had to choose a route through a set of cobbled islands, and then came within sight of the next bridge anchored by villages on both sides of the river. I steered us toward my mother and sister, who were waiting with more lobelia. With practice, their timing was improved, speckling the boat and the river around us with purple.

We had a few miles to ourselves. My father was reminiscing about when he went to high school, thinking back to his senior year and war at the doorstep, and venturing away from his family. I listened, focusing on the half swivel at the waist, inserting the blade of the paddle into the murky water, and pulling myself and the canoe to the blade, turning it just so to keep the boat tracking true, my father resting on the bow seat, his paddle across the gunwales, a faded Phillies hat on his head absorbing the August sun, and then lifting the blade back for another go. I tried to make as little noise as possible with the paddle while still maintaining a steady glide over the water.

He was writing a new haiku on the inside of the hull.

"Purple stars, love-tossed. Still currents wild and secret," he said, trying to come up with a final line.

People along the river usually look up from whatever they're doing as you slide along. There's a neighborly surprise, and you look just momentarily at them and catch eyes, thanking some god or other for the rivers connecting us. A riverbank is a back yard and a front yard; the earliest plantations were oriented toward the water because they were built from the river first, before the roads went in.

I kept us in the main channel out in the middle, though the Delaware at that point was narrow and intimate. There wasn't much traffic, a few anglers whiling away the morning's remnants without a lot of fish to show for it, but a better day, as is said, than a good shift at work.

The sun banged on the surface of the water, which was impenetrable, deflecting the light back up at us, hiding whatever was going on below. Sometimes we would drift over a rock stacked up high near the surface of the water, sometimes a log buried by a flood, mute and lurking.

"*Where else but from Nantucket did those aboriginal whalemen first sally out in canoes to give chase to the Leviathan?*" my father asked.

"*My mind was made up to sail in no other than a Nantucket craft,*" I noted, "*because there was a fine, boisterous something about everything connected with that famous old island.*"

The river wiggled right, slightly to the west, and we had a straight shot to the next bridge. There were more houses along the bank, especially on the Pennsylvania shore, where the canal still marked its path for commerce, squeezed into the narrow shoreline before the hills started. Old stone houses with white clapboards. Rustic postcards from modern times. Tourists ate it up, but there was authenticity, the echoes of barge conch shells, mules shitting on the towpath, all working together to float coal to the city. Many of the boatmen had farms along the way, and their wives would come down to furnish a meal as the men were merrying along at mule-speed. Some traded "loose" coal—not fast coal—for a pie or bottle of beer. A quarry here, a millwork there. It would be a shame, I thought, to pave over any bit of it to build houses.

We were coming to the tourist mecca, where suburbanites stared at hippies and queers, liberated for a few hours safely away from home. We were invisible, passing underneath the end-of-summer revelry on dry land; the river there was incidental to the people on shore mainlining retail, bargains on bell-bottoms and vinyl and clever tee shirts.

I scanned for a topmast of coconut heads, but there were many people on the bridge between the two towns. Someone yodeled. My mother and sister leaned over the guardrail, waving their arms excitedly, like they were helping to land a jet. Subtle they were always not, as the Deutsche would put it.

We waved back. Something came down toward us; it looked like popcorn, but the bridge was higher than the others and we were slipping underneath it by the time whatever it was landed in the water. As we poked out the other side, I told my father to plant his paddle and draw on the right. I leaned back and put my blade in the water directly behind us, pushing an arcing reverse sweep that turned the canoe so it was facing upstream and killed most of our momentum. We drifted momentarily, necks cranked backward, waiting for the womenfolk to risk their lives dashing through interstate traffic to get to the down-stream side of the bridge.

It was popcorn, drifting around us in the river and then more from the sky. Our people above us, flinging fistfuls of popcorn into the air like Buddhists celebrating a new constitution, laughing.

My father stared upward, delighted, and sang out, "Look for the girl with the sun in her eyes." He may have been a WWII veteran, but he was also in Sgt. Pepper's Lonely Hearts Club Band.

My sister, from the New Hope bridge: "You're waiting for someone to perform with," she yelled back, already on top of a new Beatles song only days old in the fast-moving stream of culture. "It's just you, Jude, you'll do."

My father shook his head skeptically from side to side. "That'll nev-er catch on," he said, squinting up into the sun at her.

I had been holding us there in an eddy formed by a bridge footing, but I let our stern catch the edge of the downstream flow, which gently pushed us loose. There was popcorn in our canoe, which my father scooped into his mouth so he could one day sit on the back porch and ask me if I remembered the time it rained popcorn on us.

I promised myself that I would try to remember it before he did, but I suspected that he would own this memory, and I was simply sharecropping.

There was another wing dam waiting for us downriver. The stream was backing up, almost lake-like, and I paddled slowly, letting us bake a little in the sun. Speedy stood up, pulling off his shirt and taking off his sneakers, and launched himself into the river. He disappeared un-der the surface, a classic Dad game, and resurfaced after it seemed too long, popping through the membrane, gasping for air but catching his breath with a few quick gulps.

"How long was that?"

"About 19, 20 minutes, Dad."

He splashed water in my direction with the palm of his hand and then ducked down under again, passing beneath the canoe, tapping it with his hand as he went by. I let the boat drift where it wanted to go, blowing sideways in a breeze from the northeast coming across my back. He popped up a few yards away, turning to find me on the sur-face. He stroked over to the canoe, which I steadied with the paddle planted on my right. As he reached up and grabbed the gunwale near the middle of the boat, I hiked out as far as I could, making a counter-weight while he hoisted himself out of the water and reached for a handhold in the thwart and he pulled the rest of his dripping person into the canoe.

"Water's great," he said, facing backward, laying his head down on the bow plate and stretching out in the sun. "Want to practice self-rescues?"

"I've got that merit badge, Dad." But the truth was that I was no longer counting merit badges and my father just smiled knowingly. It was a piece of cake for the two of us to right a capsized canoe and get back in. I had done it enough times by myself, but it was a lot of work to prove a proficiency that didn't make a lot of sense drifting along on a slow-moving river in the middle of summer.

"Well, you're supposed to be prepared," he said, and closed his eyes to bask in the sun.

I steered us into the gentle current of the river, gliding toward the middle, and still well upstream of the next wing dam that was built to keep enough volume in the canal. There was a strong hydraulic at both of these dams, but if you cruised deliberately through the middle of the opening, there was little risk. People got in trouble going over the dam itself, or monkeying around beneath it.

But that wasn't us. I saw the river folding into the break in the dam and aligned us for a straight plunge. My father was still sprawled on his back, eyes closed. "Hey, Dad, we're going over the dam," I said.

He looked as though he had just nearly touched sleep. And instead of scrambling around to face our shot through the tongue of falling river, he simply reached for a gunwale with each hand and braced himself, determined to make this passage through the birth canal upside down and headfirst, watching the sun pour around me. I held the paddle firmly astern, like a rudder, keeping us true as we tilted over the edge and fell down into the huge standing wave. We bounced and water splashed into the hull. He was beaming as we slammed into the wave train, so quickly out of the dive.

"I could do this all day long," he said.

"Me too, Dad."

As we came to the bottom of the fast water, I dug my paddle in right and forward, turning us around to look back up at the wing dam. These things never look as exciting from below, once you've been through them from above.

Facing downstream again, I saw on the river's horizon a speedboat towing a water skier. It's a big enough river and there was plenty of room for others, but from the stern of a canoe they seemed like a distant, noisy intrusion. The speedboat was plowing straight up the river; the water skier was making wide, lazy turns, slaloming out from behind the boat from one side to the other.

We suddenly felt slow.

They were heading toward us. I held my line, determined to exert my right of way as the downstream vessel and the one without power. I wondered if the speedboat driver had read the same chapter.

My father suddenly turned around and sat up in the bow seat, taking up his paddle. The speedboat began to make a sweeping right turn in front of us, still at a safe distance, its engine crowding into our quiet. Suddenly the skier slalomed toward her right, her orbit coming as close as it would to our path. I recognized the swimsuit first.

I glanced from Juliana to the captain of the speedboat. A man of impeccable timing, Vic Martine flicked a cigarette from the boat into the river and finished his turn back downstream.

It was a 1968 Correct Craft Ski Nautique, a top-of-line water-ski boat in those days. There were two other people in the boat whom I did not recognize.

"Hey!" my father yelled, pointlessly, at the retreating wake of the speedboat pulling Juliana, skipping across the waves, a bauble of gushing, youthful beauty in a bathing suit, her hair flying behind her.

He turned around to me. "Oh, we gotta catch up with them."

"It's Juliana, and that guy who wants to build a subdivision on the canal," I said, unsure whether he heard me.

"All the more reason," said Speedy.

I wasn't so sure, considering that *the pursuit of whales is always under great and extraordinary difficulties, that every individual moment comprises a peril.* But I shrugged, knowing there was no way we could catch them. My father turned determinedly to the task and began digging relentlessly into the water.

I had to switch sides to balance his enthusiasm. It took a few dozen strokes before we found a sustainable rhythm and the canoe began to track. This was not the kind of lazy paddling my father and I usually did; it was committed, like a distance runner escaping the totalitarian north, keeping stride and mowing down the fathoms.

A sunny summer afternoon kind of lunacy and I liked it. Our poetic craft bearing purple stars and popcorn didn't feel slow anymore, though Martine and Juliana were soon enough specks on the downstream horizon of the river. Chasing ghosts, we were a live, two-cylinder human engine churning down the river. My father was the muscle, planting and pulling long, even strokes that made it easy to match his beat, skipping one stroke every once in a while to keep us trimmed just off line into the gentle wind sweeping on to us.

We probably paddled 10 minutes without hesitation and I think we might have gone right past my mother and sister if they hadn't started calling us from the riverbank. With some resignation, my father stopped paddling and rested the shaft across the gunwales in front him, as I redirected us toward the shoreline.

It was the first take-out we had arranged, a narrow beach of pebbles and a path leading up an embankment through tall grass. My mother asked us if we had had enough and were ready for our picnic. My father said the picnic sounded great, but he was game for more canoeing. I knew he still had the Custom Craft on his mind. He went with my mother up the footpath to the car and fetched back the picnic. My sister and I skipped stones across the surface of the river.

We munched for a while and then my father and mother went for a swim together; she had a suit on underneath her clothes for just this purpose. They bobbed together, two heads and shoulders in the easy current, like children. My sister was rubbing the back of my head the way she used to when I was little and surrounded by women who were older than me. I wanted to lie down and doze in the warm sunshine, but I didn't want to lose the contact with her.

A butterfly or two fluttered by. Some birds. A relaxed stir of the wind. Clouds in shapes you could almost name loitered overhead under a brilliant blue sky, the kind they use for post cards. My parents came out of the water happy. I thought we were going to pack it up, hoist the canoe onto our shoulders and carry it back to the car and home.

But instead my father looked at me with unmet goals in his eyes. Without turning away, he said to his wife that we would meet down the river at the next take-out, about two miles away. It was a little more paddling than I needed, but parents are children we hate to disappoint. Speedy and I helped carry the picnic back to the car, and then my mother and sister followed us back to the riverbank.

As we settled into the canoe and pushed off into the current, my father sang, "They say everything can be replaced," dipping his paddle into the river, "yet every distance is not near."

And then we were away in search for the *proverbial evanescence of a thing writ in water*. The leisureliness and frolic with which we had started the journey were stowed away below decks, and we were soon digging downstream, hunting for the Custom Craft.

In not too many minutes, my father said, "Thar, she blows."

Thar, the speedboat churned up the river toward us. After watching them for a few seconds, my father began paddling again, aggressively. His strokes were steady and smooth, he was submerged in what he was doing, pulling straight ahead. It was up to me to calculate a point that might intersect with the powerboat, but as we chugged along I had to keep re-calibrating our course to a target nearer to us and farther from them.

When the speedboat came closer, I could see that Juliana was no longer the skier. I did not recognize the man hanging onto the tow line.

I kept resetting our course, and we were tracking straight across the river when the powerboat flew past us. My father yelled again, but he could not be heard over the engine. Juliana was in the back of the Custom Craft and Martine was at the helm. He had steered carefully away from us as he went by, giving us plenty of space. We stopped paddling for a moment as their wake came at us.

Then the water-skier lost his balance and crashed into the river. Martine's boat went a little farther upstream, slowed and circled back, edging toward the skier, but I could hear laughter now that their motor was throttled. They were about an eight-iron away.

"Let's get closer," my father said. So we began paddling again, at a steady pace, slowly trimming the gap between us.

As we got closer, it looked like Juliana and the other passenger were helping the skier clamber onto the boat. Martine was turned away from us, watching them. We were only about 80 yards away, but it didn't seem that any of them had recognized us. My father stopped paddling and stowed his paddle behind him in the hull of the canoe. He reached into his waistband, pulled out his poetry-writing marker and clenched it in his teeth.

"I'll be right back," he said, and then slid over the side of the canoe into the water. He swam steadily for a few yards toward the powerboat and then dove under the water.

I tried looking nonchalant, which isn't easy when you're in a canoe in the middle of the river staring at the only other boat on the water. The current was pushing me gently away from them. I sculled slowly, holding my position, turning a little askance, but keeping the powerboat in sight. Juliana looked around and waved to me in a neighborly kind of way, and I waved back. I wasn't dead certain whether she recognized me since she wasn't wearing her glasses. I could have called out to her, but I didn't want to call attention to the torpedo graffiti artist headed their way.

Then my father surfaced, right behind below the prow of the Custom Craft, where none of them could see him. He was steadying himself with his left hand on the hull as best he could, uncapped his pen, and began writing what I had to figure was I FLICK BUTTS.

He put the marker back in his teeth and slipped under the surface. Then, unexpectedly, Martine revved the engine and turned the Custom Craft away toward the other shore. Whew, I thought, at least he's steering away.

Then the ski-boat made a U-turn and started heading back down stream and still my father hadn't surfaced. It looked to me that Martine was on a bearing well clear of where my father should have been if he was swimming straight back to the canoe. I raised the paddle over my head and tried to call to the ski-boat but the engine was too loud.

Then my father surfaced, way off track, just in front of the Custom Craft, which plowed over him and continued downriver. On the edge of my awareness, I thought maybe Juliana had waved to me, but I was staring at the place in the water where my father had been. I was thinking he would come bobbing up to the surface with a big smile. I started paddling as fast as I could.

When he surfaced, he was floating, motionless and face down.

I came within a few yards and launched myself into the river. I swam to him and rolled him over; there was a bloody great gash on the back of his head. He was not conscious; I didn't know if he was breathing. I screamed, but the Custom Craft was already away downstream.

I first thought of trying to drag my father into the canoe, but I couldn't picture how to do that and decided I couldn't risk time trying to figure it out. I hooked my left arm under his armpit from behind, keeping his head out of the water, and began a sideways doggy paddle toward the shore.

Adrenaline turned to panic as I neared the shore. I was crying for him and screaming at the sky and the unhearing grasses and trees. I was in two worlds: one where I hoped he was okay and another in which I knew he was gone. When I could finally touch the river bottom, I wondered if this experience was what the religious people mean by God.

In my arms, he felt like he was gone. When I got him to the bank of the river, I cried with him for a minute and then picked him up in my arms and staggered up the embankment, looking for my mother.

1996 Honda Civic

After my father died, I spent the next 34 years watching people flick cigarettes from their cars with no itch to write about it. Don't get me wrong. I saw plenty of them. The ink in that pen had run dry.

Something different happened on Labor Day of 2002. I was driving a son of my own to a place in southern Maryland where we would meet with his high school theater troupe and they would go onto the lower Potomac River to film a video segment for a musical they were creating. I was in the middle of my life and the father of three—Henry, the fellow sitting next to me, was the youngest—and I had become a sort of stagehand to the project, carrying trunks and equipment to wherever they had to be, to spot where important things went unexpectedly into the woods, when intention went astray, and to hold the flag to the flagstick so that it didn't flutter and distract the putters. *I have always gone to sea as a sailor, because of the wholesome exercise and pure air of the forecastle deck.*

∞

When my father died, parts of me went numb. I managed to carry him up to the road that day we chased a Custom Craft around the Delaware River, and I was in such a state of shock that I even gave thought to carrying him back to the riverbank to look for our poetry-inscribed canoe, drifting, orphaned, toward the sea. Fortunately, an automobilist stopped at the sight of me on the side of the road with a lifeless body.

The driver took one look at Speedy and helped me load him in the back seat of his car, his banged-up head on my lap. I wanted him to take us to the next take-out, but he stopped at the first house along the road and went inside to call for an ambulance. He came back out with a stout woman who lived there and she ordered me to get out of the car while they moved Speedy onto her lawn, beneath a gently waving maple tree. I told the man as best as I could where we were supposed to meet my mother and sister. Then he left in his car and I sat there with my father and waited for the next catastrophe to happen.

I was too scared to look at Speedy. The woman knelt beside the two of us, praying, and then we could hear an ambulance siren coming from the north at about the same time the helpful driver was coming back with my mother and sister. The adults took over, which was no relief. Left alone, I no longer had Speedy to shield me from the guilt and devastation that was headed my way. I started crying when they loaded him in the ambulance.

The man never said a word, but pulled the three of us into his car and we followed the ambulance to the hospital. After a few minutes in the emergency room, a doctor made it official.

The next day, three of us walked around like zombies, putting one foot in front of the other, wondering when the dream would end. Clinically, Katie said, we were in shock. I didn't give a fuck. I was still trying to figure out how to get through the time without ever asking him, or my family, to be forgiven.

On the second day, Labor Day 1968, we went to a funeral home to pick out a coffin. I had always thought that my father wanted to be cremated, but my mother decided to have him buried, with a flag at his headstone because he was an Army veteran.

∞

For the next 34 years, no Labor Day rolled by without me thinking about him. Speedy was back again in my mind that first September Monday of 2002, a lifetime later, driving Henry to someplace he needed to be. The three of us, in one form or another, were there on the other side of the Mason-Dixon Line in a well-worn minivan.

It sometimes seemed far-fetched that Henry and I were related at all, and yet I was there at his conception and his birth. He was the one of my three children who was most Yardley and yet the least like me.

At Henry's age, I was pushing a lawnmower all day, ruminating in the droning of a two-stroke engine, watching long grass become short grass. Henry spent the summer before his last year in high school working with dozens of classmates planning, writing, and preparing to stage a musical.

He was full of talents and wonderfully skilled at working with others. When I was turning 17, I was a good walker who could barely play a radio. In 34 years, I had deftly managed my career to a point where I was the number two in a two-man consulting firm that did traffic studies for small governments.

Our minivan had served my wife for 10 years of family duty and in semi-retirement had become our cargo vehicle. Its air conditioning

stopped cooling sometime in Clinton's first term, the right-hand outside mirror was held in place with duct tape, and there was a perilous
fault line in the windshield. The radio still worked; mysteriously; however, it only seemed to play songs that I didn't know.

Henry did not drive. He was old enough and capable enough, but he
was taking a stand on what he called the petro-global jihad against the
planet. When he was 14, he made an iron-on tee shirt that said: Fuck
the PGJ. They say it skips a generation, like baldness.

We lived in Maryland, where I ended up when I couldn't stay in
Pennsylvania any longer. That Labor Day, Henry and I had driven almost free of the Washington urban core and were navigating the inter-
connected lagoons of subdivisions when a red 1996 Honda Civic
zipped past us, passing in a no-passing lane on a two-lane country road
crowned in the middle. As the Civic squeezed in front of us, the driver
flicked a cigarette into the road. And triggered a genetic response in
me.

As I said, I saw a lot of butt-flickers in the 34 years since my father
died because I had spent a lot of time on the sides of roads. If I thought
of Speedy's notepad and his bumper stickers, I would get a little angry.
They say you should follow your bliss, but all that got my father was a
stove-in head.

This time, a cigarette thrown from a car was different. Without any
warning, I wanted to get to the bottom of it. I revved the menopausal
minivan, pushing it to keep pace with the Honda, and we were soon
going fast (for me), and Henry was looking at my profile probably
wondering why the telephone poles on the other side of the road were
galloping past us with such uncharacteristic speed.

I think I might have been gripping the steering wheel tightly. In my
heart, I knew we would not keep up with the Honda unless there was
divine intervention.

We rounded a bend in the road. The traffic stopped suddenly. Road
construction. Only one lane of traffic getting through. It was our turn to
give right-of-way to the traffic coming at us from the other direction.

There was a fellow in an orange vest holding a stop/slow sign in
synch with his partner at the other end of the construction zone. This
was more than familiar to me; it was part of me. After I went to college,
I spent some time working for the highway department, chaperoning
traffic through roadwork zones.

"Dick Cheney says the risks of inaction are far greater than the risk
of action," I said aloud to myself.

"I'll be right back," I told Henry, and shoved the minivan into park—it sighed when I did that—and I unbuckled my seat belt and got out of the car. Carried ahead by tailwinds from the past, I marched determinedly to the driver's side of the Honda. A monument to plastic, bereft of chrome, a large, molded bumper designed to self-destruct at 10 miles-per-hour of impact, tinted windows, rear light epaulettes integrated silently into the smooth, boxy contour of the body. It was the hatchback, a small prairie of black glass under a little brim. Car design had leapt ahead generations since the last recorded autoflicker to discover the "box."

The Honda was throbbing a hip-hoppy salsa beat. Two thick-necked men sat in the front buckets. They were nearly as surprised as I was to find myself there, walking around in an auto zone.

"Excuse me," I said. "I noticed you threw a cigarette from your window as you were passing me back there." I was trying to echo my father's tightrope act over the chasm between neighborly civility and intrusion.

The driver looked up at me without any sign of comprehension.

"I'm an anthropologist," I said, wondering what it would be like if that were true. "Working on a research project. Can you tell me why you threw the cigarette out the window?"

"Not speak English," he said.

As far as I could remember at that moment, this was a unique response.

"Okay, well," I said, and turned back to our car, muttering, "See, this can be a rational thing that nobody needs to get upset about it."

Henry stared at me as I slid behind the steering wheel. "Write this down someplace before I forget," I told him. "When asked why he threw his cigarette out the window, the subject responded that he did not speak English, though I think he spoke at least a little bit. I believe that is a 1999 Honda Accord."

Henry did not know what to make of this.

"No, I mean it. Write that down in your notebook." Since the musical project had started, Henry was never far from a huge notebook stuffed with slips of paper that held the group's collective thinking about the musical.

Dutifully, he flipped toward the back of the notebook to a blank page and wrote something, looked at what he had written and shook his head from side to side. Then he removed the page and placed it on the console between us.

After a while, we squeezed through the construction zone and continued our drive to St. Mary's City.

When we got home at the end of the day, I went up into our baking, unventilated attic and rummaged through slowly decomposing boxes of the past, carefully handling memory fused into tangible objects, as the current pulled me faster toward the waterfall and then, sensing it before I got there, the reporter's notebook filled with notes in two different hands carefully logging the time and place and vehicle and method of littering and, importantly, the reason cited or inferred.

I inserted the sheet with Henry's entry after the last page of 1968. The study was on again.

1995 JEEP WRANGLER

Most days, Henry rode his bike to school. But it was raining a monsoon on the day after Labor Day, so I was on my way to give my youngest child a dry ride home in the minivan, thinking about how much empty space I was carting along by myself, spending down precious road bandwidth from the dwindling communal supply.

At a traffic light, I pulled alongside a young man driving a 1995 Jeep Wrangler with the top off, the rain pouring all over. He was smoking, which was some feat, given the downpour. He cupped the cigarette in his right hand, raising it to his mouth periodically and exhaling a cloud of smoke into the driving rain. As the light changed green, he threw the cigarette into the street.

This hardly seemed like littering. You can get so wet that it no longer matters what you do. Yielding to rain is a release from the narrow life, joining the will of insistent nature. Through most of our millennia here, people have gone about their business in the rain. But we have a lot more people now and very few caves.

As the Jeep drove off into the storm, I fetched the research log and jotted "ashtray flooded" as the likely cause for the flick. I reckoned I would be ordering bumper stickers soon.

∞

The rain reminded me of Speedy's funeral, when it rained like nobody's business, as though we were meant to remember him underwater. When I woke up the morning of the day of his funeral, my first thought when I heard the rain outside was how it would affect work at the country club. Then I remembered my father was due to be planted in the earth that afternoon, that my greens-keeping days were done for the season, and that school had already started, without me.

My stomach was unsettled. There were a few creepy hours when I had not much to do until it was time for Mother and me and Katie to go to the funeral home.

The Yardleys had wanted the service at the meetinghouse that my father attended until he broke ranks and joined the Army. My mother pushed a secular option, insisting that was how her husband wanted it. In the end, she had her way.

When I saw him in the coffin in the funeral home that morning, it was the first time since the emergency room. It was him all right, in a stiff, paraffin kind of way.

I had a nice, mostly one-sided chat with my father while no one was around, which seemed appropriate enough as we were in the parlor. Speedy informed me that I had a lot to learn, but it would come easily to me. I wasn't so sure.

"It's easier than it seems," he said. "Both the living and the dying."

I asked him a lot of questions: What's it like to be dead? Was it worth recording that one more flicked cigarette? Where will I look for you when I die? How do I take care of Mother? He didn't answer any of these questions, and I was afraid that I had asked too many too quickly, not giving him a chance to reply.

As his voice was getting faint, Speedy said the search for the truth was its own reward.

It's not so easy having a conversation with the dead, even if you thought you knew them so well in life. He might have said proof is a pursuit for retards.

My father's family brought Uncle James to the funeral in a wheelchair, though it was hard to tell what he was getting out of it. The minister of the church where my mother and I sometimes went—the one that sponsored my Boy Scout troop—talked about my father as though he actually knew him. In fact, they never met. I looked over my shoulder at James, parked in the aisle that parted a sea of folding chairs. His eyes were closed, which made me want to close mine. After the service, one of my father's cousins wheeled James in front of my mother and me and said they were taking him home.

"He's not going to the burial?" I asked.

"It's the rain, and we think it's all too confusing for him," the cousin said.

I looked at James, who didn't look any more confused than usual. "When he gets well, are you going to be the one to tell him that he missed his brother's burial?" I asked.

My mother put her hand on my forearm. The cousin said something about crossing that bridge when they get to. I swallowed hard, thinking I should be taking a stand. But I didn't.

∞

Back in 2002, at Henry's school, there were a few other theater parents hanging around in a hallway. Among them was a woman who was a passing acquaintance of Elizabeth, my wife. This meant that I was drawn into some kind of loop with her, as was her husband, although I often got confused about which kid was hers.

"How is Liz?" she asked, placing herself between me and the door to the black-box theater. My wife did not like to be called Liz. I assured the woman that Elizabeth was well and hard at work in the Dewey decimal system.

"Haha, the library," said she, planning for this to go on. My wife worked at a public library near our home in Prince George's County.

"I never heard the story of how you met," she said.

"Well, it's not finished yet," I said. "I'll tell you when I find out how it ends," smiling, pushing ahead into the dark theater.

∞

After high school, I tried to go to college but could not finish and after a few years, I started working for the man who still employs me. One day, I was doing a spot speed study in a residential neighborhood when a car actually broke down and stopped running just as I was timing it with a speed gun.

Elizabeth, recently graduated from college and already working in a library, was the driver. Even now, I don't know what made me a good candidate for her life plans.

I was drawn to her legs. *In no living thing are the lines of beauty more exquisitely defined than in these flukes,* said I to myself. Aloud, I asked her for a date.

"That's kinda bold, don't you think?" she said. But she was smiling faintly.

"I've heard girls like men in uniform," I said.

She laughed. "You think that hard hat and stupid yellow vest are going to get you anywhere?"

Turns out, they did.

∞

In the dark theater, the set was still at a primitive stage, but this was my first opportunity to see how the kids planned to incorporate video—like the one they filmed in the lower Potomac off St. Mary's City just the day before—with live-action theater.

They were rehearsing the opening scene of the musical, the story of Ishmael after the sinking of the *Pequod*, a sequel to Moby Dick. Henry, cast as Ishmael, sang a song about mammal love, with cast members in whale costumes dance-swimming in a circle around him. As the song ended, a screen at the back of the stage came to life with a video of a whaling ship approaching.

Any half-assed Dick Mobius knows that the *Rachel* rescued Ishmael, the only survivor from the wreckage of the *Pequod*.

But it was Juliana who pulled me out of the water.

2002 BMW 320i

Juliana was at the funeral, all the way at the back, and she drove her Fairlane wagon in the procession to the burying grounds. I didn't talk to her until after the burial, but I noticed her standing under a disturbingly cheerful green umbrella. She was wearing grown-up clothes, going-to-church clothes. I wondered why it did not seem out of place to be glad to see her.

As they lowered my father into the ground, I whispered to him to hold his breath and then he was really gone and the gravediggers shooed us away toward the cars. Mother and Katie paused to talk to well-wishers near the funeral-home car that had brought us to the cemetery. They waved to me to come along to the car—there was a reception at a restaurant someplace—but I had already decided as we were driving silently to the gravesite that I would walk home in the rain.

I told my mother and my sister that I would get my own ride. When I looked around, Juliana was still there.

We stood together under her umbrella and watched as the gravediggers filled in Speedy's grave. Then Juliana drove me to her house.

There was no one there. We had, for the first time for both of us, full-on sexual intercourse the way the missionaries teach it. I wasn't prepared for the physical sensation of it, not by my father's full-color explanation of the reproductive process or by the Boy Scout manual or by the models selling automobiles or the cheerleaders in our school turning cartwheels or by our earlier explorations or even by the subconscious wiggle through the birth canal 17 years before.

For those moments of anticipation, release and intimate collapse, I was freed; drifting heavenward on Speedy's trail, stretching behind me to stay clasped with Juliana and finally pulled back to her Earth.

It didn't make me grieve any less for my father, but it gave me something else to think about as we rejoined the funeral party at the reception.

∞

Then, a couple of generations later, I was driving toward Old Town, a place in Alexandria that was heavy on brick and cobblestone, for the making of another video for the musical. Someone—I suspected Henry, but he denied responsibility—had outfitted me in clothing intended to resemble 19th century seafaring attire. Because there would be no place to change where we were shooting, I wore my costume en route.

With us were four girls from the cast, including Meredith, who was playing the role of a missionary's daughter who is outbound on the *Rachel* when they pick up Ishmael. I wasn't sure, but I thought there might be more than a thespian thing between them. Along with her three sisters, the missionary girls would sing onstage about the better life they left behind in America while a video of that better life played on the screen in the theater.

Or so it was explained to me.

My role was to amble around in the background, looking like I was about 150 years old. In the musical, the character played by Meredith was going to fall madly in love with Ishmael after he's rescued from the sea.

The girls were chattering a mile a minute, a like-filled blur of something akin to the conversation of birds cooing on an overhead phone line. To pass the time, they rehearsed their onstage song, a parody of a 1960s girl-group ballad about boyfriends that made me think of Juliana.

∞

After we crossed the Rubicon at my father's funeral, Juliana and I were passionately together all through our senior year in high school. We even built our college plans around the Greyhound bus schedule between two central Pennsylvania colleges. The high school part of it was like being secretly married, except we had to find places to be together and I rarely had to clean the dishes. My mother was not overly inquiring about what we were up to, but we had to work like spies to keep it from her parents.

Somehow, I got us into a motel once. There, in 2002, I still had in my memory bank the image of her sitting on the commode, underwear down around her ankles.

∞

A blue-gray 2002 BWM 320i convertible was ahead of us in the boulevard. The top was down. The passenger, a young woman with carefully blonde hair and long, slender arms of tan, was smoking. The driver, sunglasses, pastel golf shirt, big watch on his wrist, was not.

The traffic was a wide, moving logjam, creeping through a gauntlet of side streets, parallel parkers and un-parkers, traffic lights and cars dodging around a Metrobus. The BMW was finless and mostly chrome-free. There was a small ornamental BMW badge in the middle of the back. It was a tidy, fancy box that symbolized the driver's entry into the pampered classes. The 2002 model year was a huge seller, in the U.S. and globally.

A lot of people were knighted that year.

Then the princess casually dropped her cigarette into the road. Not a flick or pitch. Just an unconscious letting go that said, I'm done with this, let someone else pick it up. Or not.

I almost lost them at the next stoplight, which was a lot closer to red than yellow by the time I pushed through, an angry horn of protest in my wake from a car trying to exert its right-of-way from an inter-secting street. Henry looked quickly over at me, usually the most bor-ingly non-contentious driver on the road.

"What's up, Dad?" he asked.

"She's a flicker, son." The most important thing was to stay close. Joan Jett came to mind, and I realized that I don't give a damn about my reputation either.

The four girls in the back quieted down and tuned into the front seat of the minivan. A parent going off the rails. This could be amusing.

Next thing I knew, we were side by side, me in the left lane, the BMW in the right. I held my position even though the car in front of us was pulling away. BMW had to slow down for a right turn happening just in front of him.

"Hey, Daddy-O," I called. The BMW driver was at least 20 years younger than me. When he glanced my way, I mimed the roll-down-your window signal, even though his windows (and his roof) were al-ready down. He looked away, pretending he hadn't seen my gesture.

"Your girl dropped a cigarette back there."

A double take. He was trying to pay attention to the car in front of him. A car behind me barked: I held my ground.

"She threw her cigarette in the road," I repeated.

I could feel the intense focus of high schoolers aft and starboard, unable to look away from a social shipwreck. It is written somewhere that minivans, especially when they are captained by middle-aged men dressed as ancient mariners, are not supposed to harass BMWs.

The BMW found clear space and zipped ahead. But my harpoon was in him. He had the jump on me, but I held on a few yards behind his left bumper, cutting off a lane change. We pulled alongside again; I was looking aft, careful of the traffic. I could feel Henry staring straight ahead, wishing perhaps that this wasn't happening. Then the BMW suddenly turned right onto a side street, too quickly for me to follow. I caught a wave of intuition and zipped ahead into the right-lane space that he would have occupied, and sped toward the next intersection, hurriedly turned right and then made the next right, thinking I might catch him coming in the opposite direction.

It was a tree-lined residential street a block off the boulevard and the BMW was at my mercy, rolling straight toward us. I edged toward the middle of the street, which was narrow anyway because cars were parked on both sides. He probably could have squeezed through, but an entry-level luxury car paint job is a hard thing to sacrifice to a lunatic baby boomer dressed for serving fish and chips. In the battle of nuttiness, I had gained the upper hand.

Our slow-motion jousting match brought us closer together. As we came driver-to-driver, I held up my left hand peacefully. I stopped directly alongside him, and though he obviously didn't want to, he stopped as well.

"Hey, man. I just want to know why the first mate dropped her cigarette in the road."

The pretty young woman was looking furiously straight ahead, and she turned once to glare at me in utter disgust, as though there ought to have been somebody around in a position of authority to deal with me.

The BMW driver was stuck. "Well, uhh, you know. People just do things."

"This is research. For science." The science card can be powerful. I nodded sideways toward Henry. "We don't care what your names are, and we're not taking license numbers. We've heard all kinds of explanations. Is that your answer then, 'people just do things'?"

The young woman was fuming. "Yeah," she said, louder and getting her fur up. "People just do things. And what's up with that stupid hat?"

Unconsciously, I looked up as though I could see the black tri-corner on my head. "We're theater people," I said, shrugging my shoulders. "Have a good day."

And then, we captains each steered our vessels through the narrow channel between cars docked to the curb.

"What was that?" asked Meredith from the middle row of the minivan.

"It's a research project I started with my dad a long time ago," I said and clasped eyes with her the way people do in rearview mirrors. She had a distant look as though she was trying to imagine how someone as old as me could have a father and an existence in the blurry, sepia-toned long-ago. Maybe my old-timey seafarer hat helped her orient herself between my father's time and the present.

I didn't think any of them would have believed me if I said he gave his life for this project.

That afternoon we filmed at a couple of locations in historic-looking spots in Alexandria. After we dropped off the girls, Henry informed me that the logs of whaling ventures recorded isolated cases in which women, disguised as men, joined the forecastle crew of whalers. "It wasn't common, for sure," he said. "Whaling masters sometimes took their wives with them, or took wives from the islands."

Historical context was important to him.

"Life was very hard before the mast of a whaler," he said. "It would have been a desperate choice for a woman to make."

1998 DODGE STRATUS

Our consulting firm was hired to assess handicap access at some downtown monuments. The boss said there wasn't much doubt that the architects had done their job, but someone up the food chain wanted proof from an independent third party, which was us.

I had the plans for the Korean War Memorial in hand and was there, feet on the ground, to see that reality matched the blueprints. And it gave me a chance to observe traffic in real time, as in olden times, instead of parsing data recorded by electronic monitors, a more accurate, thorough and boring process.

Everything seemed to be in order; the ramps ramped where they were supposed to ramp. There were only a few visitors, so I couldn't make any judgement about people flow. I tried to imagine a crowd filling the memorial, and then I turned and really looked around myself and realized I was in what had been Resurrection City back in the summer of 1968.

At the memorial, there are 19 ghostly stainless-steel soldiers in ponchos that look like 38 when you count their reflections on the wall, one for each degree of latitude that marked the terms for stopping the fighting. A woman came up a ramp pushing a wheelchair with a man who could have been her husband, soaking in the monument. He wore an Army veteran's hat.

I wondered how much of the war Uncle James had seen as a Red Cross observer.

∞

Jimmy never recovered from his surfing catastrophe. A few weeks after my father died, my uncle began to regress and was moved to a hospital. Dr. Matthews had no answer for it and said we should make him as comfortable as possible.

One day, my mother and I got a call from my grandfather that Jimmy had died.

It was complicated. At his end, there were so few glimmers of his true self in the wreckage of his being that it was tempting to think death had freed him. At the same time, no one was better off without the guy he used to be. And I'm not proud of this, but in my 17-year-old head I had a sense that something was after us and I was the next male in line for my disaster.

Everywhere I went after Jimmy died, people looked at me with sad, consoling eyes. There were a lot of sighs. I think Juliana was freaked out by it all. She came to his funeral but then left straight for school instead of going to the burial and the gathering at my grandfather's house. I couldn't really blame her, though I was disappointed. After I left the Boy Scouts and lost my virginity, I became a callow, self-indulgent fellow. Just like the rest of you.

There was a smaller crowd at James's funeral service; he had spent most of his adult life far away and no one seemed to know anyone from that life. I thought that Mrs. Crick, his anonymous benefactress, would show up, but she did not, and I figured she was intent on taking her generosity to the grave.

My sister, Katie, gave a good little speech about how James was judged harshly by some for his work with doctors who were studying psychoactive drugs in behavioral therapy. "There are a lot of ways to come to the truth," she said, sounding more like Speedy than I could bear. "We can't dismiss the striving of people of good heart who are trying to help others."

So I was there to help stow away the remains of the last of the Yardley brothers and try to make sense of a world that snuffs out bright candles too soon. The best I could come up was to tell myself to avoid the Heroism of Misguided Causes, like the ones that doomed those poor saps on the *Pequod*. Those kinds of pursuits might be all right for novelists, I thought, but had a life to live. A fucking life to live, as Juliana would have reminded me.

∞

Back in 2002, I hung around the Korean War Memorial for a while, and then headed home. In front of me, a 1998 Dodge Stratus. An uninspired rear end with a curved lid on the trunk. Like a lot of cars, it was camouflaged in gray, invisible in the September evening.

The driver in the Stratus, in slow motion, threw his cigarette into the street while we were both parked at a traffic light.

"Write that down," I said to myself, fumbling for the notepad that Speedy and I had kept, and scribbled without looking. "'98 Dodge Stratus. Driver threw cig to street just to make me notice what's going on."

When I got home, our neighbor was sitting in his car, parked in the street. I waved to him as I turned up our walkway, but he didn't respond. I detoured.

"What's up, Ted?" I asked, chatting through his open passenger-side window. He was a career Army man who still wore khaki to work. He sat behind the steering wheel looking like the last still-swimming fish in a dingy aquarium.

"I put in for retirement this month," he said, talking as much to himself as to me, staring through the windshield at an expanse of nothingness. "But the department has stopped processing retirement requests."

The Army was the only job Ted ever had. He was almost ready to leave a couple of years ago, and then his own son went in and then the Pentagon, where he worked, was attacked by zealots.

"What's that mean?" I asked.

"It means they don't want to let anybody go if they think there's another war coming."

Ted's boy was in an armored division.

1989 LINCOLN MARK VII LSC

Sitting in church next to wife Elizabeth with Henry on the other side of her. She did not force me into this church-going, but I sure was lured. Before we were married, I liked seeing her in her Sunday church clothes and afterward we would work up our own religious ecstasy. So the association gradually built up in my synapses, and I suppose there are worse reasons to say you believe in God and Jesus and all that stuff. It came in handy when we got to the child-rearing part of life to have so many ready-made answers and explanations.

You could say I was a convenience Christian and, you know, I don't think He would have minded. My mother and I went to church every once in a while just so I could claim citizenship in its Boy Scout troop.

I once tried to take Moby with me to service, but Elizabeth put the kibosh on that, so I would sometimes practice with just my deteriorating random-access memory, *calculating the driftings of the sperm whale's food, calling to mind the regular, ascertained seasons for hunting him in particular latitudes.*

Unfortunately, there on a balmy September morning in 2002, the Presbyterians were rising around me to sing, and it wasn't about whaling. I missed the cues that a person who was actually paying attention would not miss and bolted to my feet, fumbling with the hymnal, cheating on the open page that Elizabeth and Henry shared.

Elizabeth was not amused. She avoided eye contact through the rest of the service, past the handshake with the minister and into our car. At that point, more than a quarter century into our marriage, we still dressed up for church but, honestly, it wasn't as special as it used to be.

"I guess I kind of zoned out there," I said, hopefully.

"If you don't want to go to church with us, you don't have to," she said. I had the feeling this was one of those dangerous offers made by a spouse.

Before I had a chance to figure it out, Henry saved me from the back seat. "I've been thinking about going to a Quaker meeting," he told us. "I mean, you tried out a lot of churches before you picked this one, right?"

He had teed me up, and I took out my number one wood. "I will take him," I said, thinking, don't over-hit it. The shot fell safely in the fairway.

That afternoon, I drove Henry to the home of one of the kids in the musical over on the ritzy side of town. As usual, he was toting the bulging loose-leaf notebook that contained the script-in-progress full of false starts, research notes, un-pursued options, set-design sketches, rehearsal schedules, director notes, stanzas upon stanzas of lyrics that would never be sung, the sum of which was slowly taking shape as the story of Ishmael's odyssey home.

We got to the rich people's house, where the parents in residence offered to accommodate me if I wanted to stay. I said I would stick around for a little while but had an errand to run.

I watched through a vast wall of glass separating their house from the pool patio as Henry and his friends put on whale costumes: giant black whale-heads with just their legs sticking out at the bottom. Sometimes they posed themselves lounging around the pool, or wading in the shallow end. They danced and pretended they were a vocal group.

I had no idea what the point of the whale choreography was. There was slate all around the pool itself and a glass-topped table or two. That was all it took.

To blast me back to Martine's pool, watching Juliana from the cabana.

∞

After my father died under his water-ski boat, Vic Martine pleaded guilty to involuntary manslaughter. I found this out by reading about it in my father's newspaper. As far as I knew, no one from our family went to the hearing where he volunteered to go to jail for a while.

I never for a minute doubted that my father's death was an accident that could have been avoided if any one of us had done something just a little differently. But our thinking life is not fully in synch with our emotional one, and I guess on some level I blamed Martine. But not more than myself.

As it turned out, Martine and Juliana came across our empty canoe adrift in the slow-moving, nearly tidal river sometime after the accident. They towed it behind them, cruising upstream to where they had seen us, but of course they didn't know where we had picnicked or where we had planned our takeout. Juliana later told me they waited on the river until dusk, motoring up and down the Pennsylvania shore, and then they took it back to the dock and secured the canoe in a hidden place. At some point, it was loaded onto her Fairlane station wagon and brought back to our house in Acushnet.

I still have the canoe and I used to take my kids out on the Anacostia when they were little, but mostly it has sat in our back yard, resisting rust, the way a good Grumman does.

Martine did not come to my father's funeral, although I felt him there all the same. I eventually went back to caddying on the weekends at the country club and when the round came to the seventh fairway, alongside the county jailhouse, I pictured him in there staring through a tiny window to catch a glimpse of golf shots darting across the sky.

My mother and I never talked about Martine, or the accident for that matter. In those days, I think, it was still too raw. We were safe if we said how much we missed him and left it at that.

For a few weeks after Speedy's funeral, Juliana and I managed to avoid the conversation that was waiting for us. Then one day she picked me up in the Fairlane and drove me to school, and we sat in the student parking lot, her hand on my thigh, and she started crying. If you listen close enough to your first lover cry, you can feel the pain like it's your own. I had no choice but to pull her forehead into that warm place below my ear and say that I understood. Then it came out of her like a torrent, regret about being there water-skiing, about being with Martine, about not being more conscious of what was going on around her, about her goddamn nearsightedness, about drinking too much.

"She *loves to sail forbidden seas and land on barbarous coasts*," I offered.

"I helped kill him," she cried.

"I feel the same way. But it can't be undone. We can only live better because of it." This was more than I believed, but it was given to me by the preacher who had presided incongruously at Speedy's funeral.

Juliana and I were late for the starting bell that morning because we sat a long time on the bench seat of the Fairlane, long after all the rest of the high school drivers and passengers had sauntered to home room, grinding out their cigarette butts in the gravel parking lot as necessary. From her car, we could hear the first bell, and the second,

and then, when we were good and ready, we gathered ourselves for
the next go-round of education.

∞

Around the pool, Henry and his cast-mates were doing something
goofy again in their whale costumes, and I realized that all the other
parents had left. So I made some sort of exit and stopped by the pool to
ask when I should come back to pick up Ishmael and take him home.

Their house was not far from the river, so I drove in that direction,
winding up at the parking lot of the C&O canal park on the Maryland
side of the Great Falls of the Potomac. As I was walking toward the
canal gate where I could cross to the mule path, a white 1989 Lincoln
Mark VII sauntered down the parking lot toward the exit. A forty-
something black guy was huffing away on a cigarette. He had big hands
and effortlessly flicked the cigarette butt away a few yards.

Instinctively, I yelled, "Hey!"

His head swiveled around quickly, but I couldn't tell whether he
knew I was calling him specifically or if he was just reacting to the out-
burst.

"Nice toss," I said to Lincoln. I walked toward him. The Mark VII
stopped and the driver studied me crossing the asphalt between us.

I certainly had his attention. "I want to ask you about the cigarette."

"I threw the motherfucker in the road, man. So what?" He didn't
seem upset in any way, but he certainly wasn't apologetic. I figured
that he, like me, didn't have any place better to be just then.

"No big deal. I'll pick it up. Just wondering why you didn't put it in
your ashtray."

"You best leave that cigarette where I put it."

"Really? You're saying I can't pick it up and put it in the trash?"

"That's right."

He had me there. A first.

"But why not the ashtray?" I could see his gadget-laden dashboard,
compartmentalized in a boxy, clinical grid. There was an ashtray just
to the right of the steering wheel.

"Man, what's your problem?" He was lathering up, but the transmission was still in drive. There would be a tipping point when the
gearshift went to park, like the cocking of a revolver.

"This may be hard to believe, but I started asking people why they
throw cigarettes from their cars more than 30 years ago. You are part
of history."

He stared at me and suddenly I wasn't worth his time anymore. "Aw man, I just threw the shit out. The window was open."

"Just one more thing, if you don't mind." By the looks of things, he did. "Would you put a bumper sticker on your car so I don't count you twice."

He said "Fuck you, motherfucker" in the everyday way people have of tossing these words around.

Then he drove off faster than he'd arrived. The 1989 Lincoln Mark VII had the spare-wheel bump in the trunk, which would remind some people of Secret Service agents climbing up the back of a Lincoln in Dallas to shepherd the lady in pink back to her seat. It was a design lost in the 1970s, all boxy and rectangular, with an iron-pumper's stance. The roofline tried to lift the car visually, but there was just too much holding it down, rooted in steel, flexing its muscles.

I couldn't remember whether anyone had previously said they'd thrown a cigarette into the street just because the window was open.

Along the C&O canal, there is a mule-drawn canal barge for tourists, a lot like the one in New Hope. I watched from the towpath as the barge captain began his spiel for the modern generation of canal-history buffs.

A mule not far from me shat. The teenager dressed in 19th-century clothes who walked along the towpath with the mules didn't seem to notice.

The barge crew moved to pull in the gangplank that connected them to dry ground. It crossed my mind that I would like to try vaulting across a canal to a barge before I die.

Instead, I dashed to step on the gangplank before it was unmoored, and I boarded the barge.

When they pulled in the board, we were tethered to the land only by ropes pulled taught by a pair of honest, god-fearing mules. We lightened up on the cushion of fluid that held us free off the earth. Free of the cares of life, I settled into an old wooden barge-pew worn warm by generations of lore-seeking tourists like myself, and with my new shipmates set off for barbarous coasts.

45. TUESDAY, SEPTEMBER 17, 2002

1999 FORD TAURUS

Driving home from work with the radio on. A journalist reported that Switzerland had decided, after many years, to join the United Nations. By a public referendum, the Swiss figured it was time to swallow their concerns about compromising neutrality and join an organization that could help the human race deal with peace, terrorism and environmental degradation.

I was interested in all things Swiss because my mother and Katie lived there.

∞

Not long after Uncle James died, Katie got a fantastic job offer to work at a research hospital in Basel. It came completely out of the blue; she wasn't even looking for a job, but it paid well and offered her opportunities to work in mental health research.

Katie was gone before Christmas 1968, and before very long Mother was planning to visit her. She was there for several weeks, and when she came home she told me that she wanted to go live with Katie in Switzerland.

I graduated unremarkably from high school and went back to work as a greens-keeper at the country club. The plan was that Mother would stay until I left for college and we would rent out all but my bedroom in our house in Acushnet so I would have someplace to stay when I came home from college.

In the weeks before I left for college, Mother and I sifted through our household belongings and divided them in piles: things going to Switzerland; things that would stay in the house; and things to get rid of.

All that summer, Juliana and I stayed true and tight and hopeful that separating for college would not be the end of us.

The second weekend of my freshman year, I hitchhiked to visit her at her school and we were both excited to share our new lives. It was as though the only thing that had changed was geography.

A few weeks later, she took the bus to visit me, but there was something different. There were new roots trailing away from behind her.

Over Thanksgiving, I tried staying there in Acushnet with strangers at the only home I had ever known, but it was too weird. I ended up having the ritual feast at Juliana's house and sleeping on the couch in her family's rec room. On the day people call Black Friday, she said she wanted us to see other people. I had no particular interest in other girls; I figured that she was already looking around.

There was always that afternoon of water-skiing in our history. In my heart, I didn't think either one of us could carry that for a lifetime.

Yet I resisted. Sex will make you do that. And I won her back on Thanksgiving Saturday and we had a magical day tripping through the woods and visiting our old landmarks. That night, I crept up to her bedroom to celebrate.

In the morning, there was a firing squad in the kitchen. We were overheard. Very sternly, I got my marching orders. Juliana, mortified, made no effort to resist. Her dad took me to the Greyhound bus station in a matter-of-fact way. Phillies fans come to expect little good from life, I suppose.

There were some phone calls on the pay phones in the hallways of our dormitories, but neither of us had the stomach to fight her parents or the fast-moving stars.

∞

Back in my grown-up life of 2002, when I got home from work I parked in the street in front of our house and noticed Ted, the neighbor the Army wouldn't let retire, sitting in his car again, smoking a cigarette.

I waved to him and then he threw his cigarette into the street. I set off in his direction.

"What's happenin, Ted?" I asked at his driver's window. The lazy, curling smoke signal from his cigarette disappeared a few feet off the ground, where the breeze obliterated whatever message had been in it.

He was wearing his Army khaki. He looked at me, calculating my interest in what was on his mind. "You heard what your pal Dick Cheney said?" He knew enough about me to know I probably was not a Bush-Cheney man, but he always called all politicians "my" pals. I didn't know why.

"No."

"He said, 'Weapons of mass destruction in the hands of a terror network or a murderous dictator constitute as grave a threat as can be imagined.'" Ted let that sink in.

"It's really a very clever sentence," he continued. "He ties together a terror network—al Qaida—and a murderous dictator—Saddam—even though there is not one goddamn shred of evidence that they have any relationship at all. But this is how you fabricate truth; just keep saying something often enough and it takes root. Like selling cigarettes to teenagers." He looked at the cigarette still smoking on the blacktop.

"Constitute is a nice verb, sounds very legal and, you know, patriotic," my neighbor continued. "But the genius is in the phrase 'as grave a threat as can be imagined.' The grave speaks for itself, but the scope and terror of the threat is whatever we can imagine it to be. Think of the gravest threat and then imagine something worse. And that's the trouble we face here now in River City."

He fell to ruminating.

"How's your boy?" I asked.

"Still in one piece, for now."

"I didn't know you were a smoker, Ted."

"Hunh?"

"Cigarettes. I didn't know you smoke them."

"Yeah, well, I quit years ago. You want one?"

"No, thanks. Just wondering ... do you always throw them in the street?"

He looked at me. I was not the kind of neighbor to bother anyone about a bit of litter or weeds in the flowerbed.

"My dad and I had this thing; we used to keep track of people who threw cigarettes from their cars."

"What was the point of that?" Ted was a goal-oriented kind of guy.

This paused me. "I don't really know. Now I'm stuck picking up the slack because he's dead."

"Well, there's one for your collection," he said, nodding to the nearly spent butt in the street.

"We don't, I mean, I don't collect the cigarettes. We ask the people why."

Ted mulled this over for a few seconds. "Honestly, I don't know. But now that you ask, I do like the way it lays there smoldering away to nothing.

"Probably, I just didn't want it in the car," he added.

A memory came to me, un-summoned. "One night I remember sneaking through the woods with my dad to put a bumper sticker on our neighbor's car after Speedy saw him throw a cigarette from his window."

Ted's eyes closed, *because no man can ever feel his own identity aright except his eyes be closed.*

"Never mind" I said.

The cigarette, like a fuse on a dud bomb, had given up its brief burning life on the street. I turned back to our house. On our front porch was a package from the company that had made my I FLICK BUTTS bumper stickers. I ordered fancy magnetic ones. My father made each bumper sticker on the spot, each a little different.

At dinner, Elizabeth and I asked Henry about the musical.

"We were working on Scene 4 today, the one where Ishmael is booted off the *Rachel* because the missionary discovers him with the missionary's oldest daughter in a position that missionary daughters aren't supposed to be in."

I thought this was ironic, which must have been the point. "The missionary?"

"Yeah. The *Rachel* is taking a family of missionaries to a south Pacific island, but the oldest daughter falls in love with Ishmael. But when the captain agrees to put Ishmael off the ship at the next port of call, the daughter sneaks away with him."

The sinking of the Pequod might have been the best thing to happen to Ishmael, I thought to myself.

That night, after dinner was had and homework was attended to and my wifely administrations were concluded, I tried to keep myself awake until all the lights in Ted's house darkened, but his Ramadan was taking too long. I set the alarm on my wristwatch for three in the morning and went to bed.

It was one of those sleeps with one level of consciousness keeping watch over my shoulder, waiting for the alarm to go. When it did, I knew right away why, and I don't know whether I was ever asleep, or what sleep is if you're not in a summer heat coma near the 16th green. I slid out of bed, pulled sweatpants and a tee shirt and padded into my son's room, remembering a story we used to read to the kids, lying side-by-side in a child's bed, embalmed by the warmth of infancy.

"Hey, buddy," I whispered, and stirred Henry's shoulder.

"What's up, Dad?" Disorientated, but not particularly surprised.

"I got a mission for us. It'll only take a minute."

Henry was in pajamas. We headed down the staircase single-file and at the front door he asked what we were doing.

"I want to leave something for Ted's car."

It was balmy and wonderful outside in the pre-dawn. I had a magnetic bumper sticker in hand. We paused to study Ted's house for a minute. No lights. There was the hush of a household making sawdust. I crouched down, for no goddamn reason, and crept to the back of Ted's Taurus.

"Should I come along?" Henry asked.

I shushed him, index finger to lips, and waved him to follow me. But instead of crouching and creeping, he just walked to my side.

The Taurus was the biggest-selling car in the U.S. for several years, but by the time this model was dispatched in 1999, it was losing ground to the Toyota Camry, and sales depended mightily on fleet purchases by risk-averse, cost-conscious bureaucrats. Its rear end featured a burglar's mask arrangement of lights and a roundness free of personality. By 2002, it had become a car's ass that America was tired of looking at.

My magnetic bumper sticker would not stick to its plastic bumper so I made due with an uneven patch on the trunk.

"There," I said.

Crawling still, I crept back toward our front door, the teenager in pajamas and bare feet walking along behind.

2000 Chevrolet Suburban

I drove with Henry to pick up his friend Leonard, the cameraman and editor of the videos that would be shown at various times during the musical. They had been friends since primary school, and they were the major writers of the project. By that point, I thought Leonard could have been one of my kids if I had married someone else.

As they were seniors, there was a lot of attention to college, although Elizabeth had been more involved in our kids' decisions about school, for good reason. From the middle seat of our minivan, Leonard asked me about my college experience.

Henry laughed. "My dad's been to a lot of colleges."

One of our family's running jokes was the number of institutions of higher learning I had attended without ever getting a degree. As a tourist scholar, I had grown to like community colleges and evening extension programs more than traditional undergraduate courses at full-time universities.

In fact, I was taking an anthropology course on mythology during the fall semester of 2002.

"I don't necessarily recommend my approach," I said to Leonard via the rearview mirror. "I finished my first year in college and got a job with a highway construction company and decided I would go back in another year or so. One thing led to another and I took a class here or there when I could schedule it, and the next thing I knew I was married and working full time and my boss didn't care whether I had a diploma."

∞

I barely made it through my first and only year as a full-time college student. When summer break arrived, I went back to work at the country club, though I hated being in Acushnet after breaking up with Juliana.

One day in 1969, I was hitchhiking back to our house full of renters and got picked up by Martin Brady, my father's editor.

He asked what I was up to.

I said I was supposed to be going back to college, but my heart wasn't in it.

"Don't do it if you don't mean it," he said. "Your father didn't need a day of college to be a good reporter, and most people barely remember the crap they learn for tests. Of course, with our new publisher, I couldn't hire anyone who doesn't have a degree."

"There's a new publisher?" I thought of the 1963 Rambler Ambassador who ran the place when my father worked there.

"Some corporation that buys family-owned publishers and puts them under one brand. The new boss is likeable enough, but he doesn't know a damn thing about the news."

I wondered how my father would have fared with a different owner. "I'm sorry I never finished that story about the canal people," I said.

"You had bigger fish to fry, Izzy," Brady said. The last time we had talked was when he talked to me about the accident for the article he wrote about Speedy's death in the newspaper. At the funeral, he just clutched my shoulders with both hands and stared into my eyes.

"It was a good idea, though." Brady pulled a cigarette from his shirt pocket, and reached ahead to push in the lighter. "But you know, at least that sonofabitch Martine didn't get his goddamn housing project built."

Oddly, I never thought of Martine as a sonofabitch. "No?"

"The county shut it down."

I liked Brady because Speedy did. I thought I could trust him, and that his advice in 1969 about doing only the things I believed in might be as good as I was going to get. It was about all the push I needed to go off the college plan.

So I found a job listing in the newspaper for a road construction laborer and asked for an interview, and within a week I was riding in a pickup truck with someone I didn't know to a job that was not a summer job. It was an open-ended path, and it didn't keep going around the same goddamn 18 fairways.

∞

But three decades later, I didn't want to put radical thoughts in these kids' heads. I turned on the radio in the car.

A man said that Keiko, the "killer whale" who starred in a popular movie, had been spotted off the coast of Norway. After his movie career was over, Keiko was trained by do-gooders to survive in the wild, at considerable trouble and expense, and was emancipated with great ceremony near Iceland. But the poor fish had spent most of his life in captivity and was "discovered" while working at a theme park, and soon enough he reappeared off the coast of Norway, looking for attention and catered meals. This was making problems for Norwegian fishermen.

The radio man said the government was considering moving him to his own personal fjord as a tourist attraction.

The boys thought this was remarkably interesting and weighed its possible use in the script.

"What are you filming today?" I asked.

"Later on in the story, when Ishmael is finally on his way back to Nantucket, he's sold to pirates," Henry said in a nonchalant way.

"He's really having a rough go of it, isn't he?" I remarked.

"Well, they're environmental pirates who are opposed to whaling," Leonard explained.

Of course, I thought.

Ahead of us, as we slogged through weekend traffic across the city, the driver of a 2000 Chevrolet Suburban was smoking a cigarette. The Suburban's tinted windows were rolled up, sealing its occupants from the environment.

The driver's side window, however, would periodically roll down an inch, belching a white puff of smoke and then the tip of a cigarette would emerge, tapping ash into the street. We pulled behind the Suburban at a stoplight. When the light turned to green, the cigarette fell into the street as we, the traffic, moved forward ensemble.

I committed myself to stay close to the Suburban. When my father harpooned an auto-flicker, I knew it right away. I wondered if Henry had figured out the signs yet.

"You want me to put this in the notes?" Henry said. When I turned to look, he had already pulled the notebook from the glove box and was writing something down, peering at the Suburban.

"We're never going to know any more about them now they've gone back into their cave," I offered, almost ready to give up the chase.

"If you live in a coffin, you got to keep it clean," my son said.

"What are you talking about?" Leonard asked from the middle pew.

"We are doing research for a behavioral study," Henry volunteered. "Why people defy God by throwing cigarette butts from their cars."

"Cool."

"I'm a frustrated social scientist," I said to the middle row, wondering when this had become about god.

Then, suddenly, the Suburban pulled into a small parking lot next to a collection of run-down stores that had once held loftier commercial aspirations. I swerved in behind the Suburban.

From a box in the Pennsylvania dirt, my father could still yank my steering wheel.

The three of us sat in the parking lot silently concentrating on the Suburban. After a moment, the driver's door opened. A short, foreign-looking woman climbed down from the cab, straightened out a tube top that looked too small to be comfortable, and trudged daintily on sneakers toward one of the markets.

Was there anyone else in the sport-utility vehicle? I reached for the pile of bumper stickers on the floor between the two front seats.

"I'll do it, Dad," Henry said.

But I couldn't send him out there into enemy fire.

"Keep the engine running," I said, easing open the door. "Tell Mom I love her if I don't make it back." I walked toward the Suburban. I couldn't see anything through its tinted windows. As surreptitiously as possible, I slid the magnetized disk onto the left hip of the Suburban and then made a 180-degree turn back to the minivan.

"Smooth, Dad," Henry said. I was already pulling the gearshift into gear and maneuvering us toward the street when the Suburban driver re-appeared stage left, momentarily looking straight at me, and I at her. But she turned away immediately, schooled not to make visual contact with strangers, and I watched in the outside rearview mirror as she walked around the back of her vehicle without noticing the new ornament there.

Then we were back in traffic, headed toward our next assignment, only a small detour for science on the path to art. We went to a marina on the Potomac where a motley collection of musical-theater pirates was waiting on a cigarette boat that looked ready to fly.

When the captain turned the engine over, everyone within a nine-iron turned their heads.

Henry and Leonard climbed into a smaller, saner inboard cruiser and followed the go-fast boat out toward an open expanse of the river to film it coming closer, full of pirates.

I kinda wished I was on the fast one.

1999 VOLKSWAGEN NEW BEETLE

It was Saint Jonah's day, and the last day of summer in the Northern Hemisphere. I drove Henry to his second Quaker meeting, and I did not go in. We had both attended the week before, and it only made me realize how little I cared about the church I had been going to for the last 25 years or so. Gershwin may have had it right when he questioned whether Old Jonah made his home in dat fish's abdomen.

Long ago, before we were married, going to church became one of the things Elizabeth and I did together, not long after the date we arranged when her car stalled in front of my speed gun. Mostly, I liked being with her, although I had some latent curiosity about what people saw in it.

Church was baked into Elizabeth at an early age. So when we began to think about getting married and having a family, I figured that maybe this was a way for a flawed individual such as me to be a good husband and father. I loved Speedy, and I never stopped being his son, but there are a damn lot of trails through the woods.

And it didn't hurt too much. I married Elizabeth in the church where her family had been going for a long time. I never thought of myself as converted; it was more like being diverted.

Before I knew what was happening, the first child, Herman, came along, a bubbly creature who turned suddenly somber when his sister Isabel was born a couple of years later, and then Henry.

I was a silent but not unwilling co-conspirator as we subjected our children to rituals that I never faced: baptism, christening, Sunday school and confirmation. No one ever thought to ask whether I had any of those merit badges. People assumed that, since I was married to Elizabeth and attending church regularly and putting something in the collection plate and hanging Christmas lights and hiding Easter eggs and trying not to fart in bed, I must have been saved at some point. To keep this pretense going, I nodded appropriately and as much as seemed necessary. If I had to, I mentioned the Boy Scout church.

Jesus wasn't a Christian, I told myself, yet he managed to be a decent fellow.

The problem with the Quaker church, as that would-be draft dodger called it long ago, was that they didn't believe it either, but they kept coming back to make sure. Plus, it reminded me too much of Speedy. So after that first Sunday meeting with Henry, I opted out altogether. If Emily Dickinson could take the Sabbath at home, surely it was okay for me, a 51-year old perpetual undergraduate, to waste Sundays out in the sunshine.

That Saint Jonah's Day of 2002, after Henry went into the Friends meeting without me, I turned the key in the ignition of our decrepit minivan, thinking about those tireless electrons racing to the spark plugs, the crank turning, fuel releasing into the pistons, blastoff. All systems go.

This was too easy. I shut down the engine. I got out of the car, locked the doors with the front windows rolled down and threw the car keys onto the front seat. This was the parking lot at a Society of Friends meetinghouse, after all, during a Sunday meeting.

With neither prayer nor plan in my head, I sauntered down the drive to the undulating two-lane road that was reminding me of up-county roads where I grew up, or tried to.

I was beached at a terrible place to hitchhike. The road was narrow and had no shoulder. Traffic hurtled at me around a curve and pitched headlong down a slope toward a bridge that spanned a tributary of the Anacostia. There was no place for a driver to pull over and little opportunity to even see me there before it was too late. All of which was peanuts given that this was late September 2002, the beginning of the second year of the Great Fear, decades removed from a time when kids still hitched, and generations after a time when the Depression and the war effort had socialized adults to the point that they would stand by the road and ask a neighbor for a ride.

I stood there anyway, thinking my chance of getting a ride was so remote that I was, in effect, just vertically sunbathing. Yet it was liberating to cast my thumb-bait to drivers as they poured over the hill and curled around me onto the bridge. Most of them probably didn't see me, or couldn't put together enough context to sort out what I was doing. A few may have put it together but were just too dumbstruck to do anything about it.

None of which really mattered because that limited stretch of asphalt where I waited was connected to all the others going places by being rooted on the roadbed.

Then a 1973 Audi Fox began to slow as it headed into the turn. I was out of shape and it took me a few seconds to realize that the driver was decelerating for me. He pulled halfway onto the driveway to the meetinghouse as I headed for the passenger-side door.

"Where ya going?" he asked.

He had me there. Unprepared, I muttered something about down the road and pointed forward through his windshield.

"You don't see hitchhikers much anymore." The driver looked to be a fellow traveler in the baby boom. There was a golf bag in the cargo area.

"I haven't done this in 30 years," I said, remembering the protocol. Talk if talked to. Be small and keep your odor to yourself. Watch for signs of weirdness. Don't get too comfortable, but don't be uneasy. Just two oxygen breathers hurtling down the road. It was different being an adult, or at least of adult age, but even more different was the fact that I was hitching a ride without any particular place to go.

"*And jolly enough were the sights and sounds that came bearing down before the wind,*" I said.

"I've got a golf game," Audi Fox said, turning off in the general direction of a golf course that I had vaguely noted in the many years I had lived in Prince George's County. Subconsciously, I was still mapping ways to earn a few dollars, in a pinch, on a weekend.

"I guess I'll just hang out there for a while and then head back," I said. "If that's all right with you."

It turned out it was alright with Audi Fox. He parked and changed into his golf shoes while sitting on the back bumper. I considered whether I should offer to carry his bag for him, at least to the clubhouse, but I feared that once back in the yoke, I might get lost and not find my way out again. So I walked with him for a little way toward the clubhouse and then said so long and lurked off toward the nearest tee.

After so much of my youth misspent on golf courses, this was the first one I had been to since I walked away from the country-club summer job with Brady's advice in my back pocket.

I watched a foursome of middle-aged guys in varying stages of being overweight and adorned to the gills in golf paraphernalia. They had two electric carts, as did the next several groups lined up behind them.

I looked out over the course and saw no caddies anywhere. As it was Sunday morning, there were no greens-keepers either. A golf course left almost entirely to the golfers, running amok in their gay, motorized carts, simulated automobiles with no onboard ashtray. This must be a public course, I thought to myself.

Here and there, someone was walking, bravely dragging a bag of clubs behind them on a two-wheeled cart.

I rediscovered that I liked watching golf balls smashed off and away from their little wooden pedestals, even the deformities that sliced and hooked hideously astray. If the soul of a golf stroke is the arc of its trajectory, do such atrocities reflect evil, or are they just the output of lousy artists? Or did they exist only to draw a contrast to beauty, those wondrous efforts launched bravely into the cerulean September heaven, climbing to a peak and then settling with self-confidence in the fairway, inviting its maker to attack the green?

I sat down in the chemically pimped-up grass, watching without trying to look, as another group ascended the tee box, stepping through their rituals. I sank back on my elbows, feeling old roots in the earth, relishing a perspective closer to the ground and glad that I had no fiduciary duty to watch where the hell the balls ended up, or to throttle down a lawn mower in order to be paid the minimum wage. The golfers loomed like actors or celestial beings against the impeccable sky. It was easy to be subverted by such prosperity, even when people around the world were scratching in the dirt for something to eat and walking miles through the bush for a bucket of rancid water, and our own boys and girls were dancing across minefields to give what-for to the zealots.

After a while, I decided I was thankful that I wasn't a golfer and I picked myself up off the plush grass. I ended up walking all the way back to the meetinghouse, as I knew I would, trudging backward with my middle-aged thumb in the road, practicing a dying social art.

Henry was sitting on the hood of the car, talking to a girl I didn't recognize and there was new illumination in my mind about his interest in the weekly meeting. He introduced us and we smiled at each other and shook hands and I was glad that he had put his waiting to good use. Further confirmation of my hypothesis that a foremost reason for going to church is to meet girls. For all I know, this may apply to temples and mosques and ashrams as well.

Henry and I drove toward a marina inside the city limits. There was a political talk program on the radio. The topic was the incessant drumbeat in those days for going to war in Iraq. A radio voice was interviewing a man named Scott Ridder, who had been a United Nations weapons inspector in Iraq and a critic of the Bush administration's claims about Saddam Hussein's weapons of mass destruction. He was a former Marine.

The interviewer said some of Ridder's critics were labeling him the "new Jane Fonda," and questioning his manhood and patriotism, and taunting him by wondering aloud what he would call his exercise video.

Or at least that's how Ridder took it. "If they want an exercise video," he said, "then they should come here and ask me to my face. I'll give them an exercise video called 'Scott Ridder Kicking Their Ass.'"

My son looked up and smiled. Even pacifists relish a good smackdown. "You know, dad, we've been flying missions over Iraq for 11 years. Not a lot of people realize that. It's like the last war never ended."

I was among the lot that did not.

On our way downtown, we came upon a white 1999 Volkswagen New Beetle driven by a woman puffing away on a cigarette. We ran before the wind on a four-lane city boulevard; the lights synchronized in our favor.

"Go get her, Dad," Henry said. He was grinning.

I dug my spurs into the minivan to keep up with the New Beetle, which was zipping merrily along. I was afraid that we would lose her at a traffic light; she looked like the kind of driver who accelerated on yellow, while I was the kind who braked. But if you want to make your mark in social research, you have to be willing to change how you drive.

She threw out the cigarette at nearly 35 miles per hour. I edged closer to the wide, round bumper and the big haunches behind the rear wheels. I followed her through a light that was turning red. A siren went off somewhere. I thought at first it tolled for me, but when I looked in the rearview mirror, it wailed for someone else. The next light turned red. The VW stopped abruptly.

I reached between the front seats and fished out a bumper sticker. I got out of the car. The sun and the clouds and the birds all stopped and stared at me, I was pretty sure.

She was a nice young woman, plump and comfortable-looking. No ring on the wedding finger. The car looked like it didn't often carry male cargo. She gazed at me in wonder.

"You threw your cigarette into the street."

"Hunh?"

"I have a bumper sticker for you. You'll like it." Then I surprised myself and flipped the magnetic bumper sticker, Frisbee style, onto the passenger seat of her car.

The signal had changed. She was frozen there, waiting to see what I would do next. "Have a good one," I said. "We should move on now."

This was apparently interesting enough that the drivers stopped up behind us didn't bother leaning into their horns. As I closed my door, the new Beetle jolted away down the road. I yanked the gear lever into Drive and resumed our journey.

"Why did she do it?" Henry asked.

"She didn't say."

We drove to a place where a commercial tour company with a handful of refurbished World War II amphibian vehicles started their tours of downtown sights. After tooling around on city streets for a while, the "ducks" rolled into the river and chugged along looking at more sights from an aquatic perspective and then emerged, dripping wet, back onto the streets.

The Moby troupe had rented one of these ducks for a few hours. The motorboat for the cameraman was already there. Actors clambered aboard the ducky and I helped load gear into the motorboat and watched wistfully from the pier as they launched into the channel and headed off toward the open river.

The Volkswagen was so well built that it could float for a few minutes. But they can't sail their yachts, I hummed to myself, cause the taxman's taken everything they've got.

On the way home, Henry explained that the ducky would be a native vessel from Queequeg's home island that would rescue Ishmael after he is set adrift by the pirates.

Though few who have read Moby Dick would agree with me, I was beginning to think Melville ended his story too soon.

1968 DODGE CORONET

In the office, I was reading my homework for the night-school myth class. The Inuit tell the story of Big Raven, a god in human form, who came upon a beached whale. Big Raven asked god to help him get the whale back to the sea and thereby restore the proper order of things. Big Raven was told to go in the woods and eat a particular mushroom, which would give him the strength to lift the whale back into the sea.

∞

Probably due to a lack of imagination, I tried to press the persistent myth of my childhood onto my own children. I read Moby with each of them, but only Henry took the Dick Mobius hook, and I guess that led him to the idea of a high school musical featuring whales lounging like 1960s hipsters around a pool.

All three of them, Herman, Isabel and Henry, scared me when they emerged from the womb. They never look the way you think they might before the doctor holds them up above the white hospital sheet covering your wife's lower half. But there they are, in total confusion about the rush of air into their lungs, awed by the new state of lightness, of having grown too big for the inner sea, squalling for the mother ship.

I was afraid that these children would love me as much as I loved my father, only to be crushed or worse, disappointed by my frailty. Little man, I said in my head to Herman, the first, don't get too close. And again a couple of years later to Isabel, and finally to Henry. But it was pointless; we are made of the same stuff. I could no more resist their charms than a first mate can hold back when the whale breeches across the waves and the boats are lowered for the chase.

∞

On the drive home from work, I came upon an electric-blue 1968 Dodge Coronet throbbing at a red light in front of me. A man of indeterminate age was driving and smoking. Windows rolled down, casually blowing smoke out the window. The Coronet had been through a lot

of changes since Chrysler introduced it in 1949, from excessive orna-
mentation to winged-out fantasy to muscle car. The 1968 had rounded
tail lights arranged like space-age bowties. I wondered if this fellow
had the model with one of the most powerful engines ever mounted in
a production car.

The driver threw his cigarette out the window as the light turned
green. There was a good deal of open street ahead, which he did not
waste. The Coronet rocketed away from me as though it were a different means of travel. When it rolled off the assembly line, that particular car was just one presidential election away from peacetime gas
rationing and the long sorry road to our first code-orange alert.

"That car was just too damn fast to hold cigarette butts," I said to
myself. "Never would have got a bumper sticker to stick to it."

I was the first one home that evening and began to make pasta
sauce with what I could find in the refrigerator and then slowly my
family came home, first Elizabeth and then, as it was getting dim outside, Henry on his bicycle. We ate outside. It was one of those evenings
of low-flying clouds, the city lights reverberating as an umbrella of
pinkish orange.

Henry was telling us about the scene when Ishmael lands on
Queequeg's home island and meets the harpooner's family and falls
under the trance of paradise. Picturing myself there, I was happy that
Ishmael was finding some peace after all he had been through.

"It's getting dark again," Elizabeth said. "And Henry is getting home
late from rehearsal."

A little slow at connecting the dots, I didn't answer right away.

"You should give him a ride to school and pick him up. We don't
have to wait for winter."

Henry was shaking his head. "I'm fine, Mom. I have lights on my
bike and you know I stick to the side streets."

I was neutral on this, but inclined to let the kid decide.

"It's such nice biking weather now, and most of his trip is in day-
light," I said.

1998 TOYOTA CAMRY

Henry wanted to try out the Friends meetinghouse in the city, so I sat in the minivan on a shady side street reading up on myths. A Buddhist teacher told a young man that he was god. Enlightened, the young man went for a walk. He came upon an elephant, also a god, coming in the opposite direction with some people aboard. The people called for the boy to move out of the way. But the student reasoned that, as god, he did not have to move out of the way of anything. So he kept walking

The elephant picked him up and threw him aside.

Bruised, the student went to his master and asked why he should have to move aside if he's god.

Because god told you to, the teacher said. You fucking retard, I thought.

They have better stories than we do, remembering my mother throwing popcorn from a bridge over the Delaware. Just then, my consciousness was diverted by the limbs swaying high above, the soft intercourse of rubber and asphalt, and the remembrance of being with Elizabeth and the children in a tent under a gentle rain, our dog posted outside. Herman, the oldest, must have been about 10 and Isabel was 8 and Henry a couple of years behind. With all that experience under their belts, the kids were telling stories of past camping adventures while Elizabeth and I, on opposite sides of the tent, were listening, all woven together. The kids were too young to know anything else, or that god could be an elephant telling us to get out of the way or that, with the right kind of mushroom, you can carry a whale back to sea.

Herman, sure of his certainty, remembered the day we saw a man drive his car off the edge of a back-country road and we tried to help him hoist the front end back onto the road surface. And Isabel, striving for accuracy, noted that we had stopped to inspect a spring of water coming out of the hillside. Henry said we had pancakes that morning and the wind was blowing so hard off the lake that it made whitecaps in the batter. I could see Elizabeth clearly, chattering away while the waves broke in our impending breakfast on the Coleman camp stove, its back turned into the wind off some northern lake. I failed utterly in my attempt to keep these people at arm's length.

Now they were growing beyond me: Herman was in an internship on Wall Street and Isabel was halfway through a ROTC program that she hoped would lead to a nursing career—nurses with guns!—and Henry, the last of the Dick Mobius in our clan, helping his aimless father try to finish a long deferred and probably pointless study of people who throw cigarettes from their cars.

I might have been sleeping. I certainly wasn't reading. Henry came out of the meeting and climbed into the seat beside me.

We started driving home and came upon a black 1998 Toyota Camry with an arm slung out the passenger's seat window at the end of which a cigarette smoldered.

Henry saw it the same time I did. This was getting worrisome.

"I'll get this one," he said, pulling himself into a more athletic position in the seat, ready to spring. I tried to close the traffic gap between us, but the Toyota pulled off to the right, luring us off our path. For an instant I let go of it in my mind and then found myself turning to follow.

We followed the Camry for several blocks, moving and stopping. Sometimes, it seems to take a long time to smoke a cigarette. We harpooned the Camry at a four-way stop sign just as the passenger flicked the butt into the gutter.

"I'm on it, Dad." Henry was jumping out of the minivan with a bumper sticker before I had a chance to stop him. The Toyota pulled away, and we rolled up to our turn at the four-way. My son sheepishly got back in the car.

"I don't know what I was thinking," he said. We waited as the cars to the left and right sauntered through the intersection. Then we lurched ahead toward the Toyota.

"Your brain is pure and car-free," I said. "That's a good thing. Any moron can drive a car."

The Toyota was gone. "He pitched it because he knew our reaction time would be slow," I said.

Just ahead of us, the police had barricaded the street. On the other side, there were people milling about and I picked up enough clues to realize this was a protest. There was an open parking space within reach, a chorus of elephants and whales nudging me toward it. As I parked, Henry related that, in the musical, Ishmael would wed an island princess and there would be a grand procession. As I maneuvered us into our berth, I reflected that it been a long time since I had marched with malcontents.

At first, Henry and I didn't know what we were protesting. In fact, it was a march sprung from opportunity. A bunch of like-minded people had been in the city for the past few days railing against the International Monetary Fund, and many of them decided to double down and spend an extra day demonstrating against the coming war in Iraq, which seemed a foregone conclusion even though most people who answered polls were still saying they opposed invasion.

The first day of the IMF protests had not gone well. The city police were intent on making sure the rallies would not become a massive disruption, as IMF protests had in other cities. According to the newspaper, the police outnumbered the protesters by two to one on Friday, and they made over 600 arrests, some of which might have involved actual lawbreaking.

Most of the arrests were "preemptive," like the Gulf War itself, which, according to Henry, had never really stopped.

Saturday, the second day of the IMF protests, was subdued. Four people were arrested for reportedly trying to make a bomb in an alley, enacting with their lives a Dylan lyric. A few hundred people listened to speeches and fumed about a grab-bag of complaints and then marched to the IMF offices, which were safe behind prophylactic fences. The protesters danced and yelled. A few built a Trojan horse, but its head broke off on a tree limb.

On the third day, because a butt-flicker had drawn us there, Henry and I joined the protest as it headed up Massachusetts Avenue to the vice president's residence. I was regretting not having a wet towel in case the tear gas started flying when I saw her in the crowd. A hyperlink tried to land; my viewfinder refocused: A gray-haired woman in a crowd of mostly younger people, her profile leaning forward with excitement. Marching for peace and justice as she had that day in 1968 when my father and I drove with her to Washington for the Poor People's Campaign.

Given a chance, my memory pushed Ms. Bennett's name to the surface.

I waved to her but didn't catch her attention.

I tried to keep track of her. It wasn't a huge crowd by any means, but it was big enough. When I couldn't find her again, it made me wonder if I had seen her at all, or whether I was transposing associations from one memory to another as though they were only connected to me and not rooted in any reality.

As my son and I marched, I tried to angle us toward where I thought she might be. And then, when we reached the fenced boundary of the vice presidential residence, the marching became a standing-around rally. I was half listening to the speeches when there was a tug at my sleeve. Up close, Ms. Bennett looked older than she had from a distance. Before I had a chance to do anything other than submit, she was reaching around my shoulders and pulling us together in a firm, lingering hug.

"Imagine that," she said.

"It's so great to see you." And I meant it. It was like an embrace with my father, by someone who had hugged him in his day. "Are you still in Pennsylvania?"

"Oh, yes," she said smiling. "I've got nowhere else to go."

"I live here now, in Maryland." I had raised my voice without thinking about.

"Yes," she said, as though this wasn't news for her.

"I'm here with my son," I said, pulling Henry in front of her.

"Is he in the Boy Scouts too?" she asked, grinning.

"No. Theater is his thing."

"The uniforms are better, I suppose," Ms. Bennett said. "Do you hear from your mother?"

I got a letter every month from Switzerland and I called her in between. For many years, most of the news had come from my side of the exchange. "Well, yes. We stay in touch all the time. She'll be here for Christmas."

"You must miss her," she said.

"Yes, but, you know, I've gotten used to it," I said.

"We all loved your father so much." Then I remembered this was exactly what she had told me at his funeral. "And he is still here." She put her palm on my chest.

It felt a little weird, and maybe the water was rising up around my knees. It got quiet around us, the sense of something stirring or even stampeding outside the bubble of awareness.

Somebody inside me asked her: "Were you his girlfriend or something? I mean, I always wondered about you and my dad."

Ms. Bennett smiled, tapping her fingertips lightly into my chest and looked down at the ground between us. "We had a time when we were young, but he had his own path to follow."

"When we went to that protest in Washington, it felt like we were together, not just three people in a car going someplace at the same time."

"There were things he wanted to know about his brother, your Uncle James, but I'm afraid I wasn't much help."

"You know, I saw you two together once, at a diner. I was with my mother, on the way home from the country club."

Ms. Bennett was sorting through file cards in her head. Her face turned from side to side, unable to connect the dots. "I don't remember that." Then something came to her mind. "Do you know that nice Mrs. Crick died a few weeks ago?"

And then it was my turn to think back 34 years. I saw "Crick" on a golf bag tag in the members' storage area long before I imagined her writing checks for the care of Uncle James. "I didn't know that," I said.

"I went to her service because, you know, she was so generous with Jimmy, but no one from her family seemed to know anything about it." Ms. Bennett thought this over a few seconds. "In fact, they seemed a little suspicious. They said she hadn't any money to give away for many years, that she had been left in a difficult situation when her husband died."

I said I hadn't thought about any of that in such a long time.

Then the crowd jostled itself, re-configuring. Our conversation came undone.

An outsider who knew Ms. Bennett threw herself upon us and drew her away, and the crowd flexed again on one of its myriad axes. My father's boyhood friend tossed a glance over her shoulder and waved as crowd gravity pulled her away into a different orbit.

Driving home with my son, I told him about the Poor People's Campaign and the tear gas and my father finding me in the crowd and tugging me back to fresh air and high ground. I skipped the part about being hauled into the police station.

2002 HONDA CR-V

On my way into work there was a bizarre story on the radio. Soviet scientists were organizing an expedition to find a meteoroid that had crashed in Siberia. It took a few days for the first eyewitness reports to surface, but people in a place called Mamsko-Chuisky had witnessed an extremely bright illumination in the early morning sky, a light so bright that it hurt to look at it.

It was raining out there in Siberia. Some described a sphere at the head of a tail. Visible from as far as 45 miles away, it lit up the sky in white or, from some perspectives, blue and red light.

There was electrical interference, and the meteoroid crashed with an explosion loud enough to impress the miners who lived out there, people who knew more than the average Siberian-in-the-street about explosive noise. A shock wave swept over the region. Windows shook 25 miles away. U.S. satellite imagery revealed a swath of damaged pine trees in the endless forest near the Vitim River. Although there were some exploratory parties already looking for the meteorite, those efforts were expected to kick up a gear when the rivers froze.

It was encouraging to think that the world was big enough to absorb a meteoroid here or there without everybody making a big fuss about it.

I was just settling in at my desk when our ancient receptionist patched a call from Elizabeth to my phone.

"Henry's been in an accident on his bike," my wife said. I thought I knew all her nuances, but this was a new one. Any panic or fear she may have felt at first had been wrapped in a layer of calm. Still, there was all the urgency of pulling a baked potato out of a fire with bare hands.

"Is he okay?"

"I'm on my way to find out. He's in the emergency room at Children's Hospital."

"I'll meet you there." Thinking through the Boy Scout manual. "Is there something I should bring or something to do before I go?"

She was pulling it together on her end. "Well, if you think of something, do it. I'm leaving now." None of us had a mobile phone, so when you hung up, you were really hanging up. I was left there staring at the handset, picturing Henry busted in a dozen pieces. As I headed to the parking lot, I couldn't come up with anything I could do but drive to the hospital.

I had been going to church for all those years and acting the part of a good monotheist, but at no time during the 18 minutes I was driving to the hospital did I ask for heavenly intervention. I thought about speeding and running stop signs, imagining what I would tell the policeman who would stop me. But I was a traffic analyst, not a physician or a nurse, and I figured that's whom Henry needed. It didn't really matter whether I got there in 18 minutes or 16 minutes.

Unless those two minutes were the difference between me talking to him alive and something else. As I drove, I remembered the feeling I had in the Delaware River, carrying my father to shore. I never really figured out whether that uncertainty—was he still alive?—was a state of grace, but I had no interest in going back to have another look. If that feeling was god, the rest of the world could have him. Or Him, as the case may be.

Turns out, those two minutes didn't matter. Henry had been "doored," as the bikers say. A passenger in a stopped car opened his door just as Henry was passing—legally, in a designated biker lane—on the curb side. Henry was knocked onto the sidewalk and instinctively threw his right arm forward to break the fall. Which snapped his right collarbone.

Elizabeth and Henry both looked calm when I found them in the waiting room. Henry was more annoyed than in pain; he was one of those peculiar kids who actually wanted to be in school. Elizabeth was anxious, but the simple fact that they were sitting in the waiting room, no great gory mess of blood around them, was a relief. This wasn't a life-changing moment, or so it seemed.

He told me the story, and Elizabeth said they were waiting for his soliloquy in front of the x-ray machine. The admitting nurse had admitted that it looked like a broken collarbone. The waiting-room hell that Dante failed to imagine: the ones who aren't that bad off have to wait the longest.

Finally, a nurse came for Henry and guided him away, his right arm hanging oddly from the rest of him. Elizabeth leaned toward me and clasped my hands together in hers.

"Let's pray," she said.

"He's getting an x ray," I noted for the record. In hindsight, I probably should have just bent forward and pretended to close my eyes and stare at the linoleum floor.

"Don't you want God to help him?"

"Really? If this is all God's got to do, he ought to look around. It's bound to scare him."

She looked up at me with those eyes I loved. Only a little less loving than usual. "What's that supposed to mean?"

"It means I've been thinking I ought to be honest with you about my so-called religion."

"Yes?" Those eyes waiting for me to say something acceptable.

"I don't have one," I confessed. "I never have. I've gone along all these years because I wanted to be a team player." I was regretting this as I said it, yet glad to get it out there in the antiseptic waiting room.

She was having trouble processing this. "I don't get it," said my wife, the person I loved above all others.

"It's not about you. I don't love you any less." I had to look away. "I just don't want to keep pretending. *Truth hath no confines.*" I thought about an evening long ago when I had interrupted my parents in the kitchen. "I don't want you to change. I don't want to change us."

Elizabeth waited. She was not someone to rush into things. "If you're saying you don't believe in God, I don't see how it doesn't change us. Because I sure do."

There, in that moment, I had to decide whether to throw my marriage in front of an onrushing the bus or go on the way I had.

"Never did," I affirmed, with not a trace of hostility or superiority. "Never will."

The unintended consequence of confessing my atheism at that moment is that it may have erased any fleeting impulse in Elizabeth to remind me that she had suggested only days before that I start driving Henry to school. Not that she was that kind of wife.

Instead, we sat in silence. She was hurt, but I thought it was important to be honest. I moved to put my arm around her shoulder. She acted as though it hadn't happened.

Eventually, Henry came out of the x-ray room to find his parents more busted than he was.

We stood up on each side of him, using him as a buffer, and that allowed Elizabeth and me to move on. It did not make the rest of the day anything less otherworldly for me, or, I suppose, for her.

There is nothing to do for a broken collarbone but take some of the pressure off with an arm sling, which Henry wore with some disgust as I drove him to the scene of the accident. He had had enough forethought to lock his bike to a tree—and without ever being a Boy Scout!—and he insisted on helping me load it into the back of the minivan. Then I drove him to school and tried to get through the rest of my day.

I went to pick up Henry after rehearsal. On the way home, the radio had another peculiar story, just as weird as the meteoroid smashing so far away in Siberia that they had to wait for a river to freeze before they could get a look at it. A man about my age had been shot in the parking lot outside a grocery store in a Maryland suburb. It was a rifle shot, from long range. The police had no explanation, the radio newscaster said.

At that moment, there was a 2002 Honda CR-V in front of us, a practical box that sat up almost high enough to see through the bigger SUVs and pickup trucks that were taking over the streets. The box was smoothed over with aerodynamic, curved edges. It carried a spare wheel on one side of the rear hatch, a throwback to a more utilitarian era and a nod to the rare notion that the two hemispheres of a car do not need to be symmetrical.

This one was darkish red. The driver had the window partly rolled down and was blowing smoke into the great outdoors. We followed it for a while, far out of our way, and I began to think we had either missed the cigarette toss or the driver had used the ashtray. Then, on a quiet residential street in the city, the CR-V stopped ahead of a parking space and its turn signal came on. I swung around and rolled slowly onward, paying more attention to the rearview mirror than to the life in front of me. I was fairly sure I saw the cigarette glow arc into the street as the CR-V began backing into the parking space.

I circled around the block with time on my hands. "No one is certain what CR-V stands for," I told my wounded son. "Some think it means compact recreational vehicle, but others say it's a comfortable runabout vehicle." By the time we made it around the block, the CR-V was parked and its occupants had left. I stopped alongside and handed the one-armed boy a bumper sticker.

When we got home, there was trouble. Given so much of the day to think it over, Elizabeth had determined that it was not acceptable for me not to believe in God. I tried to tell her that I was studying the issue as best as I could, reading about mythology, which is next to god.

That made things worse. "The problem with anthropologists is they think they know a lot of facts about belief, but they don't believe anything," Elizabeth said. I couldn't argue with that.

We three suffered through a tense dinner. Henry repeatedly said he was alright, and that his shoulder wasn't hurting. When he went upstairs to do his homework, I settled into the dishes while Elizabeth found someplace else to be.

It seemed like a good time to go check up on the houseboat.

Elizabeth came from a family of lifelong Washingtonians, and her father had a houseboat parked at a marina along the Anacostia River. He named it the *Beeping Sleuty* because of some joke he used to make when he read bedtime stories to his kids.

Ironically, after we were married, I used to hang out there with him and watch the Orioles on a small black-and-white television. He had a love-hate relationship with the Birds; they were the nearest club around, but they were once arch rivals of the Senators. Then the Senators abandoned the city. Twice.

The past few years, her dad wasn't up to keeping the houseboat shipshape, and increasingly it had become my job, *that I may in some sort revive a noble custom of my fishermen fathers before me.*

So when the dishes were done, I called upstairs that I was going to the marina. After a pause, there was an "okay" from the second floor in Elizabeth's detached voice. I drove to the marina with the reading for Thursday's myth class and settled in there as the breathing river beneath me rose and fell.

1939 Plymouth

On the morning commute, the world tilted further toward the bizarre. By the time I delivered Henry to school, a landscaper had been shot while mowing grass at a car dealership somewhere else in suburban Maryland.

I was downtown counting cars along a street that might someday get speed bumps when a motorist waiting in traffic told me there had been another killing, a taxi driver filling his gas tank. And before this news had been fully digested, a pedestrian asked me if I felt safe working outside.

"He shot another one, a woman sitting on a bench at a bus stop," the pedestrian said. "She was reading a book."

"*Though of real knowledge there be little, yet of books there are a plenty,*" I suggested.

It was creepy on the street, and I began looking for rifles in the back seats of the cars that swam by.

At the end of the day, I took refuge in the darkness of the theater at Henry's school, checking on the show's progress. They were rehearsing a scene in which Ishmael, on Queequeg's home island, realizes that all westerners—missionaries, whalemen, merchants, himself—are destroying paradise. In the musical, Ishmael decides to go back to whaling. Idly, I wondered if there was some way I could move onto the houseboat.

On the way home, news of another sniper killing, a young woman shot while vacuuming her minivan at a gas station. The radio said the public schools were in lockdown. It was unsettling, to say the least.

Henry and I came upon a 1939 Plymouth coupe convertible. The driver—an elderly woman who could have started her driving career in that car—was lighting a cigarette with the window rolled down. She drove very, very slowly through the residential streets near where my son went to school. She and her car looked as though they had been sailing those streets together for decades, through the tail end of the

Depression, the gas-starved war years, the buoyant can-do fifties, the getting-our-act-together sixties, the excellent dance moves of the seventies, the cashing-in of the eighties, the numbing glide into the nineties and now the little old lady from the Northwest quadrant and her rocking black Plymouth convertible were drifting along the leafy streets, oblivious to the snipers and the weapons of mass destruction and anthrax in the mail.

We followed, but I never thought she would pitch her smoke into the street; in fact, she didn't seem to be smoking it at all. Hers was a two-door Plymouth convertible with a rumble seat folded neatly into the trunk space. It was the first American-made convertible to include a power roof, and it helped Chrysler survive the Depression as a low-cost economy car with a few extras. The Plymouth badge was based on an image of the stern of the 17th-century transoceanic voyager that landed in Massachusetts, but the name was said to actually have come from a company that made a twine popular with farmers.

The '39 had a stunning, ship-like prow that featured layers of horizontally arrayed chrome strips and, in the automotive vernacular of the time, a look of disjointed parts welded together as a whole. But from the back, it had a modern, unified look—although the skirts over the rear wheels were hopelessly out of date and exaggerated. It had running boards and a tidy chrome bumper.

We followed the Plymouth to her anchorage, down a narrow alley behind a row of center-hall colonials with narrow yards all in a row. We sat in our ridiculous minivan and watched her tap decades of motor memory to back the Plymouth into its berth, completely oblivious to us 21st-century intruders.

I shifted my transmission stick into park and swung shoe leather out onto the paved alley. She was still in her driver's position. The Plymouth was smoldering a burned, oily aroma, the engine block cooling down in tiny crackling sounds. Plymouth had upgraded to six cylinders to keep up with the competition, and that may have helped keep this dinosaur on the streets for more than six decades.

She looked up with a smile, blue eyes resounding in the light of early evening, the sounds of the city hushing down around our ears.

I said hi. So did she.

"You seem too old to be smoking cigarettes," I said.

She laughed, girlishly, under all the time gone by. "I don't smoke them," she said. "I like to smell them burning."

"You mean you smoke but you don't inhale?"

She giggled again. "I light them in the car, but I don't smoke."

I looked inside because she didn't seem to care. The ashtray had several butts.

"And you never throw them out in the street while you're driving?"

She was affronted, as if I had accused her of child abuse or the defrocking of priests. "Of course not," she said.

I admired her indignation.

"Well, then, I guess I can't give you a bumper sticker."

She was shaking her head. "Oh, no, my husband was strictly against bumper stickers."

I smiled. "My dad was too," I said, "but he changed his mind after a while."

That night, I didn't have to run away to the houseboat to be alone. I bolted from the dinner table to my weekly anthropology class at the university. As far as I could tell, most of my classmates were actually trying to amass credits for a degree, but there was another fellow of about my age, a community-college English teacher, who said he was auditing the myth class after he had been sailing around Greece that summer.

"I've been thinking of taking my father-in-law's houseboat out for a few days," I said.

"There are many great voyages," he said. "Just don't go on one of those gluttony ships. They will drown you."

52. MONDAY, OCTOBER 7, 2002

1990 CHEVROLET CAPRICE

Elizabeth and I spent a couple of days avoiding each other as much as we could, and then she broke the ice.

"Is anybody going to go to church with me?" she asked Henry and me at dinner on Saturday. Her voice had been softened by the stress of Henry's accident and the sniper shootings and my fall from grace. She was trying to pull our family back together. Henry paused, waiting for a cue.

Speedy had inadvertently taught me there were bigger things than just the truth. "Sure," I said, wondering if we could go back to not talking about it.

That night we had a strange sort of lovemaking that seemed distant, even scripted. In the early hours, I woke suddenly and she was sitting up on her side of the bed in an attitude of prayer. Her eyes were closed and her lips almost silently whispering her message to heaven. I watched her for a while and then rolled slowly over on my side of the bed. At least she didn't have a harpoon by her nightstand.

The three of us went to church the next morning and it was worse than I feared. All during the service, I felt scrutinized, though she was probably stewing over her own feelings more than wiretapping my faithlessness. I could not wait to get out of there and probably did a lousy job of hiding it.

On the way to the parking lot, I took her hand and told her that I didn't feel any different than I had at the emergency room, but that I was glad to share the morning with her. In my head, I was asking myself whether we couldn't be doing something else together.

I could feel in her pulse that this was not what she wanted to hear.

Henry did most of the talking on the way home. Elizabeth said she was going to go to her mother's. I gave Henry a ride to his friend Leonard's house and then went down to the marina.

It was a warm day and the houseboat was musty. I threw open all the windows and began to attack the place with a spray bottle of all-purpose cleaner. At some point I noticed a young woman in cut-off jeans and tank top working on the cabin cruiser tethered next to our houseboat.

I went outside and took a seat in a deck chair. I was just watching her, barely trying to be discreet. This may have been the effect of the all-purpose cleaner fumes.

She had a Mediterranean look, I decided, about the same age as my daughter. I was having a pleasant, middle-aged guy's daydream when she looked straight at me and smiled.

I waved.

She waved back, enthusiastically.

"I'm Izzy," I called. "Who are you?"

"Evelyn," she said. Apparently glad that I cared.

She had a tattoo on her shoulder, I noticed.

"*Beneath the unclouded and mild azure sky, upon the fair face of the pleasant sea, waited by the joyous breezes, he floats on and on, till lost in infinite perspectives,*" I said.

She seemed amused. "What's that?" she asked.

"Moby Dick," I said.

"Say again?"

"You know. The novel. Moby Dick." I enunciated with an abundance of caution. "The white whale."

Not sure this made a mark either.

"It's just some old book I've read a bunch of times."

She didn't know what to make of this. I headed for firmer ground.

"Is that your boat?"

She laughed. "No. I just clean it."

"Yeah, me too," I said, gesturing about the houseboat.

Evelyn seemed ready to resume her boat cleaning, and I figured I couldn't just sit around on the deck ogling her. I went back inside and plugged away at my tidying up of the in-laws' mostly forgotten week-end getaway. I stopped only a few times to check up on Evelyn.

My cleaning was half done when I went to pick up Henry and drive us to Elizabeth's parents' house.

By Monday, I had forgotten about Evelyn. Later that morning, while I was counting illegal right-hand turns on a busy downtown street, the sniper shot a student outside a high school in Maryland. By then it was accepted that these were connected shootings and they had become a public obsession. Later, it would be revealed that the police found a

Tarot card and shell casing at the school shooting. The card was in-scribed "to the police." It said: "Code: Call me God."

After-school activities were being canceled and football games postponed all over the area, but there was a sense of futility in these precautions. Where can you hide if a god, even a false, self-proclaimed one, decides he wants a shot at you?

At the end of the day, I picked up Henry from school. On the way home, we fell in behind a 1990 Chevrolet Caprice. Weighed down by an excessively heavy chrome bumper and a bank of lights beneath a square flap overlapping a large trunk, there was little capriciousness about it.

The driver, an older guy with a baseball cap, was smoking a ciga-rette. We trailed him as long as we were both going in the same direc-tion. He turned right before our next turn, and I thought about follow-ing him, but it turned into one of those myriad tiny decisions made from the brain stem, long before it ever made it to the thinking part of my cranium.

"Why didn't you follow him?" Henry asked.

"He wasn't going to throw if anybody was watching," I said.

"How do you know that?" the boy asked.

"Just intuition."

"*When night obscures the fish, the creature's future wake through the darkness is established in the sagacious mind of the hunter,*" Henry opined.

"Sagacious is a reach, but I did have a picture of his flick in my mind."

"Does that mean we put it in the report?" He was retrieving the notebook from the glove box.

"There was a flick in some reality, even if the guy himself never ex-perienced it. Why should this not count? We need all the data we can get."

Henry was scribbling. "Some kind of Chevy, wasn't it?"

"A 1990 Caprice, I think."

1999 FORD FOCUS

While I was driving Henry to school, the radio informed us that the war in Afghanistan had been a rousing success and, after just one year, we had routed the Taliban and set the land-locked collection of frequently squabbling clans on the path to democratic government.

Henry had adjusted remarkably well to his broken wing. The show must, you know, go on. He was wearing a sling, off and on, and though I don't think he needed it anymore, the kids were thinking about keeping him in it, to create a level playing field with the one-legged Ahab.

"But Ahab went down with the ship," I pointed out.

"You think Ishmael wasn't scarred by what happened to the *Pequod*?" he asked.

Surely, I thought. After I dropped Henry off, I headed downtown to the Department of Transportation to read research journals in its library. My boss didn't want to pay for these publications, and I couldn't blame him, but he didn't mind if I tried to keep up with things. Even after a lot of this material went online, I still preferred to make my rounds in person.

I was at a library desk anchored to government linoleum in a room of dust motes drifting like pollen from stacks of DOT bulletins and desiccated impact studies. Before me, an annual transportation study, hundreds of pages of numbers, a shock-and-awe display of statistical prowess. But I knew where I was going in that book, the same place I went every year.

Only 32 waterborne fatalities related to vessel collisions, a low for recent years. I was never sure whether a vessel and a swimmer would constitute a collision, but it was good to know that the number was going down. Small-boat casualties were up, however; maybe because kayak and jet-ski traffic was increasing.

I wasn't counting either of them.

It got to be lunch time. I rose from my reading table and re-shelved the reports myself. The librarians frowned on users doing this, but there were fewer of us passing through the library every year.

I decided to go to the houseboat for lunch. *Beeping Sleuty* was getting to feel like my property; I had stowed away some food and, now that it was turning cooler, there was less and less chance that Elizabeth's father would show up while I was there.

I sat on the sagging, webbed vinyl deckchair and ate a sardine sandwich, admiring the October sunshine, listening to half-hearted waves lapping against the hull. Not many people around. Sea gulls gulling about, being shiftless bums. I knew how they felt.

I had resigned myself to going back to work, picking up some data boxes and taking them back to the office to download. Then the owner of the cabin cruiser next door showed up, marching down the planks.

We knew each other enough to nod and wave. "How's it going?" I ventured.

"Great. What a day, hunh?"

"Ahab stood forth in the clearness of the morn; lifting his splintered helmet of a brow to the fair girl's forehead of heaven," I said.

"What's that?" he asked.

"We've been thinking about getting a cleaning crew over here," I said. This was mostly ridiculous, for ours was a rundown, aging houseboat that rarely putted away from the dock. "Who do you use?"

Captain cabin cruiser was eager to help. "There's a girl who comes every few weeks as necessary. I can give you her number."

And that's how easy it was to find out that she was Evelyn Fuentes, and she had a phone number. And after trying to pretend for a few hours that I wasn't going to call her, I finally did. I had the feeling she didn't really put together my voice on the phone and my face that Sunday afternoon or the Moby gibberish I had offered up.

On the phone, it's easier to be someone else, arranging to meet a girl at your father-in-law's houseboat. I was as giddy as a Girl Scout, at the same time realizing what an ass I was being. Well, we'll just stick to the cleaning proposition, I told myself.

That evening, Henry and I gave Rachel, the actress playing the missionary's daughter, a ride home. Henry sat beside her in the middle seats of the van, leaving me chauffer-like and alone in the front. This allowed them to go over the script of the musical.

In the musical, the missionary's daughter had also been picked up by the pirates, who would get drunk and set her and Ishmael off in a canoe to find their way to the shore of Nantucket.

Henry and Rachel were more deferential to each other than was likely if their relationship was just about the musical. I was thinking about the ladder leaning in the night against Juliana's windowsill.

We got to Rachel's house too soon. There was some flustered rustling of paper and the trappings of teenage life, but I kept my eyes straight ahead, as a good caddy should. Self-conscious farewells until tomorrow and a "thanks" from Rachel as she disembarked.

"You should find a reason to be with her at the door, son," I said. Maybe he didn't need this push.

Henry hurried to the door.

At home, I sat on a kitchen stool reading the paper aloud as Elizabeth finished making supper. The Bush administration was going to nominate a devout Christian physician to a key job at the Food and Drug Administration. Because the nominee had written books about women's health in the context of the teachings of Jesus, some smarty pants were questioning his suitability for a panel that would steer government policy on reproductive issues, including drugs to terminate pregnancy.

I foolishly brought this to my wife's attention. "I suppose anybody named to that job is going to bring some kind of religious orientation," I said.

She took it defensively. "Jesus isn't an old sweatshirt you can put on whenever you feel like it," Elizabeth said. I <u>was</u> at that moment wearing an old sweatshirt that my wife had been trying to throw away for years. "He was the son of God, and until you accept him as your savior, no amount of treading water at your mythology class or going to church just to be nice to me will bring you closer to salvation."

It may have been a flash of honesty; or mere prudential policy which imperiously forbade the slightest symptom of open disaffection. Like a good underwater swimmer or yogi master, I held my breath.

Later that evening, there was an emergency that required me to go buy milk. I drove Elizabeth's car, which needed gas, and while I was loading my credit card into the machine, a 1999 Ford Focus sped impatiently to the other side of the island of pumps. The driver, a woman, was smoking a cigarette. This looked familiar. She got out of her car, dropped the cigarette on the ground, and intentionally stepped over it, rather than grinding it out.

We traded meaningless smiles when our eyes crossed.

"You left your cigarette burning next to the gas pump," I said, still smiling.

She looked at me questioningly, not getting my drift. Was I someone she knew?

"The cigarette. Shouldn't we put it out?"

She shrugged and went on with the gas-pumping procedure. Whoever I was, I didn't matter.

"I've got a bumper sticker for you, but it's in my other car," I said, making sure she heard me, without trying to bear down too hard. She was an accomplished ignorer, however.

When I got back in our car, there was a news alert on the radio. The sniper had gotten another victim, a man killed while pumping gas at a service station in Virginia. Later, they identified him as a white guy of about my age. Coulda been me.

When I got home, I realized I had forgotten to get the milk.

The Beeping Sleuty

In myth class, we had been considering whether early Christianity had as many roots in lost Greek religions as it had in the Old Testament. I looked across the breakfast table at Elizabeth that morning and decided to keep this below deck. Instead, I asked if she could pick up Henry at school, or if he could come home on the metro.

"There's something I gotta do for work," I lied.

After I dropped Henry at school, the sniper killed another middle-aged man pumping gas at a service station near Manassas. A Virginia state trooper was parked nearby at the time of the shooting.

Filling stations had become dangerous in the public mind. There were among us folks who would only use the pumps farthest away from the open road, thinking they would make a more difficult target. Some people claimed they were pumping gas more quickly than they used to. Gas stations turned their surveillance cameras away from the pumps, where they were trained to catch thieves, to the horizon, in hopes of catching snipers.

There were so many suspicious things that we citizens were being asked to be aware of and report to our authorities. The snipers and the zealots were turning us into a nation of snitches.

In spite of all the danger, I quit work early and went to the houseboat.

It didn't really need much cleaning. I could have easily finished the job myself, and even gave thought to messing it up a bit for Evelyn's sake.

Since I quit the Boy Scouts, I was unprepared for a lot of things that came my way. That Friday, playing hooky, I had been imagining Evelyn in cut-off jeans and a form-fitting blouse. But friend, that's not how she arrives. Evelyn comes in pumps and a short black dress and there is nothing janitorial about her. She stalks down the boardwalk and pauses briefly before she takes a long stride across the great aqua-blue and pronounces herself upon your deck.

"Hi," said I, unsure who was the spider and whom the fly.

She unfurled a mighty smile, part customer relations, part something else to my addled mind. Unmoored by her physical presence, I somehow managed to show her around our nautical premises, pointing out the dirt as I saw it, and apologizing that there wasn't more.

"It won't take long to clean this up," Evelyn said succinctly.

"I'm sorry," I responded. "You seem overdressed for this."

She looked down at her feet. "I wasn't planning to clean it now," she explained. "It's Friday night."

Of course. Fumbling, I asked her what she did when she wasn't cleaning boats.

She said she was in college.

"Me too," I nearly exclaimed. "I've been going to college for over 30 years now, off and on."

Evelyn laughed. "I hope it doesn't take me that long."

A pause. "You've got things to do," I said. Then our eyes locked and I couldn't look away and words came spilling straight from my head. "You should be in front of a camera, not cleaning boats."

Most people like to be complimented, especially if you mean it. Evelyn smiled, looking ridiculously young.

She asked me if I wanted to party.

I was too ignorant to know what this meant. Evelyn was grinning knowingly all over the place and I was watching her legs disappear under her hemline and falling headlong again into her brown eyes.

"Of course," I said.

She took my hand and steered me onto one of the vinyl-covered benches in the "stateroom" of the houseboat of my father-in-law. And she opened her purse, fished out a tiny case and opened it before me. Inside were a half dozen or so pills of varying colors and dimensions. Already, I was pretty sure this was a dream.

Which made it okay for her to pull two capsules from the tiny box and say this was a good place to start and hand one of them to me as she popped the other into her mouth, which, I noticed, was lined with lipstick a particular shade of red I could not identify. My pill sat there on her palm as I ruminated over what I would do. Casting caution overboard, I took the pill and hoisted it onto my tongue, imagining rocket boosters flaming to life, lifting me on a journey in search of what ... whales? weightlessness? a reason why my father died in a slow-moving, relatively shallow river?

My first reaction: nothing. This was a bullshit conspiracy by the government and the media to convince us that dangerous mind-altering drugs were dangerously altering the minds of our youth. But wait, I thought, ain't I one of those youth? Not anymore, you sap, says my sadder but wiser self. No, I am not that old, I answers, and suddenly found myself saying, out loud: "Do you want something to drink, Evy?

Evelyn was mellow on the vinyl bench. I was amazed by her knees. She may have said something, or maybe not. I went to the small refrigerator and pulled out two beers of indeterminate vintage.

In the interest of scientific objectivity, I should report at this point that I had no direct experience of psychedelic drugs in my life other than the few disjointed attempts at smoking reefer with Juliana. Beyond that, I was a total rube. I sometimes drank beer if I was thirsty enough.

Marriage to a monotheist can do this to you. But it doesn't have to.

I sat on the bench within the scent of Evelyn and promptly decided I ought to be on the armchair a few feet away. She leaned in a little toward me, holding the beer at a distance as she popped the top. Some cleavage presented itself. She took a sip and handed the can to me.

"I really just wanted to wet my whistle," she said. "Do you want to share this one?"

"Not much of a beer drinker myself." I took a sip and rose to return the unwanted can to the fridge. The *Sleuty* felt wobbly under my feet. Sometimes when a big boat went by too fast, the wake would rock us. Sometimes when I took drugs from women I didn't know, the wake would come my way.

On the way back, I settled into the armchair. Evelyn asked if there was any music aboard. The old teevee didn't count—it still had rabbit ears—and there was only a decrepit tabletop AM-FM radio as an option. This was a disappointment to her, but these young people are not deterred for long. She dug into her purse and pulled out an iPod, plugged in her earbuds and approached me on foot as she dialed up something on the device.

Evelyn found what she wanted and then turned directly in front of me and slowly settled her derriere onto my lap. She pulled a plug from her right ear and gently pressed it into my left ear. But it was hard to tell which sensation was strongest: her swarming pheromones, her bottom on my thigh or the jarring, unrecognized music pumping into half of my brain. Then there was the small matter of my consciousness coming unpinned, *the current carrying me to those sweet Antilles.*

It was pleasant. She would bounce every now and then to something pouring half into her brain and half into mine. When I dared to look, I noticed blemishes in her skin plastered over with some cosmetic or other and, unless she shopped at a very old thrift shop, probably not made from the whale spermaceti. From time to time, I heard something outside our little world, an inboard engine rumbling to life down the row of pleasure craft, a distant alarm sounding emergency, Ishmael with a broken collarbone trying to paddle his way back to Nantucket with the missionary's daughter, Quentin laughing at my bell-bottom pants, the Fifth Dimension, my oldest child Herman standing up on his own steam for the first time and staggering across the floor in the hallway upstairs in our bungalow in suburban Maryland, Isabel streaking down the soccer pitch on a break-away, the people who had brought Evelyn there to my lap on my father-in-law's houseboat.

We decided to get up and walk around. My head was spinning, but staying put. We were holding hands, like lovers do, but it was more like two kids in a pitch-black room. I felt connected to her—not because of the channel of music split between us—but more like shipmates clamoring into the same lifeboat as the *Pequod* was spiraling in the maelstrom toward its heaven and hell. The October sun was spinning gold overhead, on its way into the west. We paused to watch yachts sway in their stalls as the tide-infused river pulsed inland. A chill seemed to be creeping toward us.

At the end of the gangplank, we stopped and watched the sun splinter into the clouds over Virginia. I pulled Evelyn close to me, my hand around her hip, and she leaned in willingly, warming each other against the breeze in our faces.

"How do you like ecstasy?" she asked.

"It's as good as they say it is," I answered. I was glad to have a name for it. Like Elizabeth, she felt delicate in my arm. We stood there for a while and then I took the earpiece out of my head and inserted it into her left earhole, separating us by another fraction of experience. Evelyn was still tied into something that I was no longer a part of.

She was a loose fish; I was fast to one at home.

The sunset purpled a little farther into the west. We turned and walked slowly back to the *Beeping Sleuty*, still clenched together, but our brains were off on separate orbits. When we got back to the houseboat, we sat and embraced on the vinyl bench, and she slung her leg over mine and pressed her face into me. Our lips kissed, but I closed my eyes and thought of Elizabeth. Their tongues are pretty much the same, in the end, but their techniques and tastes are as different as snowflakes.

The happily-married guy's fantasy.

This went on for a while, but one or the other of us eventually grew bored. Evelyn drew back and looked in my eyes again. I was tripping like nobody's business. But I remembered what my father told that kid at the Magical Mystery Tour and was getting used to it.

"I need to get going," she said.

"At some point, I need to go home," I said, wondering how long it would take until I could possibly do that. It was nearly dark outside.

Evelyn stood up and straightened her dress. I wondered where she was off to as she staggered toward the door. I followed after her.

Evelyn fished in her purse and pulled out a cigarette. I wished that I had a lighter, but of course, I did not. She lit her smoke and we stood there quietly while she smoked. I was surprised that I enjoyed being downwind of her as much as I did, wondering why people complain about second-hand smoke.

Finally, she flicked the cigarette into the water.

I had to ask.

"This is a non-smoking vessel," she said, as though she had been deputized her to enforce maritime law.

"Are you going to be alright?" I asked.

"Sure," she said, and I was convinced that she actually was. I watched with great pleasure as she hopped from the *Beeping Sleuty* to the marina gangplank, waved happily to me and vamped toward the rest of her evening. We had never set a time or price for her to maid-up the houseboat. It hardly seemed important.

I pulled the other vintage beer from the refrigerator and a bag of stale potato chips and watched a baseball game involving the Anaheim Angels and the Minnesota Twins. The Twins were one of the Senators traitors that had abandoned RFK Stadium, so I rooted—for once in my life—for the Angels. Though I didn't last to the end of the game, the Angels would homer twice on their way to victory.

At some point in the darkness, I realized I could probably be trusted to go home.

1999 FORD TAURUS

Elizabeth was not amused when I came home very late that night from the *Beeping Sleuty*. I told her I had gotten a little drunk after work and decided to wait until I felt safe driving.

"Who are you?" she asked.

"I'm still working on that," I shrugged truthfully. "Maybe this is my midlife crisis."

She shook her head, puzzled. "Who were you with?"

"A bar crowd. I don't expect to see them again. Honestly, I thought of you a few times." I reached forward and took her hands in mine. "I don't think I'm cut out for the saloon life, but I may have to try again some time to make sure." Elizabeth looked back, her eyes still faithful, and sighed.

She was cutting me a lot of fucking slack.

Somewhere between my trip with Evelyn and that Saturday morning, the sniper shot a woman as she was crossing the parking lot of a home-improvement store in Virginia. It was as ruthless and random as all the others, but this time there were reports of an eyewitness.

Later, it turned out that the person had not witnessed anything. And so a couple million of us looked once again over our shoulders for ways to not be a target.

We three Yardleys sat around the kitchen table waiting for Leonard, and then Rachel—with another friend—to arrive. I was driving the four of them to a beach on the Chesapeake Bay to record more video.

On the way, the radio newscaster said the Nobel Prize for Economics had been given to a cognitive psychologist who studied irrational economic decisions. In one study, most people said they would travel 20 minutes to save $5 on a $15 calculator, but they would not go the same distance to save $5 on a $125 jacket. The cognitive psychologist, as if to prove something about rationality, raced out of his house after hearing that he had won a Nobel, forgetting his keys and locking himself out.

They gave the Peace Prize to Jimmy Carter, in part, it was said, because he wasn't George W. Bush. There was a raging debate among people who rage over national policy on whether the intelligence about Iraq had been discovered or invented by the CIA, and whether it was being distorted by a war-hungry White House.

At the beach, the kids climbed into their whale-head costumes and rehearsed a number in which they sat around on beach chairs. They were playing the Velvet Underground's "I Waiting on My Man" on a boom box and then they got up and walked single file, fingers snapping, into the water.

They did this several times, complaining every time about how cold the water was. The actual singing would be taped over the video.

On the way home, I asked how this fit in the musical.

"Everywhere Ishmael goes on his journey home, there are whales in the background," Leonard explained. "Sometimes they react to what's happening to Ishmael."

"Sometimes they cause something to happen to him," Henry added.

I delivered Leonard to his home and then followed directions to the other girl's house and then Henry cleared his throat and asked if he could accept Rachel's invitation to hang out at her house. I said sure and was forgotten before they were halfway to her front door.

Nearly home, the car in front of me threw a cigarette into the street. I had not even noticed that it was neighbor Ted until he parked his 1999 Taurus in his usual spot. I rolled past him, cranking down my window.

"How's it going, Ted?" I asked.

"Just great," he said. "I haven't been killed yet by the sniper."

"Did he get someone else today?"

"Probably. If he didn't, somebody else likely did."

I would have asked about his cigarette littering again but I was distracted by an unfamiliar car, with Pennsylvania plates, parked in front of our house.

Inside, my wife was in the kitchen talking to Juliana as though this sort of thing happened all the time. In the corner of my eye, Elizabeth looked happy to see me with Juliana, and for a brief moment I was just there, alone with my first girlfriend in the camouflage we had put on over time.

We spent a few moments filling in a lot of blanks as I tried to imagine what she was doing in our kitchen.

"I'm glad you got home. Juliana was just saying she has to leave soon," Elizabeth said. "She's driving back to Doylestown tonight."

Juliana pulled an envelope out of her bag. "Do you remember Lee, the Korean guy who worked for Vic Martine?"

I said I did.

"About a week ago, he showed up at my door with this." She handed me the envelope. It had my name on it, written with a typewriter. "He said Martine is in grave danger, and that you must see him."

I guess I looked sufficiently at sea. "As far as I can tell," Juliana continued, "Lee had no idea where you lived, but he remembered taking me home that night and so he went to my parents' house. My mother still lives there, and she told him where I live now, in Acushnet."

"Don't tell me. He ran to your house." I was trying to imagine how old he must be by now.

"It sure looked that way," said my old girlfriend.

Thirty-four years later, I did not think very often about the guy who killed my father. "What's wrong with Martine?"

"Lee said he is very sick," Juliana said. "Very sick and needs what he called 'paper help.' Then he pointed to the letter and told me I had to get it to the boy who used to carry Mr. Vic's golf bag."

I had not seen Juliana for many years, since a chance encounter in Doylestown some time after we had broken up. "It wasn't easy finding you," she said, as though that was my fault. "I thought somebody on the high school reunion committee might know where you where, but you're among the missing as far as they're concerned."

I had not intentionally disappeared from that life, but on the few occasions when I went back there, it seemed I knew fewer and fewer people.

"There aren't that many Yardleys, and I found one who is a cousin or something and she said you lived here in Maryland. I guess I could have called first or something, but I just decided to drive here."

I got the feeling that Juliana was enjoying this mission and springing herself on me.

"Aren't you going to open it?" she asked.

There was a lot running around in my head. The envelope looked old, and the glue yielded easily to modern inquiry. Inside was a letter that bestowed upon me the power of attorney to act in the best interests of Victor Martine in the event that he is declared incompetent.

It was dated May 1969.

"It's a power of attorney," I said, handing it to my librarian wife, who managed our legal paperwork. "What am I supposed to do with this?" I asked Juliana.

"I had no idea what was in there, Izzy," my first girlfriend said, with a serious look. "But I knew it was important to Lee. He said not to mail it, but to take it to you in person. He wanted to be sure of that."

Elizabeth knew pretty much the whole story about Martine and Juliana and how my father died under a water-ski boat. She didn't know that Juliana used to call me Doris or that she picked me up hitch-hiking and wrote her phone number with a ball point pen on the palm of my hand and left the top button of her waitress uniform open.

Wives and husbands don't need to know everything. Often, they're gonna think they do anyway.

The ex-girlfriend and I went outside to reminisce some more next to her car with Pennsylvania plates. She said she was pressed to get home to her family, yet she kept lingering. The lights came on. Elizabeth came out on the front porch and asked if Juliana would stay for dinner, and that became a sign for her to actually get on her way.

"Will you come up and see him?" she asked, turning her face toward mine outside her window. Her blouse was buttoned all the way to the top.

I knew I would, but I was clinging to a smidgeon of resentment that Martine could reach back through all this time and pick me to carry his bag again.

After dinner, I sat in the dark on the back porch enjoying the night sky and listened to the radio, thinking about the yawing and pitching deck under my life.

The news came on, full of a new development in the sniper attacks. During a press briefing, the chief of police addressed the sniper directly, asking him to "call us." It had been previously reported that the sniper left messages at one or more shooting sites, and the on-air experts widely agreed that establishing communication with the sniper was a positive step.

This seemed like Boy Scout common sense to me that even a sniper could figure out.

56. FRIDAY, OCTOBER 18, 2002

SOME WHITE CAR.

My dad, Isaac Yardley, said I should write down any cigarette throws that happen when he's not around. For the past few days, he hasn't been around much. He says he's spending time at the houseboat because he can think better there and he's got some paper to write for his anthropology class. My mom says Dad has some stuff to work out. I didn't ask her about it, so maybe she had to say it. She took me to meeting last Sunday and most days she has been picking me up from school.

Mom and me were riding home from school when I saw somebody smoking a cigarette in a white car in front of us. Dad knows all about car models because he's been watching traffic for 30 years or something like that, and he and my grandfather, who I never met, had this thing about catching people throwing cigarettes. I don't know anything about cars and don't plan to.

Anyway, I asked Mom if she would follow the car with the smoker. I had to tell her about the research project, which was news to her. So we followed the white car and it seemed to take a long time for the driver to finish smoking. But Mom kept after him and I could tell she was getting into the chase, and I realized how much I missed Dad. He has harpoons stuck in a bunch of us, and I thought how much he must miss his father.

The white car gave us the slip, and we never saw the cigarette fly into the street. I wish I could say what it looked like and what it represented in the evolution of car design, but they all look the same to me. Mom seemed bummed about it, but I told her that was all part of the research. We have to take the negative results along with the positive.

Because we were in Mom's car, I had to write this down on a scrap of discarded script from the musical.

Scene 16. Ishmael and the Missionary's daughter, drifting in a canoe.

Ishmael: Again, I am a buoy bobbing on Mother Ocean, waiting to be rescued.

Sings: *Till gaining that vital centre, the black bubble upward burst;*

and now, liberated by reason of its cunning spring,

and owing to its great buoyancy, rising with great force,

the coffin like-buoy shot lengthwise from the sea,

fell over, and floated by my side.

Missionary Daughter: It can't be so bad if we're together.

Ishmael: No, I ain't complaining. Tis heavenly to be here with thee, facing the perils of the sea.

Missionary Daughter: Heavenly might be a stretch.

Ishmael: *It is only when caught in the swift, sudden turn of death, that mortals realize the silent, subtle, ever-present perils of life. And if you be a philosopher, though seated in the whale-boat, you would not at heart feel one whit more of terror, than though seated before your evening fire with a poker, and not a harpoon, by your side.*

Missionary Daughter: The evening fire sounds pretty good right now. Especially the bit about the poker.

Ishmael: So I intend to paddle us there, my love.

Missionary Daughter: (Leans forward.) Keep saying that Ishy, what rhymes with fishy.

Ishmael: It was the death of Queequeg and Stubb and Starbuck and Pip and even Ahab that lifted me up from the deep, hitch-hiking to the carefree afterlife. I never felt levitated, I never felt light, until my crewmates ascended into the *unclouded and mild azure sky, upon the fair face of the pleasant sea,* unweighted *by the joyous breezes,* where *that great mass of death floats on and on.*

Ishmael and Missionary Daughter: (Duet, based on "Sea of Love,"
as recorded by Phil Phillips)

Sail with me, my love
'cross the sea, and take my love
I don't know yet know
How much I may love you.
Find us a cottage in Aquarius
Just some place where we can get hilarious
I want to find out how much I love you.
Come with me, to the sea
of love.

1992 VOLVO

That morning at the breakfast table, Elizabeth said to me in a tone, "Are you going to Pennsylvania, then?" I had already told her so, but my heart was mixed with annoyance and curiosity.

My wife, however, was looking at me in an amorous way. I felt a flush rising. Had my blood pressure got a hold on me or was this the way it's supposed to be? And sometimes, drifting out there in space, the heat is all over my face, giving way to grassy glades, where something in me begins to roll around in new morning clover, kicking its heels in the air, rocking and rolling in the cool dew of the life immortal.

"Hold on a minute, wifey," said I. "I am about to become a genius."

She was too well-read for the likes of me. "That's Balzac and intellectual constipation," she answered.

Being married to a librarian has its ups and downs, but the chick could still get my spine out of place.

"A soul is the orphan of an unwed mother who died in childbirth," I said. "The secret of our father lies in his grave, and when the part of him inside us dies, we finally learn it."

Elizabeth looked at me over her coffee. There had been another sniper shooting that night, a man hit outside a chain restaurant 90 miles south of the city of Washington. Where would the sniper snipe next? This time, the victim survived the attack. Was the sniper getting bleary-eyed staring through his rifle scope? The police found a rambling letter in the woods.

That's a good place for rambling letters.

"Are you saying you think you have a soul?" Elizabeth asked, pursing her lips to blow over the coffee mug before her, regardless of whether the brew was hot or not.

It was spectacularly bright and blue in the outside sky that I could see through the back window. "I think doubt is a form of gospel, and maybe the truest form," I said, knowing I was better off being pithy than expository.

She mulled this over, pushing a slice of bagel around on her breakfast plate. It was an interlude; it didn't matter what conclusion she came to. I had come up with a tiny thing over which her brainy microbes were swarming.

I ventured out on ever thinner ice. "Maybe it's not just the vices that are enumerated. Maybe there's a list of the virtues and one of them is doubt."

Elizabeth smiled. "Don't push your luck, Bucky." Which is what she called me when we were having, or about to have, sex. I reached across the table and pushed my luck anyway, taking her hand in mine.

She was on the same page. We went upstairs and had to be quick about it. I had still to take the boy to school, and then get myself off to Pennsylvania.

Henry was late for school. I am pretty sure he knew why.

Then I was driving north on a classic stretch of American highway: Raise your hand if you have driven I-95 from D.C. to Philadelphia or beyond.

On the radio, astronomers were reporting that they had found a large black hole at the center of our galaxy.

The doubters knew it was there all along.

On Monday that week, the police arrested two guys in a white van near Richmond, and for a few hours we millions of sheep crossed our fingers. But they turned out to be just two illegal aliens who had not snipered anyone, and they were simply deported. During a televised press conference, Police Chief Moose—no novelist would dare give such a name to a character—read a precise and exact response to the sniper, something about not being able to understand everything that was said.

Big deal, I thought at the time, I don't understand most of what I hear.

On Tuesday, a bus driver was shot dead standing on the steps of his bus in Aspen Hill, Maryland. Chief Moose read part of the sniper's most recent message. "Your children are not safe," he reported, "anywhere, at any time."

Later that day, the U.S. introduced a United Nations resolution authorizing the use of force to disarm Iraq. It seemed like a dicey proposition, the experts said. Various U.N. Security Council members were opposed to it. But Al-Qaeda was everywhere: in Iraq, reputedly, and, in some minds, telling the snipers what to do.

A Congressional resolution to wage holy war is a terrible thing to waste.

There did seem to be demons a-plenty creating havoc, but as an elementary student of mythology, I liked the Greek take on it. Daemons be good or evil, depending on where and when you come across them. The sniper was twisted and malevolent, but he had at some point been a squalling newborn, attached umbilically like the rest of us, full of promise and love.

Before I knew it, I was driving along the River Road not far from where Geo. Washington improbably crossed the Delaware on Christmas Eve and thrashed a bunch of drunken Germans with work permits for the British Empire and not all that far from the stretch where Speedy and I met his Moby. The driveway to Martine's house was smaller than I remembered, more dusty, less awe-inspiring. This is how memory works.

The garage doors were closed. I wondered if the Maserati was still in there.

I knocked at the door. And even though I was expecting him, I was startled by Lee, now ancient, still wearing a white jacket.

He was not surprised to see me. He turned and gestured me through the foyer into the living room, where a wire from the Electrowriter once led to a machine that spat out something we would later call a fax. Lee steered me through the patio door outside to the swimming pool, which was covered over for the season. Maybe forever.

The same patio furniture was there, waiting.

I sat down, but Lee remained standing, as though expecting me to order something. I pulled the envelope from my jacket pocket and put it on the glass tabletop.

"Why don't you sit down?" I asked, nodding toward the chair across the table from me.

He hesitated, but then gave in.

"Where is Martine?" I asked.

Lee looked down and took a moment. "Mr. Vic in county hospital."

"What happened?" I asked.

"He gone long time," Lee said. "He call and tell me where he is sometimes. Sometime he come here for a while, but never stay long. Last time, I think he doesn't look so good. But he leave again, and then for long time I don't hear something." He reflected upon what he had told me, fact-checking.

"Then police come and say Mr. Vic found on boat in canal. I tell them, bring him home. This where he live. But they say I must have papers to bring him home from hospital. Smell very bad there."

When he said "papers," he pointed to the envelope with my name on it.

"Have you seen him? Is he sick?"

"We go, you see. Mr. Vic somebody else now. Head all empty." He gestured above his own skull.

"I'm not keen on seeing him now," I said. "You understand that he was driving the boat that killed my father?"

Lee looked down. "That hurt him. Then Jimmy die and Mr. Vic become empty. Going someplace I never see before. He go to prison to make it right, but still broken when he come out."

Until then, I had no idea that Martine's houseman had so much to say.

"I think some of him die there in prison."

We each sat with our thoughts for a moment.

"So, he's in a county hospital now, and you can't get him released because you don't have the paperwork for it?" I recapped. "But I do."

Lee looked happy. "Yes."

For a fleeting moment of which I am not proud, I considered letting Martine rot in the county hospital. And that was all it took for me to finish hating him.

"Lawyer man fix everything when you show him paper," Lee said, pointing again to the envelope.

"Then take me to the lawyer," I said. So Lee eagerly ushered me out to my aged minivan so we could drive to an office in Doylestown where there resided a gaggle of attorneys just a few steps from where my father used to hammer away at his typewriter, trying to put words to images of truth.

The newspaper wasn't there anymore. It had been moved somewhere, and developers had came and gutted the Victorian brick fantasy and implanted modern office space into it.

Apparently, this lawyer had just been waiting for me to show up and wave the magic document and produce valid identification. He explained that Martine had been diagnosed with advanced Parkinson's, and that Lee and other friends wanted to move him from the county hospital back to his home, and get him the best nursing for as long as it took.

But none of them had legal authority to direct his medical care. The system of laws had determined that he was not capable of making his own decisions, although it had also discovered that a medical care directive had been created. With my name on it.

The lawyer called in a paralegal who was a notary public. There was a stack of papers already prepared, authorizations for various parties to perform various duties, most of which drifted through me as I signed and watched the notary press her stamp onto the paper.

My ears perked up when the lawyer slid another document across the conference table and said in a matter-of-fact manner that it authorized Dr. Steven Matthews to serve as a consultant to the primary physician on neurological matters.

"Dr. Steven Matthews?" I asked. "Is he the same guy who worked with my uncle, James Yardley?"

"I don't know him," the attorney said. "All of these documents were prepared at the request of Lee and other friends of Martine."

I looked at Lee. His face was empty. "Did you arrange all this?" I asked him.

Lee nodded, unconvincingly. I turned to the lawyer. "Who are these other friends?"

"Mr. Martine has a personal attorney and some financial advisors," he said. "As a practical matter, they are my clients, along with Mr. Lee. I firmly believe they have Mr. Martine's best interests at heart."

I know a stone wall when I see one. The stack of notarized paperwork was substantially thicker than the pile still in front of the lawyer. He and the notary were too professional to show impatience if I wanted to question any of the decisions that had been reached by others.

But I had a long drive home and no reason to get any more involved in this than I already was. If some clique of rich-guy friends of Martine wanted to take him to fucking Switzerland to find a cure, what did I care?

"So I can, at any point, *on a foolish, ignorant whim,* undo any of these directives?" I asked. Thinking of Speedy decades ago and a few doors away—you want a revolution, well, I'll have you know, we all want to change the world.

The lawyer was, justifiably, confused for a moment. "Yes, you have a unique health-care directive, as far as we know," he said. "You can make any decisions about Mr. Martine's health care, unless a court determines that you have acted recklessly."

"It's been a long time since I did anything reckless," I said, though it had just been a few days. I signed the document that would allow Dr. Steven Matthews to administer to Martine. "I hope he does a better job this time around," I said.

I finished signing papers without further incident and drove Lee back to the estate that he had been taking care of for the past 34 years. He was happier, and nearly chatty. He insisted that he make a cocktail for me.

"Then make it a Manhattan," I said. "One for each of us."

So we sat on the slate patio around the pool in which no one ever swam anymore and sipped bourbon and I wondered whether this was all orchestrated by Martine. He could have been watching us from the cabana, for all I knew. Yet, legal matters cast aside, it was pleasant to sit with Lee without talking, listening to the evening settle into the woods.

When I said I was leaving, Lee asked me to wait a moment and he retreated into the dark house. He came back, reverently holding a bundle wrapped in paper, tied-up with twine.

"Mr. Vic want you have this," he said, holding it toward me with both hands.

"What is it?"

Lee shook his head. "He say long time this package for you, Isaac Yardley, if you ever come back here."

I shrugged and took the package. It felt like a book.

We, the caddy and the houseman, shook hands in the driveway. As I drove off down the winding, wooded driveway, I wondered whether Lee ever turned the lights on in the big house when it got dark.

I was thinking I would make good on a promise I made to Juliana to stop by her house when I went to see about Martine. I was headed her way, nearing Doylestown, when I came up behind a gold 1992 Volvo sedan driven by a man hurriedly smoking a cigarette, as though he was in a race to finish. His window was rolled down, and he kept faking me out by tapping ashes out the window. This was almost too easy.

We turned right at some point near the middle of town and followed a street I didn't know very well, but a lot had changed. Volvo threw the butt in the street just as he turned into the parking lot of a sprawling, one-story office building, somewhat modern and altogether practical. I parked as quickly as I could, but Volvo knew where he was and made headway to the entrance of the building.

"Pardon me," I said, hustling toward him.

He didn't want to stop, but he did.

"Can you give me a minute?"

"I'm on a deadline," he said, and leaned toward the door. I then realized that this was the new home of the newspaper that put peanut butter sandwiches in my lunchbox for all those years.

"Is that why you threw your cigarette in the street back there?"

"Sort of. This is a no-smoking property. The bosses say it makes a bad impression." The fellow on deadline was moving for the door again. And thus, the oppression of the proletariat became a reason for cigarette littering. Karl Marx, it may be of some interest to point out, was a contemporary of Melville.

Having been tugged to its doorstep, I went inside the newspaper office. It did not look much like the brick museum where my father worked, and inside there was not a whiff of tobacco or perspiration. Instead of the clacking hum of electric typewriters, the white noise of clicking keyboards.

There was a woman gate-keeping behind a "RECEPTIONIST" plaque. "Can I help you?"

Before I even knew it, I had an idea. "Is the obituary writer around?"

She immediately went to her phone and rang up someone in the forest of cubicles behind her. After a moment, the receptionist looked up and said "she" would be right with me.

After a little while, a short young woman with glasses and a pencil stuck in her hair came to the fore, looked at the receptionist, who nodded at me, and then presented herself.

"Are you interested in a death notice?" she asked.

"Not yet," I answered. "Did you write the obituary for Mrs. Crick?"

The obit writer looked back at me through her eyeglasses, ruminating through the scores of dead people whose lives she had described in one, two or three paragraphs, depending on the customer's preference and budget. "Widow. Heart failure. Long-time Doylestown resident. Her husband was somebody." This emerged from her cranial databank almost involuntarily.

"They had money, didn't they?" I asked. "I remember that she was involved with charities."

A frown in the forehead of the young obituary writer. I realized I could have fallen in love with her, under somewhat different circumstances.

"There were next of kin," she remembered aloud. "The family had owned some business that fell on hard times, though I didn't put that in the death notice." She re-focused on me. "I don't think they had money, no."

One can probably trust the instincts of the obit writer.

"Did you know her?" she asked.

"Believe it or not, I caddied for her about a million years ago."

"That's right, I forgot. She was a member of the country club."

"Everyone thought she had money, but then a friend of mine said maybe not." I tried smiling. "So I thought I would ask."

She shrugged. "I don't really remember anything else about her."

"Thanks for your time," I said, She had a preoccupied look about her, as though people were giving up their lives all around us with no one but her to summarize them in one, two or three paragraphs.

We shook hands because I couldn't think of any other way to end it.

When I turned for the door, I faced a montage of photographs from the newspaper's archives mounted on the wall. I scanned them, looking for Speedy's fingerprint on the camera shutter. I mostly paid attention to the ones with people who had the right hairstyles and clothing to have been at some point in his viewfinder. None of them jumped out at me; I guess what I was hoping for was a picture of him, not by him.

I spotted his old boss, Martin Brady, in the background of a photograph of men in front of the old newspaper office downtown. The caption indicated that this ceremony represented the sale of the newspaper by the McCaffery family to its new owners. I recognized Ed McCaffery, with a smug look, shaking hands with someone who looked vaguely familiar and must have been the new owner. But I was studying more closely Brady's look of thinly disguised skepticism about the transition.

Which one of these sonsofbitches was the new editor-in-chief he had to report to, I wondered.

When I turned around to ask if the receptionist knew anything about the photograph, there was no one behind her desk.

It seemed my wander down memory lane was done.

I got back in my minivan and went cruising on the interstates.

On the way home, I picked up a radio signal talking sniper news. Police in Tacoma, Washington, had seized a tree stump in somebody's back yard. All by itself, this stood out as remarkable. Do tree stumps have civil rights or, more importantly, standing in court? Experts speculated that the stump had been used for target practice with the same rifle implicated in the sniper attacks.

It had the vibe that we were closing in on something.

1997 Dodge Caravan

We did not listen to the radio or have a television running in our house in the morning.

So Henry and I were both stunned when we got into the car and learned that Maryland state police that dawn had surrounded a blue Chevrolet Caprice parked at a highway rest stop. They apprehended two suspects thought to be the snipers. This was amazing stuff because all the experts had been telling the citizenry to pay special attention to white tradesman vans, the presumed vehicle of sniping.

My son and I looked at each with a mixture of awe and relief and excitement. Henry immediately dug into the auto-flicking logbook, and confirmed that we had trailed exactly such a car on October 7.

"You don't think so, do you?" he asked.

But as more details trickled through the radio—a middle-aged man and an unrelated teenage boy, a hole in the back of the trunk, a car strewn with the residue of two people living on the road—we concluded that our Caprice was not the snipers' Caprice.

Glee spread over the land. A new sense of ease took root, lifting us troubled mortality to an era of peace, love and understanding.

A 1997 Dodge Caravan on the tarmac in front of us loped along all saggy-buttocks through residential streets, piloted by a middle-aged woman with a passenger smoking determinedly beside her in the front seat. The driver signaled for a turn that we were not planning to make. The way the passenger was holding the cigarette outside the car and consciously exhaling smoke out the window made it clear that the driver was a nonsmoker and the rider was doing what he could to not be a jerk.

We had both seen enough to know this guy was a flicker.

"Go ahead and follow him, Dad. It's no big deal if I'm late."

"How much is left on that cigarette?" We followed the slowly burning fuse as they turned right. After a few blocks, the driver made a Hollywood slowdown at a four-way stop sign and the cigarette fell furtively to the gutter. I braked to a full stop because there was a city police-man a sand wedge down the block from the intersection. He waved the minivan ahead of us to the curb.

I watched for a moment, but there was traffic pushing from behind. The driver was nodding, bobble-headedly arguing her case. I edged through the intersection, watching the proceedings as we rolled past. The police officer glanced up at us.

"Do you think he pulled them over for coasting through the stop sign or for littering?" I asked.

"Who gets the ticket for littering: the driver or the litterer?" Henry answered.

I wasn't sure. "In Switzerland, passengers in a car driven by some-one who's drunk get tickets along with the driver," I said. "They are accessories to DUI."

After dropping my son at school, I continued to the office, a run-down suite in a nondescript building about 20 years past its prime. There are a lot of glamorous business addresses in Washington; ours was not among them. My boss was a few years older than me, thinking about retirement and not trying too hard to drum up new business.

Professionally, I was losing interest in trying to make traffic flow more efficiently, preserving a non-replenishing supply of stored car-bon. At some point, all the whales will be gone and the oil wells dry and those who still remember how will just have to walk, or carry rich people where they want to go. Biking will eventually become safer, but not until we've torn up every last shred of creation that stands be-tween us and our oil.

On my way out of the van, I grabbed the package Lee had given me the day before. When I got to my desk, I unwrapped it and found a dog-eared, clothbound book entitled "Handbook for the Therapeutic Use of Lysergic Acid Diethylamide-25. Individual and Group Procedures." On the inside of the front cover Uncle James had written his name and an address in Vancouver, British Columbia.

I was so happy to have something of his in my hands that it took a moment for me to realize that this had come from Martine's house. In halting increments of understanding, I realized. They must. Have known. Each other.

The text was heavily annotated; Jimmy underlined all over the place and commented profusely in the margins—using diverse pens and pencils. It had the look of a journal that had been referred to often and annotated over a long period of time.

It was a manual for LSD research. The authors laid out guidelines they had developed through their own work and the work of others for using the drug in psychological and psychiatric therapy. I pictured Uncle James with a white lab coat and this handbook stuffed in the pocket, watching patients rocket around inside their brains, pulling a pencil from behind his ear to scribble something he thought was important.

Jimmy had underlined a passage describing the necessity for a patient to understand that his present state is inadequate and then summon the strength to get through "the difficult and painful process of coming to understand and accept himself."

Ain't that the truth.

James had underlined a sentence stating that the therapist cannot do these things for the patient. In the margin, he wrote, "so don't even try."

The authors thought there was an underlying factor that would explain the range of experiences people had from the drug. But they acknowledged that, as of 1959, they hadn't yet come up with an explanation. They thought it had something to do with self-acceptance and the willingness to surrender it.

The LSD manual described six levels of experience with the drug, and James had jotted down initials and dates alongside these descriptions that may have referred to actual sessions he had attended. The sixth level described a richer interpretation of reality and the feeling of complete accord with it.

In the margin, James had written "light." In myth class, we had discussed the theory that the Eleusian mystery religion of the Greeks, practiced for some 2,000 years, was facilitated by an ergot-infused drink, basically, wine laced with "natural" LSD. On my misguided little trip with Evelyn, I had not stumbled across anything remotely like an epiphany, but that didn't necessarily mean there hadn't been one there. Perhaps I was just too damn inexperienced to know one when I saw it. I was neither baptized nor christened, and I didn't have a college degree. On the plus side, I had a bunch of merit badges and had at least been wedded under the watchful gaze of the holy ghost.

All of which was less compelling than the question of how my uncle's book had come into the possession of Vic Martine. Best I could figure, they had known each other sometime before James was sent comatose back to Pennsylvania by the violent intersection of his surfboard and a rogue wave.

If they were friends, I thought, Martine could well have been in-volved in his care.

It kept my middle-aged brain, showing wear at the heels and run-ning thin in the sole, busy for the rest of the day. *From beneath his slouched hat Ahab dropped a tear into the sea; nor did all the Pacific contain such wealth as that one wee drop.*

A PARK SERVICE HORSE

Henry and I were heading downtown to meet the rest of the musical crew and the camera team. There was a protest near the Vietnam Veterans Memorial against the administration's efforts to start a war with Iraq or, according to Henry, escalate a conflict that had never really been extinguished in the decade since the Gulf War.

We parked the minivan several blocks away and walked to the mall. I asked my son how an antiwar protest fit into the musical. He explained that when Ishmael finally gets back to Nantucket, he signs up for another whaling voyage. But before they cast off, he tries to rouse the crew to take a vow not to kill any whales. The insurrection fails, Ishmael is charged with mutiny and driven off the island by a mob of angry Nantucketeers.

"Mutiny was more common on whaling voyages than people realize," Henry said as we neared the gathering. "Usually, it happened because the captain abused the crew, or didn't give them enough food or drink. A big complaint was not enough time for recreation in port."

I thought of Evelyn guiltily.

The protest was a significantly bigger assembly than the one we had been to a few weeks before. It was less vehement and included quieter, better-shaved suburbanites with baby strollers, older folks with sensible shoes and middle-school kids with homemade, heartfelt signs. It marked the third time I had lowered in protest on the Mall, coincidentally, the same number of times the crew of the Pequod set off to hunt down Moby.

The musical cast was dressed in their 19th-century whaler costumes, and there were stagehands and others associated with the production—including a few parents—along for the event. We milled about with the crowd, and the real protestors had polite questions about the costumes.

My son carried a placard that read "Grand Contested Election for the Presidency of the United States" and then "Whaling Voyage of One

Ishmael" and finally, "Bloody Battle in Affghanistan." I recognized Henry's handwriting.

Inevitably, there were speeches. Some actress who looked familiar. The crowd liked her, but we were gathered for the marching, not the standing around and listening. A body resists stillness, seeks motion. Waiting for Juliana on the rotating stool at the diner, spinning in the air conditioning with a dusting of dried sweat coated over me. The windows hand-cranked down into the door, and dark summer pouring across a country ride, past mailboxes, running along a shoulder-less road with a ditch to channel the downpours, a low-fidelity radio purring music produced for mass consumption into the teenage night.

I found myself with the others, straining for a march.

Finally, it came. There were some encouraging shouts from the stage, a kind of call and response, and we set off at a pace that wasn't going to jolt the jingoism out of anybody, much less our country's executive leadership at the time—or the vast, unwashed electorate busy watching the World Series—but we were marching again, dadgummit.

The theater troop stayed on the perimeter of the crowd, where they could be filmed by Leonard, walking backward. Step by step, I slid deeper into the center, aware that I was drifting away from the kids and losing myself among people I didn't know.

In the back of my mind, I might have been looking for my father's friend, Ms. Bennett. But image-recognition wetware is eerily accurate, even if it doesn't always at first light up the right words in the data bank. My brain caught up and the results came tumbling at me across 34 years, her face still glowing like the headland waters of West Virginia in the evening, rivers trickling out of the mountains and forests and doggedly pushing themselves ever closer to the center of the earth until they joined up and made recognizable, nameable creeks that only the people who lived nearby knew and then hooked into streams of a similar nature and poured themselves into second-generation rivers that tumbled into the big water falling and drifted all the way to the sea. Where the graves of whalers be.

She saw me at about the same time.

"Hey, you," she said.

"I knew if I came back here a few times I would see somebody I knew," I said. Our smiles were feeding one another and, instinctively, I sized Charlotte up. Not proud of it, but there you have it.

"What have you been up to?" she asked, and reached out with both arms wide open, and when our cheeks nestled there was a heavy-artillery flashback, like re-discovering an ice cream flavor you really liked but had forgotten.

"I'm here with my son and his friends." I turned around and realized they were not in the place on my mental map where I had left them. "Well, he's around here somewhere."

Charlotte and I stopped. The march was going on all around us.

She laughed. "Are you worried?"

I wasn't. "No, I'm in good hands. We've been lost here before."

Her eyes were still sparkly, framed now by a weathered face, brown from the outdoors, and when I leaned in, she smelled natural, unscented.

"I have to confess, I thought I had forgotten about you," she said.

I could have been put off, but I wasn't. "I hope that wasn't intentional," I said.

"No, no. It's just, after that day, I thought I would hear from you. And by the time the summer ended, and I didn't, well, I kind of wrote it off."

"I shoulda told you from the start that I had a girlfriend." I gulped a little. "But I wasn't thinking about her that day we spent together." I took half a step back from her. "And I'm married now. Somebody completely different."

"Me too!" She was happy about this.

"So that means we won't be wading in the river today." I recalled her underwear hovering in the sun glistening off the surface of the Potomac.

"Well"—a sly grin—"I didn't promise him I would stop wading."

"Maybe after we stop this war dead in its tracks, then."

She smiled. "Yes. After we do that."

We kept marching and talking and got around to where we lived, which revealed something odd, something that in my mind tilted this meeting away from nearly pure chance.

It turned out that Charlotte and I were neighbors, our houses less than two miles apart, and that we knew some of the same people. For nearly 30 years we had been plodding along the same streets and parks and grocery stores—though none of our kids' schools matched up—without ever having even a distant inkling that there was a co-conspirator nearby.

She and her husband were professional pacifists, running a nonviolence program for kids in the basement of their house and, wherever they could, dispute-resolution workshops for older folks.

I told her that I studied traffic, but I was thinking about looking for something else.

"Weren't you an Eagle Scout or something?"

"Almost," I said. "I have almost done a bunch of stuff."

We were stroll-marching again with the rest of them.

"I did something kinda mean," she said, looking down at the macadam unfurling slowly under our feet, where the cars usually go, shedding cigarette butts like dandruff.

"That's hard to believe," I said.

"After you left Resurrection City, my mother and I went to the police station. Momma demanded, she insisted, that they give us your wallet. At first they gave her a bunch of grief, but Momma knows how to ride the high horse, and she browbeat that poor desk sergeant into submission, and he went and got your wallet and then told us to get lost."

The few bills in my official Boy Scout wallet were inconsequential. Eventually, I had to jump through some hoops to get a new driver's license from the Commonwealth of Pennsylvania. I couldn't remember the last time I thought of it.

"But after we left, I discovered your driver's license wasn't in there. Just a Boy Scout card and a library card and some other stuff. A few dollars."

She was uncomfortable.

"I guess I could have found your address somehow, but I didn't try," she said, looking me hopefully in the eye.

"I was glad I lost that wallet," I said. "It was time to be someone else. You did me a favor."

She stopped marching and so I did. The protest washed gently downstream without us. "But attachment is important," she said, her eyes gleaming. "Let's go to the river. Bush won't notice."

I wondered for a moment whether I was becoming one of those fellows who takes up with women who are not his wife.

"As I recall, we only went in up to our knees," she said.

"Yes, and there were chaperones," thinking of her brother and sisters splashing around us as we twirled in the shallows.

She looked at me quizzically. The protest kept streaming along, leaving us pinned on a rock in 1968.

"Not that we needed them," I said. "I was a rube through and through."

She disagreed. "Not then, not now. Nor am I."

Okay, I didn't know where this was going. As usual.

I said, with little conviction, "My kid and his friends are getting away in the crowd." More protesters drifted by.

"But I reckon I can leave smoke signals under piles of stones," I said.

She smiled. The tail end of the protest march sauntered past us.

We were left alone in the street with a handful of park service police on horseback, keeping tabs on the rear of the march. Beyond them lay normal law, and no permit to march in the street.

One of the cavalry was smoking.

I took her hand. "Let's check this out," I said, and we started walking backwards from the body of protesters toward the mounted police line, stretching the assembly like taffy in a 19th-century Nantucket parlor.

As we came closer, their leader pulled a megaphone from his saddle and advised us that we would have to go back with the others so that we did not "compromise the integrity of the assembly."

He was close enough that he could have just told us that without the megaphone.

One or two of the horses shuffled, the way horses do. I was waiting for the smoker to finish because I had pretty good idea what was going to happen to the cigarette.

"We'll just be a moment," I said, and offered up the Boy Scout salute for no particular reason.

The megaphone smiled involuntarily and started to return the salute before he checked himself. Once you're in, you're in for life. From your first cigarette to your last dying day.

Then the smoker flicked his cigarette behind their line.

"No ash tray up there, I guess," I said.

He didn't answer. One of the horses snorted.

Then the posse split in two and walked around both sides of us to catch up with the rest of the protest.

Alone outside the sanctuary of the march, we gave up our plan to go down to the banks of the river.

"It was so nice to see you again," she said, inserting a semicolon into our encounter.

"I think it was even nicer for me," I said.

We turned and headed back toward the protest with more purpose in our step.

"I still have your wallet," she said, as we rejoined the back of the march.

A notion came upon me. "Maybe we can all get together, since we live so close and they've caught the snipers," I said.

Charlotte said that would be great, and from her tone, I think she meant it.

60. Friday, November 1, 2002

1998 GMC Van

We invited the professional pacifists over for dinner on the opening night of Henry's musical. Elizabeth was very interested in Charlotte, and she had her fun with me on the subject of how many more ex girl-friends she might expect to be visiting us. I told her I was pretty sure no one else would be tracking me down.

Henry stayed at school, leaving the four of us for dinner. Charlotte's husband, Bruce, it turned out, was very agreeable. He had a sense of humor about the lack of public interest in pacifism as our nation was pulled by the ring in its nose toward a war of questionable merit.

"It still surprises me that few people stand up against these wars before we get into them," Bruce said. "Then, when they've dragged on long enough, we get war-weary." We were nursing beers from bottles on our deck, watching the barbecue. He was taller and leaner and blonder than me, but I think we had about the same mileage on us. Looking at him made we wonder what it was like to be married to Charlotte.

"It's hard for Americans to say they oppose a war," I offered. "And when it's over, it's even harder to say it wasn't worth it."

He asked me what I did. I told him I was in traffic but was weary of the perpetuity of it all and thinking of leaving my job. "What kind of economy is centered on people driving around a ton or two of sophis-ticated metal and plastic, scraping ancient carbon so it can be used to pollute the thin layer of life that separates us from celestial annihila-tion?" I soap-boxed.

"I've counted them. Most people are driving around by themselves, and it doesn't look like they're doing anything really important."

"You'll get no argument from me on that," Bruce said. "What would you do instead?"

"That's a problem. I'm not qualified for anything. I don't even have a degree. I'm not really qualified for the job I have."

For two guys who don't know each other very well, our conversation was turning a little bleak. "But a lot of people haven't been held
back by a lack of talent, commitment or hard work," I said.

"You'll figure it out, Izzy," he said. Already, I was Izzy.

"What's this musical about?" Bruce and Charlotte were going with
us to see the premiere of Henry's show.

I heard myself telling him about Dick Mobius and reading *Moby
Dick* to my children and Henry taking it to heart and then, without any
provocation from me, he began writing a musical about Ishmael's fate
after the *Pequod* went down. I told him that I didn't know much about
the story Henry and his friends had cooked up.

Bruce seemed most interested in the Dick Mobius part. "You mean
you memorized the whole novel?"

"Parts of it keep coming back to me." I looked into the green neck of
the beer bottle. "*Suddenly, bubbles seemed bursting beneath my closed
eyes; like vices, my hands grasped the shrouds; some invisible, gracious
agency preserved me.*"

Bruce was grinning, enjoying himself.

"It's not contagious, as far as I know," I said.

"You know, you're the reason Charlotte and I got together," he said.

"I am?"

"After she met you, she decided to enter the Miss Berkeley County
beauty competition, she said, because your mother was Miss Delaware."

"Charlotte was a Miss Someplace?" She didn't seem the type. I
didn't correct him on my mother's actual title.

"No. She didn't get past the county competition; she only did it as a
joke. Like your mother's yodeling."

My mother didn't think of her yodeling as a joke, but I guess it may
have looked that way from the outside.

"So what was Charlotte's talent?"

"She sang 'America the Beautiful' in Swedish."

"How did that go over?"

"It was really beautiful; she has a good voice. But at the time,
Berkeley County wasn't in the mood for people messing with their an-
thems."

"But you saw this and fell in love?"

"Yup."

All through dinner, the bubbles were bursting beneath me. The
snipers had been captured and peace restored, but Mount Aetna was

erupting in Sicily and a judge in Texas refused to appoint a new attorney for a man charged with murder after his original lawyer slept through part of his trial, and an army veteran in Arizona killed three professors at his nursing school. Elizabeth's eyes kept laughing at me across the table, or with me. We barely realized it then, but this was a rehearsal for when Henry would leave for college and it would be just the two of us. The peaceniks had their own beatitude going at cross-currents over the dining room table: Indulge those who lack awareness, for their noses may merely be stuck to the grindstone.

More bubbles drifted up. Watching race horses throw themselves around a perfect track circling an emerald of grass.

Elvis Presley and Babe Ruth both died on August 16. Different years.

It got to be time to go to the show. As we headed out the door, Charlotte gasped, grabbing my arm and reaching into her bag. "But I have something for you!" she exclaimed. We waited on the front porch while she rooted around and then, with a look of triumph, retrieved my Boy Scout wallet and held it in front of me.

"There you are," I said, talking to the wallet.

"I should have found out where you lived," she said, glancing away. "But I forgot about it until we moved my mother from her house a few years ago. I found it in a box of things she kept for me."

It felt oddly at home in my hand. I looked inside. There were a couple dollars and a black and white photograph folded over several times so it would fit in the wallet. It was a picture of 1960s men looking confidently into the future as one of them appeared to be making a speech. Martine was among them, looking not at the speaker but at someone else. And then I remembered seeing this photo in the back seat of my father's '55 DeSoto on the way to the Poor People's Campaign. I must have folded it up and put it in my wallet, although I didn't remember that part.

I realized that Charlotte and Elizabeth and Bruce were staring at me, holding the four of us in a frozen tableau on the front porch.

"Sorry," I said. For no goddamn reason, I began to cry. "This is a picture my dad took. A bunch of people at a rally on the canal. One of these guys was a man I used to caddy for."

My wife came back up the steps and leaned onto me, looking over my shoulder. I pointed to Martine.

"That's Martine?" she asked, caressing my neck.

"Yup." I felt strangely glad to see him again. In my heart, I had known all along that he never meant to run over my father, that he might very well have given his own life instead if he'd had the chance. That is something that people who go to war are sometimes called to do.

Then I looked at the photo more closely. Martine was standing beside some guy who looked familiar, and my brain went to work combing through the decades to a night at Martine's house parking cars and a man with a Jaguar who had a stock tip and then, at once, I realized I had just seen the same face in a photo on the wall at the new office of the newspaper that Speedy used to work for.

I had this to think about as we drove to the metro station. Trying to put together how this friend of Martine showed up at the rally on the canal and again when the newspaper was sold to new owners. I was moving toward the conclusion that I would have to go back to see Martine after all.

We giggled like yuppies hopped up on espresso on the train ride across town to the station nearest Henry's school. The four of us rode the escalator up toward the night sky, leaning on the moving handrail like we had nothing better to do, ascending into the cool, leaving the underground weight behind us. At the street corner, a white GMC tradesman van was waiting for the light to change. A young fellow with blond hair to his shoulders and tattoos was smoking in the passenger seat. This was the kind of vehicle that had been erroneously identified as the sniper's ride.

He dropped his cigarette into the gutter.

"Hey, man. You dropped something there," I said.

"Fuck you, asshole," he said in a matter-of-fact way.

Elizabeth surprised the hell out of me. "Did you jerks get pulled over much while the snipers were still on the loose?"

"Man, you better keep that leashed," the smoker said to me.

"Why did you throw your cigarette in the street?" I said, and suddenly the other three were forming up behind me in an assault of baby-boomer rage. Lennon was singing in my head, asking if I wanted a revolution. Weirdly, we were inching closer to the van.

"I'll remind you that you're under oath," said Charlotte.

"You all need to chill," the long-hair said as the light turned green and the van rolled off into the traffic.

"That went pretty well," I said.

I would like to provide an unvarnished review of Henry's musical for the record, but many people have told me that I cannot. First, he is kin. Second, Ishmael, the hero of the play, is practically one of my family, after so many decades of close observation.

Third, I was wowed.

The musical opened with Ishmael adrift in the sea, whales circling round as he sang a song that sounded like Canned Heat's "Going Up the Country" but was really about the state of his soul under the crushing weight of November. From the video screen appeared the *Rachel*. Ishmael is brought aboard and introduced around, inspiring a song by the daughters of the missionaries getting passage on the whaling ship. There, in the background video, was me in my 18th century maritime getup.

The missionary's daughter falls in love with Ishmael; they are found in a compromising position. Her father decides to set her ashore at the next port, and Ishmael jumps ship as they drop her off. It is a rough port, full of mutineers and corrupted natives, and Ishmael puts the girl on the first respectable-looking ship that's heading back to America. He meets someone on the island who knows the place where Queequeg came from and decides he must go visit his family.

Ishmael ships with another whaler but becomes sick on the first whale hunt. The captain wants to cast him off, but relatives of Queequeg show up to rescue him. He discovers paradise on their island, and sings of floating in a bright light. He is wed to an island princess and joins the royal family.

Then missionaries arrive and begin dismantling paradise. Ishmael realizes that westerners are ruining the island and decides that he can't escape who he is and signs on with another whaler. Again, he is sickened by whaling and when the ship is attacked by pirates, the captain sells Ishmael to them. The pirates are Greenpeace-like anti-whaling activists who had previously captured the missionary's daughter. He feels at home for the first time since the Pequod, and sings about it.

The pirates are heading toward Nantucket. One night they get drunk and decide that they cannot land on the island. They put Ishmael and the girl in a canoe. There is a scene at night when Henry and the missionary's daughter sing "Sea of Love." The next morning, they land on the beach at Nantucket, where the widows of Starbuck and Ahab are waiting for the Pequod to return. The four of them vow to end whaling.

Ishmael signs on with another whaler, but before the ship leaves port he tries to inspire a mutiny. He and the girl and the widows are driven off Nantucket by an angry mob, some of whom were marching in a video against the impending war in Iraq, including a pair of middle-aged folk who used to be teenagers twirling in the river to cool off from the summer heat.

As the four of us stood in the crowded hallway waiting for the cast to emerge after the show, I held tight on to Elizabeth and told her that I love her.

1952 15-foot Grumman double-ender

The floorboards were cold beneath my feet when I got out of bed on the morning after the debut of Henry's musical. Curiosity was pulling me, but still I was looking for an excuse not to follow it to Martine.

I called my mother in Switzerland. Katie picked up the phone.

"I'm going to go to Doylestown to see Vic Martine," I told her. She wanted to know why.

"He's sick, apparently. Maybe dying." I told her about being summoned to serve as his medical care agent and finding the old pictures of him. "He has harpooned me," I said.

"Do you want to talk to Mother?"

My mother had become a quiet old person who spent a lot of time by herself.

"Hello," she said, perhaps not sure who was on the line.

"It's Isaac, Mom."

"Oh. How is your family?"

I told her about Henry's Moby Dick musical.

"Speedy would have loved that," she said.

I agreed. "I'm going to Doylestown today to see Vic Martine."

Quiet for a moment. "I wouldn't know what to say to him," she said, as much to herself as to me.

"I know. But if there's anything you want me to say ...."

"No, Izzy. You'll figure it out."

Elizabeth joined me in the kitchen and listened to half of the telephone conversation, her arm draped over my shoulder. After 30-some years, her morning smell seemed like my own.

My wife helped me load the ancient Grumman canoe with my father's fading poetry onto the roof of the minivan. "Good luck fishing," she whispered in my ear as I made for the helm of the minivan. In the back of my mind, I was telling myself I might get back from Pennsylvania in time to see Ishmael's homeward journey set to music again that evening.

Beneath the upside-down canoe lashed to the roof, the souls of my 1968 poured around me as I motored north on Interstate 95. The shockwaves of my father's death obliterated most of everything that had gone on around it, which was now welling up from the open road flowing beneath me.

Cars are a bitch, I thought, but the highway justifies the means.

Even when it's littered with cigarettes. "This world is going to end someday," my father told me once, when I was very young. "It's one thing the bible-thumpers got right."

Before I knew it, I was rolling up the Main Street hill toward the center of Doylestown. I parked the van near the office where I had signed papers to let doctors take care of Martine. It was Saturday and the lawyer's building was shuttered.

I hiked over to the country club, remembering streets I hadn't seen in some time.

The clubhouse looked as it had when my mother mixed cocktails there, but the pro shop had been torn down to make room for a more glorious version. Gentlemen were still teeing off from the first tee, trying to see how far over the rise they could drive it, and I remembered how much I liked caddying in autumn, when fat, fallen leaves captured golf balls like brown and gold stars on a heaven of green. I watched for a while and saw no one who looked even a little familiar.

I headed back to where I had parked the minivan and watched a recent model Chevrolet with a smoking driver roll down Court Street toward the diner where Juliana had worked. On foot, I would not catch up with him. But a coffee sounded good.

I drove to the diner, which had somehow become smaller. But the waitresses still unbuttoned the tops of their blouses, and there was still an undertow of pop music wheezing through tinny speakers. Also, the lawyer for whom I had signed papers was eating lunch in a booth with only a newspaper to keep him company.

"Remember me?" I asked, standing respectfully outside his booth.

"Mr. Yardley." He extended his handshake and gestured to the empty bench across from him.

"Did they move Martine to his home?" I asked.

"Yes. I think they would like to see you, if you have the time."

"I thought I would head over there. I mean, that's why I came up here."

"There are some things that belong to you at his house," the lawyer said. He was wearing a suit with no tie.

I couldn't imagine what things of mine were still at Martine's house, and I guess it showed.

"The thinking is that Mr. Martine wants to return them to you personally," the lawyer explained, pausing over his BLT.

"Is he doing any better?" I asked.

"I have never met him. From what I'm told, he's more comfortable at home, and getting very good care."

It was odd to me that the lawyer had never met Martine, but I reckoned that this was the way of a compartmentalized existence. "I'm glad to hear that," I said, wondering if my legal status as medical care agent required that I care.

The lawyer hovered over his sandwich, waiting to see if there was more from me. He was a nice-enough fellow for an attorney, but not nice enough that I wanted to watch him eat.

I could have visited our old house or swung by Juliana's new house or paused to wonder what they were up to at the high school, but I did none of these things. I followed a route I vaguely remembered toward the Delaware River at a point somewhere between New Hope and Washington's Crossing, at about Lock 7, where the River Road hid a discreet residential driveway winding back through the woods to a clearing, leaves brought down by November, a small field to the north where cars could be parked, a three-car garage where a Maserati could be housed, and a stone-clad house with a swimming pool, surrounded by slate, like a jewel reflecting the third eye of heaven.

There was a 2000 Jaguar XKR in the visitor parking area. My creaking Dodge minivan coughed as I shut off the engine beside it.

By that point, I nearly felt at home. Lee answered the door. I think he might have smiled.

It was cool, appropriately, but warming in the sun, and he led me to the patio, where Martine was perched in a wheelchair beside a familiar figure sitting on a patio chair. Martine's friend, an older gent, rose and extended his hand toward me for a shake. He was the man in the picture in my father's photograph in the lost wallet and the man in the picture on the wall of the new newspaper building and, I confirmed, the man who sauntered out from this house when I was a no-nothing 16-year-old making his first and only effort at being a parking valet.

I was putting this together. "What happened to Marcia?" I asked him. Once a Jaguar, always a Jaguar.

Roger was nonplussed. "I can't say I know what's become of her." He smiled. "I have a new Marcia now."

Vic Martine was wrapped in a plaid blanket. Beneath the years and the gray and some hard living there still was the glimpse of glory, a man in his prime who hit it farther and straighter than anyone I had ever carried, with a charm that infected the unwary.

"What's it like to have a stroke, Mr. Martine?" I asked.

It was my one shot, my only swing at him.

He tried to say something, but the words came out as gibberish.

Roger, a lifelong friend, said, "He has trouble talking. But Matthews thinks he's getting better. "

Still, I held the power of attorney for health care, for reasons I had yet to understand. "This is the same Dr. Matthews who was involved in treating my uncle?" I said.

"Yes," Roger replied.

"So, can you connect the dots for me?"

Roger took a breath, but he must have expecting this. "Vic met your uncle in Korea, during the war. They were friends." He paused. "When James was hurt in the surfing accident, Vic did everything he could think of, and that included bringing in Matthews to help with his care."

"And Mrs. Crick?"

Roger looked at his friend. "Vic had reasons for wanting to stay in the background. So he arranged for Mrs. Crick and Matthews to collude in the pretense that they had cooked up this arrangement on their own."

I could not tell from Martine's eyes whether this was true, though he seemed to be following the conversation. I had no reason to think it wasn't.

"Why would anyone not want to admit to being Uncle James's friend?"

The best questions, Speedy used to say, were the ones that make people consider how to respond. It took Martine's friend a moment to figure out an answer. "He wanted people to think his interest was in developing the acreage along the canal."

He hadn't answered my question, yet he his answer pointed in a different direction. I knew that the canal development project had been abandoned. I didn't know that it was never intended to happen.

"I think I can see a little into the springs and motives, which being cunningly presented to me under various disguises ... cajoled me into the delusion that it was a choice resulting from my own unbiased freewill," I offered.

If you want to trump people you meet in the ordinary intercourse of society, just throw some Dick Mobius at them. Roger was stymied.

Lee spoke up, unexpectedly. *"No more of this blubbering now, we are going a-whaling."*

Both Roger and I, and Martine for all I knew, were caught off guard by this interjection from the North Korean deserter. I thought of the Grumman still upside down on my minivan.

"There is one other matter," Roger said. "I gave you a stock tip some time ago." Sitting on a fence rail listening to a party. Drunk people swaying in the predawn light.

"I remember that," I said.

"Vic took your winnings from the racetrack and invested them in 1971 when the IPO came out." I was scrambling to remember, not so successfully. "You had $772 in winnings. He bought $1,000 of common when it was first offered and put it in a trust, of which you are the beneficiary."

This didn't mean a lot to me.

"Over the years, the account has grown substantially," Roger said. "He wants to dissolve the trust and give you the stock."

It seemed to me that the scrambled wits of Vic Martine were at that moment confirming what his friend had said, with some unformed glee. I thought I saw him wink.

It was probably just my imagination. I asked the crass question. "What's that mean?"

"The stock has split a few times, and the dividends have been very good. Your holdings are worth about $860,000 at yesterday's closing prices."

This was more money than I was used to thinking about, so it took me a moment to parse the decimals. In the distance, I saw horses running around a track and Juliana thumping forehead-first onto a tabletop.

Martine seemed to be grinning there under his blanket in his wheelchair. Maybe he was thinking about golfing, hitting them long and straight, or piloting his waterski boat with a fulsome 18-year old girl giggling on the end of tow rope, or sloshing down gin-and-tonics on a flagstone patio at the country club.

"What's he been doing all these years?" I asked, nodding toward Martine.

Roger looked at Lee. "After he got out of prison, he went to sea."

The sun settled a little over the woods, reflecting off the pool. "We did our best to keep up with him, but he was floating, lighter than life itself, bounding over the oceans, with Greenpeace and the merchant marine and boarding new voyages as they presented themselves."

He paused. "I think he was looking for absolution." Another pause. "Which only you could give."

Great, I thought. I have to be fucking Father Mapple for this sinning sonofabitch. This is the sorry state of salvation in the modern age, to seek forgiveness from atheists.

"Well, I'll forgive him if he goes paddling with me," I said. Half jokingly.

Before I could put a stop to it, Lee was leaning into his boss's face and asking if he wanted to go for ride in my canoe and then, imperceptibly, Martine must have somehow said yes, because they were soon at wheeling him toward the driveway.

Still, there was some Boy Scout left in me. "But we don't have a personal flotation device for him," I protested. As though it was going to make any difference. Lee was soon enough rummaging around in the garage and pulled out a vintage PFD. In the shadows, I thought, a Maserati lurked beneath a canvas cover.

Do they make canoe racks for those things, I wondered.

Then Lee and Roger lifted Martine out of his wheelchair and placed him in the leeward chair amidships in my minivan. Lee rooted himself in the starboard chair, and we were waving farewell to Roger as we rolled down the winding driveway toward the River Road.

I was lost for a while, but then I found the place where my family had made its last picnic. I parked the minivan on gravel that had launched a million portages. I hoisted the Grumman to my shoulders and carried her to the water's edge. It took two of us to maneuver Martine out of the minivan and carry him down the narrow path to the pebbled beach.

We gently placed Martine on the bow seat. There was nothing to really secure him there, so Lee put his employer's hands on the gunwales and looked at me.

"That should work," I said.

"I run with you," he answered. I took this to mean that the former long-distance runner for the Democratic People's Republic of Korea would more or less keep pace with us by running along the canal towpath.

But before he left, Lee lit a cigar and put it in Martine's lips.

I grabbed the tow line at the bow and walked backward into the water, sliding the canoe down the gravel until it floated free. It was badly unbalanced until I clamored into the stern.

And so I began paddling upstream into the negligible current of the Delaware River, with the wasted, smoking shell of my friend Vic Martine uncertainly perched in the bow of our family's canoe, north toward the mountains where men and mules had dug anthracite out of the rocks and shipped it downstream on the canal so genteel folks could light their parlors and heat their homes.

After a bit of paddling, I paused and reached fore, taking the joint from Martine's face and indulged myself in a puff before throwing it into the river, thinking that I would spend my newfound inheritance in Intel Corp. to take Elizabeth on a long sea cruise aimed at one or another of the truths about love.

CPSIA information can be obtained
at www.ICGtesting.com
Printed in the USA
LVOW03s1458031217
558470LV00010B/907/P